PROLOGUE

Two men were following him, Winston was sure of it. He quickly turned to look out of the corner of his eye without letting on that he had noticed the two men as he walked faster down the street. The remains of the medieval gatehouse were just up ahead and the hotel just a little ways beyond that. It was the same suspicious pair he had seen earlier while he was eating at the cafe. They were both younger, late twenties if he had to guess. One had quite a posh appearance about him while the other looked much rougher, the typical gangster type- a man you didn't want to be following you down a dark alley. Unfortunately, a dark alley was where he was about to find himself but it was the only option he had at that point.

After passing through the remains of the centuries-old gatehouse he quickly turned left and picked up his pace as he made his way through a maze of small, twisting, alleyways. Winston hoped he remembered the layout of the town enough to make it to the hotel. Hopefully he would be safe in his room. He began to run.

He had come so far, why was this happening now? Well that was just it wasn't it- he had come too far. Winston had always expected to stumble across something he shouldn't have and find himself in this situation. His mum had always told him to leave well enough alone. Winston was stubborn though and hardly ever listened to his mother. She'd certainly be surprised when his discovery hit the papers though. If he could only lose his pursuers and get to the Codex.

It had taken Winston years of research, scoffers' ridicule, and most of his academic credibility to figure out the location of the Codex and it would lead him to what was likely the most significant artifact in human history. He wasn't about to lose it now. Not when he'd come so far. If only he hadn't stopped for so long in Southampton. He had found what he was looking for quick enough but he had wanted to share his discoveries with Amelia; it was a shame that she was apparently out of the country. Winston knew he should have just called first.

There it was, like a beacon of hope in a dangerous storm- the rear entrance to the hotel. He ran as fast as he could and made his way through the door, slamming it behind him. He winced at the noise. Surely this late at night someone would have heard the noise and would have been startled. Winston quickly made his way to the stairwell and avoided the elevator.

Winded, Winston finally made it to the third floor and his room door was in view. He was almost safe.

A chime signaled that the elevator had reached the floor, and as the doors opened, his two pursuers stood before him. Hope bled away.

"Der ya ah professa," said the rough looking man in an even rougher dialect. "'Tis a good ting we watched ya comin' outta 'ere earlier or we woulda lost ya in the alleys."

"What do you want?" he asked knowing full well what they were after.

"Wha yer 'iding."

"You don't have to run," said the other man. He had a northern but much gentler accent. "Give us what we want and no harm will come to you."

"Seeing as how I will probably be harmed anyway for what I know I don't see how your promises are much of a comfort. I would rather die than let the scum of the earth trample on the sacred."

"That can be arranged," said the gangster as he produced a pistol that had been tucked in the back of his belt, hidden by his coat.

Winston's eyes were transfixed on the barrel as beads of perspiration began to appear on his forehead even though all the warmth had left his body.

"That is not necessary nor prudent," said the other man. "Not only do we need him to tell us what he knows, firing that thing will alert the entire building and most of the block to what we are doing."

"Not a problem," the gunman replied as he produced a small metal cylinder from his inner pocket and began to screw it onto the barrel. It was a silencer.

Despite the other man's protests, Winston was fairly certain he was not going to survive until the morning. Whether or not he told these men anything he was going to be shot dead because he knew too much. He needed to think of something, anything.

"Seeing as how I have no choice, I will give you what you want. It is in my room."

"After you," said the gangster with a wave of his gun.

As Winston passed between the two men the gun had been lowered and was no longer pointed at him. He seized this opportunity to grab a hold of the nearby fire alarm.

The assailants were stunned by the sudden bells and Winston ran down the hall. As he was making to round the corner he heard a sound louder than the fire alarm that raised a greater amount of fear. Within a fraction of a second that fear had been realized as Winston jerked forward and felt the bullet pierce through his lower back, tearing flesh and tissue as it damaged his insides. Despite the pain and terror, he continued to run.

Whether or not his attackers followed he did not know or care. Winston knew he was dying. When he reached his room door he winced in pain as he came to a stop. He touched the entry wound and pulled back a hand covered in thick red blood. The world around Winston went hazy and he could tell he was going to lose consciousness soon. He would not let his discovery die with him. He was not a failure and the world must know the truth. His legacy would live on even if he wouldn't.

Winston fell to his knees, he no longer had the strength to stand. He took the folded up piece of paper from his jacket pocket. The picture he had sketched the other day was all that he had. It had started this whole mess hadn't it? No matter. Winston began to write a message to the one person he knew would be able to follow his trail. She would finish what he started and acknowledge his life's work. His mum would be proud yet.

THE
JANE AUSTEN
CODE

THE
JANE AUSTEN
CODE

A NOVEL

J.D. Gregory

FIRST EDITION

ISBN-13: 978-0692375631

ISBN-10: 0692375635

CHAPTER 1

It is a truth universally acknowledged... "That I'd rather be anywhere than in this office," said Anna as she sighed and closed the book before returning it to the place on the shelf where she had found it. Begrudgingly, she grabbed a book on medieval romance literature. *Pride & Prejudice* would have to wait. Anna took one last look with longing at Amelia's beautiful collection of nineteenth century Jane Austen novels and returned to her professor's desk to continue her research.

Spending long hours in a musty office pouring over less than riveting old books was not quite how Anna envisioned her Summer in England. She much preferred the traditional American vacation between semesters. Unfortunately, the British system saved the Summer for the rigorous task of researching and writing one's Masters dissertation while the warm weather and sunny days mocked from outside. When it actually *was* sunny and warm that is. English summers were much more akin to Spring in the American Midwest- mostly cool and rainy. Why Anna left St. Louis to study in Southampton she would never know.

"Why not study British literature in Britain?" she said to herself in a mocking tone while looking down from the third floor window. People were walking down the street soaking up the rare rays of sunshine. Anna was a single 23 year old American girl living abroad in Europe; she should be living it up. She signed at the thought; at least she wasn't stuck in the library.

Her course director and dissertation advisor Amelia had offered to let Anna use her office for a couple of weeks while she attended a series of conferences in the States. Amelia's personal collection of books was much more helpful to her research than those in the University library, which appeared to lack anything substantial that had been written on her subject in the last thirty years. Anna still found it absurd that they had barely any recent books on medieval alchemic philosophies or Arthurian romances. Perhaps with alchemy she understood but King Arthur was the most famous character in the history of British literature. She supposed it was her own fault for assuming that a university library would have an up-to-date collection.

Anna continued the tedious work of reading and jotting down notes to use in her writing later on. The first draft of her dissertation was close to completion, she had about a third left to go before Amelia returned from her trip and reviewed her work. Anna would then have a month before the final product was due and she would then return home to Missouri. She was left wondering where the year had flown off to.

Her productivity was interrupted by her cell phone receiving a text message. It was her friend Olivia. *Drinks at the Cove, 5ish?*

Anna had to admit that the offer sounded quite good. The buy-one-get-one free cocktails at the local island-themed restaurant, Pirate's Cove, were hard to pass down. Anna sent her affirmative reply to Olivia and was about to return to her research when she was startled by a knock at the door.

"Dr. Lockhart, are you in?" a deep male voice said with authority and urgency. "Amelia Lockhart?"

Anna quickly opened the door to see two men dressed in suits who looked to be on some official business. One had a stern pale face with short graying hair while the other was taller and appeared to be of Indian descent. They both had police badges hanging around their necks.

"Dr. Lockhart," the shorter one began. "I am Detective Murphy and this is Detective Mandviwala."

"I'm sorry," Anna interrupted before the detective continued. "Dr. Lockhart is out of the country right now. She is letting me use her office while she is away."

The detectives looked at each other a moment before turning back to her.

"And your name is?" asked Detective Mandviwala.

"Anna Lewis," she replied. "Dr. Lockhart is my program director."

"I take it you are from the States?" asked Detective Murphy in an assuming tone.

"Yes, I'm from St. Louis, Missouri." Murphy took out a pen and notepad from his suit jacket's inner pocket and began to write things down.

"When will Dr. Lockhart return?" asked Mandviwala.

"Two weeks from yesterday," Anna replied. "May I ask what this about? I may be able to contact her."

The two detectives looked at each other another moment before Murphy answered.

"A murder was committed in town at the Dolphin Hotel. A man named Winston Leigh was found shot dead in his room. A note was found in his coat pocket with the name of Amelia Lockhart and her office number on the back."

"What did the note say?" asked Anna without thinking. The shock and mystery of the situation had immediately captivated her. She realized she seemed far too eager and felt herself going red. "I might know what it means or can relay the message to Dr. Lockhart or someone else."

Detective Murphy looked hesitant but produced two photographs of the front and back of the note from his jacket and handed them to Anna. She immediately began to look them over.

Eighteen in these Halls. A Mystery Hidden Behind Susan's Balls. In Sacred Winchester She Found Rest. Turn the Key and Reap the Harvest.

"That's it?" asked Anna aloud with confusion. "Not much of a note." She looked at the second picture. The victim had apparently written his cryptic message to Amelia on the back of a sketch drawing. The image was strange to say the least. It appeared to be of a man with open wings like an angel with the head of a lion that breathed fire. A snake was coiled around his legs which appeared to be standing on some sort of cracked egg shape that also had wings. In his left hand he held a sickle and in the right a pair of keys. It was quite a peculiar image but one that Anna felt looked somewhat familiar.

"Do you have any idea as to the meaning?" asked Murphy. "Has Dr. Lockhart ever mentioned either Winston Leigh or a Susan?"

Anna shook her head in the negative. "I'm sorry, no. Not that I know of."

"And the image on the back?"

"I don't think so but it does look familiar," Anna replied while straining her mind to recall where she had seen a similar image. After a few seconds she could finally see it in her mind's eye. "It's not exactly the same, but I have seen similar images in medieval alchemic manuscripts that I have seen at Oxford."

"Interesting," the detective replied however Murphy's facial expression revealed his annoyance and disappointment that he had revealed information to an outside party that was not able to add any new information to the case. He quickly took the photograph back and returned it to his jacket pocket. From the same pocket he produced a business card and handed it to Anna along with his pen.

"Please write down Dr. Lockhart's contact information if you know where to reach her. I would appreciate it if you did not contact her before we have a chance to question her ourselves."

Anna nodded and wrote down the two email addresses for Amelia that she knew of.

"We will be in contact if we need you to answer any further questions," Detective Mandviwala said while they made ready to leave Amelia's office.

"I'm sorry I wasn't much help," Anna replied but the two detectives paid her little mind as they walked down the hall without closing the door behind them. She figured that they were pretty concerned with the murder investigation but they didn't need to be inconsiderate.

After closing the door Anna immediately wrote down the mysterious message in her notebook alongside her research while it was still fresh in her mind.

She attempted to remain productive for the next few hours and continue with her research but she found it quite difficult to focus her mind on anything other than the murder, the message, and its connection to Amelia.

Amelia Lockhart did not strike her as the type to be caught up in a murder investigation or that would know anyone likely to be murdered in a hotel room. Amelia was the typical highly educated middle-aged woman from the south of England. Receiving her degrees from Cambridge, she had all the air and appearance of a successful woman and paragon of the educated feminist ideal, often championing the cause. She also had a strong affinity for gin, as evidenced by the half empty bottle currently sitting on her desk. From the many talks that she and Anna had had over the year though, it was obvious that in spite of the fervent feminism, Amelia was a girly-girl at heart just as Anna was. The two of them had often bonded over such topics as baking and romance novels. Jane Austen was a particular favorite of Anna and Amelia's as the exquisite collection on the shelf could attest to.

Anna finally decided that she wasn't getting much done in her current state of mind and packed up to leave. She took a few books from Amelia's shelves to read later on, put them in her bag with her notebooks, and locked the office door. Instead of heading for the elevator as she had intended to a moment ago, Anna made her way to the computer lab just down the hall.

Upon entering the room she saw various students working diligently on their own dissertations. She recognized a few familiar faces and hastily waved the obligatory hellos before she sat down at an empty computer by the window. Anna wasn't in the mood for small talk.

She quickly entered in her network login information then waited for the computer to boot up. She took her notebook from her bag and turned it to the page she had written the message down alongside the name of Winston Leigh.

When the computer was finally ready Anna opened the internet browser and typed Winston Leigh into a search engine. The results varied- social media accounts, the address of a man from Chichester; nothing that pointed to the man who had been murdered. Anna wasn't the savviest person when it came to searching the internet. She barely knew how the internet actually worked. She decided to add the words "Dolphin Hotel" and "Murder" into the search engine and met with a bit more success as she was lead to various online news articles about the event in question.

From what Anna gathered, Winston Leigh had lived in Hammersmith and was described variously from a Cambridge-educated author to a conspiracy theorist and all around nutter. Who and whatever he had been he apparently had crossed paths with the wrong person and ended up dead. Anna immediately wondered if he had been caught up in one his own conspiracy theories. She shook her head to remove the thoughts. She had read too many mystery novels lately instead of the books that she was supposed to have been reading for her dissertation.

Anna looked down at the time in the corner of the computer screen and realized she only had twenty minutes before she was supposed to meet Olivia at Pirate's Cove. She logged off the computer and made her waves goodbye to the people she knew in the room before making her way to the staircase.

As Anna passed Amelia's office door a thought occurred to her- Amelia and Winston Leigh had both graduated from Cambridge. It was possible that they had known each other at school.

Anna opened Amelia's office and inspected the framed degrees that hung on the wall. She had earned her PhD in 2000 which meant that she had probably spent the majority of the 90's at Cambridge.

Anna locked the office again and immediately returned to the computer lab to continue searching the Web. After several minutes of failed attempts she finally discovered that Winston Leigh had also earned his PhD at Cambridge in 2000, in Medieval Literature. He and Amelia had been in the same program and graduated the same year. They had to have known each other. Anna pondered the possibilities of their relationship as she made her way into town.

OOO

"What do you think? Zombies and Wenches?" Olivia asked Anna from across the table. It didn't sound like the first time that she had asked the question. There also appeared to be an impatient server standing beside them that she hadn't noticed.

"Hmm?" Anna replied before realization dawned on her. "Oh, yeah sorry, that's fine."

"You ok Anna?" Olivia asked with concern in her voice after the server had left. "You've been acting spaced out ever since we got here. You are feeding into the blonde stereotype and we can't have that."

"Yeah I'm fine," she replied with a chuckle. "Right after you texted me a couple of detectives came by Amelia's office to talk about the murder that happened in town this morning. I've just been thinking it all over ever since they left."

By the look on Olivia's face she obviously had not been expecting such an explanation. Dissertation stress- sure, maybe even homesickness, but definitely not a murder investigation. She appeared to be so confused that she ignored the strands of her auburn hair that had fallen in front of her eyes.

"Elaboration please," she finally said as she went to move her hair from her view, tucking it behind her ear.

Anna relayed the encounter with the detectives to her friend while they waited for their drinks to arrive. As she described the note that the victim had left for Amelia the server brought their four drinks to the table. Two dark greenish brown colored drinks were placed in front of Olivia while ruby red drinks were placed in front of Anna. The two girls immediately traded one for the other. For some strange reason the drinks were buy-one-get-one-free but one had to order two of the same drink even though all of the cocktails were the same price. England was nutty like that.

"I saw the story on the news in the Stag earlier. The guy was shot in the back. I guess running is your only choice when only the criminals get to arm themselves."

Anna smirked at her friend's comment. Olivia Campbell was also from the States, born and raised in New Hampshire. Anna loved her friend but she was a walking stereotype of the typical rich white girl from New England- complete with a beautiful home on a lake and a ski chalet in the mountains. To be fair, Olivia had said the chalet was on the *public* mountain. She was also quite a scholar. Olivia had already been accepted into Harvard's Ancient History PhD program straight out of Undergrad. She deferred it for a year to do a masters in Social Archaeology at Southampton. It still boggled Anna's mind. Olivia even had to turn in her dissertation a month early in order to fly back to the States to start her new program at the end of August. That date was less than a month away and she didn't even seem concerned. She would probably receive the highest marks of distinction as well. Olivia might have been privileged in ways that Anna hadn't been growing up but she was a hard worker and a true scholar and deserved all of the recognition and honors that she had received.

"What do you think of the message?" Anna asked her friend. If anyone would have an idea it'd be Olivia.

"Well it's obviously meant to say more than it does. No one is that cryptic by accident."

"Yeah, but if the victim was running away from a guy with a gun he might not have had the time to write out what he really wanted to say."

"Exactly my point," Olivia replied. "If the guy really meant what he wrote he would have said 'Help, so and so is trying to kill me, he lives at such and such address.'"

"I guess you have a point," Anna relented.

"It's some sort of coded message that Amelia was supposed to have figured out." Olivia had a mischievous look about her. "Maybe they used to be lovers and only she knows the secret truths."

"Amelia?" said Anna in disbelief." She doesn't strike me as the type to have long lost lovers. You've been reading too many steamy mystery romance novels."

"Oh you loved the one about the sheik and the lady explorer and you know it," Olivia retorted.

"I only read that one because your mom told me to. I trust her judgment when it comes to lady-porn."

"She does know the good ones," Olivia said in agreement before attending to her drink.

Anna took a sip of the dark green-brown zombie cocktail before reaching into her bag to pull out a notebook and a pen.

"So if the message is coded then obviously we have the main keywords- 'eighteen,' 'secrets,' 'Susan,' and 'Winchester.'" Anna wrote down each word and circled them on the piece of paper as she wrote them. "Now we just need to figure out their connections and what they mean."

"Why are you so into this murder investigation?" Olivia asked with a smirk. "Shouldn't you just let Amelia or the cops figure it out?"

"Because it's much more exciting than my dissertation, that's why."

"Yeah I can see that. If I had to read about medieval romances all day I would be looking for someone to put me out of my misery."

"Hey now," Anna replied. "The annals of King Arthur and his knights are infinitely more interesting than your boring purse of Roman coins that someone found in their backyard."

"But *who* buried them and *why*?" Olivia retorted with either genuine or fake excitement, Anna couldn't tell for sure. "Was it a native Celt looking to keep his meager earnings safe from the Imperialist tax collectors or perhaps they were buried as an offering to the gods to insure a fertile harvest."

"Does it really matter?" asked Anna after taking a long sip.

"Of course it does! Why wouldn't it?"

"Because you can't really know anything about those coins for sure other than the relative dates of them and that they were buried in the ground at some time after that. Medieval Arthurian romances inspired centuries of poets and authors and arguably influenced the entire European age of chivalry. What did your coins do except collect dirt?"

"They got me into Oxford's ancient coin collections and numismatics labs," Olivia replied with a smug smile.

"Well at least there's that." She took another sip of her drink. Anna and Olivia had had many debates concerning their chosen fields of study over the course of the year and frankly Anna was tired of them. Most of the Archaeology majors she had met over the year had had a level of pretentiousness about them implying that they thought their subject was the most important thing in the history of the world. Anna admitted that some aspects of the study were interesting but the majority of it was digging in the dirt looking for ancient peoples' garbage and then arguing with people about what it really meant. She would take historical documents over garbage any day.

"Ok, so a girl was eighteen here," Anna repeated to return the subject to the murder." "Do you think he meant Southampton or specifically the Dolphin Hotel?"

"I guess it could go either way," Olivia replied.

Anna gazed out the window and into town.

"You want to walk over there don't you?" her friend asked.

"Of course I do," Anna quickly replied.

"Ok fine," Olivia relented. "Let's get the checks."

The server took just enough time with the bills for the two of them to finish their drinks. After they made their payments they walked the short distance further into town towards the Dolphin Hotel. It was 6:00 in the evening and most of the shops in the center of town were closing or already closed. Anna was still amazed by the fact that the majority of shops in England closed by 6:00 on the weekdays. She was used to American stores that were open until 9:00 or later.

As they neared the Dolphin Hotel they passed under Bargate- some of the last remains of the medieval city of Southampton. The light-stone structure had once been one of the gatehouses into the city and had served several purposes over the centuries including watchtower and guildhall. Unlike many of the cities in England, that still boasted near-complete medieval city walls and town structures, Southampton had very little that still remained. As an important English port, the city had seen extensive bombing in both world wars. Since the rebuilding of the city occurred after the advent of the automobile, Southampton felt more like an American city at times- spread out and not easily accessible without a vehicle.

Anna could see a commotion that was still going on outside of the hotel as small crowds still gathered around and various news anchors were reporting to their television audiences. Other reporters appeared to be asking questions of the people, likely workers at the hotel and the policemen standing about. Anna doubted that she and Olivia would be allowed to enter the building; the doorway was roped off with caution tape.

"Well what now Sherlock?" Olivia asked with sarcasm.

"I'm not too sure," Anna replied. "I wasn't expecting there to still be a lot of people around. I thought we'd at least be able to go in."

"Tell them you're a consultant."

"Funny."

"I'm serious," said Olivia. "Drop those two detectives' names and see what happens."

Anna shrugged. "Worth a shot." She didn't know if it was the excitement of the investigation or the strong cocktails she had just ingested, but Anna had thrown her normal sense of caution out of the window.

Anna approached a tall, dark, male uniformed police officer. He gave her a look that suggested he was annoyed and had been turning people away from rubber-necking the crime scene all day.

"My name is Dr. Anna Lewis and this is my associate Miss Campbell," she began before the officer could protest their arrival. "Detective Murphy asked me to come down and consult on the crime scene.

The officer appeared to be thinking it over and Anna was getting nervous.

"Go on up," he replied finally. "Third floor and down the hall to the right."

Anna didn't know if it was the name dropping or adding the Dr. to her name with the American accent to sound official but she was glad that it had worked. They quickly made their way to the elevator trying hard to not look back.

"I can't believe that worked," Olivia finally said as the elevator doors closed.

"It was your idea!" Anna exclaimed.

"Yeah but I didn't think it would actually work." She was beginning to look positively giddy with excitement. "We are going to get to see a crime scene!"

They reached the third floor and found the room in question, which appeared to be 311. Many people were still in the room investigating the scene looking for clues. Anna had seen enough crime dramas on television to recognize forensics teams at work.

Anna gazed about the room but was horrified when her eyes met those of Detective Murphy. He did not appear to be pleased that she had showed herself in to a crime scene and brought a friend along with her. He immediately made his way to the two ladies

"What are you doing here?" asked the detective but did not wait for her to answer. "Who authorized you to come up here?"

"I um..." Anna's voice was caught in her throat and she didn't know what to say so she just went with the truth. "I thought seeing the scene might help me figure out what the victim's message to Dr. Lockhart meant."

Detective Murphy did not look pleased.

"If we want your help we will ask for it. Now please get out."

The two of them quickly did as the detective asked and quickly went back downstairs without saying a word to each other. As they made their way to the door a sign caught the corner of Anna's eye and she walked over to get a closer look.

"The Jane Austen Assembly Rooms," she read aloud. "I didn't know these were here." The excitement of seeing something Jane-related almost made her forget about the angry police detective upstairs- almost.

"We'll come back later," Olivia said as she pulled Anna out the door. Her friend was eager to leave the scene before they were in any serious trouble.

Once outside Anna noticed a large black placard on the side of the building with white writing. She stopped to read it but Olivia kept on walking.

"Come on," her friend pleaded. "Let's get out of here. We can't get arrested- we're foreigners."

"Wait a sec. I want to read this."

Olivia walked back over to her friend and the two of them read the placard in silence,

City of Southampton
Jane Austen
Author: 1775-1817
Dolphin Hotel
It is said that Jane celebrated her 18th birthday here in the ballroom of the Dolphin on 16 December 1793 with her brother Frank. Jane was staying with her cousins, the Butler-Harrisons in

St. Mary's Street. John Butler-Harrison was twice mayor of Southampton in the winter of 1808/09. According to Jane's Letters, she attended two other dances at the Dolphin ballroom, a beautiful bow-windowed room on the first floor.

"Did you see that?" Anna asked aloud.

"What? That Jane Austen danced here and that her cousin was the major? What of it?"

"Jane celebrated her eighteenth birthday here. Jane Austen was eighteen here at the Dolphin Hotel."

"You can't be serious." Olivia's expression as she looked at Anna suggested that she doubted her friend's connection to reality.

"Oh I am," Anna replied with an excited smile. "The message has to be about Jane Austen."

"Beside the fact that Jane's birthday party was at the Dolphin, what on earth do you have to go on that would make you so certain?"

"Besides the hidden mystery bit the other parts of the message can be related to Jane."

"How so?" Olivia asked, obviously skeptical.

"Jane wrote two novels that she called *Susan,* an early work called *Lady Susan* that went unpublished in her lifetime. Also, the first draft of *Northanger Abbey* was called *Susan* as was the main character before she became Catherine Morland.

"Finally, Jane is buried in Winchester Cathedral- 'sacred Winchester.'"

"That is such a stretch Anna," said Olivia who remained unconvinced.

Anna ignored her friend's comments as a thought dawned on her.

"*Northanger Abbey* was published by Jane's brother a few months after she died."

"What does that have to do with anything?"

"Don't you see?" Anna was surprised that Olivia hadn't figured it out yet. It was so simple. "Jane Austen discovered a secret that she kept hidden, probably in the pages of her books. *Northanger Abbey*, or *Susan* as she called it at first, must have the main key to the secret within it and was only to be published after she died in Winchester in 1817."

"This is crazy Anna," Olivia replied. "Jane Austen did not leave a secret code behind in her books."

"That has to be the truth of it." Anna was adamant. "Winston Leigh was a conspiracy theorist who graduated in the same year from the same program as Amelia, who is an avid Jane Austen fan."

As her mind began to ponder the connection, Anna began to remember bits and pieces of conversations that she had had with Amelia over drinks at the pub. One in particular from a few months back stuck out. She had just been privy to the opening of an exhibit at a gallery in London concerning Jane Austen's letters. She had attended a lecture given by a friend of hers concerning Jane's use of encoded letters. The exhibit featured several letters that Jane had written to her sister and nieces in different coded formats for fun. The author was apparently fond of creating codes and puzzles for her nieces and nephews, a skill that she had learned from her father in childhood once he had taken charge of his children's education.

After a couple of drinks Amelia had mentioned that her friend believed that Jane Austen might have been caught up in a conspiracy that had kept her from marrying and caused her to publish her works anonymously. Anna began to wonder if the lecturer had been Winston Leigh. It had to have been. It all made sense.

"Winston Leigh had followed Jane Austen's clues and found out something that he shouldn't have. He was caught up in his own conspiracy theories and was killed for it. He left Amelia the message so that she could figure it out and discover the truth."

Since Amelia was out of the country for two weeks it was up to Anna to follow and decipher the clues as there might be a time limit to them. She would unravel the secrets that Jane Austen took to her grave.

Chapter 2

The next evening Anna sipped her glass of red wine as she gazed about the seminar room looking for familiar faces. She only knew a few, mostly people that she had met through Olivia. Her friend was the only reason that she was attending an archaeology seminar.

"You could at least *act* like you want to be here," whispered Olivia to her less than enthusiastic friend. Anna must have looked a little too bored.

"Oh I'm sorry," replied Anna with a mock apology then sat in what she assumed to be a more dignified manner. "I'll just sit up straight in judgment while I think about how wrong the speaker is. Isn't that what you Archaeology people do?"

Olivia made that squenched face that she usually gave to people when she was annoyed.

Anna smirked. "Tell me I'm wrong."

"We don't *always* disagree," her friend admitted.

Anna returned to sipping her wine and pondering her thoughts. Olivia had made her negative opinion of Anna's theories concerning Jane Austen quite known and wasn't very supportive of her decision to continue with her investigations. Anna wasn't about to give up though simply because her friend didn't agree with her. She did convince Olivia to accompany her to Bath in the morning, if Anna agreed to attend the evening's seminar. She couldn't imagine a worse torture at that point in her life. At least there was booze.

While she waited for the presentation to begin the city of Bath was all that occupied Anna's mind. Throughout the course of the day, since she had awoken that morning, Anna had been contemplating Jane Austen's secrets and how she could have revealed them to those who knew where to look. Winston Leigh's message had pointed to *Susan*, which could only have meant *Northanger Abbey*, a particular favorite of Anna's.

The story itself had been written as a satire on Gothic novels, such as *The Mysteries of Udolpho,* that were popular in Jane Austen's day. Such works often centered on characters caught up in suspenseful adventures of physical and psychological terror. They involved crumbling castles, scheming villains, and persecuted heroines. The principle character of *Northanger Abbey*, Catherine Morland, was a young girl obsessed with Gothic novels and viewed herself as one such persecuted heroine looking for adventure among scheming villains. While staying in Bath with family friends, Catherine becomes acquainted with new friends that invite her to their home- Northanger Abbey. She expects to find crumbling ruins and to unravel a mysterious history but such things do not come to pass. Catherine eventually discovers the folly of expecting life to turn out like her stories and by the end of the novel matures a great deal. Anna had often wondered at the relationship between Catherine Morland and Jane Austen and if the heroine was a reflection of the novelist herself. The two women shared many of the same characteristics and background. The description of the Morland family and Catherine's upbringing was practically identical to Jane Austen's own life. Around the year 1800, Jane's father abruptly quit his longtime occupation as a minister in the village of Steventon in county Hampshire and moved the family to Bath in north

Somerset. Perhaps it was at this time that Jane had been caught up in her own Gothic adventure and had decided to disguise it within the pages of the satire of *Northanger Abbey*. The answers might be found in Bath.

Anna was brought out of her thoughts by the gradual silencing of the room as the people in the crowd finished their conversations. The seminar host, a short middle aged man with thin, graying hair and a boyish demeanor, stood up to begin his introductions of the night's speaker.

"Hello all and thank you for coming this evening," he said. Anna could feel the man's awkwardness from her seat. "Our speaker tonight is in the second year of his doctoral research, which is also the focus of his presentation." The man looked down at a piece of paper and continued on. "Before coming to Southampton to complete his masters program he received his undergraduate degree from the University of Aberdeen, which is also his hometown. Speaking tonight on the topic of mystery cults in Britain before and after the sub-Roman period, I give you Fraser Adams."

With the introduction finished, those present began to clap, welcoming the speaker. He then stood from his seat in the front row and turned to acknowledge his audience. Fraser Adams was a slender man of average height who looked to be in his mid-to-late twenties. He wore a brown-green tweed jacket over a white-blue patterned shirt with no tie and collar opened. He also wore slim-fitting khaki trousers with brown leather shoes. His dark brown hair was cut short and clean, styled in that old-fashioned way with a part and swooping bangs to the side. It was the perfect complement to his stern yet handsome face. The man's posh, old-fashioned-yet-modern look and stern demeanor made him seem to Anna that he thought too much of himself.

"Thank you for the introduction Timothy," he said with a quick nod without giving the man an acknowledging glance. "I have spent much of my life fascinated with various aspects of religions, both ancient and contemporary. What captivates me are the aspects that transcend notions of time and place, those that radiate within all spheres of human history. Epic tales of gods and heroes often share common threads and mysterious rituals that spread across history, speaking to people on a primal level regardless of people group. Personally, however, I find no other time period in history as fascinating for the study of religion than the second through fifth centuries AD."

By his enthusiasm the man seemed to care a great deal about his topic. Anna settled in to be bored out of her mind but at least he had a nice voice. Fraser spoke with just the right amount of his native Scottish accent. He was eloquent, easy to understand, and Anna had to admit he was also quite sexy. She would find him exceedingly attractive if he did not have such a thick air of arrogance and pretentiousness about him.

"At the apex of the Roman Empire, human religion reached a height from which it has steadily fallen into darkness. It was a time of uncertainty and awakening as many people groups were spread across the Empire, living together and sharing their native religious ideas and practices. Contrary to how Rome is often painted in popular Christian histories, the Empire did not seek out those with beliefs different from their own to be thrown to the lions or put on crosses. In fact, they often embraced new beliefs and made them their own. It was the Christians' wish to be isolated from the rest of the religions of the world and their unwillingness to compromise with authorities that made them martyrs, not the whips of Empire."

Fraser began to slowly pace around a few meters as he began using the slides of his computer presentation. Unlike many presenters, Fraser did not use them as a crutch by simply reading information off of them to the audience. In fact, the slides had little information to read and consisted mainly of pictures, illustrations, and charts.

Fraser had such a grasp of his topic that he sounded as if he were a seasoned professor that had given this lecture a thousand times. He spoke with a passion that kept his audience captivated even though many probably knew very little about ancient religions. Anna herself almost found the lecture interesting although not enough to hang on to Fraser's every word. He had lost her some time into his explanation of the cult of the Roman mother goddess Cybele. She did find his slides interesting though as they contained many frescos, mosaics, and sculptures- the infinitely more interesting parts of archaeology. From what she had gathered, ancient mystery religions were cults that had various strange initiation rituals. They also promised to reveal to members the secrets of the gods that would insure happiness in the afterlife.

After what felt like two hours but had in reality only been roughly thirty minutes, Anna's attention was grabbed by the picture of a particular stone sculpture. It was of the same winged, lion-headed creature that had been sketched on the back of Winston Leigh's message to Amelia. This one was surrounded by what appeared to be depictions of the Zodiac.

"Here we have a rather unique carving of an enigmatic persona that has often been equated with Aion and Phanes of the Orphic traditions and Ahriman of the Persian religions. Whatever its true identity, this being was an important aspect of many mystery religions of the Roman Empire. This particular piece was found at Ribchester, Roman *Bremetennacum*, in what is often assumed to have been a temple of Mithras."

Fraser didn't give the sculpture as much attention as Anna had hoped he would and left her with many more questions. He continued on for a few minutes longer but Anna paid little attention as her mind was occupied with notions of the sculpture and its connection to Winston Leigh.

Anna was brought out of her musings as the awkward man, Timothy, stood up and announced that it was time for the audience to ask Fraser questions. Without giving it much thought, Anna's hand immediately went up.

"Yes, you in the back," said Timothy pointing at Anna.

She was caught off guard and probably looked like a deer in a car's headlights. She hadn't expected to be picked first and her question wasn't formed in her mind yet.

"Yes um," she hesitated. "The um winged lion-headed thingy." She winced. *Smooth Anna, real Smooth. You sound like a real genius.*

Fraser's face revealed his impatience for Anna and her apparent lack of intelligence. He obviously thought she was wasting everyone's time, especially his own.

"Yes, what about the lion-headed thingy?" he said with a slight tone of mocking.

Anna's embarrassment gave her focus. She refused to be treated like an intellectual inferior.

"Is there a connection between the concepts of Aion-Phanes and the Persian Ahriman and why do you think images of him have been found in cult places across the Roman Empire?"

"Many books and much research has gone into asking just that question. I have spent a great deal of time on it myself but I will try to condense it enough for you."

Anna caught his veiled comments that he would need to dumb down the answer for her. She was also quite certain that her face revealed to everyone in the room that she was beginning to strongly dislike Fraser Adams.

"Many mystery religions contain an aspect of the heroic god overcoming a personified chaos to bring order to the universe. The rituals enacted within the cult were meant to help the individual achieve that act of heroism within their own lives. By being united with the god ritualistically, they brought divine order to their own chaotic lives. They were cults of salvation parallel to the Judeo-Christian tradition before the Church snuffed them out when they had the power to do so. The winged being represents the primordial chaos that must be overcome in order to reach the divine.

"Next question," Fraser asked, looking about the room.

"I'm not done," Anna said while raising her hand again to grab his attention. Fraser looked none too pleased but appeared to not want to be too rude to her in front of his peers.

"Alright," was all he said.

"You said that the being represented chaos to be overcome and that the Church snuffed out the mysteries. Do you think it is possible that you are wrong?"

Fraser's eyes betrayed his indignation at Anna's notion that he was wrong. She continued on in spite or perhaps because of it.

"You say that the Church wanted to eliminate and supplant the salvation teachings of the mystery cults and that they all but died out once Christianity became the only legal religion. However, many of the images you showed appear in the philosophical alchemic writings of the Middle Ages, many of which were written by clergymen. Do you think that it's possible that the winged being in fact represents the union of the physical world with the divine and the ability to transform matter as the alchemists attempted to do- creating the Philosopher's Stone and Elixir of Life."

Fraser's wall of arrogance was breached as he stood staring at Anna with his mouth open without an answer to give.

"Em...I suppose that is possible." It was all he could muster before Timothy pointed at someone else with their hand raised and they proceeded to ask a question of the now slightly flustered Fraser Adams.

"Nicely done," Olivia whispered in her ear. "I've ever seen Fraser squirm like that before."

Anna was so content with herself that she didn't even hear the next question asked. She enjoyed watching the pretentious man, who had seethed arrogance at his own knowledge, flustered by the fact that she had taught *him* a thing or two. It certainly helped that she had an extensive well of knowledge of her own to draw from. She had spent weeks studying medieval alchemic philosophies and their connection to Arthurian Romances. She didn't know if there was any real connection between the teachings of the mystery cults and the alchemists but she certainly made it sound possible. Fraser Adams would not be treating her like an intellectual inferior any longer.

More questions were asked and Anna found little interest in them as they were mostly people trying to sound smart and innovative in front of their peers. What occupied her mind was the possible connections between Winston Leigh's clues about Jane Austen and the drawing on the other side. Was the Aion creature connected somehow? If so at what point? In ancient times, the medieval period, both, or neither? There was just too many variables to consider and Anna needed more information. Hopefully she would find it tomorrow at Bath.

With the seminar finally concluded many attendees left but several remained behind to continue to drink wine and socialize. Olivia had stayed, forcing Anna to do so as well.

"Well that was certainly interesting," said Olivia. Anna wasn't quite sure if her friend was being sarcastic or not.

"Only you and five other people in the room probably found that interesting," she replied before a long sip of red wine.

"What do you mean? You had a very intriguing insight back there. You sounded like you were enjoying yourself."

"Oh no. I thought the seminar was more boring than watching paint dry. I enjoyed making that pretentious ass feel stupid for treating me like an idiot."

"I have seen some breathtaking dried paint," said the Scottish accent from behind her and Anna winced as Fraser joined in their conversation with glass of wine in hand.

"Olivia," he continued. "Care to introduce me to your friend who does not seem to care much for Roman mystery cults?"

"Anna Lewis," she said with an outstretched hand before Olivia could answer Fraser. "I'm quite capable of introducing myself."

"Of course you are," Fraser replied as he gently took her hand into his and shook it in that dainty way that men usually do with women. "I've not seen you at any of the previous seminars before. Are you in the Archaeology department?"

"No. I am in Medieval Studies."

"Ah, of course you are," he said with a smug look that suggested her answer made sense.

"What is that supposed to mean?" she asked with veiled indignation.

"Well it certainly makes sense in regards to your comments earlier about medieval alchemic philosophies. Also, my material bored you as it appeared to be a little over your head."

Anna could hardly believe that this guy was serious but he was, and it made her fume. She hoped that her anger wasn't rushing to her face making it go red. She did not want to give Fraser the satisfaction of getting a rise out of her.

"Yes well," Olivia stepped in. "I can certainly feel for Anna. Whenever she goes on about Arthurian romances and crusader poetry my eyes glaze over."

"What does your research center on?" Fraser asked Anna, appearing to genuinely want to know. She certainly hadn't expected him to care.

"I am discussing the philosophical connections between chivalric romances in the West and the crusaders coming into contact with the culture and teachings from the East. I'd go into it more but I wouldn't want to try and condense years of study into an explanation that would probably just go over your head."

Fraser's only reaction was a slight smirk.

"Why did you choose to attend a seminar outside of your program?" He asked Anna.

"I owed Olivia a favor and she didn't want to come alone," she replied.

"I see." He appeared to be studying Anna like an ancient sculpture in a museum. Something about her was interesting to him. It made her feel equal parts embarrassed and uneasy.

"Yes a small price to pay for subjecting me to your craziness in Bath tomorrow," said Olivia.

Anna shot her friend a glare for bringing up her investigation, especially in front of Fraser. Olivia gave Anna a slight apologetic look in return. It was all she was going to get from her friend.

"Ah, Bath is lovely," said Fraser ignoring the obvious awkwardness between the two ladies. "Will it be your first time visiting?"

"Yes for both of us," Anna replied after taking a big gulp of wine. "I had meant to get there all year but I've always been too busy."

"Be sure to visit the ruins of the Roman baths that give the town its name. They are fascinating."

Anna couldn't imagine anything she would rather do less in Bath than see Roman ruins, especially after Fraser's lecture.

"Sounds like fun," said Olivia. "If you aren't doing anything tomorrow you should totally come with us and give us a guided tour."

Anna shot her friend another glare that could have killed a small animal but she wasn't worried by the offer. She was quite certain that he would rather be anywhere else tomorrow than in Bath with the two of them.

"I'd love too," he replied and Anna didn't have to imagine something she would rather do less than seeing Roman ruins because it was going to be her reality. She was going to have to spend a day with Fraser Adams.

CHAPTER 3

Anna sat on the train to Bath, gazing out of the window as the green countryside whisked by, still quite ecstatic that Fraser hadn't shown up at the station that morning. Following the declaration that he would like to join the two ladies on their trip, Olivia had given him the train details that she and Anna had agreed on. The train was to leave at 9:15 in the morning and they couldn't wait for him if he were late. It pleased Anna to no end that Fraser hadn't made the train.

"You certainly look happy," said Olivia. "I told you he wouldn't actually come."

"I still can't believe you asked him in the first place."

"He's smart and his accent is hot," she replied with a shrug. "Plus, I thought he might have been interested in you after he came over to talk to us last night."

Anna squenched her face as she usually did when she heard something shocking or unbelievable. Olivia's comment was both.

"You can't be serious," she replied. "He just sauntered over to make sure I knew he was smarter than me." She crossed her arms and mumbled, "Over my head..."

"Well you certainly gave it back to him," replied Olivia. "I don't know, I think you might have made an impression. I've never seen him with a girl, not romantically anyway. He's usually pretty standoffish and unapproachable."

"Probably an introvert," said Anna. She'd seen the type many times over the years. Fraser and his ilk tended to like being alone and didn't bother to spend time with other people. "It was probably the first time an intelligent girl had talked to him in a while."

"I don't know," Olivia said and appeared to be trying to recall something. "He comes to parties and stuff that people in the Archaeology department throw. I've even talked to him at a few of them. He just always seems to be having a bad time or looks bored."

"Then why does he even go to them?" Anna asked. "Wouldn't he have more fun reading in the library or something?"

"Maybe he can't say no to invitations," Olivia said with a smirk.

When the train pulled into the station of Bath Spa Anna was amazed by how beautiful the city was. The large amount of elegant Georgian architecture reflected that the heyday of the town had been the eighteenth and early nineteenth centuries, before the Industrial Revolution. It was an era of elegance and sophistication in which many people of all social classes made journeys to Bath for either socialization or for health reasons. The city's natural spring made Bath a popular destination for healing and recovery in both ancient times and in more recent history. Jane Austen had lived in Bath for a number of years; before and following her father's sudden death in 1805. She had also written of Bath in her novels, notably *Northanger Abbey*.

Anna and Olivia made their way through the crowded streets of Bath, peering into the various stores along the way. As with just about all of the more famous cities in Britain, the streets were packed full of people- both domestic and foreign. Within the first fifteen minutes of walking around the city, Anna had heard seven different languages spoken in large groups. She had also been either cut off or bumped into by three different groups of French children without so much as an apologetic hand gesture. Such was life abroad in Europe. Anna had gotten used to it after a couple of months.

When they finally reached the area of the Pump Room, one of Bath's more famous assembly rooms, a large crowd was gathered around a troop of entertainers dressed as medieval mummers performing their antics. They wore tattered multicolored cloths and different masks. Anna made out a devil, some sort of fat noble woman, and a monk. She wasn't quite sure of the others. The musicians accompanying them wore plain white masks and played the guitar, fiddle, and accordion. Anna was thoroughly pleased with the performance and dropped a few coins into their tip bucket. She gave Olivia a look and her friend reluctantly did the same.

"Well, where do you want to go first?" asked Olivia

"Since it's right around the corner, we should probably take a look at the abbey first. Then I thought we could make our way to the Jane Austen Center for the tour and tea time."

"Sounds good to me."

As they rounded the corner and walked under a pillared arch, they walked into an open area that was dominated by the beautiful medieval church building towering above them. To the sides were various shops and tea parlors. One building to the right of the church entrance appeared to have a long line of people to get into it. The sign above the door indicated that it was the entrance to the ruins of the Roman baths.

"Well I know where I *don't* want to go first," said Anna with a laugh that caught in her throat when she spotted something that gave her a start. "You have got to be kidding me."

"What is it?" asked Olivia with concern.

Her question was answered as Fraser Adams walked over towards them from where he had been standing by the entrance to the ruins.

"Ah there you are," he said when they were near enough. "I expected you to show up about twenty minutes ago but no matter. How was the train?"

"You weren't on it," Anna said quickly without thinking. The shock of his presence had apparently killed her inner monologue.

"Yes, sorry about that," he replied, apparently mistaking her comment for concern. "It's good to see you didn't decide to wait for the next train. I was running a little behind and had no way to tell you as I don't have either of your mobile numbers. I decided to drive myself instead to save time."

"I didn't know you had a car," said Olivia. "I miss driving myself places."

"It is terribly convenient most of the time," he said while looking at his watch. "Are we ready for the tour?"

"I suppose we are," Olivia replied.

Anna looked back at the beautiful abbey that was going to have to wait. She sighed and turned to Olivia. She gave her friend a look that Anna hoped conveyed adequately enough how deeply irritated she was. She still could not believe that Olivia had actually invited Fraser to their day at Bath. She began to make her way to the end of the line for the ruins.

"Oh don't worry about the line," said Fraser. "I reserved a time slot. I was also able to get the fees waived."

"How'd you manage that?" asked Anna. "Nothing in this country is free."

"I told them you were working on a school project and I showed them my university archaeology pass. It lets me get into most sites without paying."

"Why didn't I get one of those?" asked Olivia. "I have to pay all the time."

"They are usually only issued to lecturers and doctoral students."

"Figures," she replied.

The three of them walked inside, past the line of people, and into a richly ornamented room covered in Neoclassical artwork and decorum. White, grey-veined marble pillars topped with gilded Corinthian capitals held up the high white domed ceiling that was elaborately engraved. In each of the four vaults that held the dome was a picture of a Roman goddess. In two, the goddess was flanked by the wind and the sun while holding a vine. They stood on what appeared to be a winged sphere with three symbols on it that Anna didn't recognize. In the other two, the goddess was encircled by the vine, the sun appeared more intense, and the wind was gone. She stood on the same winged sphere but the three symbols were different. Anna was reminded of the cracked egg with wings that the lion-headed Aion creature was standing on in Winston Leigh's drawing.

Overhead was a balcony that Anna could tell was a part of the Grand Pump Room that was located upstairs. Inside, the line wounded several lengths of which they bypassed and approached the ticket desk. Fraser showed the attendant his reservation ticket and they were given three tickets and an explanation about the complimentary handset that accompanied the tour that explained the ruins and artifacts.

"You won't need that," said Fraser as Anna reached for her set. "They tend to just cause people to stand about in the way and are usually rubbish anyways."

Anna shrugged and took her hand back. "If you say so."

After they walked through the initial doorway and into the tour proper, they were on the second story of a somewhat open area that looked down over the dark tan limestone ruins of a large ancient plunge pool of green water. People walked about looking at the ruins, posing for pictures, or sticking their hands in the water in spite of the signs warning them not to do so.

"So here, looking down, you have the ruins of the Roman baths that gave the city today its name. The town itself was first established by the Romans with the name *Aquae Sulis*, which means 'the waters of the goddess Sulis,' sometime around AD 60, roughly twenty years after the Romans conquered Britain. The evidence suggests that the hot springs had been sacred to Sulis even before the Romans invaded."

"Who is Sulis?" asked Anna. "I've never heard of that goddess before."

"Apparently she was a native Celtic water goddess associated with these springs. Not much is known about her other than that. The Romans called her Sulis-Minerva, equating her with their own goddess."

"I thought Minerva was the goddess of wisdom and battles," said Olivia. "I haven't known her to have many aquatic characteristics."

"Most likely the Romans sought to integrate the Celtic goddess into one of the more important members of their pantheon to better influence the natives with their culture. Minerva, as Athena, was traditionally raised by Poseidon, so it's possible that they used her association with the great god of the Sea to give her Sulis' qualities."

"Interesting," Olivia replied.

It was certainly anything *but*. Anna felt herself spacing out there for a second. She had just wanted to know who Sulis was; she didn't need Athena's life's story.

Fraser's tour continued on, as boring as Anna had expected it to be. As they made their way through the museum, he glossed over many of the more interesting pieces such as sculptures and mosaics and spent more time than was needed on small finds such as brooches and hairpins. He also felt the need to overly explain the Latin inscriptions on the tombstones even though the translations were right in front of them. Anna couldn't have cared less but Olivia appeared to be in seventh heaven, even going as far as debating some of the Latin with Fraser. After the third time Anna's impatience was apparent enough that Olivia had let it go from then on.

As engaging as Olivia was with Fraser's tour, he did not appear to be as enthusiastic about it and seemed to be losing patience with her as much as Anna was. He had apparently been more prepared for the two of them to be fascinated with his information, rather than being critical as Olivia was or Anna's not appearing to care.

The three of them eventually made their way into an underground building complex. According to Fraser, it had once consisted of various structures along a main street that lead to the temple of Sulis-Minerva and the sacred spring next to the bath house. Not much remained of the buildings themselves though, save for some pediments and carvings and such.

"We are now standing in what was once a type of market area leading to the temple precinct. Many ancient temple complexes had areas such as these, in which pilgrims could purchase sacrifices and offerings for the temple, or religious souvenirs to take home."

"Even the ancients had their obligatory gift shops," said Anna.

Fraser smirked at her comment. "Religion has always been a very profitable business. Just meters above us stands the abbey's store, where tourists of today buy their mementos."

As much as Anna hated to admit it, Fraser had a point and it was an intriguing thought- that the people of this city were connected in such a way across the better part of two thousand years.

"What was on the site of the abbey in Roman times?" asked Anna.

"Unfortunately, the abbey makes it impossible to conduct extensive excavations so we do not know for sure. Various artifacts have been found in the foundations over the years such as pottery and mosaic fragments."

"I'll probably regret this," Anna replied. "But what is your educated guess?"

With a fresh smirk Fraser gave his opinion. "Given the layout of the precinct, and what we know from other sites across the Empire, it is most likely that a basilica once stood on the site of the present abbey. As basilicas were large, open, public buildings that were usually cross shaped, once Christianity was the only legal religion many of them were converted into churches."

"Seems logical enough," said Olivia. "No sense in wasting resources."

Anna didn't know why she was so interested in what ruins the abbey was covering. Maybe there could be a connection to Jane.

"When were the Roman ruins found?" she asked.

"Well, different parts were found and excavated at different times. The first of the major discoveries were made in the eighteenth century, many when working on the Grand Pump Room which opened in 1799."

The year before Jane Austen moved to Bath. Anna had to admit that it was too interesting of a coincidence. Something had made George Austen suddenly quit his career as a clergyman in Steventon and move his family to Bath. Could he have been interested in the excavations of the Roman ruins? Perhaps the hidden truths that Jane had concealed had been first unearthed in the midst of where Anna was standing. She needed to investigate further.

They continued on their way through the museum and the ruins until they came upon where the temple of Sulis-Minerva had once stood. Currently, only a small amount of the front of the temple remained on display. At the top of the small staircase that once let into the temple was a podium that held the gilded head of the goddess- all that remained of the statue which had once stood within the sacred building.

A small doorway to the left took them out of the temple complex and into a small room that overlooked where the original sacred spring fed into the baths. The building material around them did not appear to be Roman but also did not look to be a part of the museum building either. A certain symbol on one of the stone blocks caught Anna's eye- a sickle crossed by a key. She had seen similar symbols used in churches all over England and the rest of Europe as the mark of a particular mason or school of masons.

"When were these structures put into place?" asked Anna.

"I'm not entirely sure," Fraser replied. "My guess would be sometime during the construction of the Pump Room. Why do you ask?"

"Something about that mason's mark. I feel like I've seen it before."

The look on Fraser's face seemed to imply that he was impressed that she knew it was a mason's mark. Anna couldn't believe him. She was a Medieval Studies major for crying out loud. He apparently did not have much faith in the mental capacity of females.

"I'm not certain, but I think I once heard that these initial buildings were designed by the same architects that designed the Circus and the Royal Crescent. Have you seen those parts of the city yet?"

"Not yet in person," Anna replied. "We were going to head up that way after the baths and the abbey."

"The Jane Austen Center is on the way I think," said Olivia. "We can still have our tea."

"Sounds good to me," said Anna before turning to Fraser. "How much is left?"

"We haven't even gotten to the actual baths yet," said Fraser with a look of amazement that Anna would be ready to leave without seeing the best parts of the ruins.

"Well let's be on with it then," she said waving her hand.

As they continued on their way, there was a small window that overlooked the Queen's Bath. Anna took a quick look out of it and saw a pool of green water below. On the far end of the bath was a strange looking statue in a niche overlooking the water. It was of a man wearing red robes and a king's crown, with a strange maniacal expression on his bearded face. The panel next to the window explained that the statue was of King Bladud, a legendary pagan king from before Roman times. He was supposedly the first to discover the sacred spring and founded the city of Bath. Anna remembered reading about him once in Geoffrey of Monmouth's pseudo-historical chronicle of the kings of Britain. She had been spending a fair amount of time in that particular medieval work for her dissertation; it was one of the earliest accounts of the deeds of King Arthur. Of course, Fraser passed by the intriguing statue without a single world.

When they entered the baths Anna had to admit that they were pretty interesting. A large pool of water was surrounded by stone pillars; various other rooms flanked the open area. Anna could only imagine what it would have been like to be a Roman lounging about the baths.

They walked into one of the dark side rooms and it contained multiple rows of ceramic squares stacked on top of each other.

"This is one of the *caldaria* or hot rooms- the Roman version of a sauna. What you see are the remains of the hypocaust system used to heat the room. These rows of ceramic tiles held up the floor. Fires would be lit and hot air would be pumped underneath to heat the room. Many hot rooms also had flue systems in the walls to heat the room as well."

"Now that is pretty cool," said Anna. "Too bad that technology was lost during the Middle Ages."

"In this part of the Empire anyways," said Fraser. "In the East, Roman baths continued to be in use for centuries after Rome fell. They still use them in countries like Turkey."

"That's the downside of invasions and wars," said Olivia. "The Saxons and Vikings simply didn't know how to live in Roman cities and would usually build their new villages outside of existing towns that had indoor heating and working sewage systems."

"It's a shame," said Anna. "Many people died from the cold in those days. They don't call it the Dark Ages for nothing I guess."

The three of them continued on through the baths until they reached what appeared to be the end of the tour, where people could sample the sacred spring water that was pumped out of a metal fountain. Anna took one of the white paper cups provided and filled it with some of the water. It certainly smelled like most well-water she had experienced before, with the rotten-egg aroma of sulfur.

"May the waters of Sulis heal us of our infirmities and strengthen our bodies," said Olivia sounding like a lame toast among history nerds.

Anna took a sip and it tasted like drinking a cup of liquid copper pennies. "Yep. I don't see how people thought that was good for you. Especially during the Enlightenment."

"It is what it is," said Fraser with a shrug. He seemed to Anna to have softened since the tour was finished. He no longer had his usual air of pretentiousness. Not as much of it anyway.

They left the museum through the obligatory gift shop at the end and made their way back through the square to the abbey.

Bath Abbey appeared to have been constructed out of the local light yellowish Bath stone as was most of the buildings in the city. While sharing many of the typical characteristics of the Gothic cathedrals that Anna had visited so far, she noticed that the church had very unique features as well.

"It really is a magnificent building," said Anna to the others. "The low aisles, nave arcades, and very tall clerestory give off the opposite balance typical to perpendicular Gothic church architecture."

Olivia and Fraser just looked at her without saying anything, appearing to be stunned that Anna had such an extensive knowledge of medieval church architecture.

"What?" she said with a shrug. "I had to take a class on this stuff in my Undergrad."

"And I thought my class on buildings and society was boring," commented Olivia.

Fraser just looked at Olivia without saying much of anything. He seemed to agree with her. He also seemed to be impressed by Anna and it made her smile inside. At least she hoped it was inside.

"Hey! I just listened while the professor here prattled on for over an hour about hairpins, brooches, and pottery. I also recall having to listen to the two of you argue about tombstones. The least you can do is let me impart my own brand of knowledge to enlighten *your* areas of ignorance."

Fraser smirked and nodded his head. "As you wish," he said while gesturing with his hand for Anna to precede before them into the church. "Lecture on *professor.*"

Anna smirked back and they continued on. As they walked the inside perimeter she explained some of the finer details about

Gothic architecture and what, in her opinion, made Bath Abbey unique. Olivia looked about as bored as Anna had been inside the ruins of the Roman baths. Fraser, however, appeared to be hanging on to her every word. He seemed genuinely interested in her explanations. Anna began to feel horrible that she hadn't given him as much enthusiasm.

Before she could feel too terrible, an interesting coat of arms caught her eye. Over a lower doorway with an open large wooden door that was likely centuries old, was a blackened shield with a white key crossed with a sickle, flanked by peculiar white birds. Anna walked over to the doorway and peered in. A small staircase led down into a cold, dank, and dark chapel.

"This must be one of the oldest parts of the church," she said with excitement, caring very little whether the others followed her or not as she descended below. She began to smell the musty old stones and feel the dampness typical of subterranean chambers under churches- usually crypts.

The lighting wasn't the greatest, with only a lamp in the far corner and some candles at the shrine providing the only illumination. From the pillars and the vaulted ceilings, Anna could tell that the chapel had once been a part of a Norman church, probably built sometime in the 12th century. As she made her way to the back of the room, she noticed that the masonry was quite rougher and appeared to be much older- possibly Anglo-Saxon, but she couldn't tell for sure. Another low archway led into a smaller room. Anna peered in and could see various worn carvings on the stone walls. She could barely make them out without more light but they appeared to be saints or other biblical figures. On the back wall was a worn image of some sort of man holding a key in one hand and a staff of some sort in the other. It was probably St. Peter, an often venerated saint who held the keys to heaven. Anna thought something was off about the image though.

While Olivia and Fraser were looking about the outer chapel, Anna crept deeper into the back room and pulled out her mobile phone. With the touch of a button, her phone produced its flashlight and Anna shone it over the image of St. Peter. The head was badly worn and she couldn't make out the typical bearded face of the saint. She could also see, though barely, the outline of wings that were once attached to the figure. Wings were definitely peculiar as very few saints were depicted with wings, certainly not Peter.

Anna realized that what she had mistaken for a staff was actually some sort of scythe or sickle. The image also appeared to be standing on a sphere of some kind. She wasn't sure but she could almost see a serpent coiled around the legs.

"Fraser over here," she yelled back. "Look at this."

Fraser came quickly with Olivia close behind.

"Well that certainly is interesting," he said as he inspected the image.

"What's so interesting about some worn down saint?" asked a confused Olivia.

"It's not a saint," said Anna. "It's an image of Aion."

"Nice discovery Anna," said Fraser with excitement in his voice and then looked around the small chapel. "This chamber looks to be quite a lot older than the Norman foundations surrounding it. The dimensions are typical of *Mithraea* found among the forts of Hadrian's Wall but I've never heard of one being found in Somerset. The only temple known in the South is the one found in London"

"Typical *what* now?" asked Anna. "You've lost me."

"Oh yes sorry," Fraser apologized. "Temples of Mithras, a sun god of mysterious eastern origins. Mithras in some form or another has been worshiped for thousands of years from Britain to Japan. In Roman times, the mystery cult was popular among the military and merchants. It was also exclusive to males. The groups tended to be small, less than twenty members or so per temple, with seven levels of initiation."

"Sounds like one of the campus fraternities during undergrad," said Anna with a smirk.

"Actually you aren't far off," Fraser replied. "I'm not too familiar with such groups myself as we don't do that sort of thing at colleges in the UK, but I've seen them in movies. Weird initiation rituals, a sense of brotherhood, drunken parties full of debauchery- standard mystery cult practices."

"That's all well and good," said Olivia. "But why is there a temple of Mithras under a church?"

Anna offered what she thought was a plausible explanation. "Whoever built the first church probably thought there used to be an older church on the site and confused the images with biblical figures. Winged beings, robed figures holding keys and such- not too far off."

"You are probably right," said Fraser. "Patron gods or patron saints. Ironically, they both tend to have the same tokens in their icons."

"Why hasn't anyone noticed this temple until now?" Anna asked. Before the question could be discussed further they were startled by a shout.

"This area is off limits!" said an angry middle aged man.

Anna thought he was probably a priest or something but after a better look he didn't appear to be clergy. He wore a blue suit with a long, grey tweed coat. He looked more like a businessman. Anna thought it strange for a man to be wearing a long tweed coat in the summer but perhaps such a thing was normal in England.

"The door was open and there was no sign," said Olivia in their defense.

"Yes well, whoever left it open will be severely punished I can assure you, now please return to the rooms above."

"Sure thing," said Anna and the three of them were escorted from the undercroft ruins by the less than pleased man.

When they reached the surface he quickly locked the ancient wooden door behind them with an equally antique key that he produced from his coat's inner pocket. Fraser's eyes were squinting as if he were studying the man.

"We should leave," said Fraser suddenly. Anna gave him a confused look and was about to ask why before she was cut off. "Questions later, we go now."

The three of them quickly made their way out of the abbey, through the gift shop, and into the square. The mummers had moved their show into the area in front of the abbey; there was now a man on a high unicycle juggling torches. If Anna hadn't been flustered she would have stopped to enjoy it. Fraser ushered them through the crowds and down a few side streets before they slowed their pace.

"Are you going to explain why that man freaked you out so much?" Anna asked finally.

Fraser's eyes betrayed little but Anna could tell that he was choosing his words carefully.

"I fear we may have stumbled upon something we shouldn't have," he replied. "There is a reason those ruins haven't been made public and are apparently under lock and key."

"Why would people want to hide archaeological discoveries?" asked Anna but she already knew possible answers- antiquities dealers made a pretty penny.

"There are many reasons to keep ruins hidden," Fraser replied. "But I had the feeling the man in the church was trying to hide something more than a Mithraeum."

"What do you mean?" asked Olivia.

"You don't study mystery cults for long until you realize that they didn't really die out when Christianity tried to extinguish them. On the fringes of the Empire, they simply became less advertised and grew into secret societies. Many lived on in secret within the Church itself, or under the Church in this case. Mystery brotherhoods thrived within the walls of the monastic orders in the sub-Roman period."

Anna smirked. "Next you're going to be talking about Templar treasures and Freemason conspiracies."

Fraser didn't appear to be amused by her comment. In fact, it seemed to agitate him.

"That's exactly what I'm talking about," he replied. "The mystery brotherhoods lived on in monastic orders and especially thrived during the Crusades. They still exist today in secret and wish to remain so. The Freemasons are a large organization and many groups honor the ancient pagan ways within Masonic lodges while the greater brotherhood is none the wiser."

"And you think one of these mystery brotherhoods meets under Bath Abbey?" asked Anna. Her words sounded skeptical but as she said them she realized that certain things were making a lot of sense.

"It looks like you might have been right after all Anna," said Olivia.

"Right about what?" asked Fraser, curious. The question pulled Anna out of her thoughts and she shot Olivia a look meant to keep her quiet but it was too late.

"Anna thinks that Jane Austen left clues in her books about some kind of conspiracy. That's why we came to Bath."

Anna closed her eyes and sighed, preparing herself for the snide comments that were no doubt about to spew forth from Fraser's pretentious mouth.

"Well that's certainly an interesting theory," he replied with genuine sincerity. "Care to explain?"

Anna opened her eyes and blinked a few times in disbelief. He actually seemed to want to know. Olivia had ridiculed her the first time that she had mentioned it and she was her friend. Fraser Adams was an arrogant prat. Why did he care?

"Yeah sure, but can we go?" Anna looked over her shoulder. "I'd like to keep a move on."

As the three of them continued on their way through the city walking uphill, Anna explained to Fraser everything that she knew- which wasn't much, and everything that she suspected- which was a great deal. She told him of the murder of Winston Leigh and the message that he had left for Amelia. Fraser was particularly interested in the fact that a drawing of Aion had been on the back of it. When they neared the edge of Queen's Square Park, they stopped for a moment of respite and Fraser thought over Anna's theories.

"So you think that Jane Austen's father had been caught up in some conspiracy here in Bath and that she stumbled upon it herself as well?"

"Exactly," Anna replied. "It seems likely that it had something to do with that mystery brotherhood meeting under Bath Abbey." A thought dawned on her as she spoke. "Winston Leigh must have discovered the temple as well and drew the Aion." It certainly made sense.

"Yeah and he's dead now," said Olivia with fear in her voice. "What's to stop us from ending up the same way?"

Anna had to admit that she had a point. She hadn't stopped to think about the consequences of following the clues left by a murder victim. They were likely now in danger because of her delusions of grandeur.

"That's why I wanted to leave the place," said Fraser. "We did as we were told and didn't act like we were suspicious of anything. They had no way to know that any of us recognized the ruins as anything but part of the church. We did not seem a threat and I doubt we were followed."

"I don't really care," said Olivia, getting heated. "I'm about to start a doctoral program at Harvard in a month and I really don't need to be murdered before that, thanks. I'm going back to Southampton." She turned to leave and walk back to the train station.

"Olivia wait," Anna pleaded and her friend stopped to look behind.

"I'm done Anna," she said. "Stay and keep investigating if you want. You might not end up like that poor man in the hotel but I'm not willing to take that chance." She continued walking in the direction of the train station.

Anna wasn't quite sure what to do and as the distance grew between them, apparently so did her resolve. She could go back to Southampton with Olivia, give up on the investigation, and continue working on her dissertation. She could also solve Jane Austen's mystery and possibly bring the people who murdered Winston Leigh to justice. As Olivia rounded the corner and was no longer in view, Anna made up her mind. She turned around to continue up the hill and realized that she had forgotten about Fraser. He wasn't leaving.

"Are you going back too?" Anna asked, not entirely sure why she cared.

"You've piqued my interest Anna Lewis," he replied. "I want to see if you are right about this Jane Austen business."

"Aren't you worried about winding up dead?"

"Not really," he said with a shrug. "I know how to not draw attention to myself."

"That must be hard for you," Anna said with a smirk. "I bet you love attention."

"Well, I guess that depends on whose attention I have," he replied with a smile as he gestured with his hand for her to walk on. "Shall we proceed?"

Anna wasn't quite sure how to take his comment. Was he flirting with her? Did she even want him to? She walked on and tried not to think too hard about it. Instead, she tried to think about what they were going to do next. She had been right about Bath having its secrets, but how did Jane fit into them? The answer appeared in view as if from an unspoken prayer- the Jane Austen Center of Bath.

"As obvious as this sounds, I have a feeling we may find out something useful about Jane in there."

"If we don't they might want to rethink their business," Fraser replied and Anna smirked.

As they approached the building, which was a Georgian townhouse converted for the purposes of the center, they were greeted by a statue of a regency era woman in a blue dress and a bonnet that could easily have been any female character from an Austen novel. Anna preferred to think she was Elizabeth Bennet.

Through the course of the tour, Anna learned much about Jane Austen that she hadn't known before but nothing too incredibly exciting for their purposes. Jane had grown up in a loving family with several brothers and her sister Cassandra- her closest friend and confidant. Her father encouraged his children in all their pursuits both educational and recreational, often creating puzzles and games for them to enjoy. The family would play together and put on small performances for each other as well as for relatives and neighbors. At a young age, Jane developed a love for stories and even tried her hand at writing plays and histories for her family and friends to enjoy. Jane loved her life in Steventon and apparently did not adjust very well when her father uprooted them to live in Bath.

The final presentation was to take place during a high tea, which Anna had been looking forward to since the moment she had gotten off the train that morning.

When they walked into the tea parlor, Anna felt as if she could not imagine anywhere else she would rather be. The room was simple yet elegantly decorated with paintings of various regency era scenes and peoples. Small rounded tables with white cushioned chairs were set up around the parlor with white tablecloths and napkins, with saucers and teacups also all in white. Above the fireplace was an oil painting done in the likeness of the only Mr. Darcy that mattered- Colin Firth.

Anna and Fraser sat at a table by the window and as the server handed them their menus Anna couldn't help but smiling.

"Well, you seem quite pleased with yourself," said Fraser. "Even though we haven't learned anything I would deem useful yet."

"Don't spoil this for me," she replied with a stern but playful look. "Enjoy your tea like a good Englishman. Maybe we'll learn something during the final talk."

"I'm Scottish," said Fraser with a hint of annoyance.

"Then ask for a deep-fried candy bar or something. I don't care."

"I am so sick of the deep-fried candy bar stereotype. One place in one town in Scotland does it and the whole country is attributed with the love for deep frying candy. It's disgusting."

"And what do you call haggis?" asked Anna with disbelief that the Scottish could find anything disgusting.

"A delicacy."

"Uh huh," she replied and opened her menu; Anna was not about to debate the edibility of sheep stomachs.

She was torn by the options. She could get "Tea with the Austens"- a selection of cheese and cucumber finger sandwiches with a slice of cake, or "Lady Catherine's Proper Cream Tea"- scones served with Dorset clotted cream and strawberry jam. While tempting, Anna had partaken of Cream Tea quite a bit while living in Britain so she decided on "Catherine Morland's

Savoury Tea"- a warm cheese scone with prosciutto and cream cheese. She thought it a fitting choice as the heroine of *Northanger Abbey* was central to Anna's life at the moment.

When the tea was served, a woman entered the room and stood beside the far white wall which had then begun to be used as a projector screen for her presentation.

"I trust you are enjoying your tea," she began in a proper accent of southern Britain. "We at the Jane Austen Center are glad to have you with us today and hope you enjoy this final discussion of Jane's subtle allusions to the intrigues of Bath during the era in which she lived here."

Anna quickly turned to Fraser and smiled with a sense of satisfaction. He smiled back although with significantly less enthusiasm and they continued to listen to the speaker while they enjoyed their tea.

According to the speaker, *Northanger Abbey*, or *Susan* as Jane had originally called it, was most likely begun during the years 1797 and 1799- the Austen family's earliest known visits to Bath.

Although not specifically stated within the novel, central to the story is the heroine being mistaken as the possible heir to the vast fortune of the well-known "Man of Bath" Ralph Allen. The politician and shrewd businessman was largely responsible for making the city the pinnacle of Georgian Neoclassical architecture that had earned its place as a World Heritage Site. With the help of the architect John Wood, Allen ushered in the use of the popular Bath Stone that could be seen in most of the buildings in the city. As Allen owned the quarries, he made a vast fortune but did not have any children to leave it to. In Jane Austen's day, the Allen fortune was thought to be held by some distant relatives living in the country. The heroine, who accompanies a Mr. and Mrs. Allen, is mistaken by the fortune seeking braggart Mr. Thorpe as the young heiress of Old Allen's vast wealth. Jane Austen would have been familiar with the legacy of Ralph Allen as her mother's great uncle James Brydges, the first Duke of Chandos, was his contemporary and fellow patron to the architecture of John Wood.

The manuscript of *Susan* was finished sometime around 1803, when Jane was living in Bath. She then sold it to a publisher who held unto it for quite some time with the novel never going into print. It wouldn't be until 1816 that Jane's brother Henry could buy it back. He would finally publish Jane's first completed novel soon after her death in 1818.

As they left the Jane Austen Center, Anna found herself unable to read Fraser's reaction to the tour or the final discussion. He had appeared attentive and looked to have hung onto the speaker's every word but as they made their way downstairs and out onto the street he had been silent and uneager to discuss anything.

"Any thoughts?" Anna asked finally.

Fraser certainly appeared to have them even though he was choosing not to voice them. He was staring across the way in the direction of the dark obelisk in the middle of the small park at Queen's Square.

"Several," he replied. "But I'm not entirely sure they'd be of any help. You're the Jane Austen expert and her conspiracy is your theory. What are *your* thoughts?"

"Well, I do wonder if Jane's manuscript had been kept from being published for some reason. Maybe her clues were noticed by someone at the printing company or someone with power had known of Jane's possible discoveries. Her allusions to Ralph Allen without mentioning the man and his legacy by name are also interesting."

"Yes I thought so too," Fraser replied. "We should investigate his life further. If he and John Wood were responsible for most of the more famous Neoclassical buildings in Bath, they may have had something to do with the building of the Grand Pump Room and the other buildings surrounding the Roman ruins. I also had no idea that Jane Austen was related to the Duke of Chandos."

"Is the Duke important?" asked Anna. She could tell that Fraser had more to say on the topic and was processing information in his head.

"I've seen his name pop up a few times in my research," he replied. "As I said before, you can't study mystery cults long before you realize that they still exist in some form or another. For some reason, during the period following the Enlightenment, ritualistic mysticism grew in popularity among the aristocracy."

"That's ironic," said Anna. "Weren't people supposedly throwing off the 'shackles' of religious superstitions in favor of reason and intellect?"

Fraser shrugged. "Who knows why people do what they do? Regardless, various 'brotherhoods' sprang up in the centuries following the Protestant Reformation with varying degrees of paganism and ritual. Some were more deist in character like the Freemasons, who only recognize a universal architect, while others like the Hellfire Club, were purported to have worshiped Bacchus and engaged in drunken pagan orgies that would have rivaled any in Classical times."

"Sounds more like just an excuse to party to me," Anna replied.

"Most members probably thought along those lines but there were many scattered among the groups who toyed with much grander notions."

"Like what? World domination?" said Anna sarcastically and laughed. When Fraser didn't even smirk she stopped laughing and felt awkward.

"Not exactly domination," he replied. "More like influencing the civilized world into tearing itself apart so that they could help to put it back together the way they thought it should be."

"You can't be serious," said Anna in disbelief. "Next you'll tell me it's the Illuminati that killed Winston Leigh because he found the lizard men in the center of the earth that orchestrated Nine-Eleven. Do you have your own YouTube channel?"

"While most of what you read about Illuminati conspiracies is complete nonsense, the principles behind the theories are built upon facts. It isn't a new concept now and it wasn't a new concept then. Since the dawn of human civilization, there have always been groups of 'enlightened' people who thought they knew what was best for the world. Some were very skilled at working in the shadows to achieve their goals. Others, like Hitler and the Nazis, chose more direct approaches that put them in the spotlight."

"I guess you have a point," Anna replied. "But what does this have to do with the Duke?"

"Like Ralph Allen, the first Duke of Chandos- James Brydges, was well known for being an antiquarian and patron of the arts. He was also a Grand Master of the Masonic Lodge. He even employed Handel as his house composer for a time. Learned men from all over Europe came to stay at his estate and discuss and debate various topics."

"In France they had salons, in England they had rich peoples' houses," said Anna jokingly. "So, you think the Duke may have been involved in the secret brotherhood of Bath?"

"It seems likely," Fraser replied. "That doesn't really help us right now though. Where do you think Jane Austen's clues lead?"

"I have no way to really know for sure, but, in *Northanger Abbey* Catherine thinks she's a heroine in a Gothic novel. As she's making her journey to the Tillney's estate, Henry sort of plays with her preconceived notions about their house by telling her that she might find a secret passage that leads to underground chambers and long hidden secrets."

"Does she?" asked Fraser, ignorant of the novel's outcome. He apparently wasn't a Jane Austen fan.

"Nope," said Anna. "But that's the satirical point. Northanger Abbey turns out to be a normal manor with normal wealthy people and Catherine's naivety almost causes her to offend the people who invited her to stay at their home."

"So, you think that Jane Austen covered up her true experiences with notions of satire?"

"Exactly. I think that while Jane was in Bath, she was invited to stay at someone's home, then found a secret passage to hidden mysteries, just like Henry Tillney joked with Catherine about in the book." Anna looked around the area of Queen's Square Park. "Where was the Duke's house?"

"Somewhere just outside of London I think," Fraser replied then shook his head. "It couldn't have been the Duke's house though. It was demolished and sold off piece by piece by his son. It didn't exist in Jane Austen's day."

Anna's mind was struck by epiphany and pulled the notepad from her purse on which she had taken notes during the tour. She flipped through a few pages and smiled.

"The Duke's house might not have been around but Ralph Allen's was, and still is."

If Anna was right, and Jane Austen had visited a wealthy estate and then stumbled upon secret passages uncovering mysteries long hidden, then they were likely hidden beneath the home of the Man of Bath himself- Prior Park.

CHAPTER 4

"This isn't getting us anywhere," Anna complained as she closed the book she was reading. She put it on top of the stack of other books that she had already glanced at without finding useful information. "We need to be looking around for secret passageways."

Fraser sighed and closed the book that he was reading as well. He had been jotting down several lines of notes.

"We can't simply go from room to room looking for hidden doors Anna. Someone would find us, think we were nutters, and telephone the police. We are lucky this place was turned into a school or this process would be even more difficult."

Fraser was right of course. Anna was just anxious to move on.

Prior Park hadn't been far outside of the city of Bath. It would have taken too long to walk, though, so they had driven there in Fraser's car- a black, 'sporty' Peugeot hatchback that was some years old. The car certainly wasn't as pretentious as the man himself. Anna had half expected his car to be some two-seated roadster from the 70's that he had restored himself.

When they arrived, Anna was surprised to discover that unlike most of the touristy estate houses that she had visited over the year, Prior Park had been turned into a Catholic boarding school sometime in the 19th century. It was a pleasant surprise, and a nice turn of luck, as Anna and Fraser were able to use their status as university graduate students to secure reading rights in the school's library. They used the cover story of researching their dissertations.

While not as extensive as Southampton's library, it did have a good collection of books pertaining to the history of Bath and its peoples. It also had books that had once been a part of Ralph Allen's personal collection.

Though she was anxious to continue on, Anna had to admit that she had learned quite a great deal since they had arrived, particularly about the architect John Wood the Elder. In addition to being the architectural genius essentially responsible for what the city of Bath became, he was also an accomplished antiquarian scholar that had written on a wide range of subjects from the Romans to Druidism. He had even conducted surveys of Stonehenge and other ancient stone circles. His list of architectural accomplishments was vast, including many in Bath such as St. John's Hospital, Queens Square, the Circus, and the building they were in currently- Prior Park. The Royal Crescent, the half-moon of wealthy townhouses built on a hill just west of the Circus that overlooked Bath, was designed by the man but executed by his son John Wood the Younger. The son was also an accomplished architect. In addition, Anna learned that the building that currently housed the sacred Roman spring was also designed by John Wood. The man's fingerprints were everywhere in Bath.

Anna closed her eyes, giving them a rest from staring at books, then let her mind think on the day's events. She had come to Bath looking for connections to Jane Austen and possible conspiracies that the novelist may have uncovered. So far, she had found little apart from a pagan shrine hidden under the abbey that was apparently still in use. She didn't know for sure, but Anna was quite certain that Winston Leigh had also found the shrine. He had drawn the depiction of Aion on the wall using the same piece of paper on which he would later write his cryptic dying words to Amelia.

Anna flipped to the page in her notebook that she had written down the message immediately after the detectives had left her.

"Find something?" Fraser asked. He seemed interested in what she had written down.

"Just thinking on Winston Leigh's message again."

"Any thoughts?"

"Well, I'm pretty certain the first part is about Jane Austen and her hidden secrets. I still have no idea what 'turn the key and reap the harvest' means."

"It is quite cryptic I have to admit," Fraser replied. "It does sounds like standard mystery liturgy though."

"What would it mean to the cults?" Anna asked

"Anything," Fraser said with a shrug. "It's all about the soul's journey into mystery. Those sorts of metaphors were used by cults all over the ancient world, even Christians. Jesus himself used open door and harvest imagery many times."

Anna remembered seeing said biblical imagery earlier in the stained-glass windows of the abbey- Peter with his keys, Paul with his sword. In one image, Christ held a sickle in one hand while reaping stalks of wheat representing people.

"That's it!" Anna exclaimed but was immediately embarrassed that she had yelled in a quiet library. A few students had turned to look at her with silent, judging, expressions that were typically British before returning to their books.

"Yes?" asked Fraser in a smug, joking manner.

"The key and sickle," Anna replied then proceeded to draw the symbol in her notebook then held it up for Fraser to see. "'Turn the key and the harvest reap'- Leigh was telling Amelia to look for this symbol."

Fraser looked skeptical. "What makes you so sure?"

"I keep seeing it places," she replied. "First, I saw it at the sacred spring; I thought it was a mason's mark. Then I saw it over the old doorway that led to the shrine underneath the church." Her eye caught a particular book sitting on the table and her mind was filled with notions. "It has to be a symbol of the mystery brotherhood; one that John Wood was particularly fond of. He designed the building around the sacred spring. He also designed this house for Ralph Allen; if there is a secret passageway to some underground chamber it is probably marked with the key and sickle."

"You certainly are a clever one Anna Lewis," said Fraser with a smile. "And not just a pretty face. It's better than anything *I've* come up with."

Anna felt heat go to her cheeks and she hoped that they weren't flushed. That would be embarrassing. He gave her a veiled compliment, so what? Although, even a veiled compliment about her intellect from a man as smug as Fraser Adams meant more than accolades from her friends. Why was she so determined to think poorly of Fraser? Because he had made a *horrible* first impression, that's why. Anna pushed the thoughts from her mind.

The two of them tidied up their table, then placed the books they had been using on the return carts before making their way down the hallway.

"Ok mystery-cult expert," said Anna with a quiet but playful tone. "Where would *you* hide a secret passageway?" She was concerned by how flirty that had sounded. Anna certainly didn't want Fraser to think that she was flirting with him.

"Well," he replied while looking around as they walked. "Many of the secret passageways and hidden chambers that I know of tend to be reused from older structures, like a medieval castle or church ruins."

"That's basically what Mr. Tillney describes in *Northanger Abbey*," Anna replied.

"The problem is that Prior Park was a whole new creation from the minds of John Wood and Ralph Allen, so it will be difficult. It was fashionable among the intellectual elites of the day to build all sorts of puzzles into their homes, especially into the furniture. Desks and cabinets could have all sorts of hidden compartments inside of them. The home owners knew that guests liked to snoop and made it a sort of game that rewarded those that had the mental capacity to solve the puzzles."

"So basically a hidden doorway could be anywhere," said Anna with a hint of frustration. It wasn't going to be as easy as she had hoped.

Knowing Jane Austen's love for puzzles and mind games, it sounded very likely that she could have been wandering around Prior Park looking for possible mysteries to solve. Her father and mother had taught her to use her mind quite well. George Austen in particular invented all sorts of puzzles for his children to solve. If he was somehow connected to the goings on at Prior Park, perhaps it was his lessons that had led to Jane being able to solve the mysteries of the manor house.

Anna and Fraser continued walking around for quite some time but found nothing. As the manor house had seen several renovations and alterations since the Church first purchased the estate in 1828, it was hard to determine how much of the building had remained the same since Jane Austen's day. They were also not able to be as thorough with their investigation as they would have liked to be as they didn't want to draw attention to themselves. They were walking around a boarding school after all. Luckily, it was summer sessions and the majority of the students were not staying on campus. The main rooms and hallways were virtually empty, though they would occasionally pass a priest or a nun.

There were several rooms that had plaques with information about Ralph Allen, John Wood, and Prior Park, but very little of any use. Most contained information that they had already gleaned from the books in the library. A pamphlet Anna had picked up, however, had some interesting information about the fate of the estate following Ralph Allen's death. Allen left no immediate heir so the fortune went to his favorite niece, Gertrude, who had married Allen's friend William Warburton. The couple had lived at Prior Park for quite some time prior to the deaths of Ralph Allen and his wife. After inheriting the manor, William and Gertrude were forced to move out of Prior Park and let the house to an Irish aristocrat. They also sold off much of the contents of the house to liquidate assets in order to fulfill the further inheritance wishes of Ralph Allen. Following the deaths of her husband and young son, Gertrude returned to Prior Park. A woman in her fifties, Gertrude gave the gossips quite something to talk about when she married a young clergyman named Stafford Smith who was twenty years her junior. She died childless in 1796 with the estate going to her cousin's children, though they chose not to live at Prior Park. Instead, it became the home of Lord Harwarden, Sir Cornwallis Maude, an Irish Viscount who had married Ralph Allen's other niece, Mary, and had sired nineteen children by three different wives. Though he had not owned the property at the time, it was the quite fertile Lord Hawarden who had lived at Prior Park during Jane Austen's days in Bath.

"I'm about to try every cliché in the book," Anna finally said in frustration.

"What do you mean?" Fraser said with a laugh.

"You know, pulling on suspicious candlesticks, twisting busts on mantles; that sort of thing."

"Have at it," he replied with a wave of his hand. "Though, I doubt there is nearly as many of those things about this place as there probably had been in the Regency era. Perhaps we should return to town and try to look for other leads."

Anna sighed in frustration. "No. This has to be the place. It just makes too much sense." She had to be right; she knew she was. Jane Austen had found something hidden in that manor house and she would find it as well.

"I'm going back to the library," she said while quickly turning. She then began walking down the hall without giving Fraser time to protest.

"I admire your tenacity," he said from behind. "But we should probably return to the Roman ruins. We are more likely to find something useful there than continuing to search this place. Even if there had been a secret chamber hidden somewhere on the grounds, it's likely not there anymore."

Anna ignored him and marched back into the library, bound and determined to be right. Fraser knew nothing of her theories and nothing about Jane Austen for that matter. Who was he to tell her that she was wrong? He just wanted to return to the Roman ruins because that was his area of expertise. Could she really blame him though? Anna would probably feel much more comfortable looking for clues amongst medieval alchemical manuscripts and Arthurian romances but she would need to spend the day in the libraries of Oxford to do that.

It was then that she recalled the Aion iconography that she had seen among her research at Oxford. Anna had almost forgotten about it. Perhaps she could find some sort of clue among those manuscripts. If only she had written down which ones they were. They hadn't pertained to her research so she had dismissed them. She would need to make a trip to Oxford soon. If anything else, it would give her an excuse to at least *try* to be productive and work on her dissertation.

The library appeared to be one of the only areas of Prior Park that had seen little alteration over the years. As such, it was the best place to have a final look. Anna was good to her word and tried every cliché that she knew of. She went about every part of the library touching, pulling, or turning anything she thought looked suspicious. She looked behind paintings, searched for a lever somewhere around the area that appeared to have once been a fireplace, and knocked on the walls while listening with her ear to them. She was pretty sure she looked insane.

Fraser simply shook his head, each time giving her an expression that either meant he couldn't believe that she was trying something, or couldn't believe that she was touching so many things that she shouldn't be.

When she had tried everything and searched every nook and cranny, Anna finally gave up and sat in a reading chair in one of the back corners of the library. She then put her face in her hands in frustration. Fraser simply stood in front of her.

"Don't say a word," she said in an irritated tone.

"Wouldn't dream of it," he replied. "However, I do believe there may have been a chair over by the door that you haven't leaned back in yet."

Anna wasn't amused and gave Fraser a look that let him know it. He was just so smug. His accusing eyes made her feel stupid and it infuriated her even more. Was she wrong about all of this Jane Austen nonsense, or just about Prior Park? She had no other leads.

It was then that she saw the symbol engraved in a stone above Fraser's head; it could only be seen clearly from the angle Anna was sitting.

"There it is," she said with excitement, pointing. "The sickle and key symbol." It looked almost identical to the mason symbol she had found earlier in the sacred spring.

Fraser turned around and hunched down to look at it for himself.

"Yes, but all that tells us is that John Wood was responsible for the building's construction and we already knew that."

Anna ignored him and began to search around their immediate area again, knocking on every stone and piece of wood along the way.

"You can't be serious Anna," Fraser said in frustration. "Ow! Really?" She chopped his shin with her hand to get him to back away.

She knocked on the floor where he had been standing and it sounded strange. There was a small, finger-sized hole in it as well.

"If you want to continue fooling around in this place, by all means go ahead. I'm returning to Southampton with or without..." his words were cut short as Anna pried off the small piece of floorboard that she thought had sounded suspicious, revealing some sort of mechanism that looked like a sundial.

"Turn it ninety degrees to the left," said Fraser as if he had not just threatened to leave her there.

Anna turned to look at him.

"Do it," he said as if commanding her.

Stunned by his tone, she quickly did as he asked and turned the dial 90 degrees to the left. After she did so, Anna could feel, and hear, various gears and levers moving underneath the floor. Moments later, a portion of a wall moved behind a shelf of books to reveal an entryway into darkness. The bookshelf, which had apparently not originally been there, was barring their path.

"How did you know to do that?" asked Anna is disbelief.

"I've seen similar devices before," he replied. "You turn the dial to the East, to welcome the Dawn."

Anna waited for a further explanation but Fraser quickly went to one side of the bookshelf. He pushed with his might to move it, giving them just enough room to squeeze through. He quickly went beyond the entryway, not wasting any time.

"Are you coming?" he asked irritated after popping his head back out.

"Yes sorry," Anna replied. For someone that had been so determined to be right, she was stunned to find that she had been. She squeezed in behind the shelf and Fraser, this time with Anna's assistance, moved the bookcase back into place so that no one could see the obvious hole in the wall behind it.

Once inside, Anna could see that the doorway immediately led to a stone stairwell that went down into a chilly darkness. It was much like the stairwells that led up to the bell towers of medieval churches, but in the opposite direction.

Fraser took his mobile phone from his pocket and turned on its built in flashlight, illuminating their path downwards. He began to descend the steps with no apprehension whatsoever and Anna followed close behind him. She braced herself against the cold stone walls for balance while trying hard not to slip on the smooth steps.

When they reached the bottom, they found themselves in an open, vaulted, stone chamber that appeared to run the length of the library above. The floor was caked in dust and dirt. It was solid but felt more like ground than the stones that lined the chamber walls. The place must have been built upon the bed rock. The air was stale as the place had apparently not been visited in quite some time. There were also no visible footprints anywhere on the grimy floor. Whatever was down there had remained undisturbed, possibly for close to two centuries.

Fraser continued to flash his light around, revealing the chamber to be relatively empty.

"There isn't anything down here," he said in frustration. "Whoever used this place cleaned it out of anything useful ages ago."

"Shine the light back over there," said Anna pointing. Something in one of the side chambers had caught her eye but Fraser moved too quickly for her to see it clearly.

When the light shone back in the area it revealed an old wooden armoire, rotting from either age or termites- probably both. It looked like it was about to fall apart at any moment. Also in the room were other pieces of old rotting wooden furniture- a small table and a few stools. They went in for a closer look.

"I've seen a similar piece to this one before, at a townhouse I visited in York last spring," said Fraser. "It had secret puzzle compartments built into it." He rubbed the area around his mouth with his hand as he inspected the armoire. "Now let's see if I can't figure this out."

Anna watched Fraser for a moment. She could just imagine the proverbial gears inside of his head spinning while he contemplated the puzzle of the secret compartments. It was cute really. They were in a secret subterranean chamber looking for lost mysteries and Fraser Adams was trying to solve a puzzle cupboard.

Anna walked over to the corner of the room and reached down to pick up a large piece of stone that had crumbled off of the wall. She held it high over her head and then walked over to the armoire.

"Watch out," she warned Fraser.

"What're you..."

Anna didn't give him time to finish his question before she brought the stone down with all her might, smashing the front of the wooden armoire to bits. As it had been rotting for centuries, it hadn't taken much for her to plow through it with the stone. Much of the remains began to crumble and fall apart. She snatched Fraser's phone from his hand and shined it about the debris.

"How could you?" he asked in astonishment.

"It got the job done didn't it?" Anna said in reply.

"Americans...," said Fraser while shaking his head. "You probably just destroyed whatever was hidden inside of that thing."

"Nope," she said smiling. The light glimmered on a small black object lying underneath the pieces of wooden debris. She scooped it up then brushed off the dirt and wood particles. It was a case, about a little less than a foot long, and looked and felt to be made of some sort of smooth stone or marble. She turned it over to see a small metal plate on one side had an engraving on it.

"Obsidian," said Fraser who had probably noticed Anna's look of confusion.

Anna rubbed the grime off of the metal plate so she could made out the inscription. After a few moments she could finally make it out- *Isabella Elizabeth*.

"Isabella Elizabeth..." said Fraser. "Does that mean anything?"

"Perhaps," Anna replied. She was too focused on the case to give the name more thought. She immediately opened it, revealing a lady's fan- certainly not what she had been expecting to find.

"That's it?" said Fraser in surprise and frustration. He apparently had not expected a fan either. "After everything, that is all we find? A bloody fan?" He kicked a stone in his anger and sent it flying. Anna heard it hit a wall at the other end of the subterranean chamber. "Winston Leigh threw his life away for a stylish accessory."

Anna was a bit surprised that Fraser was taking their discovery, or lack thereof, so badly. He had only just found out about the whole business a few hours ago. She wasn't even certain he had truly believed her until she had found the hidden doorway in the library. Anna took the fan out of its case and carefully opened it to have a closer look at it, shining the light on it as she did so.

"I wouldn't be giving up just yet," she said and Fraser looked at her with confusion.

She turned the fan and shined the light on it so he could see it better. One side had a map of the city of Bath printed on it. It was not an uncommon item to own as it was fashionable in the days of Jane Austen to have fan-maps while visiting popular destinations. At times, it had been hard to keep track of the many dance halls and assembly rooms one had to attend in a town. What was uncommon about this particular fan-map of Bath was that, marked out in red, were the streets that ran through the Royal Crescent, the Circus, and the Queen's Square. All had been designed from the mind of John Wood and looked to be in the shape of a sickle and key. A small red X had been drawn where the key was pointing.

"Now quit whining and let's go," said Anna with a wide grin. "I'm pretty sure this stylish accessory is a treasure map."

OOO

Anna almost ran into another group of French students standing about in the way while she was inspecting the fan-map against her tourist map of Bath. They were almost to the place where X marked the spot.

She and Fraser had wasted little time since finding the map. When they returned to the library, no one had been the wiser that they had stumbled into a long forgotten secret chamber. Luckily, turning the sundial switch back to the position they had found it caused the stone wall to return to where it had been as well.

Before they had made their way out of the library, Anna had noticed an old map hanging on the wall that looked very similar to the one on the fan. Upon closer examination, Anna found that it was a common map of the late eighteenth century by a man named Thorpe. She had made the connection immediately upon reading it- Isabella Thorpe, an important character in *Northanger Abbey*. By using the name, Jane Austen had alluded to the map of the mysterious Isabella Elizabeth.

Anna looked up to see a familiar troop of mummers and minstrels. She had been there hours before- standing in front of the entrance to the Grand Pump Room and the exit to the Roman Baths gift shop. She looked at the map again. The X was just down the street and to the left.

"It's that way," she said to Fraser while pointing.

"That's the area of St. John's Hospital," he said and then reached into his bag. He pulled out the notebook he had been writing in earlier at Prior Park and glanced through his notes. "The hospital was one of John Wood's earliest projects. The man who financed the project also had Wood remodel his townhouse, which was adjacent the hospital. It was the Duke of Chandos."

"Jane Austen's great uncle?" asked Anna, more out of surprise than an actual question. "That is obviously not just a coincidence." Excited, she began to quickly walk in the direction of the hospital without giving Fraser much chance to respond. He was right behind her.

St. John's Hospital was a two-story building of Bath stone with a heavy ground-floor arcade of round-headed arches on pillars. It was built next to hot springs called Cross Bath.

They moved quickly down the alleyway and into the area behind the hospital in which the townhouse was located.

The house was separated from the hospital building by a small park no bigger than Anna's front yard back home. When they reached the front, Anna could see that the building in which the duke had once lived was larger than the typical Georgian townhouse and in most respects was the size of a proper house.

Built of stone and faced with white plaster, it was three stories tall with five windows on each floor facing the street and twin chimneys on both ends. The building, which matched the style and architecture of the almshouse behind it, also appeared to have been taken over by the hospital and used for shelter housing. As they had just spent a fair amount of time searching around a boarding school, Anna was not looking forward to traipsing around a hospital drawing suspicion.

To the left of the house was another small park area. Anna could tell by the layout of the area, that when the house had been built, there had most likely been other buildings to the left and right of it. Like much of Britain, the area likely saw much bombing during the world wars. Chandos House had withstood the test of time while its neighbors became park land.

As she was gazing on the kept grass and flowers, Anna noticed a stone in the wall close to ground with some sort of engraving on it. She quickly jumped the small fence to have a closer look.

"What're you doing?" asked Fraser looking horrified.

"I jumped the fence to look at this," she replied. "So what?"

"Fences are usually a good indication that you are not allowed to be someplace."

"I'm pretty sure we weren't supposed to be traipsing around a subterranean chamber underneath a manor-turned-boarding-school, but we did that anyway didn't we?"

"Just don't let anyone catch you," he warned.

Anna rolled her eyes and shook her head. She had definitely learned over the course of the year that the British had some strange complex about following simple mundane rules. If an area was chained off or a sign said "do not touch" or "keep off the grass," they would comply like a dog with a shock collar at an invisible fence.

She moved in for a closer look at the image on the stone- it appeared to be in the shape of an X. *X really does mark the spot,* Anna thought to herself. She then realized that the X was in reality a weathered carving of the now familiar sickle and key. The stone also had cracks in it as well- likely bombing damage. The section of the house was patchy and Anna could tell that the war-damage had likely been repaired, and quickly, as some of the mortar was cracking.

"Keep a look out," said Anna with a smile. "I'm going to do some more stuff I probably shouldn't be doing."

Anna picked up a rock about the size of a softball with a pointed end then began chipping away at the mortar around the engraved stone. It wasn't long before the stone was loose enough for her to pry it out with the help of the pointed rock. The stone did not go back as far as she had expected. The area behind it was dark and deeper than the block. Anna reached in with her hand and prayed that there were no spiders or other creepy crawlers living inside. Eventually, her fingers touched a solid object that felt similar to the case that held the fan. She moved it closer, bit by bit, until Anna could grab it with her hand and pull it out completely. Out came a black box, most likely obsidian as well, that was roughly a foot long, 6 inches wide, and about 2 inches thick. A metal clasp on one end held it shut.

Within moments of pulling the box out, Fraser had jumped the fence as well, caring little for breaking the rules now that Anna had found something.

She unfastened the clasp with no trouble and opened the box. Inside was a sheet of silver metal, about a fourth of an inch thick, with numerous markings all over it. It looked to Anna to be some sort of language- one she was unfamiliar with. She gently pulled the sheet out of the box to look it over. The language was written on both sides and two holes were to one side at the top and bottom.

"It looks like a piece of a codex," said Anna as she studied the find. "But I have no idea what language this is."

"It's Demotic," Fraser quickly replied. He had a wide smile on his face as he stared at the sheet of metal.

Anna had never heard of that language before but she didn't want to make her ignorance known to Fraser. It sounded to her like he had said *Demonic*. She wondered if it was some sort of cultic language invented in the Middle Ages for summoning demons. It had been known to happen.

"It's also known as Egyptian script," Fraser continued, apparently deducing her ignorance. "It was the common written language of Egypt during the Greco-Roman period."

"Not quite the treasure I was expecting, but cool nonetheless."

"Indeed," said Fraser as he looked it over. "I would put that back in its box. I will put the stone back before someone notices us."

Anna carefully returned the silver sheet to the box and clasped it shut while Fraser went about fixing the wall. As she did so, her eyes caught those of another walking on the other side of the street then panic filled her. It was the man in the long grey coat from the abbey and he had recognized them.

"We need to run," she said, grabbing Fraser's hand then pulled him up from his crouched position. Before he could reply he also noticed the man from before. They ran, hand in hand, behind Chandos House and into the inner courtyard of the Hospital. Anna quickly turned to look behind and saw the man jump the fence and look at the wall where the engraved stone was. As they rounded the corner, before he was out of site, Anna could see him take his mobile phone from his coat pocket.

"He's making a call," she said with a huff as they ran. "He's also chasing after us."

Fraser turned to look for himself and said "shyte" once Anna's report was confirmed. He suddenly broke stride and turned right, down a tight alleyway, dragging Anna long with him. A few moments later, they were back onto the street filled with mummers in front of the Grand Pump Room. Before Anna could process what was happening any further, Fraser pulled her to him, against a storefront wall, then took her into his arms and kissed her fervently.

Stunned, Anna did not immediately know how to react. Fraser Adams, an egotistical Scottish prat she had only just met the previous night, was kissing her- quite well in fact. When the shock wore off, Anna realized that it was an attempt to blend in with the crowd while keeping their faces out of direct view. *It always works in the movies*, she thought to herself and then returned Fraser's kiss, with a bit more enthusiasm for authenticity. Anna brought her hands up to caress his back, feeling the toned muscles under his shirt as she did so. Fraser's hand went to the small of her back, slightly caressing the bare skin that had been exposed as her shirt rose slightly with her arms. Anna was surprised by how soft his touch was.

With one eye slightly open, Anna saw their pursuer pass them by none the wiser. He stopped a moment in the square to search for the two of them, but not being able to make them out, he turned right and kept running towards the train station. Fraser must have noticed too and as Anna's tension relaxed, he broke the kiss and she pulled away. When their eyes met Anna realized that her cheeks had flushed considerably.

"I think we lost him," said Anna feeling slightly awkward.

"I've always wondered it that would actually work," said Fraser with a smirk on his face.

"Ducking into a store would have worked just as well," Anna replied with indignation that she wasn't quite sure was genuine or not.

"Well, we can do that next time if you would rather." He glanced down at his watch. "We should leave quickly before he doubles back once he finds we aren't at the station. We've found what we needed to I think." He looked at her with a grin. "I hope you enjoyed your day in Bath."

Anna didn't smile back but had to admit that she certainly had enjoyed her day. Underground ruins, elegant houses, treasure maps, and a fine tea time. Where else would this mystery lead her she wondered?

Chapter 5

Anna sat at a table in Oxford's Bodleian Library, books spread out and open all around her person, with a notebook in front of her. The white, lined, pages were blank though and she had been holding a pen in her hand for quite some time. It had been tapping much more than writing.

Anna shook her head. Her mind had been wandering again. She had accomplished very little and her deadline was approaching fast. She would need to put the Jane Austen mysteries away on the shelf for a while so that she could focus on her dissertation. She would need to have her first draft turned in to Amelia in a few days and she had a third left to write. She was also having troubles thinking of an adequate conclusion.

She glanced at her cell phone to check the time, but also to see if she had by chance missed a message. She hadn't heard anything from Fraser in days. Anna assured herself that she only cared because she was waiting on the translation of the text. Why would she care if Fraser stayed in touch with her or not other than that? She barely knew the guy and couldn't really stand being around him all that much. Although, Anna had frequently found herself thinking about their kiss.

After the excitement of Bath, their drive to Southampton had turned out to be quite an awkward experience at first. Since Olivia had left Anna alone, Fraser had offered to drive her back to the university. It had been chivalrous but also the only sane thing to do as they were likely being chased by murderers. If he had made her ride the train home, Anna may have been stabbed in the crowd then left on a bench at one of the small stops along the way.

At first they had talked very little during the long drive. Anna hadn't been able to tell if he had been simply lost in thought or had just not wanted to talk to her. Whatever the case, Fraser must not be one for making conversation. They had discussed the Jane Austen investigation for some time but when she had exhausted her theories the conversation went south. She had attempted to make small talk on a few occasions but his replies had been short and nondescript.

Anna had been determined to not sit in awkward silence for hours so she decided that there was only one real way she could get Fraser to talk at length.

"So what made you go into Roman archaeology?" she asked and then settled herself in for the long haul.

"My gran actually," he replied. "Her father was an antiquarian scholar that specialized in the Roman military, specifically- their religious life. Their family vacations consisted mainly of trips across the Mediterranean world while he oversaw excavations at various sites. On the off season they would be dragged all over the British Isles. While many in his place would have simply ignored his family and left them at home, my great granddad never wanted be away from his children. He saw it as an education more valuable than the most expensive private schools. History and family were very important to him."

"He sounds like a great man," said Anna.

"He was. I wish I could have known him."

"So I take it your grandmother became a scholar as well?"

"Not in the traditional sense," Fraser replied. "As highly educated as she was, she still lived in an era when academia was heavily dominated by men. As you can imagine, traditional old

English gentlemen did not appreciate it when a young Scottish woman had a better grasp on Greek, Latin, and Classical civilizations than they did."

Anna certainly understood what that was like. Even in the more "modern" era, women were not always treated with the same respect in the professional world than the majority of their male colleagues. There were many brilliant women scholars, but Anna felt as if females had to set themselves far and above their male competitors in order to be recognized.

"What did she end up doing?" Anna asked.

"The Second World War broke out and she was asked to join a group of military scholars that were a sort of a British counter intelligence unit. They were an answer to the Nazi Thule Society that had been scouring the world for artifacts and relics. As she was young, highly educated in antiquities, and spoke French and German fluently, gran was ideal for the group."

"Wow, that's awesome. She was like a lady James Bond mixed with Indiana Jones."

"Something like that, yes."

"Was she able to tell you any of what she went through or was it highly classified?"

"Some statutes of limitations had run out before she died and she told me many amazing stories when I was growing up. There were still others that she either wasn't allowed to speak of or were too hard for her to talk about."

"Tell me some of them," Anna had pleaded.

"Alright," Fraser replied and then began to tell some of the tales that his grandmother had told him of her adventures during the war.

Over the course of the drive south, Anna heard many amazing stories about Fraser's grandmother- Miranda Mackenzie Fraser, whose family he had been named for. The tales were filled with danger, intrigue, and suspense enough that Anna had no doubt that she could easily sell the movie rights. One particular tale peaked her interest the most- the story of how she had met her husband. Miranda had been on assignment in Rome when she met a fellow Scot named James who had been working in the Vatican archives. The two literally ran into each other while being chased by fascists. They helped each other escape and fell in love.

When they reached Southampton, Fraser had offered to walk Anna to her room. For some reason that she still did not understand, it had given her butterflies in the stomach. She had chalked it up to the Scottish accent and gentlemanly behavior. Regardless, she had not been about to let it go any further since she had just met him the previous night. When at her door, however, Fraser had simply asked if she had a scanner and if she could quickly make him a copy of the silver sheet. Anna wasn't certain whether she had been disappointed or not, but regardless, her ego had certainly taken a hit.

Once Anna had made the copy, he told her that he was going to take it to an Egyptologist friend of his to translate and that he would be in touch. That had been almost a week ago.

The previous night she had gotten frustrated with waiting, and in combination with the university library's inadequacy, she decided to take a trip to Oxford for the day. She had extended an invitation to Olivia to join her but her friend had turned her down. Olivia hadn't left her room much the past few days. She claimed to be working hard on her dissertation but Anna knew that she was also trying to play it safe. Olivia could be very paranoid sometimes. Anna had decided not to tell her friend about Prior Park and the silver manuscript. If she had been that concerned about being seen in the chamber below the abbey, she probably would not like to be involved in the rest.

Anna surveyed the books in front of her, deciding which ones she needed and which ones she could put back. She closed a few, put them in a stack, and then placed them on the return cart. She sighed and went back to search the shelves again for useful books. At the libraries of Oxford, Anna found that she had the opposite problem that she usually had- too many interesting books. She often found herself going back to her table with a pile of books simply because she stumbled across them while looking for one in particular. Though Anna wished she could sit and read each one in its entirety, she had to skim them for useful information or she would never leave the library.

She stopped in a particular section devoted to alchemy and hermeticism then scanned for anything useful on the Holy Grail or the Philosopher's Stone. Her eyes caught a particular leather-bound tome of significant age called *Oedipus Aegyptiacus*. As Egypt was in the title, it was likely on mysticism, and Anna was easily distracted onto the Jane Austen mystery. She quickly took the book from the shelf and inspected it.

The book had been published between 1652 and 1654 and was comprised of three volumes of studies by Athanasius Kircher. From the picture inside, the man appeared to have been some kind of church scholar. Anna quickly, but carefully, flipped through the book. It was filled with all sorts of strange pictures, charts, and letters, typical of such works from the period. She thought it was worth a closer look and took it back to her table.

After looking through it for some time, Anna grew fascinated by much of what she saw. As it was written in medieval church Latin, she didn't understand the work in its entirety but she knew enough from her undergrad days to figure out the gist of it. Kircher had claimed that he had deciphered the mysterious Egyptian hieroglyphs that had eluded translation since roughly the 5th century AD. Anna had read similar works in her studies as it was a common thought in the Middle Ages that the Egyptians had invented alchemy and had passed on their secrets in their mysterious symbolic language. Any alchemist worth their salt had claimed to have deciphered the Egyptian language. Unfortunately, all of their efforts proved to be in vain once the language was truly deciphered with the discovery of the Rosetta Stone less than a century after Kircher had lived.

Anna flipped through several pages of supposed translations of various Egyptian texts. She found them to be quite strange and eccentric but also fascinating. Many sounded like instructions for a ritual to transform the soul, but Anna figured that in reality it was probably more likely to be some dead person's grocery list. After turning a few more pages of alchemical charts she saw it- an illustration of Aion, or something quite similar. It was not exactly the same depiction that she had seen before; many details were missing such as the sickle and key. Also missing was the lion's head. Many of the essential details were there, however. The illustration depicted a youthful, angelic, being with a snake wrapped around its legs with either a halo or the sun's rays shining behind its head. It also was breathing some sort of flame, or perhaps a beam of light, onto what looked to be farmland. She could also tell that there was an implied geometric element to the lines and shapes as well. The whole scene just left Anna confused. She took a quick picture of it with her cell phone and jotted down information in her notebook.

She closed her eyes and sighed. She was getting nowhere on both of her projects. Unfortunately, she found she had little focus for her dissertation- the more important of the two at the time. Amelia had tried to warn her that she might have been biting off more than she could chew in a master's dissertation. She was writing on the Holy Grail *and* the Philosopher's Stone after all- a fool's quest indeed.

Anna began perusing through her notes, as she usually did when she felt stuck in her arguments. She looked over her outline, wondering if her thesis was strong enough. The Holy Grail, the cup that was thought to have held the blood of Christ, was believed to be able to heal any wound and essentially bestow immortality on the one who continually drank from it. It was a legendary relic that was central to many medieval romances, the most famous being those trials of King Arthur and his knights. The Philosopher's Stone, likewise, was a legendary item of great power sought after in the late Medieval and Renaissance periods that was believed to have the power to transform iron into gold and could also create the Elixir of Life, which granted immortality. Anna believed that the Holy Grail and the Philosopher's Stone were one and the same legendary item of power and not to be taken literally. Instead, she viewed them as literary devices used to inspire people to transform their mundane life into something immortal and divine. Amelia had loved her proposal but had warned her that she could fill several books with such a topic. She had been right though and Anna was feeling overwhelmed.

She looked at her watch- it was getting late. At Oxford, life didn't shut down as early as it did in Southampton but she wanted to be back to the dorms before dark. After she had packed her stuff and returned her books, she noticed her phone blinking- she had missed a call and had a text message. It was from Fraser.

Where are you?

Oxford, she replied.

Anna made to leave and was surprised by his quick reply.

Meet me in front of Radcliffe Camera in 5 minutes.

Anna was surprised to find that Fraser was in Oxford. She pondered the situation as she left the library. The Bodleian was situated along Radcliffe Square and she could have even taken an underground tunnel to the camera building if she had wanted to. She had done so on quite a few occasion just because she could and she thought it was cool. She didn't this time, however, as it was quicker to just go the normal way above ground. Anna walked through the Bodleian courtyard and under the archway that led to the entrance of Radcliffe Camera- a circular, Neoclassical building of yellowish stone with a faded blue dome. She loved walking around this part of Oxford, with its centuries old complexes of Gothic buildings and cloisters. Honestly, it made her feel like she was walking around Hogwarts.

When Anna saw him, Fraser was leaning beside the black, iron fence that encircled the building. He was wearing light tan trousers and a blue blazer with red stripes on the cuffs. He looked like he was going to a yacht club or a job interview.

"How did you know I was here?" she asked as soon as he was close enough.

"Olivia told me," he replied.

"You drove all the way here to talk to me?" she asked, a bit flattered. "You could have just called."

"I was already here visiting a friend," he quickly replied and the feeling of flattery evaporated. "I did my undergrad work here and was a member of Brasenose College, just there." He motioned with his thumb to the complex of Gothic buildings to his right, opposite the Camera.

"Did this friend happen to translate our item?" asked Anna, laying on a small hint of irritation. "It's been almost a week and I've heard nothing from you."

"Sorry about that," Fraser said apologetically while trying to hide some sort of embarrassment. "I was visiting the very friend in fact, but his translation was...less than pleasing."

"Why?" she asked.

"See for yourself," he replied then produced a folded piece of white paper from his jacket pocket.

Anna took the paper and opened it. It was indeed a translation but the words made little to no sense in English.

"It's gibberish," she said. "Why would they hide gibberish?" She continued to read it over until a thought occurred to her. "Unless it's encoded somehow."

"My thoughts exactly," Fraser said with a smile. He looked pleased with her for a moment and then the smile quickly left. "The only trouble is, we have no idea where to find the cipher to unlock the code."

"That is a problem." Anna crossed her arms in thought and learned against the railing next to Fraser. Where in the world could they find the cipher?

"Any Jane Austen related theories?" asked Fraser with a look of anticipation.

"I'm not sure," she replied. Anna had exhausted her knowledge of secrets hidden in *Northanger Abbey*. They had followed the trail that Jane had left and found the map leading them to the codex piece. She was fairly certain that well was now dry.

"Let's try and think like conspiracy theorists," Anna suggested. "Winston Leigh was one and he was right after all."

"I think I may be a little too academic for that exercise," Fraser replied.

"Could you *be* any more pretentious?" asked Anna shaking her head. "I'm not asking you to think that aliens built the pyramids. Just think about Regency-era politics, philosophies, and what a mystery brotherhood might want to cover up."

Fraser narrowed his eyes at her. "I'm not pretentious."

"Keeping telling yourself that," said Anna laughing. "Maybe it will come true."

"Fine," said Fraser crossing his arms. "Let's say Jane Austen's father was caught up in some conspiracy involving this mystery brotherhood of Bath. They found this piece of silver codex and then hid it until they could figure out what it meant, which wouldn't be very likely as Demotic hadn't been translated yet.

Somehow, Jane Austen found out about the hiding place or the map on this Isabella's fan."

"Oh right," Anna interrupted. "I did a little information gathering about her over the past few days." She rummaged in her backpack for the notebook that she had written the information in. After finding the pages she had written on she continued. "Isabella Elizabeth Maude, born 1779 to the Lord Hawarden's third wife. Like Jane Austen and her sister Cassandra, Isabella remained unmarried until she died in 1859. She was only a few years younger than Jane and would have likely come into contact with her during her time in Bath. It was probably Isabella that invited Jane to stay at Prior Park and inspired the scenes in *Northanger Abbey*. One of the main characters of the novel, Isabella Thorpe, is probably a veiled clue to the Thorpe map on Isabella's fan."

"Definitely possible," said Fraser who was mulling over the information in his mind.

"Also," Anna continued. "I never thought about it until now, but at the end of Mr. Tilney's description to Catherine Morland, he says she might find the confessions of a wretched Mathilda, which is another name for Maude."

"Isabella Maude..." Fraser repeated, making the connection. "Fascinating. To think that all of these clues were in one of Jane Austen's books."

"It's no wonder that *Northanger Abbey* was caught in publication limbo for so long."

"Indeed," said Fraser continuing to think things over. "It seems likely that Jane, Isabella, and possibly Jane's sister, were in on this conspiracy together. It's a strange coincidence that the three ladies never married; especially Isabella, who was a lord's daughter."

"Maybe they made a pact or something," said Anna. "A secret sisterhood to exist alongside the brotherhood of their fathers."

"They must have talked about it with each other in letters or something," said Fraser with a bit of excitement."

Anna shook her head. "Jane told Cassandra to burn all of her letters when she died."

"An obvious move if one is trying to hide something," said Fraser while rubbing the sides of his mouth with his thumb and forefinger. "Is there any way Cassandra could have kept them hidden and told everyone that she burned them?"

"It's possible," said Anna thinking it over. "If she kept them hidden then they are most likely in Chawton somewhere."

"Where is Chawton?"

"A little north of Southampton, outside of Alton. There is a museum there now in the house that Jane Austen lived before she died."

Fraser looked at his watch. "If we hurry we can make it there before they close up for the night."

The walk to Fraser's car did not take them very long and they were soon on the road south back to Hampshire. Without Fraser spinning adventurous tales about his grandmother, the atmosphere within the car quickly grew awkward and Anna found herself staring out the window at the Oxfordshire countryside.

Eventually, Fraser turned on the radio and Anna felt relieved- for a brief moment. He had chosen to listen to some sort of talk show that was currently discussing the mating habits of garden snails. Anna touched a preset button to change the channel.

"I was listening to that," he said and then quickly changed the channel back.

"You can't be serious," Anna protested. "This is the most boring thing that can possibly be on the airwaves."

"Radio Four is not boring," he replied with an air of condescension. "I prefer to learn something while I drive. People who listen to nothing but commercial radio rot their brains."

"So, you are telling me that because you would rather listen to some guy talk about the mating habits of garden snails instead of the Top Forty, you are not an idiot?"

"Something like that," he smugly replied.

"Not from where I'm sitting," Anna replied with a wry look.

Fraser looked to be ready to reply with a smart remark but it was caught in his throat as he looked in the review mirror. "I think we might have a tail."

Anxious, Anna turned around to investigate the cars behind them on the motorway for anything suspicious. As she did, Fraser suddenly jerked the car and entered into the left lane. The movement sent Anna forward against the dash and she felt motion sickness embrace her. She sat herself forward again and closed her eyes while trying to breathe her body back to calmness. Fraser jerked the car a few more times and the sickness grew worse. Anna folded her arms across her chest and put her head between her knees.

"I've either lost them or I was too quick with my judgments," said Fraser after a while. "Are you ok?" He must have finally noticed her position.

"Just a little carsick," she said from between her knees. "It will go away eventually."

A moment later, Anna felt Fraser gently caress her back with his fingers. As she focused on the soothing touch of his hand she felt the motion sickness begin to dissipate. The caressing stopped for a brief moment and relaxing classical music began to play. He had changed the station for her.

It was not long before all traces of nausea left Anna, but she found herself unwilling to let Fraser know about it immediately; she let him continue to rub her back for a few more moments.

"Thank you," she said with a smile as she returned to her upright position. When their eyes met, Fraser looked to want to say "you're welcome" but his words caught in his throat and he just nodded. Anna turned the channel back to Radio Four and let Fraser listen to his "educational" programing. She was asleep within minutes.

Anna awoke just before they reached Chawton, a little before 17:00. Fraser parked his car just down the street from Chawton House and they quickly made their way to the building. To Anna's surprise they were about to close for the evening.

"You can't be serious," she said aloud in frustration. "It's only five o'clock and there's like four hours of daylight left. Why would they close?"

"I was afraid they might have closed," Fraser said. "Small towns tend to close up rather early."

"That makes no sense. How can they expect to make any kind of profit if they close when the majority of people just get home from work? When else would people be able to visit the place?"

"The weekend?" Fraser replied like it was obvious. "You Americans expect too much out of your businesses."

"Well, you can't expect to only have visitors on the weekends; that's ridiculous. What about all the tourists and foreigners that want to visit Jane Austen's house? She has a world-wide fan base. Imagine how much more money they could make if they stayed open an extra two hours on the weekdays."

"If you stop talking about profits, I will take you into that pub across the street and buy you dinner. We can talk about what to do next."

"Ok," Anna said with a smile and the two of them walked into the pub, the Greyfriar, to have a bite to eat.

The pub turned out to be nicer than Anna had expected. They were seated in an upstairs dining room with lace drapes and white table cloths that suited a tea parlor more so than a tavern. After looking the menu over, Anna decided on a steak and ale pie that turned out to be the best she had had so far in England. The kitchen had run out of the usual puff pastry typical of meat pies and had cooked it in the fashion of desert pies. The result had been exquisite. She also had a hot mulled wine to drink to make the meal perfect.

"I'm glad to see you are enjoying yourself," Fraser said with a chuckle as Anna smiled wide after taking another sip of her wine. "Ready to figure out what to do next?"

"I was thinking we could have a look around the old church we passed coming into the village. It won't be closed and I'm sure Jane and her sister spent a lot of time there."

"Sound plan," Fraser replied. "Finish your wine and let's be off."

Anna downed her last few sips and the two of them left the pub and began walking down the street to where she had seen the church. The church was down a small road lined with tall lush trees and was next to a large Elizabethan-style manor house made of stone. Along the way, a pair of beautiful Clydesdale horses stood next to an old wooden fence eating grass. As Anna neared the horses they did not make to move away so she crouched down and pulled a hand-full of grass from the ground to feed to them. One of the horses looked up at her and then gently took the grass from her hand. Anna smiled wide; it always felt nice when animals trusted her.

She turned around to see Fraser standing with his arms crossed, smiling at her. It was a warm look that she had not seen from him before. It confused Anna for some reason and she quickly made to continue on their way towards the manor house.

"That's probably the house that Jane Austen's brother lived in," said Anna upon realization.

"How is that?" Fraser asked. He was probably wondering how the poor son of a clergyman ended up living in a manor house.

"Chawton was owned by the Knights, who were rich cousins of the Austens that had no heir. They offered to adopt Jane's brother, Edward, as their son. When he inherited the estate, he let his mother and sisters live in Chawton Cottage. Until then they had bounced around various places after Jane's father died. They continued to live in Bath for a time, but it was too expensive for them. After that, they lived in Southampton under the care of another brother until Chawton became available."

"Convenient for them to have such connections," said Fraser.

"I suppose so," Anna replied. "Those few years after her father's death were apparently hard on Jane. She didn't write very much and shelved many of her projects."

"I wonder if her mind had been occupied with other, more mysterious, pursuits," said Fraser, thinking it all over.

"That seems very likely."

Just before the manor house, a stone path veered to the right towards the church that was situated in front of a large, open field of green grass. Along the path of stones leading to the entrance gate of the churchyard, was a pointed wooded shelter that look like a tiny covered bridge. Next to the shelter was a blue sign that described the St. Nicholas Church of Chawton, which belonged to the Diocese of Winchester and the Northanger Benefice.

"Northanger Benefice?" asked Anna aloud immediately upon reading it. "What exactly is a benefice?" she asked Fraser. She barely knew anything about how the Church of England operated.

"I believe it's a group of churches, smaller than a diocese, which are overseen by a single clergyman."

"Northanger pops up again. This can't be a coincidence." Anna began to ponder the implications in her head.

"Didn't you say she lived here *after* she first sold the rights to publish *Northanger Abbey*?" asked Fraser. "How can there be any connection to her codes?"

Anna thought it over. He had a fair point.

Anna shook her head. "She had called it *Susan* at that time. It wasn't until just before her death that Jane changed the main character's name to Catherine and the title to *Northanger Abbey*. No, this is another clue. Jane meant for someone to come here to find something hidden."

Fraser continued to read the sign. "According to this, Jane Austen's church had stood on this spot since the thirteenth century but a fire destroyed most of it in 1871. Only the chancel and the sanctuary survived."

"Hopefully, what we are looking for was hidden in those areas," Anna sternly replied to give herself confidence. It would have been a shame if Jane's secrets perished in the fire.

They walked into the churchyard and Anna began to investigate everything she saw. As the church building itself postdated Jane Austen, she had to force herself not to spend too much time staring at the gargoyles and grotesques that decorated the outside. Instead, she decided to look for clues among the older tombstones. Many appeared to be quite old and weathered. Many looked intriguing and appeared to date from the Middle Ages, however, upon closer examination Anna realized that they were from the early twentieth century. The Regency-era grave markers were much simpler in appearance and were usually small stone crosses with various engravings. One particular cross, that looked to be made of Egyptian granite, was situated under a gnarly old tree that looked to be made of many smaller trees coming together at the trunk and branching all about. She moved in for a closer look.

"Anna over here," Fraser called from the far left corner of the graveyard and Anna made her way over to him, leaving the gravestone for later.

"It's her mother and sister," she said upon reading the tombstones. Cassandra Austen, who died the 18th day of January 1827, aged 87 years. Cassandra Elizabeth Austen, who died the 22nd day of March 1845, aged 72 years.

"How much longer did Jane's sister live after she died?" asked Fraser.

"Almost thirty years," Anna replied. "It's sad. Jane was her best-friend. She lost her mother nine years later."

"I wonder why she never married. It would have made their lives much easier."

"Cassandra was engaged for a time in her early twenties but her fiancé contracted yellow fever and died somewhere in the Caribbean."

"Tragic," Fraser replied. "What about Jane? She seems like she would have been witty enough to attract an intelligent gentleman."

"She was engaged for a day actually, to a wealthy man from Basingtoke, just before her father died. She called it off the next morning for some reason and no one really knows why."

"Interesting," he said. Anna couldn't tell if Fraser was actually interested in the love lives of the Austen women or not but she certainly was.

"Some say Jane never got over her first love- an Irishman named Thomas Lefroy. He was a relative of some family friends."

"What happened there?"

"They were in their early twenties, flirty, and got on rather well. Tom's rich uncle was basically financing his law career, and didn't want his time and money wasted by his nephew marrying a poor girl with no connections. Once Tom's affections became apparent, he was shipped back to law school and they apparently had little contact with each other after that."

"Why do people think that there was anything deeper than flirting?" he asked.

"Jane never really showed the same affections for anyone else," Anna replied. "Also, he named his first daughter Jane."

Fraser shrugged his shoulders then bent down to investigate the immediate area around the gravestones and Anna did the same. The markers for the Austen women stood over a small, square plot with moss covered dark-gray stone squares. Graveyards in Europe were quite different than those typical in America, which had only existed as a country for a few centuries. Many graveyards in the US were in large open fields, with a church often being built at the time they were established. Typically, the deceased were buried with their loved ones side by side, with family members buried in the immediate vicinity. In Europe, graveyards were smaller and used around already established churches, many existing since the Middle Ages. As such, it was not uncommon for family members to be buried on top of one another. Some lone tombstones could have the epitaphs of entire families on them.

Fraser began pulling at one of the square stones and it filled Anna with shock.

"What're you doing?" she asked.

"Being an American," Fraser replied with a grin.

"We just break rules when we have to," Anna replied with fervor. "We don't go around desecrating graves all the time."

"They're dead; it isn't like they actually care," he said and continued flipping over stones.

"Yeah but still..." Anna's words stopped short when Fraser upturned a stone which had a rough engraving on the other side of it. She leaned in for a closer look. "What is it?"

"I don't know," said Fraser as he wiped away the damp soil to reveal a clearer image. "It looks like some kind of chalice or an urn."

"The Holy Grail?" she asked. It was the first thought that popped in her mind and Anna almost winced at how ridiculous it sounded. She had been reading about the Grail a lot lately.

Fraser looked at her with quizzical judgment. "I probably wouldn't go that far." He stood up and grabbed a stone from closer to the fence and placed it in the bare spot. It didn't match up completely but it was less conspicuous than the exposed earth. He handed the engraved stone to Anna. "Here, we might need it later."

Anna took the stone and looked it over. It did sort of look like the Grail; she might not be completely wrong.

"We should probably have a look around the inside of the church," she said.

Fraser nodded his agreement and the two of them made their way to the front of the church, then pushed past the large wooden doors into the interior of the building. The inside was typical of most of the parish churches that Anna had visited over the year. Wooden pews flanked a central aisle on both sides but the church had only one side aisle, on the left side, and only one row of stone pillars holding up the arches. Wooden beams that almost looked Germanic lined the ceiling above their heads, and stained glass windows with various saints and biblical characters lined the outer walls.

They made their way to the back part of the church, the sanctuary and chancel, as they had been the only parts of the church present in the days of Jane Austen. Above and to the left was the typical pipe organ, and on both sides were the wooden choral seats. Directly in front, was a pillowed kneeling station in front a low wooden banister, behind which was the Eucharist altar. To the left was a large, white and gray, marble tomb. The owner of the tomb, whose visage was captured in the same white marble, lounged above like a specter relaxing from a long day of haunting. The man wore a curled wig and his style of dress suggested that he had lived sometime in the eighteenth century. Anna's eyes rested on the top of the monument. Held atop pillars on both sides, were what appeared to be grails or urns.

Anna held up the engraved stone and compared the shapes. The stone sketch was rough but all of the essential curves and shapes were present. "It's the same urn," she concluded.

Fraser walked over beside Anna and placed a hand on her shoulder as he inspected the two. "Looks to be," he said.

The touch of his hand surprised her and made her tingle, or shiver. Perhaps she had just felt a draft. Anna was unsure how exactly she felt about the placement of Fraser's hand. Regardless, she let it stay where it was. After a moment she stepped forward and he quickly took his hand back. She looked up at each urn. The one on the right appeared to be completely solid but the one on the left looked to be made of two pieces. Throwing caution to the wind, Anna climbed the marble effigy and reached up to inspect the left urn. Just what she thought- the top portion came off with a little force, revealing the inside to be hallowed out. Anna reached in with her hand and felt around. Her fingers immediately came into contact with what felt like parchment. She carefully pulled out the contents of the urn, revealing a handful of wax-sealed envelopes and a small, leather-bound journal that was wrapped closed with a leather cord much like a bootlace. The red wax seal on the letters appeared to be of a deer or stag sitting atop a crown.

Anna carefully broke one of the seals, and with equal care, pulled out the folded paper within to inspect it. She was amazed by what she found.

"These are some of Jane Austen's lost letters," Anna exclaimed. Cassandra hadn't burned the entire collection after all.

"We've found what we need then; excellent," said Fraser beginning to look nervous. He looked to the entrance of the church. "You should probably be less American now and hop off the man's tomb before somebody walks in."

Anna carefully placed the letter back into the envelope, then put the collection of documents into her bag before resealing the hiding spot. She climbed down from off of the marble effigy and back onto the solid floor of the sanctuary.

"Ready when you are," she said with a smile and the two of them left the church and made their way back to Fraser's car to return to Southampton.

Safely in the car and with light still left in the day, Anna decided to spend the drive home inspecting the treasured correspondence. She carefully took the items from her bag and looked them over. The handful of letters appeared to have been composed at various dates over the course of a few decades. The earliest was dated to March 1801, while the latest was June 1840. It was nowhere near the amount of letters that Cassandra had supposedly burned, however. The ones that Anna had found must have been the most important ones that Cassandra had felt needed to be kept for some future generation to discover, long after Jane's death.

Anna took in hand the envelop that she had already opened, dated March 1801, and carefully took out the letter within then began to read it.

My Dear Cassandra,

You have not written in some time and I find myself quite distraught. I long for your return though I know it is likely we will not see each other until we are both residents of Bath. Why my father chooses to uproot his poor family from the only home they have every known and move them to such an ill society, I shall likely never know. I fear I shall faint again! I have pressed him fervently yet he responds the same way. He claims that his age does not allow him to care for the parishioners under his authority as well as he would like and that it is time for the more leisurely pursuits of retirement. I suspect there is more than what we are lead to believe, if not simply that father wishes to help James. Our brother has seen much hardship of late and will find the rectory a soothing balm.

We have heard again from Frank and his letter has agitated our father greatly though he will not let mother or I read the portions that have upset him so. He assures us that Frank is indeed safe and well and remains sailing amongst the ancient pharaohs. Our brother should return soon. You will likely see him before he meets us in Bath as he has made plans to visit Kippington after he makes port.

Father spends much time in his study since receiving Frank's letter. Though somewhat distant he took the time to read the latest portions of 'First Impressions' and gave his opinion regarding the latest additions. I long for your good opinion as well though I fear it will not come soon enough. Whilst father was occupied my glance lingered on the papers on top of the desk. He appears to be occupying his time looking over dusty tomes of vitruvian architecture and making sketches the like of Da Vinci. Perhaps our father aspires to be an accomplished artist in his old age. This could likely be his reasoning for desiring to live among the faux classical atmosphere of Bath, though I think not. Father noticed my gaze and declared his tiredness to me and that he must finish the additions on the morrow.

I wish to write of more however I grow tired of waiting for your letter and hope to inspire you to quickness. I long for us to be together.

Yours affectionately, J. A.

Anna returned the letter to the envelope, and setting the others to the side for a moment, unwound the cord from around the leather journal. She carefully opened it to find, on the first few pages, small caricature drawings of regency-era peoples. On the first page was what looked like a chubby little boy in a red military coat, wearing a white powdered wig, and playing a flute. The second page had a drawing in the likeness of a French aristocratic woman with a ridiculously large pompadour wig. As Anna continued to flip through the pages, they gradually became filled with less pictures and scribbles and more with small paragraphs of descriptive notes. Some pages seemed to describe observations of etiquette, while others had names of individuals and a short one sentence description, or a note about a coat or a frock. Some names were only described with one word such as Whig, Tory, or random French words. When her eyes scanned various character descriptions that she was familiar with, Anna realized beyond a doubt that she held Jane Austen's notebook in her hands. She sat back and held it with a sense of reverence while letting the gravity of it all sink in.

For a time all thoughts of mysteries, hidden secrets, and murder faded from Anna's mind as she stared at the some two centuries old musings of one of the world's most beloved novelists. Jane Austen herself had written on these pages with her own hand over the course of decades, possibly from a young age, as the early drawings and scribbles attested to. It was so much more than simply a journal that Jane had kept to chronicle her life. This was so much more intimate. The pages that Anna held were a gateway into the person that Jane Austen had really been- what she found truly interesting in life, her imagination, her creative spirit, her soul. Anna didn't feel nearly worthy enough to continue turning the pages.

"Are you alright?" Fraser asked, noticing that she hadn't moved for quite some time. "Are you sick again?"

"No, I'm alright," she replied. She let out a long breath that she hadn't realized she had been holding in. "I'm just a bit awestruck. This is Jane Austen's personal notebook- one of her most precious possessions in life."

"Have you found anything useful in it?" he asked.

"*Useful?*" Anna repeated as if his question were ridiculous. She was almost appalled. In her lap was probably one of the most important finds of the modern literary world, not to mention Jane Austen fans, and all Fraser Adams could think about was the mystery brotherhood and the silver codex. "This contains the notes, personal thoughts, and insights into the creative process of one of the most beloved and important female novelists in the history of literature. Whatever that club of glorified stuff-shirt frat boys is hiding, it is *nothing* compared to the value of this book and these letters."

Fraser softened but still seemed unconvinced that her fervor was entirely necessary. "I suppose you do have a fair point. Those items alone are worth a fortune. I doubt Winston Leigh was killed over Jane Austen's memoirs and lost letters though."

"I'm not entirely sure Leigh even knew these existed," Anna replied. "I'm fairly certain he meant for us to follow the clues in *Northanger Abbey*, which led to the silver codex page. He might not have known that it would translate into gibberish though."

"Have you found anything about a cipher yet?" asked Fraser.

"Not with my first glances, no," replied Anna. She thought he was being rather pushy. "I've mostly just come across old sketches and character profiles."

Anna soon recognized familiar Southampton areas and realized that Chawton had only been less than a half an hour car ride away from where they lived.

Fraser pulled his car up to the curbside in front of Anna's dorm building and parked the car. He unbuckled his seatbelt and Anna knew that he was likely wanting to walk her in again, probably to make copies.

"No need," she said as she quickly opened the door and stepped out. She leaned down and poked her head back into the car to talk to Fraser. "I can walk myself up. I will study the notebook and the correspondences further. I will call you in a few days with my findings."

With that, she shut the door and waved goodbye. Anna walked up to her room with a triumphant smirk on her face. Regardless of what she would find and when she found it, she would make Fraser Adams wait to know it.

CHAPTER 6

"I'm so glad it's finally over," said Olivia after sipping from her cup of tea.

"Yeah me too," Anna replied while gazing hazily into her own cup of barely drank tea.

"You're finished with your first draft?" Olivia looked confused and Anna realized that she hadn't really been listening to her friend.

"Oh, no," Anna replied after blinking away her daze. She returned to her surroundings- the quaint little garden café just outside the gift-shop in front of Winchester Cathedral. "I'm just glad you are finished so we can hang out more. I feel like I haven't seen you in ages."

"It's only been like a week Anna," she replied. "I'm surprised you haven't been holed up in your room too, or in the library."

"Mostly," Anna replied. "It's just nice to get out for the day."

Olivia had finally called Anna that morning and apologized for ignoring her. She claimed that she had been too stressed out with her dissertation to see any other human face to face for more than two minutes, though Anna still suspected that there was more to it. Olivia had made her opinion on her investigation into Jane Austen rather obvious when she had stormed off in Bath. Whatever the case, Anna was glad to have her friend back and the two of them had decided to spend the day in Winchester, only a fifteen minute train ride from Southampton. They were currently enjoying a cream tea before touring the cathedral.

Anna took a sip of her delicious earl grey and noticed her phone vibrating on the table. She didn't have to look to know who it was.

"You're quite the popular one now," said Olivia. "That's the third text you've gotten while we've been sitting here."

"It's just Fraser," Anna replied. "He's being relentless."

"Why Anna Lewis," said Olivia with a grin. "You must know what you're doing if you can get a guy like Fraser Adams wrapped around your finger."

"What are you talking about?" Anna replied out of shock.

"Just saying, you had to have rocked his world pretty good."

"I haven't slept with him!" Anna replied, the notion being quite ludicrous. "I've only known him a week. Plus, he's kind of a prat."

"That's never stopped a lot of girls," said Olivia with a shrug. "He's smart, hot, and Scottish." Her devilish grin returned. "While he shows you how it's done in the Highlands, you can make him call you his *Sassenach*." She was referring to one of their favorite steamy historical romance novels. It brought to Anna's mind certain images of a more rugged Fraser, in a kilt, taking her in his arms as he did that day in Bath. She felt herself going flush and shook the thoughts from her mind before she was bright red.

Olivia must have noticed her embarrassment and kept the grin as she continued her interrogations. "Well, if there's nothing going on between you two then why is he in full on stalker-mode?"

"He just wants something," Anna replied then sipped her tea.

"Obviously," said Olivia, raising an eyebrow.

"Not me!" said Anna in protest. "It's purely professional. Even when he kissed me in Bath it wasn't because he liked me." As she said the words, it sounded as if Anna was trying hard to convince herself rather than Olivia.

"Wait, he kissed you!?" her friend asked in shock. "Why was that not immediately the first thing you told me this morning?"

"Because it wasn't a real kiss...Well it *was* real kiss, a really good kiss in fact." Anna was pulled back to thoughts of the moment their lips touched but shook them off. "I mean...It was just a diversion."

"I'll bet it was." Anna wished Olivia's stupid grin would just go away.

"We were being chased," Anna admitted and Olivia's face became somber. She found herself missing the grin.

"So, you really are continuing on with this Jane Austen nonsense?" She shook her head before sipping her tea. "How you convinced Fraser to buy into it is beyond me. He certainly never seemed the type. Maybe there really is something to your feminine wiles Anna."

"It's not nonsense," Anna replied in a softer tone. "Also, I do *not* have feminine wiles. Charm perhaps, but not wiles."

"Well, it's nonsense that will get you killed, charm or not." Olivia shook her head. "It's just not worth it Anna."

"Let's just say that I've already found evidence that Winston Leigh was right, and that alone was worth it."

"Yeah, what?" Olivia looked very skeptical.

As much as Anna wanted to tell her friend the entire truth about the codex, the brotherhood, and Jane Austen's notebook, it was much safer for Olivia to know nothing about it. She had been right that day in Bath- the less she knew about the whole business the less danger she was in.

Anna shook her head. "It's best you don't know."

Olivia pursed her lips appearing to be annoyed, but at what exactly, Anna could not tell for certain. Was she upset that Anna wouldn't reveal the truth or was it that Anna hadn't given the whole thing up entirely? "Well, let's just finish our tea and wander around the cathedral, shall we?"

Anna smiled and nodded in agreement.

The two ladies finished their tea and left the café and gift-shop behind them to enter into the cathedral courtyard. Winchester Cathedral was of a grand design, containing one of the longest central naves in all of Europe. The church had seen several major restorations over the course of its almost thousand year existence. The present structure was first built by the Normans overtop the ruins of a much smaller church from the Saxon period. The Romanesque Norman architecture could still be seen in the towering sections in the middle, while the rest of the cathedral had been updated with the Gothic features from more recent eras.

As Anna and Olivia walked around the inside of the church, she noted the features typical to most cathedrals- patrons entombed under the floor, marble effigies, shrines for the bishops of Winchester. The stained glass windows at the front of the church were unique, however, as they appeared to be comprised of a hodgepodge of pieces put together as if someone had glued together various pieces from different puzzles. As they neared a tour guide speaking to a group, Anna could heard the elderly gentleman explain the significance. During the period of the English Civil War, Oliver Cromwell's soldiers shot out all of the windows, believing them to be a form of idolatry. The townspeople of Winchester snuck inside and saved the remains of their beloved windows then attempted to restore them once Cromwell's regime came to an end.

When they reached the north aisle, Anna found the grave that she had been looking for- that of Jane Austen herself. She stopped in front of the black granite slab for a moment of reflection and to read the inscription.

In memory of JANE AUSTEN, youngest daughter of the late Revd GEORGE AUSTEN, formerly Rector of Steventon in this County. She departed this Life on the 18th of July 1817, aged 41, after a long illness supported with the patience and the hopes of a Christian. The benevolence of her heart, the sweetness of her temper, and the extraordinary endowments of her mind obtained the regard of all who knew her and the warmest love of her intimate connections. Their grief is in proportion to their affection, they know their loss to be irreparable, but in their deepest affliction they are consoled by a firm though humble hope that her charity, devotion, faith and purity have rendered her soul acceptable in the sight of her REDEEMER.

Anna was moved by the words of the inscription. She was surprised to find that it didn't mention that she was an author, but quickly realized that Jane had not wanted recognition and had published her works anonymously. As such, her accomplishments would not have been engraved upon her tombstone.

"She did so much in her life and no one ever knew it at time," said Anna aloud to Olivia.

"Are you on about her mysterious codes again?" her friend replied.

"Not entirely. She's had millions of fans since she died but while she was alive she published her novels simply as 'A Lady.' She didn't write her stories so that the name of Jane Austen could live on long after her time. Her gifts to the world were so much more."

"You aren't going to get all existential on me are you?" asked a wary Olivia. "I don't think I can handle 'All are one who read Jane.'"

"Not quite," Anna said with a chuckle. "Maybe I will write my next dissertation on that topic though." The notion of her dissertation brought Anna back to reality. Unlike Olivia, she wasn't finished and needed to be- in days. She let out a long sigh. "We should go. I need to get back to the library."

"Sucks to be you," said Olivia, her grin returning.

"Sure does," said Anna, taking one last look at Jane's final resting place. She would soon bring her a final, lasting peace. Her *magnum opus* would be revealed to the world. For now though, Anna's quest would need to be put on hold. She followed Olivia out of the cathedral- the library awaited her.

OOO

Anna finally made herself blink. She wasn't entirely aware of the last time she had closed her eyes but they were very dry. She had been staring at her computer screen for quite some time.

She looked at the clock in the bottom right corner of the screen- 19:30. Although she had been in Europe for almost a year, she still had to do her quick mental calculation to figure out what time it really was- 7:30. *Is it already so late?* she wondered. Anna leaned back in her chair and gave her body a stretch. She looked about the quiet library. It was nearly empty save for herself and a handful of Asian students at a table across the way. Since the undergrads had returned home following the close of the spring semester, the library had become extensively less populated and Anna found herself enjoying her dissertation writing much more amongst the books than in her dorm room. Even though she was being productive, it felt like she was out doing something.

She finally met her word count goal for the day and decided to take a quick break. She would likely continue writing more into the night. Her deadline was fast approaching and she was almost done with her first draft, sans conclusion. Eagerly, she took out Jane Austen's notebook from her bag and placed it beside her own. Since the discovery, Anna had needed to force herself to keep on track with her dissertation by setting herself daily goals and routinely scheduled breaks to investigate Jane's letters and notebook. If she hadn't done so, she would probably never finish her work and would have wasted a year's program.

It had been a few days since Chawton and Anna had learned much regarding Jane Austen's secrets, although the letters raised many more questions than they had answered. She also had yet to find any sort of clue to a cipher.

The stack of letters included not just those written by Jane, but also a few written by a handful of others. Other than Cassandra and their brother Frank, Anna had been unable recognize any of the names of the authors. They included a Mathilda, Juno, Minerva, the Maiden, and the Countess. She had scoured several Jane Austen biographies, in the library and on the web, looking for the names but to no avail. They were obviously pseudonyms meant to hide the identities of the authors and recipients of the letters. Other apparent code names were used within the letters as well, including an often-mentioned Mercury. Anna was no expert in handwriting comparisons by any means, but she could see similarities in style and had the working theory that Jane was Minerva and Cassandra the Maiden. It was also likely that Mathilda was Isabella Maude. As to the identities of Juno and the Countess, Anna had no concrete evidence. Her working hypothesis was that the Countess was Jane Austen's cousin Eliza Hancock, who had at one time been the *Comtesse de Feullide* before her husband was beheaded following the French Revolution. The others remained a mystery.

Anna had spent much time over the past few days piecing together a sort of narrative of events from the letters, Jane Austen biographies, and the notebook, although Jane's notes and squibbles were often undated and somewhat eccentric at times.

From what Anna had gathered, it appeared that Jane met Isabella Maude in the spring of 1802- a year after moving to Bath. George Austen had been an acquaintance of Lord Hawarden and they were introduced at the Upper Assembly Rooms one evening. While Jane's father and mother were away visiting relatives in Kent, she had been invited by Isabella to stay at Prior Park. The girls must have stumbled upon the secret chambers at that time. Later allusions to the experience were given in some of the letters between "Mathilda" and "Minerva." It seemed that at the time, the chambers were still in use as some sort of ritualistic meeting place but was cleared out following the death of Isabella's father in 1803. That particular year, following the sudden death of her friend's father, Jane began to investigate the happenings with a sense of gothic adventure on par with Catherine Morland. Unlike the naive Catherine however, Jane stumbled upon a real conspiracy involving members of her own family.

Anna took in hand one of the earliest letters from 1803 and read through it again.

To the Maiden fair,

The nature of this correspondence will not contain the typical pleasantries that may be saved for letters of a more common type. Such will be the protocol among the sisters in future letters. With that said I will readily convey what I have learned.

Before her departure with Mercury, the Countess wove a tail so rich with intrigue that I can hardly believe the truth of it, yet I find that it must be so for it was her original testimony that set these events in motion many years ago. The Countess received a letter that had been meant to find her following the death of her husband almost ten years past but had somehow not reached her for three years. According to the letter, the rumored confession upon his execution is indeed true. Philip, as he confessed was his name, had secreted himself as a valet in the real comte's employ on the orders of a person or group of persons named Pantagruel. He was tasked with locating a map long ago secreted away by the true comte's family in centuries past that was to lead to a great treasure. However, after he murdered the comte and took his place, Philip fell in love with the Countess and chose to remain in his new life, forsaking his mission. The political turmoil forced the Countess to leave France for good and Philip was hunted by those he once served. Before he was beheaded Philip confessed much to the Countess in his letter. He had indeed found that which he sought among the real comte's estate and had learned a great deal. The item in question was revealed to be not a map but only a page of an ancient book written in an unfamiliar tongue. With the page were centuries of writings chronicling the family's quest and findings. At the very least three more pages of the book were thought to exist scattered sometime in ages past, quite possibly the Crusades. Before he was able to flee France for all time, Philip was captured and interrogated by none other than Bonaparte himself, who may have connections to this Pantagruel. Under diabolical tortures Philip confessed all that he knew, save for the hypothetical location of a lost page among the ancient ruins of Bath! Of all places! The Countess delivered the letter into the hands of Pluto who shared the revelation with dear Jupiter. She confessed to me that they did not appear as astonished as she would have thought them to be. This event, as you should not be surprised to hear, occurred six years ago.

Since then the Countess has not been privy to much from Pluto or Jupiter but Mercury has revealed a small amount to her. It would seem that he and Jupiter will be secreted away from time to time to discuss goings on with others of a like nature. I am convinced that Neptune and Triton are also counted among this group. I am unsure if I should subtly interrogate Triton the next I see him as he would be more prone to let information slip from his mouth.

According to the Countess, Mercury and Jupiter met with Neptune when he came ashore two years ago, before his official leave. It would seem that this meeting is why we now find ourselves in our present circumstances. The Countess believes that her present adventure to the continent is a pretext for Mercury to procure more information about this Pantagruel, Bonaparte, and the other pages of the lost tome.

We will talk more next we see each other. The Countess also made mention of a trip Jupiter and Mercury took to London last year on important business. She believes that it was something to do with Neptune and an artefact acquired in Alexandria. If I remember the time correctly, Jupiter spoke little of his journey and was soon away shortly thereafter. This event will occupy my current investigations.

Until we meet again,
the wise Minerva.

Anna put the letter to the side and looked to the notes she had written thus far while tapping her pen on the table. She had written a list of the coded aliases from the letters. Minerva- Jane, the Maiden- Cassandra, the Countess- Eliza. Anna had been agonizing over the others. She had an inkling that Neptune and Triton were Francis and Charles Austen, both had been naval officers that had made it to the rank of admiral. Both being initiated at a young age into a secret fraternal organization seemed to have had its benefits. From what Anna understood thus far about the whole buisness, the brotherhood had included Ralph Allen, the Duke of Chandos, the John Woods Elder and

Younger, Lord Hawarden, George Austen, and at least a few of his sons. Anna also had an inkling that Eliza's wealthy godfather and friend of the Austen family, Warren Hastings, had also been a member of the brotherhood.

She had written a list of known members parallel to the list of code names. Anna stared at them for several moments, lost in thought, before her cell phone vibrated in her pocket and she forced herself to blink. She took out her phone to see who had texted her. It was Fraser again- *Made any progress?*

Anna tossed her phone unto the table without replying. Fraser had proved to be quite persistent the past few days. Anna had tried to explain to Fraser that, unlike him, she had to have the first draft of her dissertation finished in a few days and couldn't completely occupy her time trying to crack the Jane Austen Code.

She picked up her phone and texted a reply. *Not quite yet, I'm almost done for now. Taking a break. Come to the library if you want to join me. Fourth floor by the spiral staircase.*

Be there soon, Fraser replied a few moments later.

Anna was surprised that Fraser had suddenly become so infatuated with the Jane Austen mystery. When she had first described her theories to him that first day in Bath, he had listened to her with an open mind and did not dismiss her as a whacko. However, he certainly hadn't seem interested in becoming her partner on this adventure at the time. It wasn't until they had found the secret chambers under Prior Park, and the codex page, that he had shown his true excitement. If Anna had to venture a guess, it would be the prospect of unlocking the ancient secrets of a mystery cult. Such a discovery would certainly earn him great honors in his field of study and would provide him with the material he would need to finish his doctoral work. Such a thing would be a fine motivation indeed. Anna was close to finishing her master's work, with her doctorate still way off on the horizon. It would certainly be nice to almost be finished with school for good.

Anna took another letter from her bag to read over while she waited for Fraser. It was dated to February 1805.

To the wise sister Minerva,

The words of your last letter have not left my heart and I dwell on them constantly. I have overheard words between Pluto and Mercury. I daresay it took great skill on my own part not to be discovered. It would appear that the fever words you wrote of are indeed true and that among Jupiter's effects should be writings or drawings of what I would imagine would be of a confusing and mysterious nature. I am still unsure as to 'the Ebon Stone' and failed to deduce the meaning of those words. If you are able to discover anything at all write to me of it immediately.

They made mention of whether or not they should have 'it' moved to another location and that 'it' might not be safe where it remains. Perhaps 'it' is the item that Mathilda and you yourself once discovered and which you had detailed to me upon our last meeting.

The words were often difficult to comprehend however I am wondering if perhaps Jupiter had somehow made progress with 'it,' providing long awaited details. Only time will tell the truth of the matter.

I the Countess remain your noble sister

As Anna put the letter aside, she saw Fraser making his way towards her area from the direction of the elevators. She jotted down the words *Ebon Stone* among the code names she had yet to deduce.

"You don't look to be taking much of a break to me," said Fraser as he sat his one-strapped, brown, leather bag onto the table. He then pulled out a chair and sat down.

"Trust me," she replied. "This is infinitely more entertaining than my actual dissertation."

Fraser quirked his head to the side to look down at the notes she had been writing.

"Why do you have a list of Roman deities?" he asked thoroughly interested.

"Well, it would appear that Jane and her little cabal of inquisitive women wrote to each other using pseudonyms in the chance that someone would read their letters. From the handwriting, I've figured out a few of them. Jane is Minerva and Cassandra is the Maiden. I'm also fairly certain that the Countess is their cousin Eliza and that Neptune and Triton are the naval Austen brothers."

Fraser put his hand to his mouth and made the particular furrowed brow face that he was prone to make while he was deep in thought.

"If Jane is Minerva, then Jupiter and Juno are most likely her father and mother," he finally said after a few silent moments. "Minerva is the daughter of Jupiter's mind."

"Yes, that definitely makes sense with the contexts of a lot of what's written in the letters." Anna looked to her notes and her mind immediately began to make new connections. "What about Pluto and Mercury?"

"Mercury is Jupiter's son and Pluto his brother,"

"George Austen didn't have a brother."

"What about a brother-in-law?"

Anna shook her head. "Eliza's father died way before all of this," as she finished her sentence a thought immediately occurred to her. "But her godfather was alive. Warren Hastings was friends with George Austen and was rumored to have been his sister's true love and Eliza's biological father. He must be Pluto. That would likely make Mercury Jane's brother Henry. He married Eliza after she was widowed." Anna began to write the identities next to their code names. "That just leaves Pantagruel."

"What was that?" asked Fraser who had apparently been lost in his own thoughts. "Did you say *Pantagruel*?"

"Yeah," she replied. "Whoever Pantagruel is, they have something to do a shadow group operating during the French Revolution that seems to have been connected to Napoleon. I've never even heard that name before. It's not another Roman god is it?"

Fraser was staring at the pages of her notebook. He eventually shook his head after a moment. "No. Pantagruel was the literary creation of a heretic French priest named François Rabelais."

"Strange that I've never heard of him," Anna replied. "I'm usually wading knee deep through the writings of heretic priests of the Middle Ages."

"He didn't live at that time," Fraser replied. "Rabelais died in the middle of the sixteenth century. He wrote a series of stories that were grotesque satires of the world he knew- the Catholic Church in particular. The main characters were the giants Pantagruel and his father Gargantua. Pantagruel and his friends were like grotesque caricatures of King Arthur and the Knights of the Roundtable."

"Why have I never heard of this until now?" Anna said astounded, more to herself than to Fraser. She would certainly need to investigate François Rabelais and his works further. If not for the investigation, then perhaps for her dissertation's closing statements about the use of Arthurian legends to convey philosophical notions.

"I'm not too well versed in the curriculum of European literature found in American universities."

"It's mostly British with a splash of Dante and Goethe for good measure."

"I'm not that surprised," Fraser replied.

Over the next hour or so, Anna and Fraser went over the letters using what they knew about the identities of names mentions in the letters. From Jane's first letter and the timing of events, Anna concluded that Neptune was Francis Austen and Triton- Charles. Thus far, they determined that the contents of the letter of Eliza's husband, the fake *Comte de Feuillide*, reached Warren Hastings and George Austen sometime in 1797, inspiring Jane Austen's first family excursion to Bath. It was possible that Rev. Austen and the brotherhood discovered the codex page at that time, perhaps among the ruins of the Roman baths. In November of 1800, Frank brought troubling news from Egypt that apparently facilitated the family's sudden move to Bath. In the Spring of 1802, Jane's father and brother Henry made a trip to London at the behest of the brotherhood after which George Austen became very reclusive, spending much time in his study with strange writings and charts that Jane did not understand. Whatever he had been working on for years had remained unfinished at the time of his death in January of 1805. Eliza's letter a few weeks after his passing made reference to mysterious mutterings that he had made in Jane's presence when he was extremely feverish the night before his death. It would have been exceedingly more helpful had they been in possession of the letter that Jane wrote to her cousin Eliza, detailing her father's fever words. They only knew of *the Ebon Stone,* which had remained as much a mystery to Jane as it was to Anna and Fraser at present.

The later correspondences were few and far between each other, containing little information other than the comings and goings of various coded individuals. The most interesting bits concerned Isabella Maude making sure that "Mr. Thorpe" was secure while making a visit to her old home in 1815. Everything else contained in the letters made reference to Jane's plans to leave clues in the finished manuscript of *Northanger Abbey,* but her chronic illness had begun to get the better of her and slowed her progress. The final letter of Jane's in their possession described the characteristics of her illness, including severe fatigue, frequent fevers, troubled nights, and her skin turning, "black and white and every wrong color."

"Inheritance powder," said Fraser after Anna had read him the symptoms.

"What's inheritance powder?" she asked in reply, no doubt with a look of confusion conveying how she felt.

"It was a common name in the Elizabethan-era for small doses of arsenic that heirs would put into the food of their benefactors, if they were too inconvenient and seemed to persist on living."

"That's horrible," Anna replied.

"Sometimes it was just business," said Fraser with a shrug of his shoulders.

"So, you think Jane Austen was poisoned slowly with arsenic?"

"It definitely sounds plausible. If she had drawn too much notice to herself and her plans to reveal clues that the brotherhood wanted to keep hidden, it would have been no trouble to bribe a housekeeper or a doctor to slip the powder into her food or drink.

"Although," he continued. "The truth could also be less sinister as many medications of that era contained trace amounts of arsenic. Accidental poisonings were a common occurrence."

Anna had to admit that either option seemed likely, but her instincts wanted to lean more towards intentional poisoning by nefarious characters as it seemed to coincide with everything thus far.

"Do you think that Jane ever discovered what her father had been working on?" asked Fraser changing the subject to more academic pursuits than murder. "It's never mentioned whether she did or not in the letters."

"Since I read Eliza's letter, I've been going through Jane's notebook looking for something but it's a hodgepodge." She took the notebook in hand and opened it up to some of the more eccentric scribblings. "The pages don't always seem to be in chronological order either. It's like she would open it to random pages whenever she got an idea and wrote it down. Only she knew the rhyme or reason to it."

"Sounds like my notebooks," replied Fraser with a smirk. "Anything with strange symbols or alphabets?"

"There is this," said Anna as she turned to the page she was thinking of. "It's a drawing of something that looks sort of like the state of Ohio, with what looks to be alchemic symbols spread out in a pattern in the shape of a seven pointed star."

"Ohio..." repeated Fraser as he looked at the drawing. "That's the one that looks slightly like a heart and is always in the news during your election season."

"Yeah, it's a swing state."

"Regardless, the drawing doesn't look much like a heart." He continued to stare at it intently, searching for meaning. "It does look very familiar though. I feel like I've seen this shape hundreds of times...but I just can't think of where. It's like trying to remember something that happened in a dream right after you wake up."

"You aren't getting all metaphysical are you?" asked Anna with grin.

"Don't be ridiculous," he replied quickly. "I'm a Scot. We are a rational people. I'm just saying that I know the shape and I will kick myself when I realize what it is."

Anna wondered to herself if she could be the one to kick him. *Rational people...ha!* Anna looked to the drawing again. If this was indeed copied from George Austen's writings, it was highly unlikely that Jane ever figured out its meaning. Books detailing alchemical symbols and patterns were not typically found on the bookshelves of normal English families. The scribbles around the drawing were barely readable, but off to the side, were the words *Invisible? Faded?* and *Smoothed?,* which had been underlined. Anna had no idea what it could possibly mean.

Fraser had his eyes closed and looked as if he were having bathroom trouble.

"It's driving you crazy isn't?" she said with a laugh. "You look like you are trying to pass a kidney stone."

"That's it!" exclaimed Fraser suddenly, giving Anna a start. He leaned over and took Anna's face in his hands and gave her a quick kiss on the mouth. "The Rosetta Stone!"

Anna no doubt had the wide-eyed, deer-in-the-headlights look about her, more shocked by the sudden kiss than by Fraser's revelation.

"The Ebon Stone- it's the Rosetta Stone!" Fraser continued, as if he hadn't kissed her at all. He apparently thought nothing of randomly kissing girls that he knew in excitement. "The keystone cipher is the Rosetta Stone." He leaned back in his chair and put a hand to his head, sweeping the hair from his eyes. He was almost laughing.

He finally looked to Anna. "Have you nothing to say?" he asked confused. "Grab your wits about you woman," he said playfully. "We've almost done it!"

Anna decided to just ignore the kiss. It had simply been a sudden, involuntary act of appreciation. Fraser was thinking nothing of it so why should she?

She cleared her throat before turning the notebook to face her. "Now that you say it, it *does* sort of look like the Rosetta Stone- which is a big black stone." Anna pulled up a picture of the Rosetta Stone on her computer and compared it to the drawing. "It looks backwards though."

Fraser squinted his eyes as he looked at the two pictures, thinking over them. "You're right. I wonder why it was drawn mirrored."

Anna became lost in her own thoughts as she stared at the pages. Her eyes drifted to the words written to side. "The pattern is invisible," she said when the thought occurred to her.

By the look on his face, Fraser was doubting her sanity. "An invisible pattern on the Rosetta Stone?" he chuckled and it made Anna perturbed. "Even if the Egyptians were able to make invisible ink and highlight portions of the writing on the stone, centuries of weathering would have made it impossible to tell."

"Weathering," Anna repeated. "The pattern was made smooth over time." She continued to think as she looked at the picture. "It's not a mirror image, it's the back. The pattern was on the back of the Rosetta Stone and became weathered over time. There must have been enough of it visible in the Regency era for George Austen to notice it. There has to be a way that we can examine it for ourselves; we have tech that he didn't. I bet x-rays or something can pick up the pattern."

Fraser still looked at her as if she were insane.

"You think that the British Museum is just going to let us waltz in and let us run x-rays on the Rosetta Stone because Anna Lewis believes that Jane Austen left clues that her father deciphered a coded message leading to a treasure?"

"Well, when you say it like *that* it makes me sound crazy," Anna admitted.

"Besides," he continued. "It doesn't have to be as complicated as all that. The way the Rosetta Stone is currently displayed in its case shows it from all sides. All we have to do is a little makeshift RTI on it and be on our way without anyone ever noticing."

"You lost me," Anna replied. "What is RTI?"

"Ah forgive me," said Fraser as he crossed his arms over his chest and sat back in his chair. "I sometimes forget that you know next to nothing of archaeology."

"Think nothing of it," replied Anna with thick sarcasm.

"Reflectance Transformation Imaging. It's a computational photographic method that can reveal details on artifacts hidden to the naked eye. If there is some sort of weathered pattern on the back of the Rosetta Stone, it will show up."

"MacGyver archaeology, nice."

"Fancy a trip to London tomorrow?" asked Fraser. Anna couldn't tell if his polite demeanor was genuine or sarcastic.

"I'd be delighted," she replied. Hopefully all would go according to plan. First the Rosetta Stone, then hopefully wherever the codex would lead them. Despite her excitement, Anna almost wanted to let it all go and simply finish her dissertation...almost.

CHAPTER 7

Anna tried her hardest to stifle a yawn but failed, instinctively bringing her hand up to cover her mouth. She was so tired that she almost didn't see the familiar site of the great black gates come into view as she and Fraser neared the British Museum.

Though they had been up rather late into the night planning what they were about to do, Fraser thought it would be best if they arrived at the museum when it opened for the day. Apparently, they would find the crowds exceedingly less annoying. As a result, they had to board their train quite early in the morning in order to make it to London in time. It would have been much more convenient had they driven Fraser's car, but Anna knew all too well that driving in London was a nightmarish experience. You also had to pay a daily congestion fee to do it. She understood why they had needed to take the train, but she didn't have to like it. Anna had planned on finishing out her daily sleep schedule during the train ride, but alas, it was not meant to be. A chavtastic couple, their pram, and two rowdy children had not allowed her the pleasure of rest. Since arriving at Waterloo Station, it had been a whirlwind of sprinting to an Underground station, riding to Taunton, and then continuing their sprints to the BM.

As weary as she was, Anna never tired of the British Museum. The moment one passes through the black gates, they step into the courtyard of a grand Neoclassical building complex of columns, statues, and carved edifices. It was the typical architecture that one thinks of when picturing a museum, but the BM had been the first such building and the archetype for those to follow. As beautiful as the Metropolitan Museum in New York was, the British Museum was much older and more magnificent to look at.

Despite the hour, crowds still gathered at the entrance. The building had been open for almost an hour, letting many visitors into the inner grand vestibule to wait for the galleries and exhibit halls to open. As Fraser and Anna walked through the main entrance, they were surrounded by visitors and tour groups from all over the world. The nationalities of many groups could be determined by the tour-guides, who either held up a country's flag to let the group know where they were, or simply had a tall flag strapped to a pack on their back. Some tour guides even carried little PA systems on their backs.

As early as it was, they were still going to have a difficult time accomplishing their goal. From what Fraser explained of the RTI process, he would need to take various pictures from the same distance but at different angles. It sounded like he was going to need a wide arch of space to work in.

"You still think this is going to work?" asked Anna with a wave of her hand, gesturing to the crowd. There was already a substantial amount of people standing at the large doorway, behind which, stood the Rosetta Stone.

"It shouldn't be too much of a problem," replied Fraser while surveying the groups. "It will be your job to make sure I'm not interrupted."

"How exactly am I supposed to do that?" she replied with disbelief in her abilities to police the situation.

"Be creative," said Fraser with a grin. "I have the utmost faith in your ability to distract people."

Anna shot him an incredulous look as the clock struck on the hour and the doors to the galleries were opened. In a matter of moments, the crowd of people flooded into the Egyptian wing. The mass of people had bottlenecked, as was typical, and was now slow going.

"I don't particularly want to deal with that," said Anna. "I'm way too tired to be crushed by a gaggle of Chinese people."

"I'm inclined to agree," Fraser replied. "I've a better idea." He quickly took Anna's hand in his own, then dragged her through the crowds and back towards the museum entrance.

Anna's first reaction was to Fraser taking her hand. She had wanted to pull it back from him once he started to drag her though the masses of people, but found herself letting him lead her on. She told herself that it was because she didn't want to become separated in the crowd.

Before reaching the main entrance, Fraser turned right, leading them through a gift shop, then further on down a long hallway until they turned right again. Anna was now in what appeared to be a gallery of ancient Mesopotamian monuments. Around them stood steles and obelisks from Babylon and Assyria, as well as monstrous stone creatures with the heads of men, bodies of bulls, and wings of eagles. Looking at them, Anna was sorry that she hadn't made the time to visit that area of the museum even though she had been there many times before.

She only had a moment to take in the beauty of the ancient monuments before Fraser continued to drag her on through the galleries. They were soon surrounded by other stone monuments, this time of Egyptian make. Fraser had taken them the long way around- circumventing the crowds, which Anna could now see just up ahead, surrounding a large glass box standing upright. She could only assume that the Rosetta Stone was housed in the glass box as many people were standing in front of it having their pictures taken by their friends or family. Luckily, the back of the stone was not regarded with a similar degree of wonder.

Fraser stopped short of their destination and they held back a moment while he fiddled about in his pack.

"Here, take this," he said as he handed Anna a stick of gum.

"What do I do with it?" she asked confused.

"Chew it, obviously," he said looking up from his pack, surprised that she hadn't immediately ascertained what to do with a stick of gum.

Anna looked at him with a sideways glance as she unwrapped the gum, popped it into her mouth, and began to chew. It was spearmint- not particularly her favorite.

Fraser continued rummaging. He pulled out a fancy professional camera, which he hung around his neck, and then tied a long piece of twine to the bottom of it. Anna just continued to watch. She figured that as confused as she was, she would probably understand what was going on quickly enough.

Once Fraser had made his preparations, they made their way to the Rosetta Stone and stood behind the glass case, ignoring the crowds on the other side of it. Once in place, Fraser produced a red plastic ball about the size of an apple.

"Gum please," he said as he place his hand out while inspecting the glass without looking to Anna.

"Um, here," Anna replied as she placed the chewed gum in Fraser's hand. Anna felt a bit awkward about placing her chewed gum in his bare hand, but it was what he had asked for after all.

Fraser quickly looked around to make sure that no one was paying attention to what he was doing, then spilt the chewed gum into two pieces. He then put one piece onto the red plastic ball and reached downwards, sticking it to the glass case just below the Rosetta Stone. With the second piece, he stuck the end of the twine not connected to the camera to the middle of the case.

Almost horrified, Anna began to nervously look around the room to make sure that no one was paying too much attention to what they were doing, especially security guards.

"Ok," said Fraser turning to Anna. "Now it's your turn. Make sure no one bothers me. I'll only have a few minutes before all of the flashes draw too much attention and a security guard will show up to make us move along."

Without really knowing what to do, Anna simply nodded and turned around with her arms crossed to look intimidating. Hopefully, everyone would think that they were doing something important, that they were *supposed* to be doing, and would leave them be.

Fraser took the camera from around his neck and held it out in front of him. He then stepped back until the twine was taut and snapped a picture with the flash. He then stepped to the left and took another, stepped a little more to the left and took another, and then stooped down to take another picture, always at the same distance away.

"What is he doing?" asked an older Indian man to Anna's left. She turned to acknowledge his question.

"An experiment for class," she replied, trying to quickly think of an excuse. "We are seeing how much weathering has occurred on the Stone since it was brought to the museum." She hoped that it would be enough to satisfy the man's curiosity.

"Good," he replied. "I always thought there must be a better way to display that thing." He then quickly continued on his way.

Anna sighed in relief but quickly held her breath as she spotted a security guard across the room whose attention they had finally grabbed.

"Are you about done?" she asked in a panic. "We are about to have company."

"Yes," Fraser replied as he went about his picture taking. He was now on the other side of the Stone. "Just a few more shots."

Anna's nerves were on the edge and she could feel herself sweating as the guard came closer. He was a large, intimidating man with a full, bushy auburn beard. What was she going to do? The experiment excuse may have worked on the old Indian man, but it certainly wouldn't satisfy security.

"Done," said Fraser as he grabbed Anna by the wrist. "Grab my pack," he ordered while nodding and looking down to make sure that she understood.

As she took the strap in her hand, she was being pulled in the opposite direction of the guard. Anna was certain that she heard the man say, "Hey stop!" with a Scottish accent as they meandered their way through the crowds of people, becoming just a couple of faces.

The next few moments were a blur as Fraser pulled Anna through several galleries of Greco-Roman monuments. Eventually, Anna found herself in a large, long gallery which held various white marble friezes all around the room. At both ends were larger monuments that looked to have once been on the top of the entrance to an ancient temple.

"What is this place?" asked Anna.

"You've never been in the Elgin Gallery before?" asked Fraser with surprise.

"I've not yet had the pleasure of spending a day at the museum, staring at the ancient and classical pieces," she replied with a hint of sarcasm, though she immediately wondered at her sarcasm. From what she had seen, it would have been a pleasure to see these monuments under more pleasant circumstances. "I've only been here a few times and mostly to see the Medieval pieces."

"Ah," he replied, without the "figured as much" that Anna had been expecting. "These are the Elgin Marbles. They used to decorate the Parthenon in Athens."

"Temple of Athena right?"

"Indeed," Fraser replied with a smirk. "Not so ignorant of Classical times after all."

"The city is called Athens," she said with a smirk. "Even a lowly Medieval Studies major can make that connection." She sat Fraser's pack down on the floor for a moment. "Where do we go now?"

"The British Library isn't too far of a walk from here and I have access to a few of the document labs."

"Do you need a lab to complete the RTI?"

"No, but it should be relatively peaceful and we won't be disturbed while I analyze the data."

"Sounds good," Anna replied. "We should get out of here as soon as possible. I know it's irrational, but I feel like there is someone staring at as in every gallery."

"Probably the guards," said Fraser. "Isn't it their job?"

"Cute," said Anna with a wry smile and the two of them made their way out of the Elgin gallery. They eventually exited through the main entrance and into the courtyard outside. As they neared the black gate, Anna felt a tickle on the back of her neck and she turned back towards the entrance. At first glance, she could have sworn that she saw the man in the long grey coat that had chased them in Bath. He had been at the top of the staircase, staring at her with his arms crossed.

"Fraser," she said as she stopped walking to get his attention.

"What is it?" he asked, looking at her with a hint of alarm.

"I thought I saw," she turned back to look at the staircase but there was no one there. She shook her head. "Nothing, I must still be tired. Let's just go."

Fraser looked at her with a bit of suspicion in his eyes before nodding and they began their walk towards the British Library.

OOO

As Anna sat watching Fraser on his laptop, going about the task of analyzing the picture data from his camera, she thought that she might as well be watching someone splitting an atom for all she understood of it.

"So *that's* why you needed the red ball there," she said as Fraser's program centered on analyzing the light reflected off of the plastic ball.

"It serves as a sort of anchor for the program to determine where the light from the camera's flash is coming from. Even when doing proper RTI, with a sort of domed machine to block out everything around the object, you still need the ball for the program to work."

After the plastic ball bit was calculated by the program, the rest of the analysis took hardly any time at all. From what Anna could tell, the program compiled all of the data from each picture taken and sort of combined it into one head on picture of the object.

"Wow," said Anna as Fraser clicked an option. Before them was a picture of the back of the Rosetta Stone that sort of looked like an inverted x-ray. Instead of showing the inside, it revealed everything on the surface. Every scratch, every contour, every chip, no matter how small, stood out as if it were a topographical map showing a landscape. Fraser flicked a little ball-like object on the screen and was able to change the direction that the light and shadows were coming from, revealing even more detail depending on the direction.

"This is actually pretty terrible RTI," said Fraser. "If we would have been able to do this the proper way, we would see a lot more; but it is what it is."

"Stop," said Anna suddenly. "I can see it!" She quickly leaned in to inspect the image better. What she saw filled her with amazement. What had appeared was not the seven pointed star that had been drawn in Jane Austen's notebook, but rather, the image of a circle within a square, within a triangle, within a circle. "Squaring the Circle," Anna said aloud. "It's an alchemic glyph often associated with the formation of the Philosopher's Stone."

Anna remembered that Jane had also drawn various alchemical symbols as well, but she hadn't been able to recognize any of them. Anna took control of the mouse and played with the lighting slightly. "There," she said as symbols became barely visible. There were many more than were in Jane's notes, and occurred along all parts of the glyph- not just at the points. She recognized a few of them, but the majority looked to be a part of a more ancient script version of the symbols- if such a thing had even existed. Much was still uncertain about the history of alchemic symbolism. Below the largest triangle, written in Greek letters, was the word ΑΧΙΩΜΑ. Anna didn't know Greek but she knew enough to recognize the word Axiom.

"What does it mean?" asked Fraser finally.

"Axiom," Anna replied. "I thought you knew Greek."

"Thank you," he said with sarcasm and a wry smile. "I know it says Axiom. What does it have to do with the glyph?"

"Well, it looks similar to medieval alchemic recipes for creating the Philosopher's Stone, but much more complex. I'm also having trouble recognizing some of these symbols."

"I've seen a few of them before," said Fraser. "They look like some of the symbols for the Roman gods that I've seen on the walls of a few *Mithraea*."

"Of course," Anna replied. "Those are the older versions of the alchemic planetary symbols and their associated metals." Anna pointed at the Greek letters. "Since it appears to be a Philosopher's Stone glyph, this most likely refers to the Axiom of Maria."

"The what now?" Fraser asked confused with an eagerness to understand that filled Anna with warmth. Lately, whenever she had explained something to him about alchemy, he looked at her with eyes filled with respect. It felt good that, even though she knew next to nothing about Classical Archaeology, he thought or her as an intellectual equal in her own right.

"It's an ancient alchemic precept attributed to a quasi-mythical Roman-era Jewess named Mary," she replied. "I think I have it written down in my dissertation notebook somewhere, actually." Anna took her notebook from her bag, then rummaged through several pages until she came to a series of notes that she had taken months ago, on a manuscript of Adelard of Bath. *Bath again...* She found it odd, and certainly not a coincidence, that the city of Bath kept turning up as they were investigating this mystery. "One becomes Two, Two becomes Three, and from the Third comes the One as the Fourth."

"Well that is certainly nice and cryptic," Fraser replied.

"She was also credited with the saying, 'Join the Male and the Female, and you will find what is sought.' She believed there was great power in the union of opposites."

"Union of opposites eh?" repeated Fraser as he thought over Anna's words.

The morning hours passed by as Anna and Fraser continued with their musing and ponderings over the information that they had gathered thus far. Anna's notebook pages began to be filled with various sketches and symbol combinations in an attempt to unlock whatever cipher was used to encode the Demotic on the silver codex page.

Fraser was quite certain that the codex had been written sometime before the beginning of the 5th century AD, as it was around that time that Demotic began to be completely replaced by Coptic Egyptian. It was also at that time, that the monument that the Rosetta Stone had once been a part of, would have likely been destroyed. A particularly zealous Christian Roman emperor had ordered the destruction of all pagan temples and the monuments in them. Afterwards, the Rosetta Stone would have been buried in rubble and lost in the sands of time.

"This is impossible," said Fraser in frustration. "Even if we figure out what this glyph means, it's not going to make the codex make any sense. Not without knowing exactly what kind of cipher was used to encode the text."

Anna sighed. He was right of course. She had been staring at the symbols for hours, wracking her brain and notebook for clues to unlock this supposedly alchemic cipher. Scholars in the Middle Ages spent years, even decades, trying to unlock these mysteries and she expected to do so in a matter of hours. Although, Jane Austen's father had apparently done just that before his sudden death, or thought he had.

Anna carefully inspected Jane's notes again concerning her father's investigation of the Rosetta Stone. She was still confused as to why he had drawn a seven pointed star rather than the squared-circle glyph that they had discovered. Had he expected to find a seven pointed star? Anna was fairly certain that the man had inspected the back of the Stone and would have known the truth of it. Although, it could have been that George Austen had only been able to make out the alchemic symbols and not the glyph. If so, assuming the shape to be a star would not be a stretch of the imagination as seven symbols surrounded an eighth in the middle. It was impossible to say for sure what though, as they did not have RTI technology.

Anna spent the next hour or so researching the history of cryptology and ciphers amongst the books of the library. What she learned was quite fascinating. Ciphers had been in use since ancient times, although, they were nowhere near as complicated as they were in the modern era. The use of computers, and other mechanical code cracking devices, had made the ancient cipher types incredibly easy to crack- eventually. Before the Renaissance period, the majority of ciphers were either substitution ciphers or transposition ciphers. With substitution ciphers, letters were systematically replaced throughout a piece of writing for other letters or groups of letters. Julius Caesar had invented a famous cipher, which he used to encode his personal correspondences, by replacing each letter with the letter three positions later in the alphabet. Transposition ciphers did not change letters, but rather, scrambled them according to some defined formula or a geometric design. Anna was certain that the cipher used on the codex was one of those two types- possibly a combination of both.

She continued to stare at her notes but Anna's eyes were growing hazy. *One becomes Two, Two becomes Three, Out of Three comes the One as the Fourth.* How did the Axiom of Maria fit into all of it? What did it have to do with the Squared Circle? The union of male and female creates a life- a third. Out of the third life comes the One? Which is also a fourth life? Was the Philosopher's Stone the One and the Fourth? A bigger question had just occurred to Anna- *Did the Codex contain the method to create a Philosopher's Stone, or the location of one?* She shook off the notion. The legend of the Philosopher's Stone had only begun to circulate during the late Middle Ages. She had never even heard of such a thing even pondered before the Islamic period, although, the philosophical theories behind it had been around since the days of Classical philosopher's like Aristotle- hence the name.

Anna couldn't help but feel that everything was connected somehow. Maybe she had been studying Hermetic philosophies too much lately but everything seemed intertwined- her dissertation research, Fraser's research into Roman mystery cults, the Jane Austen Code,- all of it. It had been Amelia that had helped Anna focus on a topic for her research. Amelia's own area of expertise had been medieval alchemy. It was not unlikely that Winston Leigh had earned his degrees in something similar, as the two had graduated together and remained friends. Perhaps Amelia had guided her towards something that she knew Winston had been interested in. Did she know of his previous theories of the Jane Austen Code? The notions made Anna's head spin. She closed her eyes to regain her bearings. Amelia would be returning any day now and they were going to have a serious discussion.

"You better not be falling asleep now," said Fraser in a teasing tone, though Anna suspected he was also quite serious.

"I'm just thinking very hard," said Anna in reply. She probably could fall asleep at any moment if she wanted to though. "Have you ever heard of *Prima Materia*?"

"The first substance?" Fraser pondered her question curiously. "It's mentioned several times in some cult liturgies. It was believed to be the primitive, formless base of all matter- sort of like Chaos materialized."

Anna nodded. "The alchemists thought that the Philosopher's Stone was essentially made of *Prima Materia*. It was the perfect divine substance from which God had created everything and it was believed that he passed on the secrets of its making to Adam. It had the ability to bypass all natural laws of matter and transform any substance into another. It could also heal any disease, even death itself."

"So what does *Prima Materia* have to do with the cipher?"

"Everything? Nothing? I have no idea," replied Anna in frustration. She turned her notebook around, presenting her drawings and scribbles to Fraser. She pointed at the one that represented Squaring the Circle. "This glyph, here, circulated around Europe in the Seventeenth Century as an unsolvable puzzle for the *Magnum Opus*- the Great Work of creating a Philosopher's Stone. Such a talisman wasn't even thought of during the period in which the codex was apparently written and the cipher inscribed on the Rosetta Stone. Instead, they pondered the *Prima Materia*. Classical alchemists viewed their work as, not just experiments, but also as an esoteric spiritual experience. They wanted to *achieve* the state of *Prima Materia*. It was a journey into the Sacred."

Fraser looked pleased with her explanation and genuinely interested. "Your alchemists and mystery cultists sound like they were cut from the same cloth," he replied. "The followers of Mithras, for example, thought they could achieve union with the divine through a sort of mystic ladder of seven grades. Each was associated with a planet, beginning with Mercury and ending with Saturn, and an element as well."

"Spiritual transmutation," said Anna making connections. She suddenly found herself quite interested in ancient mystery cults. *What on earth has come over me?*

"Exactly," said Fraser in reply with a smile. "I also believe that there was an unspoken eighth grade of Mithras, probably associated with your *Prima Materia*- the Son of Aion."

"Eight grades..." Anna repeated while looking at her drawings. "Eight symbols- seven metals or their planetary gods, and the key symbol in the middle. The key is given to the one who passes through the seven states and into the eighth."

"I stand at the door and knock," said Fraser. "If any man hear my voice, and open the door, I will come in to him, and will sup with him, and he with me."

"That sounds familiar," said Anna. "Is it a mystery liturgy?"

"One could certainly argue that," replied Fraser with a smirk. "It's from the Book of Revelation."

"No wonder the medieval Church scholars saw no contradictions between alchemy and Christianity."

"Unfortunately, the Church leaders weren't as open minded in Late Antiquity. The cult of Mithras and others like it were systematically destroyed."

"Apparently they continued on in the shadows," Anna replied before a new notion occurred to her. "What order did Mithraic planet grades go?"

"Mercury, Venus, Mars, Jupiter, Moon, Sun, Saturn."

"The first four are in the same order as the actual planets in the solar system, with the exception of earth," said Anna with surprise. "That's so weird. Did they even know about the order of the planets back then?"

"I'm not entirely sure," said Fraser while thinking it over. "I've only dabbled into Archaeoastronomy but I'm fairly certain the naming of the planets didn't have anything to do with their places in the solar system. The earth was thought to be at the center well into the fifteenth century."

"Copernicus," Anna replied through a haze of pondering. Was it only a coincidence, or did the followers of Mithras somehow know the true order of the planets? Maybe there really *was* some spiritual link to the planets. Anna shook it out of her head. First she was interested in mystery cults, then she had almost admitted Astrology had some basis of truth to it. If Anna wasn't careful she'd start checking her horoscope every morning.

Anna began to stare at the symbols and the glyphs as she returned her thoughts to the Mithraic order of the planets. "The sickle and the key..." she said aloud. "The Aion statue held the key in one hand and a sickle in the other. They are, apparently, also the symbols of the brotherhood." She pointed at the symbol of Saturn, "What if the sickle is connected to the scythe of Saturn? You said it was the seventh and last grade of Mithraism. What if our brotherhood followed similar philosophies and the key is the symbol for the eighth grade? Your Son of Aion."

"It definitely sounds plausible," Fraser replied. "As you said, the philosophies of the mystery cults survived in the writings of monks and Church scholars. The early monastic orders were essentially secret brotherhoods themselves. There could be any number of ways that Mithraic teachings could have been passed on through the centuries to survive in the group we are dealing with now."

Fraser looked at her scribbles again and appeared to be thinking something over. "What if this doesn't refer to the Axiom of Maria? It could just be invoking the general philosophy of Reason."

"I suppose I could be wrong," Anna admitted. "What do you mean by the Philosophy of Reason?"

"Classical philosophers talked of the ongoing battle between Reason- *Logos* or *Axioma*, and *Thelema*- Desire. Both concepts developed into their own philosophical religious orders. Many Christian groups even viewed Christ as the *Logos* in human flesh. The more mystical of them later became known as Gnostics.

"Counter groups sprang up that edified *Thelema* and followed the creed of 'Do what thou wilt.' Many took Dionysus, the god of wine and revelry, or Bacchus, his Roman counterpart, as the patron god of their cults. What's interesting is that some of the more modern, quasi-mystical fraternal orders follow the same veins. Freemasons honor logic and reason while other orders are little more than pagan sex cults."

"So our mysterious brotherhood must be an order that was guided by the Philosophy of Reason," Anna pondered aloud. "Did the followers of Mithras lean more towards *Axioma* or *Thelema*?"

"They honored logic, though Christian writers tended to paint them as engaging in rituals of debauchery. Most of it was hearsay though. The cult was only open to men and their rites were highly secretive, so little is known of them for sure. It is highly unlikely women were ever involved in them, so you can rule out Bacchic-like orgies. The main ritual consisted of a sacred meal with bread and wine. It was so similar to the Christian mass that the Church leaders claimed that the Devil himself had inspired it as a mockery of their holy sacrament."

"Which one came first?" asked Anna.

Fraser shrugged. "I guess it depends on how much you view the New Testament as a product of the first century. Both religions seem to have gained a foothold in Rome before the beginning of the second. I don't know much about Judaism but I do know that the Passover rituals, on which Jesus' Last Supper were based, predate Mithraism by several centuries. It's my guess that later, non-Jewish, Christians saw Jesus' ritual through the lens of their pagan worldview and saw the bread and wine in a way similar to the followers of Mithras."

"That makes sense," Anna replied and continued to look at the glyph and the symbols. Maybe she *was* thinking about it all wrong. The Axiom of Maria seemed to make sense at first glance but maybe she had jumped to conclusions. She reached for the photocopy of the silver codex page and looked it over again. She opened the Demotic grammar that they had checked out and turned towards the beginning chapters, with pages concerning the main alphabet. The photocopy was pretty difficult to make out at times but she recognized a few of the letters here and there, although, she could swear that the more frequent letters didn't look quite like the ones in the grammar book. Anna inspected the table of contents and found the chapter concerning numbers then turned to it. Her instinct served her well- the majority of the letters on the codex page were numbers.

"Most of these letters are numbers," she told Fraser.

"Oh yeah?" he replied without looking up from the book that he was reading. He hadn't appeared to be too concerned with Anna's discovery.

"Yeah..." she said with a cold tone. *Screw him; I'll figure it out myself.* Anna went about translating the Demotic letters into their corresponding Latin letters and numbers, making careful note of where exactly each line stopped, and a new one began. She also preserved the small dots that occurred in between various letters. When she was done, her notebook page looked a lot like some sort of coded computer language. It did look rather familiar to her.

Anna contemplated the beginning of the first line- *S27.18K14.21*. It sounded like a barcode on an item at the store, or some sort of serial number. Anna's eyes glanced to the book she had been reading on the history of cryptology. She snatched it up then quickly flipped through some of the Chapters she had been reading. There it was, sitting in the Chapter on the types of ciphers used in and around the Regency period in England- a chart detailing Text Ciphers. The particular example used was a letter written to the American traitor, Benedict Arnold, from the commander of the British forces. It looked very similar to the letters and numbers that Anna had translated from the codex page, but had three sets of numbers separated rather than her two. According to the book, the encoder would use a particular text that the recipient would also have in their possession. The numbers referred to the page, line, and word of the text to form the complete message. The fact that Anna only had two sets of numbers cemented the notion in her mind. The text of the Rosetta Stone did not have pages, only lines.

Anna reached for a much easier to read version of the Rosetta Stone, that she had printed out a little bit ago, and began to put her new theory to the test. After plugging in the first set of numbers, Anna had a word that looked like *Senu*. She proceeded to look up the word in their Demotic dictionary- it translated as "Brothers." It appeared that Anna was correct.

"Hey Fraser," she called out nonchalantly. "Reading anything important?"

"Trying to," he replied, again without looking up. "I think I might have figured out a link between the Mithraic grades and the words on the decree of the Rosetta Stone. I might almost have it."

"Oh ok," Anna replied. "Since you've almost cracked the code with your mystery cult stuff, you probably won't care that I figured out the cipher already." She smirked and went back to working on her decipherments, waiting the few moments it would take for her words to sink into Fraser's mind.

"You what now?" Fraser asked, but Anna refused to lift up her head and continued on working without acknowledging his question. He was no doubt staring at the top of her head. "Anna," called out Fraser, with a hint of annoyance.

She finally put her pencil down and looked at him. "Oh, are you finally ready to talk to me?" she asked.

Fraser looked more irritated than apologetic. "You said that you cracked the code?" he asked with a slight tilt of his head and his eyebrows raised. He was definitely losing his patience and it caused Anna to smirk.

"It was actually pretty simple," she replied. "Nothing about the inscriptions on the back of the Stone were a clue to the cipher. As I said before, the majority of the Demotic letters on the codex page were actually numbers." She showed him her computer code-like translation. "It's a Text Cipher; the numbers point to the line and words on the text of the Rosetta Stone. The first word is 'Brothers.'"

Fraser's mouth was slightly open and he appeared to have nothing to say at that moment. It was priceless.

After a moment he gained more of his composure then looked to suspect how accurate Anna's code formula was.

"Here," she said pushing her resources towards Fraser. "Check it out for yourself."

"You'll have to forgive me if I do," he replied, with little of an apologetic tone, as he took her notebook and papers then went about translating using the cipher. "I find it hard to believe that no one could have figured out something so simple before..." Fraser appeared to be staring at what he had just written. "My god...you are right."

Anna got up and walked around the side of the table to see what Fraser had written. *Brothers of Castus, Sons of Aion.* Anna smiled to herself.

She patted Fraser on the shoulder. "I'm going to go for a walk and rest my genius. I'll leave you to the grunt work for a while."

Fraser Adams was either too stunned that Anna had cracked the code, or too concerned with the words if his new translation to pay little mind to her comments. It was true what she had said. Her mind was very tired of thinking and needed to rest. Anna took her cardigan in her hand and walked towards the elevators. Thoughts of the first lines that she had translated filled her mind as she walked. Why did Brothers of Castus sound so familiar to her? She had definitely heard the name Castus somewhere before.

Eventually, Anna found herself wandering around the bottom levels of the British Library until she was in the general vicinity of the entrance. She and Fraser had been in such a rush when they walked in that she hadn't taken the time to look around. Off to one side, Anna noticed the entrance to what appeared to be a small museum dedicated to the history of literature and composition. Her interests piqued, Anna went inside.

The small museum was more akin to a traveling exhibit than a typical collection. As Anna walked around, she found herself surprised by the random pieces with varying degrees of importance to the history of Western Civilization. She saw the musical musings of Mozart and the Beatles, some of the earliest manuscripts of the Bible, and even one of the original copies of the Magna Carta.

When Anna made her way back towards the entrance, something small and wooden caught her eye. As she approached the object, behind the thick panes of glass, she realized that it was a small wooden desk. Sitting next to it, was an old piece of writing that had yellowed with age. The label on the outside of the glass described it as Jane Austen's portable writing desk.

Anna was filled with warmth and smiled to herself as she gazed on another piece of the life of the great novelist. Jane continued to be beside her, even now, as she and Fraser were about to unlock the mysteries of the codex and follow its clues to whatever was still hidden in the shadows of time. Jane Austen's secret legacy was about to be fulfilled and Anna could almost feel her smiling beside her.

"Soon Jane," she said softly. "Soon the world will know the hidden truths you meant for us to find."

CHAPTER 8

When Anna finally found herself back in the area in which she had left Fraser, she had no idea how much time had actually passed. When she saw him he appeared to have not moved at all, diligently going about the work of translating. It looked to Anna as if he were almost finished.

"How did you translate that so fast?" she asked with shock. "I couldn't have been gone for more than forty-five minutes."

He didn't answer immediately but waited a few moments as he finished the word he was on. "I've studied Coptic, which is very similar grammatically to this particular dialect of Demotic." He put the pencil down and looked to Anna. "I'm fairly certain whoever encoded this was more familiar with Coptic than Demotic as well. Probably not a native to Egypt."

"Fascinating," Anna replied though it sounded anything but in reality. Whatever the nationality of the encoder, she was glad that Fraser was about done. "So what does it say?"

Fraser finished a few moments later and finally turned to address Anna's question. "See for yourself," he said and handed her the piece of paper with his translation of the text. Anna immediately began to read it.

Brothers of Castus, Sons of Aion. Draw in breath from the Sun's rays. You will be lifted up, ascending to the heights of the divine Empyrean. See and hear the immortal things.

The journeys of the Host we see will appear through the disk of God, Lord of Time, and pass through the birth canal of the ministering winds.

Look to the East. You will see the Great Ones staring at you waiting to devour you. Put your right finger on your lips and say

Symbol of Balance guard me! NECHTHEIR THANMELOY! PROPROPHEGGE MORIOS PROPHYR PTTETMI MEOY ENARTH PHYRKECHO PSYRIDARIO TYRE PHILBA

The Great Ones will circle and welcome you. Thunder without sound will follow and you will say

I am a spark of light shining forth from the Dark Depths.

The Empyrean will open and you will see the Throne and the Gates of Fire will be shut.

Stand before them and declare

O Fire-Walker PENTITEROYNI, Light-Maker SEMESILAM, Fire-Breather PSYRINPHEY, Fire-Feeler IAO, Light-Breather OAI, Fire-Delighter ELOYRE, Beautiful Light AZAI, Star-Tamer, ACHBA Lord Aion, OLAM, Open for me. O Immortal sound on mortal tongue EEO OEEO IOO OE EEO EEO OE EO IOO OEEE OEE OOE IE EO OO OE IEO OE IEO OE IEEO EE IO OE IOE OEO EOE OEO OIE OIE EO OI III EOE OYE EOOEE EO EIA AEA EEA EEEE EEE IEO EEO OEEEOE EEO EYO OE EIO EO OE OE EE OOO YIOE.

"That's it?" said Anna. "That must have been the strangest thing I've ever read, and I read medieval alchemic writings a lot."

"Well, it is apparently only a third of what they left," Fraser replied. "We don't even know what page that is. It could be the middle for all we know."

"Good point," said Anna. "What are all these strange words in capitals? Were those not in the dictionary?"

Fraser shook his head. "Those aren't Egyptian words. I'm fairly certain they aren't words in any known language, though they sound very Greekish. They are probably some secret liturgical phrases used by the cult. I've seen similar languages used with other groups in the Roman period."

"It definitely sounds like some sort of secret ritual," said Anna. "I've read enough campy, adventure-quest novels to know that if this codex leads to some sort of hidden temple or treasure, it will likely be guarded by a series of booby-traps. The rituals and phrases described here are likely meant for the initiates to pass through the obstacles unharmed."

"You're probably right," said Fraser. "It was typical of mystery groups to guard their secrets heavily. Even though it wasn't common, some of the more *imaginative* cults were known to set traps in their temples for the uninitiated who might stumble into areas that were off-limits."

Anna looked it over again. Such strange things, but was she really all that surprised? She once read a recipe for making a Philosopher's Stone that involved singing to the mixture while it burned.

"This bit at the end," she said while pointing to the strangest part of the text. "All these words are made up of the same letters, all vowels. Do you think it's some sort of code within the code?"

"Not sure," he replied. "It could be anything really. You sound like you might have an idea though."

"I do actually," said Anna with a smile. "What if this part is some sort of melody the initiate is supposed to sing?"

Fraser just blinked at her a couple of times, though he didn't seem to think the notion was completely insane.

"You never know," he said finally, appearing to be thinking it over. "Music was an important part of the mysteries. Ancient writers said certain musical notes and melodies sent people into ecstatic frenzies. I've never been able to figure it out, rationally, how such a thing was possible, but the human brain is its own mystery. Who knows what could happen if the right tones or sound waves were to mix together in a room designed to enhance them."

Anna remembered an article she had read a while ago about ancient constructions that modern man could still not figure out. One in particular, was a completely underground temple on the island of Malta that had been built a thousand years before the Great Pyramid. Much about the temple still remained a mystery but whoever built it seemed to have had an advanced knowledge of acoustics, as certain rooms were designed to enhance sound. Apparently a man chanting in a particular room in the center could induce a trance throughout the entire complex.

"Do you recognize the name of the brotherhood?" asked Anna. "I swear I've heard the name Castus somewhere before."

"It means 'pious one' I believe," Fraser replied after thinking over her question a moment. He quickly typed some things into his computer then looked over whatever information he had found. "It's not a very common Roman name but there are a few notable individuals known from historical records. One was a martyred saint and another was one of Spartacus' slave generals." Fraser continued to read the computer screen and then smirked. "Well well...here's one you may find interesting. Lucius Artorius Castus- supposedly the historical basis for King Arthur."

"That's right!" Anna exclaimed when her memory was jogged. "That's where I've heard the name before. I remember reading it in an article. I also think there's a movie about it."

"I'm not sorry to say I missed that one," said Fraser as he continued to compile information. "It's rather flimsy evidence at best. All we have is the man's grave inscription, which isn't even in Britain."

"Where was he buried?"

"Dalmatia...modern Croatia," he added the last bit once he realized Anna had no idea where Dalmatia was. "The inscription lists all of his military posts- the last being the governor of Liburnia, a Dalmatian province."

"Where does the connection to King Arthur come from then?"

"His post before obtaining the governorship, was as a commander in the Sixth Legion *Victrix* that was stationed at York. He probably kept that position until he was old enough to retire from the army, then become a governor."

"You're right, the evidence is pretty flimsy." Anna pondered if such a theory could have a grain of truth somewhere within. Could Lucius Artorius Castus somehow have inspired the legend of King Arthur? Could he have founded the mystery brotherhood to which Jane Austen's father may have belonged? From what she knew of the medieval legends of Arthur, there was definitely a possible link between the brotherhood and the Knights of the Round Table, though perhaps not a literal table. The Brothers of Castus were a shadowy order that supposedly guarded a secret treasure. Rumors and legends of such a group could very well have served as the inspiration for the knights of Arthur, and their quest for the Holy Grail. The link could very well be Lucius Artorius Castus. If the man had served in Britain for decades, he would have definitely sired a few children to carry on the legacy of Artorius. Perhaps one of his descendants had been the real King Arthur, who had supposedly fought the Saxons at the Battle of Mount Badon at the beginning of the 6th century. Regardless of the possibilities, Anna needed to focus on the task at hand.

"Well, what do we do now?" asked Anna. "We only have a part of the codex and have no idea where to find the other pages."

Fraser appeared to be heavily thinking things over. He was rubbing the sides of his face- something that Anna had noticed he did when something troubled him.

"Are you ok?" she asked. "You look worried. It's not that big of a deal."

"Hmm?" Fraser had been so lost in thought that he hadn't really heard her. He realized what she had said a moment later and shook the glazed look out of his eyes. "I'm fine. I may have a good idea of where another codex piece might be."

"Oh yeah?" Anna was skeptical and was sure it appeared on her face. "Why haven't you brought it up until now?"

"Because it wasn't important until now," Fraser replied rather defensively. "I'm sorry," he apologized, sincerely, after he realized how his tone had sounded. "I'd had some theories but didn't think they mattered until we were sure we could translate the pages. This is a very dangerous matter Anna. People have apparently been murdered over this for hundreds of years. Winston Leigh was only one of the latest."

"It's ok," said Anna. "I know it's dangerous. My mind has been so caught up thinking about codes and treasures that I keep forgetting that a man was killed a little over a week ago because of it all." It was true. Anna had done a fairly good job of pushing the danger from her mind. They had been chased a few times now, by people with unknown degrees of homicidal tendencies. If she really had caught a glimpse of the mysterious man from Bath at the British Museum, then they could have been followed. They could be in grave danger as they spoke. "Where to then?"

"A small village to the west called West Wycombe," Fraser replied. "It won't be easy to get to from here. It's not that far away, but we'd need to take a train to somewhere that has a bus route."

"Figures," Anna replied. "We might as well just take the train back and drive there ourselves." Smaller towns in England were always a pain to travel to, especially towards the west. She and Olivia had wanted to take a trip to a smaller town in west Somerset to see an old abbey. It was only 80 miles from Southampton, but they would have had to take a train to Bristol and then a long bus ride to the town in a complete journey roughly four hours long. In America they could have just driven there in an hour.

The two of them made ready to leave the British Library and cleaned up their workspace, putting the books they were using on the reshelf carts. With area cleaned, Anna swung her bag over her shoulder while looking around. It had been a pretty eventual day, having accomplished much of what they had set out to do. If only they could find the other pieces of the codex.

"It's still early," said Fraser looking at his watch. "There's no sense in wasting a day in London. Is there anything you'd particularly like to do? I could take you to dinner."

"Why Mr. Adams," said Anna with her best attempt at a Southern belle accent and a sly look on her face. "Are you asking me out on a date?"

Fraser shifted a bit uncomfortably but didn't seem too embarrassed by Anna's teasing. "I supposed I am," he replied while composing himself with the mock dignity of an English gentleman. He brought his hand to his chest and tilted his head downward in a slight bow. "Miss Lewis, I would be honored if you would accompany me this evening."

Fraser Adams was handsome to say the least, and his demeanor spoke of his education and background more so than any framed degree hanging on an office wall. If Anna had just met the man, she would have likely agreed to go out with him in a heartbeat. Unfortunately, she knew how arrogant Fraser could be and it was quite the turn off. She had all but walled herself to the thought of spending time with him romantically. However, the playful gentleman act combined with the Scottish accent were enough to make Anna's defenses buckle, along with her knees.

"You may have that pleasure good sir," Anna replied with a mock curtsey.

As they made their journey about town, on foot and tube, Anna found herself warming to Fraser Adams in a way that she hadn't expected. Upon their first meeting, what seemed like a lifetime ago but which had only been a couple of weeks, Anna had no interest in him at all. He had treated her like she was just a ditzy, blonde, American girl. Sure, he was refined and nice to look at, but he was a proud arrogant sort who looked down on people most of the time. For many women such traits were of little consequence, but Anna found them most unattractive.

When he had shown up at Bath to give them a tour of the Roman ruins, Anna had thought for sure that he was interested in Olivia. Even after her friend had made her opinion of the Jane Austen mystery known, and left the two of them behind, Anna thought that Fraser might have still been interested in her. He had made no real attempt on their early drives together to engage Anna in meaningful conversation, unless he was talking about himself or his research. He hadn't asked her a single question about her own family or research, other than how it pertained to their present quest.

What did she know of him really? He had grown up in Aberdeen and his grandmother had been a well-educated lady-spy of some sort, living before her time. He attended undergrad at Oxford and was currently pursuing his doctoral research concerning Roman mystery cults at Southampton. He also dressed rather well.

Anna eventually found herself in what appeared to be the Soho area of London, though with her sense of direction they could be anywhere. She had only been to that part of the city a few times and it had always been in a rush.

"I hope you're in the mood for Thai," said Fraser as they approached a little restaurant called the Thai Orchid. "This is one of my favorite restaurants in London."

"I suppose I could eat it," Anna replied. She was being coy. In truth, she could eat Asian food all day every day. There were so many types of dishes that one could eat it all the time and still have something different.

When they walked in Anna immediately fell in love with the place. The restaurant was dimly lit and decorated with various Asian plants and flowers. In the background Anna could hear Shamisen guitar music playing- it was perfect.

"How many?" asked the small, elderly Asian hostess. Fraser replied with "two" and she kindly led them to a table towards the back of the room, next to a flowing fountain made of black stones. When they sat down she placed bamboo-covered menus in front of them.

"I love Thai food," said Fraser after the hostess had left them. "Thailand is sort of the European vacation equivalent of your Caribbean. Whenever I feel like getting away for an evening, I like to go to a nice Thai place and imagine I'm there."

"I know what you mean," Anna replied. "Back home, there is just something about having some pineapple chicken and a piña colada that makes you relax."

"I suggest the Pad Thai. It's the best in the Kingdom."

"I'll take that under advisement," Anna replied while she perused the menu. Anna wasn't too familiar with Thai food and none of the dishes sounded familiar. She found that Asian food in Europe was quite different from the food at such places in the States. She had yet to find a Chinese restaurant that served General Tso's chicken.

When their waitress arrived to take their orders, they both ordered the Pad Thai and Fraser gave Anna a satisfied smile as if it pleased him that she had taken his advice. He also ordered a bottle of Riesling.

"So, what's a nice girl from the States doing in the south of England studying alchemy?" he asked as the waitress brought the bottle of wine and filled their glasses.

Anna did her best to stifle a smile as she took a sip of the crisp white wine. He had finally asked about her for a change.

"Well, I actually didn't start out with alchemy," she replied. "I studied European History during my undergrad at Wash U, back home in St. Louis. I wrote my senior thesis on early Arthurian romances and their influence on Late Medieval thought. One of the more interesting books I read during my research was written by Amelia Lockhart, so I decided to look into pursing my masters at Southampton with her. She's actually the one that steered me towards writing my dissertation on the philosophical connections between Arthur's quest for the Holy Grail, and the pursuit of the Philosopher's Stone."

"I had no idea she studied such things," said Fraser in thought. "What was her book about?"

"The French and German Arthurian romances mostly, but she postulates that the original Welsh sources might represent a link to an ancient form of British Christianity that developed before the rise of the Roman Catholic Church."

"That's certainly intriguing," said Fraser, obviously pondering the notions in his head. "I might have to pick that one up myself."

"What about you?" asked Anna. "Why did you choose Southampton for your doctoral studies and not Oxford?"

"Financial reasons mostly," he replied, a bit embarrassed. "Oxford approved my research proposal but I couldn't secure the amount of funding needed in time. Luckily, Southampton also accepted me but allowed me a little more leeway."

"You should have tried looking for a program in the States," said Anna. "They are more difficult to get in to, but it's usually fully funded."

"I thought about it, but I wouldn't have had as many opportunities to study ruins as often as I'd like. I'm also not sure how well I could have adjusted to life in America."

"You'd have to beat college girls off with a stick, that's for sure," said Anna. Once she had said it aloud, she realized that she hadn't meant to and felt herself going red.

Fraser smirked but Anna could tell that he was trying to hide the fact that he was flattered by her comment. "What about you Miss Lewis? A beautiful, intelligent, American girl like yourself should have English blokes circling her at all times."

If Anna hadn't been red before she certainly was then. What could she really say to that? *No not really?* She certainly didn't have guys pounding on her dorm room door. Apart from Olivia, she rarely socialized with people outside of classes. There were only five other people in her program and two of them were male. One, an American from Ohio, was married to another girl in the program and the other was at least fifty years old, and possibly gay. The only other guys she really came in contact with were friends of Olivia from various archaeology programs. She had even seen Fraser at a party several months ago, but Anna doubted that he even remembered that she had been there.

"Honestly, I haven't really given romance much thought the past few years. I've just been too busy." She decided to just go with the truth. "Dating seems like such a high school thing to me now. Something you did because everyone else did, and you had time to go to the movies or hang out in your basement. Since I started college, all I do is read and write papers; I don't have time for much else."

"I'm in very much the same place in my life," Fraser replied. "It's so easy to relate to others when you are young and all that matters is toys and cartoons. The longer I spend in academia, the harder it is for me to relate to people." His gaze shifted to the flickering candle between them on the table. "I find my circle of friends has become more of a fixed point in the past few years."

"I know what you mean." Anna also looked at the candle as she shared in Fraser's state. She knew very well what it was like to not be able to relate to people. Since graduating from high school, she had rarely made what she could call a lasting friendship. Since Anna had lived a short drive from her college campus, she had chosen to save money and not live in student housing during her undergrad. Her choice had likely cost her several opportunities to make friends while living the dorm life. If the past year was any indication, she likely made the right choice in the matter. Of all the students living in Anna's building, Olivia had been the only one that she had really hit it off with and formed a real friendship.

With her childhood friends, she rarely found herself having meaningful discussions with them outside of the topics of various mass media. The moment that she started to talk to them about her field of study, they would smile and then try to show her an internet video.

When Anna looked up from the candle their eyes met. Fraser looked at her with a pained smile that conveyed a bond that they shared, much stronger than one grown from hours of going to clubs or movies with someone. It was a bond shared from an isolation among many.

"That's enough self-pity for the night," said Fraser in a joking tone to lighten the mood before topping off her glass of wine, "On to more exciting topics, or I fear this shall be the worst date of your life Miss Lewis."

"Certainly Mr. Adams," Anna replied. "What do you expect to find at this West Wycombe?

"The Hellfire Caves," Fraser replied with a troubled look.

"The what?" asked Anna in surprise. "That doesn't sound like a very, um...pleasant place."

"The caves were bought and excavated by Sir Francis Dashwood, the leader of the infamous Hellfire Club, for their meetings and rituals."

Dashwood? The name immediately filled Anna's mind with ponderings. The Dashwoods were the central characters in Jane Austen's *Sense & Sensibility*. Could there be a possible connection between Jane and this mysterious group?

"Tell me about this Hellfire Club."

"They went by various names- the Order of St. Francis of Wycombe, the Monks of Medmenham, but now most people just call them the Hellfire Club. Francis Dashwood, the Earl of Sandwich, founded his group as a mockery of monastic orders centered on pagan rituals and the teachings of Pantagruelism."

"Pantagruel," Anna repeated. "The name of the fake count's benefactor. So you think the Hellfire Club had connections to the group in France?"

Fraser nodded. "Dashwood and his spiritual successors were often suspected of being French-sympathizers and conspirators. As was Benjamin Franklin, who had had a long-lasting friendship with Dashwood. He was rumored to have been a Hellfire initiate."

"Interesting." Anna wished she had been surprised that one of the great founding fathers of her nation had been a member of a quasi-pagan cult, but from what she knew of Benjamin Franklin, it made perfect sense. He may have been one of America's great early thinkers, but the man had had a penchant for the obscene in his younger days. He had once written an entire treatise on how having affairs with elderly women was much more preferable to having them with younger ones, as they were much more experienced, discreet, grateful, and that the nether regions were the last to age.

Anna shared her knowledge of Old Ben with Fraser, among other less bawdy subjects, over the course of their dinner. The Pad Thai had turned out to be quite delicious and Anna had to admit to Fraser that it had been the best she had had.

After the meal, Anna was feeling quite satisfied and exceedingly happy. The two of them had finished an entire bottle of wine over dinner, though Anna suspected that she had had a bit more of the wine than Fraser had, as she had been much more talkative than he had been.

As they walked from the restaurant Anna wasn't entirely sure of her surroundings, though she had to admit that she wouldn't have been much more aware of them had she been sober. They walked for a long time, and as they did, Fraser talked to Anna of various subjects. He pointed out interesting facts about London, the buildings they passed, or just bits of Romany things that she had little interest in. At that point, Anna was just happy listening to him talk. She would probably forget everything he told her anyway.

"Ah excellent, we made it in time," said Fraser as he looked at his watch.

"And where is that?" asked Anna looking around, trying to figure out the significance. She saw only a few office buildings and a Waitrose market.

"One final stop before we head back to Southampton." He took Anna by the hand and led her towards the Waitrose but veered to right, towards a door with a large open-sign hanging on the front. The door immediately led to a staircase. When they descended to the bottom, Anna found herself in a large, underground, used-book store. "You can have any book you want, my treat."

"This is amazing," said Anna. Fraser barely registered to her attention anymore- she was in paradise.

She immediately began rummaging throughout the bookstore. Anna adored used-book stores. Going to all the local stores back home was one of her favorite past times. She loved the anticipation, the search, and the fulfillment of happening upon a great find. Each time was a new quest. She had been sorely disappointed to find that England had a severe lack of cool, old book stores that weren't a part of a second-hand chain. She had come across a few in London, in the Trafalgar area, but they tended to be highly overpriced and contained antique books that she could neither afford nor cared to. This store was much more like the used-book stores that she was accustomed to. Though underground, it was still quite large and each section had much to offer, at reasonable prices. Anna suspected that they must be in the vicinity of a college campus as the selection was quite good.

As Anna made her way through every section that she had an interest in, she occasionally would steal a glance at Fraser. He was by her side most of the time. Even though she was taking her time and being thorough with her search, he did not appear to be losing patience with her. In fact, quite the opposite, as he appeared to have been smiling at her each time she looked at him without his noticing. It filled her with something that she did not know how to describe, other than warm and fuzzy.

When Anna finally reached the medieval literature section, something immediately caught her eye. Bound in aged, green leather was an edition of Malory's *Le Morte d'Arthur* at least a century old. She quickly, but carefully, took it off the shelf and inspected it. It even contained the Aubrey Beardsley illustrations that Anna loved. She had been searching, for years, for such an edition. Reading that particular book in high school had been what had inspired Anna to pursue British literature in college, instilling in her a love of Arthurian romance. It had been her quest to find a beautiful old edition of the book that fueled her love of old bookstores. She had hoped to find one in England, but so far, hadn't been successful. She had visited stores in Wales, and as far north as Edinburgh and York, but to no avail. It was her own, personal, Holy Grail and she had finally found it.

She flipped a couple of pages in the front. It was an edition from 1894 and priced at £75. Anna sighed, closed the book, and carefully place it back on the shelf. It was too much for her to spend and she wasn't about to ask Fraser to buy her such an expensive book.

"What's wrong?" he asked. "Don't you want it?"

"It's seventy-five pounds," she replied. "There's no way I'm letting you buy me a book that expensive, no matter how much I want it."

"Nonsense," he said and grabbed the book from off the shelf.

"Put that back!" she tried to push it back into place but he overpowered her.

"I told you any book you wanted and I meant it," he quickly made his way to the cashier at the counter.

Before Anna could stop him from making the expensive purchase, the transaction was over and he held the aged, green book before her.

"I don't know what to say," said Anna as she took the book in her arms and held it close to her chest. She looked up to Fraser, who was smiling at her.

"I take 'thank yous' and the occasional second date."

"Thank you," she replied with a smile and then held a smirk. "We might have to see about the second one."

Anna placed her treasured gift into her bag and the two of them left the store, then made their way to the nearest Underground station. After a few stops and changes, Fraser pulled Anna out of the subway car at Charing Cross.

"I thought we were going to Waterloo?" she asked confused.

"I thought we might walk the rest of the way," he replied.

Anna shrugged and followed beside Fraser while looking around the subway. Charing Cross was one of Anna's favorite stops. Each London Underground station was decorated differently and this particular stop was adorned with black and white paintings of people building a cathedral in the style of medieval artwork.

Anna and Fraser made their way above ground and into a square, in the area of Trafalgar, which surrounded one of St. Margret's Crosses. Anna looked up into the sky to see a rare sight in the skies of England- stars. Over the course of their time in the bookstore and the Underground, it had turned into night.

Fraser led the way into a storefront. Anna found herself continuing to be confused and unaware of where exactly she was going, but didn't voice it. They passed a few stores and kiosks and then she found herself in a small subway-like hallway; it smelled slightly of urine as well. The whole place felt quite rapey but they were through it quickly. When they emerged into the outside world again, Anna was surprised to find herself over the River Thames. They were on a footbridge to the other side.

The view was breathtaking. She could see Big Ben, beautifully lit up at night, the London Eye, the business district, and even St. Paul's Cathedral in the distance.

"I had no idea this was here," Anna admitted as she walked beside Fraser, making their way to the other side of the Thames.

"This is one of my favorite walks in all of London," Fraser replied. "It's a beautiful view of the city and not many tourists know about it. It's also terribly convenient as Waterloo Station is practically right at the other end."

He had been right; Anna and Fraser were soon at Waterloo Station. Luckily, they only had to wait 10 minutes for a train to Southampton Central. Over the course of the hour or so train ride, Anna flipped through her new, old *Le Morte d'Arthur* and smiled wider with each page. Fraser poured over his translation of the codex page and the notes he had written on their investigation.

When they arrived in Southampton, Fraser drove Anna to her dorm building as he had decided to drive to the station that morning instead of taking the bus like she had. It was quite the blessing as it was growing late and Anna was very tired, having fallen asleep towards the end of the train journey.

Fraser parked his car just outside the dorms and proceeded to open the passenger side door for Anna. "Here we are my lady," he said, again with mock a gentleman tone.

"Thank you good sir," she replied with her southern belle. "I had a lovely evening."

"Would you like me to escort you to your door Miss Lewis? The Lord only knows what sorts of ruffians and ner-do-wells could be roaming about these halls, waiting to prey upon a beautiful young lady."

"Sure," said Anna, who couldn't stifle her laugh. "Did you just say 'ner-do-wells'?"

"Well there *are* Americans around here," Fraser replied with a grin.

"We *are* a bunch of ruffians and ner-do-wells, arn't we?" said Anna with a smile. "That's why we're fun."

The two of them made their way into the building and up the three flights of stairs to Anna's floor. Just before they reached her room, Anna stopped and turned to Fraser.

"I'm home safely," she said. "You have done your duty as a Scotsman and I thank you for a wonderful day of scholarly investigation, and the splendid evening that followed." She leaned up and kissed him on the cheek.

Fraser smiled and looked into her eyes. She hadn't quite moved back to where she had been standing and was still rather close to him. He leaned in and kissed Anna's mouth softly- his lips touching hers, with mouth slightly open and inviting. Anna returned his kiss as she felt tingles run down the span of her body. As the sensation filled her with a sense of passion, she continued the kiss with more enthusiasm and Anna found herself reaching for her doorknob. She was startled to find that her door was open and abruptly broke the kiss to investigate.

When she gazed in, Anna felt as if someone had punched her in the stomach. Her room had been ransacked; her meager possessions were thrown about and lying everywhere. Anna knew exactly what they had been looking for- the codex page. Luckily, she had taken it with her to London along with Jane Austen's notebook and lost letters. Anna wasn't stupid.

"Look at this mess," she said before sighing and then sat on her small, unkempt bed. She felt violated but wasn't as upset as she should have been. Anna figured it was the satisfaction of knowing that whoever raided her dorm room had failed to find what they had been looking for. Sure, all of her things were thrown about her room, but all she had to do was clean it up. From what she could tell, nothing had been broken and she had taken the only other thing of consequence, her computer, with her to London.

Fraser looked furious. "This shouldn't have happened," he declared in anger while looking about the room. He stooped down to grab a hold of her desk chair and picked it up off the floor, putting it back where it belonged.

Anna looked around the chaos of her room. The shock was beginning to wear off as her mind began to dwell on the sight and fear crept its way in. If people were willing to kill over all of this, they weren't going to be above ransacking a graduate student's dorm room. She should have been much more cautious.

"If I had been here I might have ended up like Winston Leigh." Anna's words brought Fraser out of his anger and he walked over beside her and sat next to her on the bed. He took one of her hands and held it softly.

"Now that we've unlocked the cipher, hopefully this will all be over soon and you will be safe."

His words struck Anna as rather odd and they didn't bring her much comfort. "You're awfully sure of yourself. We don't even know if the other codex pages are in your Hellfire caves. Even if they are, they could lead to halfway around the world for all we know."

Fraser let go of her hand. "I'm just being optimistic I guess," he replied and then looked into Anna's eyes. "You've figured everything out this far Anna, I have no doubt in my mind in your ability to continue to do so."

Anna smiled at Fraser's compliment and leaned in and kissed him in appreciation.

Fraser broke away and smiled before standing up. "I should let you get your rest now. You've had a long day and this last fiasco could earn anyone a good sleep." He began to walk over to the doorway and Anna stood up and followed behind him. When they reached the door, Fraser turned around and took Anna in his arms and held her. For a brief moment, it had felt awkward to Anna; it was their first hug after all. She soon felt as if there was not a place she would rather be.

"Be safe," he said finally. "I will see you tomorrow." When Fraser broke away to leave, Anna pushed the door shut. She wasn't entirely sure what had come over her to make her so forward, but she knew what she wanted.

"I'll be safer if you stay with me," she said. By the look in his eyes Fraser knew exactly what her intentions were.

To his credit, Fraser Adams seemed to want to protest Anna's offer for him to spend the night with her. After a few brief moments of inner turmoil, he quickly pressed his mouth to hers and kissed her with the passion that continued on from their previous kiss. Anna reciprocated in kind as the kiss deepened and their tongues began to lightly touch each other.

Perhaps it had been the emotional trauma of the day or perhaps her extended period of celibacy, involuntary or not, but all Anna knew was that she wanted Fraser and she let him know it as she pulled him towards her bed.

Fraser continued to kiss her with passion as his hands began to caress the naked skin at the small of her back, his hands going upwards under her shirt and under the strap of her bra. The touch of his hands filled Anna with sensuous chills that ran down the length of her spine, moving downwards. She ached for his hands to continue to explore her body.

As if Fraser knew exactly what she wanted, he gently laid Anna unto her bed with one of his arms. With his other hand, he began to caress the length of her thigh under her skirt while he continued to kiss her mouth. He then broke away to kiss her neck.

Anna's body tensed as his lips and tongue touched the soft skin of her neck and she let out a soft, involuntary moan. The sound must have fueled Fraser's passions further because he quickly moved from her neck to kissing the tops of her breasts outside the neckline of her shirt. Without much grace, Anna sat up and quickly slipped her shirt over her head and then tossed it on the floor. With newfound access, Fraser's mouth took in more of her right breast while he took the other in his hand.

Anna could feel Fraser's passion for her touching the inside of her thigh as he continued to kiss her. She couldn't wait any longer and found herself unbuckling his trousers. Fraser took the cue and did the rest of the work himself. He slipped them off, onto to floor, and then pulled off his shirt.

Now fully bared, Anna took in the sight of Fraser Adams and it made her hungry for more. His body was much more tone than she had expected for someone who spent most of his days researching. Perhaps he liked to work out in his down time.

Fraser took Anna in his arms again and continued to kiss her, his hand caressing the inside of her thigh before finding what it was looking for. His fingers briefly brushed against her, sending ripples of pleasure, before he took her white lace underwear in hand, then slipped them down past her legs. He tossed them onto the floor and returned to her.

When Fraser was in place, Anna reached down and took him into her hand, guiding him to where he needed to be. With a soft thrust, he entered slightly and Anna moaned with the pleasurable satisfaction of it. When he pushed further in, the sensation took hold of her and she drove her nails into his bare back.

They continued on in such a way for a time before Anna pushed Fraser upwards and she placed her legs around his middle, so they could face each other. She snapped off her bra before continuing to kiss him. She was now naked, save for her skirt, which was now around her middle.

So much for sleep. All thoughts of cultists and killers left her mind for the rest of the night.

CHAPTER 9

Anna awoke the next morning very tired in body but quite relaxed in mind. Her arm reached out to touch Fraser but she was alone in the bed. She opened her eyes to see that he had already awoken and had put his pants on, but was still bare-chested. He was sitting in her desk chair and staring out her window, appearing to be deep in thought.

"Good morning," she said as she sat up then stretched out the rest of her sleepiness. She felt a chill and brought the sheet up to cover her naked torso. "Are you alright?"

Her words brought him out of his mind and back into her room. "Yes, sorry. I'm fine. Good morning to you as well. Did you sleep ok?"

"I should hope so," she replied with a grin. "Do you want to grab some breakfast before we head to the Hellfire Caves?"

Fraser tore his gaze from Anna and looked at her desk clock. "Yes, that sounds good. We should leave soon though."

Anna nodded and got out of bed. She held the sheet to her body as she stood but then let it fall to the floor. "Do I have time for a quick shower?" she asked.

Fraser took in the sight of her and he shifted a little before smiling. "I believe I could use one myself."

Anna and Fraser took their time getting ready in a very less than time efficient, yet satisfying, manner. When they were ready they packed their quest essentials and headed out in Fraser's car.

"Is it Friday?" Anna asked and Fraser nodded an affirmative while making a turn. "Can we stop by Avenue Campus real quick? Amelia wanted me to gather her mail and put it on her desk."

Fraser didn't protest the slight detour and they quickly made their way to the part of campus that was designated for the Humanities. Once parked, Anna left Fraser in the car and quickly ran into the Parkes Building. Using one of the keys that Amelia had given her to open the faculty office, she made her way to the mail cubbies.

Amelia's pile of mail was typical- office memos, the university newsletter, a magazine, and a couple of invitations to be a guest lecturer at some conferences. Mixed in, Anna found a white envelope addressed to Amelia in sloppy handwriting. It was from Winston. She blinked a few times while she let it sink in. Apparently, Winston Leigh had written Amelia a letter and either mailed it before he died, or had plans for it to be mailed in the event that something happened to him. The thought also occurred to Anna that it could be a set up. Whoever killed Winston had probably read his mysterious note with Amelia's card attached to it.

Regardless, Anna had to read the letter and quickly opened the envelope. If it came to it, she could just put it in a new envelope and mimic the handwriting. Amelia would never be the wiser.

Ameilia,

If you are reading this it probably means that I'm dead and I probably didn't go pleasantly in my sleep an old man. I know most of our friends thought I was crazy but you at least tolerated my theories and encouraged me to pursue them in spite of everyone else. It's for that very reason that I am trusting you with my life's work. Since I am likely dead and danger may surround you, I will keep this brief. My investigations came to a head when I finally tracked down Francis' lost letter that I had suspected to exist for quite some time. It's not important where or how I acquired it but it is now in your possession along with my journal, which I have had sent along with this letter. Since then, everything has spiraled out of my control. I knew that people would likely be after me so I arranged for you to receive my materials in the event of my death. Obviously, this is a dangerous business and I wouldn't blame you if you chose to put it all away and stay safe, but if you do choose to pursue it and unlock the mysteries, I trust that you will honour my endeavors. I also ask that you check in on mum for me from time to time and make sure she is ok.

Farewell,

Winston

Anna immediately gazed down to a package on the floor beside the cubbies- it was roughly the size of a book. She picked it up and inspected the label to see that it was indeed addressed to Amelia and had arrived from London. Anna used her keys to tear the tape on the box and then opened it to find a brown, leather-bound journal just a little bit smaller in size than a standard notebook. She unfastened the metal clasp and opened it to an old, folded piece of parchment that had yellowed with age, sitting in the front cover. Anna carefully opened it to reveal what appeared to be a letter that Francis Austen had written to his sister Jane, dated to June, 1817- a month before she died.

Anna carefully returned the letter back into the journal. She put Amelia's mail in the empty box and quickly went to her office. Anna placed the box on the desk before making her way out of the building and back to Fraser's car.

"Run into a problem?" asked Fraser looking a bit agitated that she had taken so long.

"More like a gift," said Anna holding up the journal. "Winston Leigh knew he was in danger and had this sent to Amelia if anything happened to him."

"Fair enough," he replied and the two of them got into the car to resume their journey towards West Wycombe and the Hellfire Caves.

The drive proved to be an excellent time for Anna to familiarize herself with Winston Leigh's life's work, but first she would read Francis Austen's lost letter. She carefully took it from its place in the front cover and opened it.

My Dearest Sister Jane,

I regret that I am not able to visit you in person during this troubling time and it is my fear that you should be taken from me before I am able to see you again. It is for that reason that I write to you this letter for it will reveal much that you have enquired of me for so long that until now I was not able to confirm for you. I feared for your life if you knew the truth, however, as your condition worsens that fear is very much misplaced. What will follow is a faithful account of our family's secret legacy and the Ordo Castum.

The Ordo Castum, or the Brotherhood of Castus, was founded long ago by a Roman general stationed in Britain to guard a sacred treasure of great power that God had led him to find buried beneath Bath. The treasure has been known by different names by different peoples- Pandora's Box, Osiris' Coffin, the Ark of the Covenant. The Brotherhood knows it as the Casket of Aion. When the Roman legions were called away from Britain, the Ordo Castum took the Casket to a hidden location safe from both Romans and Britons with the intention of returning one day to reclaim it and continue their guardianship. When it was apparent that they would not be returning to Britain, the brothers who guarded the knowledge were stationed in Egypt and encoded their secrets on four silver codex pages that were given to members of the Brotherhood dispersed across the Empire.

It was indeed one of these pages that you found in the bowels of Prior Park and that Charles and I had to vehemently deny the existence of regardless of your inquiries and protests. It has since been placed back where it belongs.

I do not know precisely at what time in history members of the Ordo Castum returned to Britain. I do know that they did not know the location of the Casket of Aion and chose to hide away a page of the encoded document in Bath. The Brotherhood continued to live on for centuries but would forget the page's location as well.

As for our family's association with the Ordo Castum, I believe that it was our ancestor John Austen who was first initiated into the Brotherhood along with others from the court of Queen Elizabeth. He was followed by his sons and grandson, at which point our family had for some reason cut ties with the Order. It was while studying at Oxford that father was approached by members of the Brotherhood, including our mother's father. You know very well our father's academic mind for study and inquiry. He devoted much time to investigating the Ordo Castum and the Casket of Aion and it became his obsession. Father achieved the rank of Keeper within the Brotherhood, which is much like a librarian or antiquarian for the Order.

As time went on father initiated each of his sons into the Brotherhood when they came of age. Charles and I became important members of the Order, and as we climbed the ranks within the Navy, we were sent on various missions on their behalf. On one such mission, I lead a small group consisting of fellow sons of the Order tasked with commandeering a certain vessel amidst the turmoil of the Battle of the Nile. The French vessel was named the

Franklin, in honour of the American conspirator Benjamain Franklin, and contained secret missives concerning the missing codex pages and the possible means to decipher them. It is on that same vessel, renamed the Canopis, that I had the honour of being captain. That mission led to the eventual capture of the famous stone from Rosetta that we acquired from the French at Alexandria. After the discovery of the stone father became obsessed with deciphering the codex piece in the Order's possession. It was this that prompted him to retire from the Church and move you all to Bath. Unfortunately, the Egyptian languages remains a mystery to this day and father was unable to achieve his goal before he died, though I believe that he had been on the verge of a discovery at the time.

Such has been our family's legacy and dealings with the Ordo Castum. I beg of you not to make any of the truth known to our mother or dear Cassandra. I also ask that you not let any of our brothers know that I have divulged this to you.

I pray that this letter was a comfort to you and that you will soon recover from your illness.

Your affectionate brother
Frank

Anna looked up from the letter and to the rolling green hills of the English countryside passing by in the distance. Her eyes simply gazed on, unaware of the scenery as she contemplated what she had just read. Much had been explained in the letter but many new mysteries had now surfaced. Anna wondered to herself if Francis' letter had reached Jane in time. The thought of her dying before ever knowing the truth filled Anna with a profound sadness.

"Have you ever heard of the Casket of Aion?" Anna asked Fraser.

Anna's words were apparently a shock to Fraser and he almost swerved into the van in the next lane over.

"That letter mentions the Casket of Aion?" Fraser asked once he'd regained control and Anna nodded. "It's a Gnostic legend. There was a small sect, around the third century, that believed that at the dawn of humanity the good God sent his messengers to earth with a sacred box full of divine power and wisdom. It was meant to guide them along the right path and combat the forces of the evil God, who ruled over the physical world. They called it the Casket of Aion and believed that it was opening the box that had put Eternity into the hearts of men, setting them above the animals. It also gave them the wisdom of the gods and the knowledge to build civilizations."

"Sounds like some sort of extra-terrestrial device to me," Anna joked. Fraser shot her a look that suggested he doubted her sanity. "I'm kidding!" she replied in protest and held up her hands. "I think I saw something about it on one those ancient aliens shows once though."

"Those people are usually quite insane but there is sometimes a kernel of truth somewhere in the midst of it all. Whatever it actually was, the sect believed that wars were fought over the casket, and then it survived a great flood, before eventually falling into the hands of the people of Shinar- who we know as the Sumerians."

"What did they believe happened to it?"

"Well, we don't really have any actual writings of the group- only hearsay written by early Church fathers against heresies. One seemed to think that the sect worshiped the Ark of the Covenant even though it had been lost for centuries by that time."

"The Brotherhood of Castus also seemed to believe they were the same thing," said Anna. "When was the Ark supposedly lost?"

"I'm not really sure," Fraser replied. "Hebrew Bible and Israelite History isn't really my area, but I think it was sometime before the Babylonians destroyed Jerusalem in the sixth century BC."

Anna pondered everything that she had just learned. It was all beginning to be too much and she closed her eyes to shut out the world. They had learned quite a lot in the past day or so and Anna was having trouble processing it all.

After an adequate moment's rest, Anna opened Winston Leigh's journal and began to look it over. The thick notebook, which was in fact several notebooks bound together at some point, was full of pages of various notes, drawn pictures, and newspaper articles pasted within. It was what she had expected- a hodge-podge of historical notes, observations, and the musings of a man obsessed with conspiracy theories. Anna barely knew where to start. As she flipped through she began to realize that the Jane Austen Code was only a small portion of the man's investigations into the shadowy histories of the world. Lost civilizations of elves, hidden relics, secret societies- the man could have had his own cable television show back in the States.

Finally, Anna recognized a drawing of Aion. She stopped flipping pages and began to read more closely. What Leigh knew about the cult amounted to more or less what they knew already. Below was a drawing of what looked to Anna to be Ark of the Covenant, but with more monstrous creatures gracing the lid instead of angels. After a closer look, she realized that they were in the likeness of the lion-headed and winged Aion. The drawing must have been what Winston had imagined the Casket to look like.

According to the scribbles, he had apparently believed the Casket to have originated in an ancient lost civilization, perhaps Atlantis, and given to the people from the gods. The possibility of extra-terrestrials also did not escape Winston Leigh. Anna saw the names of various civilizations with arrows pointing out the supposed path the Casket had taken through the ages- Sumeria, Egypt, Israel, the Hittites, Judah, Assyria, then apparently lost until the Roman period. Anna could see where Leigh had not known the name of his theorized Aion-cult and then had recently written *Ordo Castum* to the side. Scribbled after were the names Teutonic, Hospitallar, and Templar. *Templars, why am I not surprised?*

According to the journal, the brotherhood dispersed among monastic orders of the Catholic Church and likely took their codex pages with them. Leigh then contemplated the fates of the knightly monastic orders- the Templars were persecuted and abolished by the Vatican in 1312, while the other two survived several centuries longer. The Hospitallars, also known as the Knights of Malta, consolidated their power on the island until Napoleon invaded their fortress in 1798- just prior to making his way to Egypt. The Teutonic Knights were abolished in 1809, also by Napoleon. Anna certainly found the coincidence intriguing, as did Leigh, who had literally drawn the connections out and then circled Napoleon's name. Below the circle, underlined several times, was the name *Pantagruel*.

Anna then began to read everything that Winston Leigh had discovered about the shadowy Pantagruel Society. Though Leigh believed the group to have existed in some form or another since Antiquity, the present incarnation was apparently founded in the early 16th century by the order's first Grand Master, Alcofribas Nasier- a pseudonym of the heretic priest François Rabelais. The society appeared to have remained small, until the era of the Enlightenment, when many of Europe's philosophical thinkers were throwing off the perceived shackles of the Church and looking to a new world order. The Pantagruel Society apparently wished to free humanity from the chains of Christianity, which brought about the Dark Ages, and restore civilization to the glory of the pagan *Pax Romana*. Though their vision was skewed, Anna had to admit that it did seem as if it had been easier for human beings to coexist and thrive in eras of religious tolerance.

Pantagruel seemed to have had connections to several groups across Europe, including the Hellfire Club of England and the Illuminati of Germany. Their influence even extended into the Americas with Benjamin Franklin, a name which Leigh had written in several places connecting the American and French Revolutions to Pantagruel influence. It was apparently with the reign of Napoleon, the self-styled new Roman Emperor, that the order achieved their greatest height of power and almost conquered Europe. According to Leigh, Napoleon had been the Grand Master of the Pantagruel Society long before taking over France and embodied everything that they stood for. Though he appeared to tolerate the Vatican and was crowned in a Roman Catholic ceremony, Bonaparte was anything but a devoted follower of the Pope. In secret, he was himself the *Pontifex Maximus* and charged the Pantagruel Society with scouring the world for relics of ancient power to solidify his claim to the imperial throne of Rome. The Casket of Aion would have been Napoleon's greatest prize and he had believed it would have allowed him to rule the entire known world. Anna was glad he hadn't succeeded. Pantagruel might have very well taken over the world if not the efforts of Jane Austen's father, brothers, and the Brotherhood of Castus.

Anna flipped through a bit more of the notebook but did not manage to find anything else useful before she started to grow carsick. She stopped for the time being and closed her eyes again.

An hour or so later, they stopped at a small inn called the Pot & Kettle for a nice spot of breakfast. Neither of them had the full English breakfast. Anna decided on a couple of eggs over-easy with some hash browns and toast while Fraser substituted the hash browns for some black pudding. When Anna made her disgust known for the dish comprised mainly of congealed blood, Fraser said it reminded him of haggis- which was hard to come by in the south. Anna had laughed at how stereotypically Scottish he had sounded.

When they finally neared West Wycombe, Anna wasn't surprised to find that it was much like many of the sleepy little English villages she had visited. A small, main strip of shops and houses was surrounded by a few farms and lush park land. Within the park, Anna could see a lake with an estate-house situated beyond it. According to Fraser, it had once been the home of Francis Dashwood.

When they parked the car, Anna got out and took a quick look around while Fraser paid the parking fee. The rest of the small village was dominated by the hill just beyond. Atop it was situated a Neoclassical style, temple-like building and situated just behind it, but a little higher, a stone church with a golden orb at the top of the bell tower. Something about the sight gave Anna the chills.

"What is that place on the hill?" she asked when Fraser returned.

"The Dashwood Mausoleum," he replied while placing the receipt in the car's windshield. "The man himself is buried within it. The Hellfire Caves run beneath it."

"For some reason it gives me the creeps."

They quickly made their way through the village and towards the entrance of the caves- which seemed to have been made into a local tourist attraction.

"Sir Francis owned all this land," Fraser explained as they walked. "He probably chose this place for the site of his cult gatherings because of its religious significance."

"Was a saint martyred here or something?" asked Anna.

"Not quite," Fraser continued. "The ancient Celts worshiped on this hill and then the Romans built a temple on the site. A settlement then grew around the sacred precinct. That church up there was originally built sometime during the seventh century over the ruins of the pagan temple."

"You seem to know a lot about this place," said Anna, a bit surprised by the extant of Fraser's knowledge of Francis Dashwood and his town.

"I studied this site along with a few others during my undergrad," he replied. "I once wrote a paper on early excavations of Roman sites and their influence on the British Enlightenment."

"Sounds interesting," Anna replied. "I once wrote a paper on medieval alchemy's influence on Enlightenment greats like Isaac Newton."

He smirked and shook his head. Fraser looked at Anna in a way that a curator might look at a new piece of art. It was as if he continued to find her intriguing and fascinating. His eyes also betrayed other feelings he had for her- he was growing to treasure her. The look was quickly followed by one that Anna could only describe as anxiety.

"Let's try to do this quickly," he said with urgency. "There's no telling what dangers lurk around us."

Anna nodded her agreement and they made their way to the entrance of the Hellfire Caves. The entrance appeared to have been made to look like the ruins of an old, Gothic church. The sight did not ease Anna's nervous chill. She did not believe in demons, or that there was any power in pagan or Satanic rituals, but everything about the place just felt wrong. The mausoleum, the church on top with the caves of a mystic pagan cult underneath, but most of all the entrance itself. It was a mockery of the Church. Anna was by no means a religious person but she had respect for those who were, regardless of their creed. That the Hellfire Club was a quasi-pagan cult did not bother her but that they had chosen to mock Christianity did. Had they just chosen a Greco-Roman style entrance instead, it would have been fine. Anna couldn't say who or what, but she did believe that something was responsible for the world around her and that the Universe wasn't just some cosmic accident. Such powers shouldn't be mocked. Perhaps it was her studies, but she believed in the power of positive and negative energies and their effects on nature and people. People could worship and believe in whatever gods or religions they wanted but they shouldn't mock, ridicule, or persecute those who believe differently. Hate was a powerful and evil weapon, regardless of who wielded it.

Anna was surprised to find that others were there to walk around the caves- tourists by the look of them. She supposed that the infamous nature of the Hellfire Club probably attracted the sort who liked to wander around haunted places and such. When they walked inside, Anna looked to a board with a map of the caves. The route was sort of like a Z-shape and consisted of corridors leading to rooms of different shapes. Towards the end was an oblong room called the River Styx, leading to a final circular room called the Inner Temple.

Walking inside, Anna was immediately struck by the damp coolness of the air within and the aroma of the caves. The physical experience was familiar to Anna as she had traipsed around an old chalk mine a few years ago back in the States. As she breathed in and closed her eyes, Anna found herself wishing she were back in that mine instead.

As they continued on, the corridors were wide enough that Anna and Fraser could walk beside each other comfortably- quite tall enough for the average person to walk through without hitting their head. Fraser stood a whole foot or so from the cave ceiling above. Some corridors were also larger than others. As they walked on, Anna would occasionally see signs describing the rooms or a mannequin dressed up like a member of the Hellfire Club

Anna walked slowly through the caves while Fraser seemed determined, walking at a brisk pace. She had been left some distance behind before she realized it. Anna had been walking in a daze, not being able to shake the negative feelings she had experienced at the entrance. She shook them off and touched the cold cave wall, feeling some sort of shape. When she looked at the wall, Anna's gaze met that of a hideous creature. She let out a quick, startled scream before realizing that it was only some sort of carving. It was a simple face, like what a child would make for a snow man, but in the stone it had an otherworldly ghost-like feel to it. The sight of the face chilled Anna to her core.

To his credit, Fraser quickly came to check on Anna once he had heard her scream. Rather than scold her, he simply put his hands gently on her shoulders. "That thing creeps me out every time I see it too."

Fraser took Anna's hand and walked beside her from then on. They eventually found themselves in a larger, oval-shaped room that was designated Franklin's Cave. Fraser abruptly stopped to have a look around and Anna's mind immediately went to Benjamin Franklin, his association with the Hellfire Club, and Francis Austen's letter. Jane's brother had helped capture a French vessel, named *Franklin,* which had been carrying valuable information about Pantagruel, the codex, and their dealings in Egypt.

Fraser looked to be searching for something but then quickly stopped to look around the room, as if making sure that no one was inside the cave with them- or soon would be. Once apparently satisfied, he reached behind the rock he had been investigating and a portion of the cave wall to his left opened up, revealing a secret corridor.

"How did you know that was there?" asked Anna with a mix of surprise and suspicion.

Fraser ignored her question and stepped through the doorway, motioning for her to quickly join him. Once inside the corridor, Fraser pushed the stone door shut, once again making the entrance secret to all who walked through the caves. Anna was surprised to find that the corridor was lit up just as the rest of the caves, signifying that others knew of its existence as well.

"Like I said before," Fraser said finally. "I studied the hillside and these caves." He continued to walk along the corridor without looking at Anna. He seemed quite worried about the danger that they could be walking into. Anna had been too concerned with the overall creepy feeling that she was having in the Hellfire Caves to really address thoughts of the immediate threat. "Many thought Dashwood designed the shapes of these caves to represent the sexual union of a man and a woman."

"Ah, the triangle cave is a vagina isn't it?" said Anna, interrupting Fraser.

"Exactly," replied Fraser with a smirk. "The Franklin Cave and corridor are an ovary and fallopian tube.

"So, there should be a second ovary cave hidden away," said Anna immediately once she made the connection. She remembered the shapes of the caves on the map. The theory was certainly sound and fit well with what she had learned of Dashwood's Hellfire Club.

Fraser smiled at her sense of deduction but it soon faded as he ushered Anna on through the corridor. They soon found themselves in a room that was roughly the same shape and size as the Franklin Cave, but not empty of furnishings. Bookcases and shelves lined the walls, filled with books that looked to be centuries old and also various ancient artifacts. Anna recognized statues and busts of pagan gods from different eras and cultures-Greco-Roman, Egyptian, Celtic, even Persian and Hindu. The sight was reminiscent of the libraries of 18th century antiquarians that Anna had seen while visiting stately homes. She was likely gazing at Francis Dashwood's secret cache of antiquities, rare books, and manuscripts. Anna was quite surprised to find them in such a good state, as they were housed in a damp cave underground- not a great environment for the preservation of antiquities. They must be regularly looked after by someone.

In the center of the room stood a large, hexagonal, stone table with a carving of what appeared to be a sun in the middle of it with crooked, rather than straight, rays. Lines separated six sections of the table, each with alchemic runes and symbols carved into them. Some she recognized and some she didn't.

As Anna stood contemplating the carvings on the table, Fraser quickly made his way to some of the cases along the wall and began to rummage through them. He started opening cabinets and pulling out drawers, looking for a piece of the codex. Anna made her way to a cabinet on the opposite wall and began to do the same. What she found could only be described as a hodgepodge of mystical writings and artifacts, catalogued by no rhyme or reason that Anna could immediately comprehend. At times she found herself gazing too long at certain manuscripts, many of which she could use in her research and had not seen the like at the Bodleian, at Oxford.

"Well, well," said a man's voice that did belong to Fraser. Anna froze in fear and her heart sank. "This a right pretty sight innit?" The man's accent was rough and Anna could barely understand him.

Anna was practically paralyzed with fear but she managed to look to Fraser, who had turned around to look at the man. When their eyes met, his held fear as well but he was not overcome by it.

"The professa brought 'is sket wit 'im sir," said the man over his shoulder to a much older man wearing what looked like the attire of a clergyman, black with red trim. The older man walked up and stood beside the first man and gave him a look of displeasure.

"Thomas, if you cannot open your mouth without sounding like a crass imbecile then please keep it closed for my sake." He turned his attention to Anna and looked her over a moment before turning to Fraser. "May I enquire as to your purposes here today?"

Fraser stood silent for a brief moment as his eyes met those of the stern clergyman. He then walked over beside Anna. That he had drawn nearer to her filled her with a slight sense of calm. It was immediately shattered as he reached into her bag and pulled out the obsidian case that held their page of the Codex.

"I've brought you the page that the girl found," he declared to them with a sense of pride at his accomplishment. Anna's world shattered.

A menacing smile crept across the clergyman's face and Anna felt as if her insides had been ripped out, tied in a knot, and put back. She turned to look at Fraser, her eyes pleading for an answer to his betrayal. He would not look at her.

"Well done Brother Fraser," said the man as he took the case from Fraser's hand and opened it to inspect his prize. "Unlike some, I knew you would not fail the order."

Fraser turned to the rough man named Thomas. "I told you that I would take care of things and to not go near the girl. What possessed you to rummage through her dorm room?"

"Ease up brap," said Thomas getting indignant. "You was takin' yer right good time, wanit? The sket wanit no dangers of bein a stiff as the lastin." Anna had trouble figuring out exactly what he meant but she gathered enough.

"You killed Winston Leigh?" she asked out loud as her mind made the connection.

Thomas smirked. "Got a right 'olms bitch 'ere don weh? Mebbe she does need smokin." He reached behind his back, Anna assumed for a gun.

"We may need her Tom," said Fraser quickly and the other man stopped. "Your haste to use that thing almost caused irreparable damage the last time."

"Yeah well, If we 'adn'ta shot that bloke this bitch wouldn'ta sniffed out 'is trail. You was quite right about that."

Anna turned to Fraser, her world imploding by the moment. "You were there too?! All of this...*everything*...it was all a set up? You were just using me to figure out the code?"

He didn't answer her but simply looked into her eyes. He had no sign of remorse, or triumph for that matter. She had simply been a means to an end. In that moment, it all began to make perfect sense. Though she had barely known him at the time, Fraser Adams had jumped at the opportunity to show her and Olivia around the ruins of Bath. He was then never quite surprised enough by her discoveries and theories. The temple beneath the abbey, and then the Jane Austen Code- anyone else would have laughed and said she was crazy; Olivia certainly had. Then, when the danger seemed quite real, Fraser never baulked back from their investigations, but rather continued to encourage Anna, quite fervently at times. He had only wanted her to solve the mystery- to crack the code. Every kind word, every soft touch...it had all been a lie. She felt like she was going to be sick, and probably would have been, had her anger not began to grow rapidly.

"Why?!" she demanded. She neared him and began to pound his chest with her first "Answer me!" Fraser let her get a few in before grabbing her by the wrist.

"Doctoral programs are expensive," Fraser replied matter-of-factly. "I needed funding and the Pantagruel Society was interested in my research."

Anna smacked Fraser, hard, across the face with her free hand. The sound echoed off of the cave walls in the silence and Thomas made to reach for his gun.

"There will be none of that," said the clergyman with a wave of his hand and a glare, stopping Thomas before he made a hasty mistake. "Brother Fraser is right, the order may have a use for her." His glare seemed to cause the rough man to cower in obedience.

"Brother Thomas, I've closed the caves for the day. Take the girl to the sacrifice cells while I have a word with Brother Fraser."

"Yes Master," Thomas replied with a bow. He quickly walked over to Anna and grabbed her by the wrist. "C'mon then."

As Anna was being dragged away, to God only knew where in that underground den of madness, she could only continue to stare at Fraser. He had held his eye contact with her for quite some time, barely registering an emotion, before his attention was given to his Pantagruel master.

When he was finally out of view, the lights began to grow dimmer inside the damp caves, mimicking the turmoil that Anna felt inside as she descended into darkness.

CHAPTER 10

The faint sound of the dripping water was driving Anna mad. It also might be keeping her sane, as complete silence might have likely been worse.

Anna had no idea as to how much time had actually passed since she had been thrown into that cold cell with iron bars. If she tried to contemplate it, she would probably drive herself even crazier than she already was. It could only have been hours for all she knew, but it certainly felt as if it could have been days. Left in a cold darkness, with only thoughts of betrayal and heartbreak for company, would be a hell for any sane person to endure.

Thoughts of Hell had entered into Anna's thoughts quite often since entering the caves. Francis Dashwood had planned his Hellfire Caves quite ingeniously. Anna, forsaken and alone, cut off from her world, was trapped in a dark cell deep beneath a church. That church, penetrating into the sky on the hill above, was as beautiful as any sacred paradise in Anna's mind's eye. Heaven above with Hell bellow. Dashwood had designed these caves to be his own abomination of sacred space- a mockery of the church above ground. In these caves, he and the other bored and debauched aristocrats in the cult would engage in all manner of horrifying rituals and celebrations. Anna was being held in a cell meant for sacrifices. God only knew what innocent creatures, animal or human, were once held in that very cell before being led to their doom. What horrified Anna the most was that

Francis Dashwood and his aristocratic followers had gotten away with everything they did. Even Benjamin Franklin, one of her own country's most famous founding fathers, had apparently been mixed up with the Hellfire Club and Pantagruel.

Anna found herself dwelling much on the shadowy Pantaguel Society. Following Napoleon's failure and defeat, they had to have secreted themselves among the various fraternal orders and secret societies of Europe and the Americas, biding their time until they could influence the world again. What better way than using the Casket of Aion?

Anna had no earthly idea what exactly the Casket was or how it worked. She imagined a golden vessel, possibly given to ancient man by some otherworldly beings- supernatural creatures or extra-terrestrials, it didn't much matter. They were the same thing as far as she was concerned. I was an object of great power, able to transform mankind from tribes of hunters and gatherers into kings and conquerors that built great towers and monuments to their own glory. For all Anna knew, the Casket had the power to bore into a person's mind and take over their will. Perhaps that was the reason it had been worshiped as a god.

Anna shook her head. The darkness really *was* driving her insane. If she managed to get out of that cell alive, she might find herself wearing a hat made of tinfoil.

She was brought out of her musings by the sound of a metal door opening in the distance some ways down the corridor. It was soon followed by the emergence of the soft light of a candle, slowly making its way towards her. As no one who would care to rescue Anna even knew she was in West Wycombe, thoughts of eminent freedom did not enter into her mind. As she hadn't seen light for quite some time, Anna's eyes hurt when it grew closer and she needed to shield them for a time. When she was finally able to see, the visage of the priestly Pantagruel leader stood before her.

The man still wore his black robes with red trim and looked to simply be a wizened and kindly old clergyman, ready to wish Anna a good day. Nothing about his demeanor was different than any of the other friendly, old priests that she had met in her life. As she looked at the man, Anna felt as if he cared about her fate and would readily hear her confession of sins.

"I apologize for the discomfort of the cell Miss Lewis," he said, folding his hands behind his back. "I can have a chair brought to you if you'd like."

"The floor is fine," said Anna with defiance. She sat up strait and hugged her knees. "Who are you?"

"My name is inconsequential," he replied. "You may simply call me the Master."

"So are you the Grand Master of Pantagruel or just another link in the chain?"

"Brother Fraser was right. You *are* very astute." He looked her over a moment. "For an American."

"And proud of it."

"Ah yes, Americans and their pride," replied the Master with a smirk. "That pride is often one of my order's greatest weapons. It is so easy to manipulate."

Anna did not answer him but simply replied with silence, for there was truth in his words that she could not deny.

"What are you going to do to me?" she asked finally.

"Kill you most likely," replied the Master as if he were simply reciting a grocery list. "Once you've proven yourself no longer useful, that is. Which of course brings me to my visit." The kindly old man was gone and the Master looked down his sharp nose at Anna with the same stern face that he had used to make the rough Thomas cower. "Where is the third page of the Codex?"

Anna smiled inside, careful not to let her joy show. *They don't have them all.* She could use that to her advantage- greatly.

As long as she could convince the Master that she could figure out the last page's location they would not kill her.

"I have a few theories," Anna replied. "But I will need the notes and books in my bag returned to me, unmolested. I will also need some light."

The Master looked her over a moment. "That can be arranged," he said finally. "If you harbor thoughts of betrayal, rest assured that my order has assassinated kings and elected presidents as easy as sending a memo. Give me a reason and your loved ones will be dead within an hour."

His threat sent a chill to the core of Anna and she simply replied to him with a silent nod.

"Let's see if we can't find you some more pleasant lodgings," said the Master with a smile and the face of the kindly old man returned. For some reason, the facade terrified Anna more so than the calculating evil underneath. As the Master left the cells, taking the candlelight with him, Anna was returned to her personal Hell of darkness and contemplation. How was she going to figure out the location of the last page of the Codex? Her life was balanced on the edge of a knife.

Again, Anna had no way of knowing how much time had actually passed when she again heard the sound of someone approaching. With her mind occupied on a possible plan of escape, the time seemed to go by much more quickly than it had previously. It was interesting what a slight glimmer of hope could do for a person. Though the time had passed faster, Anna had expected the Master to return much sooner. He had made it seem that he wouldn't be leaving her in the cell for much longer.

When the candlelight came closer, the figure that appeared before her was not that of the Master. Fraser Adams had finally decided to pay a visit to Anna in her cage. He was still wearing the clothes that he had worn to West Wycombe, along with a small, leather satchel. Anna figured that she must not have been in the cell too long, as Fraser would not likely have it in him to wear the same clothes for more than a day or so. She wasn't entirely sure that she even wanted to see him. Though she had been contemplating Fraser's betrayal for hours, deciding on what exactly she wanted to say to him, now that she was confronted by him she somehow remembered none of it.

"What're you doing here?" asked Anna. It was the only question that she really wanted to know the answer to.

"I'm to deliver you to your new quarters," Fraser replied, again with little to no emotion as if Anna were only a means to an end. He quickly produced an ancient-looking key from his pocket and then used it to unlock her cell. He stepped through and extended his hand to Anna, to help her up.

"Thank you," she replied with venom in her tone. "You are such a gentleman." She refused his gesture and helped herself up off the damp dirt floor.

Fraser had no reply, no smart pretentious comment, he simply looked at her. The light was too dim for her to inspect his face properly. Anna couldn't tell from his eyes whether or not he was showing any emotion. He certainly wasn't in his demeanor. He simply stood back and made an *after you* gesture with his arm, waiting for Anna to walk into the corridor.

They walked along the dark, damp, and musty chalk corridor in silence. Anna didn't have much to say to the man who had led her on. He had used her simply for his own ends and those of his masters. If he refused to give her an explanation, then she would refuse to ask for one. Anna had gathered what she assumed to be the truth during her time in the cell.

Fraser Adams had come from a scholarly family and wished to make a name for himself in the academic world as well. From what he had told Anna, whatever money his family used to have a century ago had been squandered by his forebears. From what she knew of his grandmother, as exciting as her adventures were during the war, she hadn't gained much fortune. Fraser had told Anna of his failed attempts to obtain the required funding for his doctoral studies at Oxford, however, he had conveniently left out the details of how his funding for Southampton had come about. A poor Scot with a large chip on his shoulder- that was all Anna needed to know.

As her eyes had still not quite adjusted to the lighting of the main corridors, Anna wasn't sure of the route they had taken through the Hellfire Caves. She eventually found herself back in the antiquities room with the large stone table. Anna saw her bag lying on a wooden table to the side of the room, next to an Islamic style vase. Fraser walked over to it and inspected its contents. Satisfied, he walked over to Anna and handed it to her. She snatched it from his hand and slipped the strap across her body. Once in place, she too inspected the contents. Everything seemed to be as it should be. She saw her own notebook next to the larger, compiled journal of Winston Leigh, along with the aged notebook of Jane Austen. Anna wondered if anyone had looked through them since she had been held there. The only missing item was the obsidian case which held the codex page.

"What about the codex?" Anna asked Fraser.

"The pages will be brought to you eventually," he replied.

"Brought where exactly?" she finally asked.

"You will be put in a room at the inn in town. The innkeeper is on the Pantagruel payroll and will likely have an eye on your room at all times. It is also outfitted with CCTV." Fraser closed his eyes and shook his head. "You wouldn't believe how technology has allowed the Pantagruel Society to finally achieve their goals. They had all but vanished into the shadows after the end of the Napoleonic Wars."

"Biding their time like rats," Anna replied.

Fraser didn't have an answer but she thought he might have nodded in agreement before turning to lead her out of the room.

The Master must have closed the caves again for the day as the corridors were completely devoid of tourists. When they reached the entrance, Fraser produced a padlock and locked the front gate after they were through. After turning the key, he put it in his pocket and they quickly made their way into the town. Anna contemplated running from Fraser at that point but thought it useless. Where would she run to? She had no car and everyone in the small village had likely been bought off by Pantagruel. They would quickly put her back into their hands and then she would be taken care of, permanently.

When they reached the entrance to the inn, Fraser turned to face Anna; for what reason she cared little. Perhaps he wasn't to take her to her room but to pass her off into the care of the innkeeper.

She was shocked by Fraser suddenly taking her by the hand and pulling her around the corner. An even greater shock occurred at the sound of a gunshot, not far off. It was followed almost instantly by the sound of the bullet hitting the concrete of the curb, at the corner they had just turned.

"Shit!" yelled Fraser pulling Anna down the alleyway. "The Master had me bloody watched by Tom."

"What's going on?!"

"No time just get in the sodding car!"

It was then that she noticed that Fraser had moved his car from the car park down the street, to the alleyway just a few meters away. He quickly unlocked the car and the two of them jumped in, not bothering with the seatbelts, as Fraser quickly got the engine running. As he began to back out of the alley, Anna heard another gunshot followed by the sound of the right headlight being shot out. She felt the vibrations of the impact from where she sat and it froze her in fear. Fraser reached over with his hand and pushed her down into a more safe position, then turned around to navigate the alleyway while driving backwards. Tom fired off a few more shots as they rounded the corner and Fraser began to drive forward. One shot managed to hit the windshield, flying through it, and sending small glass particles through the car without shattering the glass. The bullet exited through the back window in a similar manner, while the other shots hit the hood of the car. Anna was grateful that Tom was a lousy shot.

Anna was too scared to move and remained where she was, on the floor of Fraser's car, for quite some time. It could have been an hour for all she knew. It had all happened so quickly. In just a short time, Anna had gone from being a prisoner in a cell, to being shot at, and was now on the run. She wondered how long it would take for them to catch up.

"I think we are safe for now," Fraser said finally. "I executed a few maneuvers down some secluded B roads. They won't be finding us any time soon. I'm not even really sure where we are exactly."

Anna took his word for it and righted herself up into the passenger's seat.

"Are you going to explain all of this now?" she demanded and then strapped herself into the seatbelt.

Fraser didn't respond right away but rather fumbled with his satchel, pulling it over his head, and then tossed it into Anna's lap. She opened the clasp on the satchel and pulled out the obsidian case. Anna quickly opened it to see that two pages now resided within.

"The second codex page- as I planned," he said with a forced smile. Anna just looked at him in reply. She may have blinked a couple of times.

"You think it's that easy?" Anna said, her anger finally reaching the surface. "You were using me from the start! You were an accessory to the murder of Winston Leigh, probably read his message to Amelia, and then started watching her office. You were probably following me the next day!"

Fraser's silent look of guilt was answer enough for Anna to know that her allegations were true. He had likely been staking out Amelia's office when the police came to question her and found Anna instead. From there, he had probably followed her when she met Olivia for drinks and then when they went to the Dolphin Hotel. *Oh Olivia...*she had played the two of them right into his hands.

"I *knew* something was off with you," she continued. "I just didn't want to admit it. For a scholar of ancient cults, you knew way too much about modern secret societies and their workings. When you knew *exactly* how the door mechanism at Prior Park worked, I was too excited to question it but I knew it was suspicious. You were also *way* too pushy about investigating Jane Austen's conspiracy when you had no personal interest in it at all. I guess I was wrong about that too. You were just going to use me to figure it all out for you and then find the Casket of Aion for your Pantaguel masters."

Fraser sighed. "You are partly correct," he admitted. "I *was* using you from the start but I never intended to give either you, or the Casket, to Pantagruel. I could care less for their ideals and their New World Order. I was purely out for myself."

"Yeah? So what's changed?"

"Falling for you wasn't really part of the plan."

Anna had to admit that she was a bit taken aback a moment by the sudden declaration, but it was hardly enough to deter her anger.

"You've *fallen* for me?" she asked with a tone that suggested how ludicrous the notion sounded. "You certainly have an interesting way of showing a girl you care about her. I was unaware that turning over a woman to a cult of psychos, to be held in a dark prison cell for god knows how long, constituted as an act of love in this country. Not sense Henry the Eighth anyways."

"I said I was sorry about that," Fraser replied.

"Actually, no, you haven't," Anna quickly retorted. "It must have slipped your mind."

"Well, I was *going* to apologize as soon as we got to the car, but unfortunately, I wasn't planning on being shot at." Fraser looked irritated and then rubbed the dashboard. "I can't believe that cretin shot my car..."

"I can't believe you! I could have been killed and you're upset about your stupid car?!" Anna brought her fist down on the dashboard. It hurt her, considerably, but she didn't wince at the pain to prove her point.

"Are you quite finished?" Fraser replied to Anna's act of aggression and she gave a relatively silent "harrumph" in reply. "I am truly sorry that I put you in danger but it couldn't really be helped. Yes, it's true that I was using you from the start and that I've been mixed up with Pantagruel for some time, but there is considerably more to it than that." He settled in for what Anna perceived to be a long explanation while keeping his eyes on the road.

"The real truth is that I've been using Pantagruel, for much more than doctoral funding, since the start. I needed to get my hands on that codex page."

When Fraser didn't elaborate further than that brief statement, Anna was quite surprised and quickly interjected. "That's it?! You just wanted the codex page? You went to all that trouble, just for one piece of a puzzle that wouldn't lead you anywhere?" As she asked the questions out loud, Anna's mind began to make connections that she hadn't quite seen before. "How *did* you know about the codex pages anyway?" she asked, probing.

"Because I've had the third page this whole time," Fraser replied matter-of-factly. "As I'm sure you've just figured out a moment ago." Anna had to admit that Fraser did apparently understand how her mind worked.

"And *I'm* relatively sure that you are going to explain to me exactly *how* you came to acquire it," Anna said, her eyes narrowing. "Right now."

"I've always had it," he replied. "It's sort of been a family heirloom for quite some time. My gran passed it on to me before she died."

Anna gave Fraser a look to signify that he wasn't at all done explaining.

Fraser sighed. "From the very beginning then?" he asked and Anna quickly gave one forceful nod in reply. "Alright then.

"I was named for my gran's family, the Mackenzie-Fraser's of Aberdeenshire. My ancestor, Alexander Mackenzie-Fraser, was a Lieutenant-General of the British forces during the Napoleonic Wars. Before that, he served during your country's Revolution. During that time, he came into contact with German soldiers serving in the king's army and gained their trust and admiration. Later, he was given the command of the infantry forces of the King's German Legion and served with several soldiers he had fought beside in America. A few belonged to a secret order of Teutonic knights that had been keepers of a page of the codex. As one lay dying, he revealed to Alexander the location of the page and claimed that the others may have been buried in the Nile Delta, at a place once called Rashit by the Coptics."

"Rosetta," Anna interrupted making the connection.

"Exactly," Fraser replied with a smile. "Alexander had heard of the Stone, but thought that perhaps the French and British expeditions might have missed a piece of the codex. He situated himself to become the commander of the British forces during the Alexandria Expedition of 1807."

"I take it he failed," said Anna, knowing that one page was found in Bath in the time of Jane Austen. The other had been in the hands of Pantagruel- likely taken from the Knights of Malta by Napoleon himself on his way Egypt.

"Indeed," Fraser continued. "While Alexander had success occupying Alexandria, his forces were massacred by the Ottomans occupying Rosetta and the British ultimately lost control of Egypt. The expedition became known as the Fraser Campaign after that, staining Alexander's reputation. He was given a few commands afterwards, but eventually died a couple of years later in the Netherlands from battle wounds. He had wished for his son to continue on searching for the complete codex but his heir had little love for his father's quest. The page was left in a case with other antiquities and forgotten."

"Children rarely live up to their parents' expectations," said Anna. Her own father had wanted her to become a lawyer like him and her grandfather. He had been quite disappointed when she had chosen to pursue the Humanities, though he tried not to show it.

"As time went on, stories were passed along through the branches of the family until my great-grandfather grew obsessed with them as a young man. He eventually found the codex page during a family visit to Castle Fraser. He went on to become a celebrated antiquarian but devoted most of his time to the study of the codex and its supposed history. In his old age he squandered what wealth he had left on his pursuits, ultimately leaving my gran with nothing but the page of the codex and a scholarly mind that developed before its time. Then, as I said, the page passed on to me and I have devoted much of my own academic career to unlocking its mysteries but have continued my family's legacy of failure."

"Until *I* came along that is," said Anna with wide grin. She meant it as a joke, with a dash of pride, but Fraser seemed a bit upset by it. She would have apologized if she hadn't still been mad at him.

Fraser sighed, his frustration showing. "I admit, every time you unlocked a further piece of this mystery where I had failed, I wanted to hate you for it. All it really did was make me admire you and endear you to me all the more. When you cracked the cipher, I could have taken you in my arms then and there."

That time, Anna felt her cheeks going flush. Fraser hadn't just declared that he cared for her out of the blue. Instead, he admitted that one of the reasons he had fallen for her was that he respected and admired her mind. That meant so much more to her than words. "Yes well, you did a fairly impressive job translating once I had."

Fraser's face betrayed a further bit of guilt. "Actually, I wasn't entirely honest with you."

"You think?" she replied quickly in a tone thick with sarcasm.

"I wasn't visiting a friend at Oxford that was an expert in Demotic. I've actually been able to read Demotic since I was sixteen."

"So, that day in Oxford you were just spying on me?"

"Not entirely," Fraser replied. "I had to check in with a Pantagruel contact at Oxford. I first came into contact with the society during my undergrad years as a member of the Phoenix Society."

"What's the Phoenix Society?"

"An organization similar to your country's fraternities and sororities. It was originally formed by Francis Dashwood's nephew after the death of his uncle, to honor his memory and that of the Hellfire Club."

"Sounds like the Skull and Bones," said Anna, reflecting on the similar organizations and their supposed connections to political puppet masters.

"Actually, we would entertain visiting Skull and Bones fellows from time to time," Fraser replied. "Whether they know it or not, I suspect that fraternity has connections to Pantagruel's arm in the States."

Over the course of an hour or so, while they drove away from danger, Fraser continued to explain to Anna his duplicitous nature and his connections to the Pantagruel Society. The shadowy nature of the group made it so that many members of the group did not know each other, or the greater workings of the order. Fraser worked with a small team of academics tasked with acquiring ancient knowledge and artifacts of power. Other members, like Tom, were assigned to such groups as enforcers. Fraser referred to them as the Brute Squad and explained that they essentially kept an eye on teams like his and made sure that they kept the order's best interests to heart. Fraser did not know exactly how the society was administered, but it was his understanding that each region was overseen by an elder called the Master, who in turn answered to an overall Grand Master of the order. The Master that Anna had met oversaw operations in the southern half of Britain, leading the quiet life of a village clergyman when not plotting the downfall of nations. Fraser did not know who the Grand Master of the Pantagruel Society was but he had the suspicion that they did not reside on the British Isles.

After Fraser had explained enough for one car ride, Anna finally grew tired from the emotional stress of recent events and closed her eyes, drifting into a dreamless sleep.

CHAPTER 11

Anna was awoken by the sudden motionlessness of the stopped car. She fluttered her eyes open while she stretched out the sleep.

"Where are we?" she asked through a yawn. Fraser had parked the car in a tiny alleyway somewhere between rows of two-story redbrick buildings.

"My office? Safe house?" Fraser replied with a shrug. "Whatever you want to call it. The place where I keep my business to myself. We should be safe here, for a while at least. I've taken great measures to make sure that Pantagruel doesn't know about this place."

The two of them stepped out of the car and then made their way towards the street corner. Anna took a quick look around, not recognizing a thing. They were definitely not in Southampton, or anywhere near a city that she had visited before. She suspected that they weren't entirely too far away from the university; Fraser would have wanted to make quick visits to this place if he ever needed to. They appeared to be in another sleepy little village off from main roads.

"What town is this?" Anna finally asked as Fraser led them to a doorway close by.

"Lyndhurst, in the New Forest," he replied as he put a key into the door and quickly opened it. "My great-grandfather owned this building and it was one of the few properties he managed to keep. He apparently liked to spend his summers in the New Forest."

"I haven't had the chance to visit the New Forest yet," Anna replied as they made their way up a flight of stairs to the second floor. Olivia had once orchestrated a hiking day through the park with some of her friends. She had invited Anna but she had respectfully declined a day of hiking through the forest.

When they reached the top of the stairs, they went through another door and into a small flat. As Anna looked about the room, she imagined it could have been the office of some Victorian antiquarian. Shelves of old books lined an entire wall while its opposite was home to cases of various items. The room reminded Anna somewhat of the Pantagruel chamber in the Hellfire Caves, though exceedingly less damp and creepy. A comfortable looking, old, leather reading chair sat next to a small wooden table on which sat a tome pertaining to the cult of Isis. By a large window, stood an old mahogany desk with various stacks of papers piled about it. Though there was much on the desk, it did not appear to be cluttered. Fraser didn't strike Anna as the type to have a chaotic study area.

"My gran used this flat as her own personal hideaway during the war," said Fraser. "Most of the books and artifacts belonged to either her or her father."

"I love it," Anna replied continuing to take it all in. She absolutely loved the smell of old books and wooden furniture. She could even detect a hint of the old, leather chair in the air about the room.

Shutting the door behind him, Fraser quickly made his way to the desk and sat in the chair behind it. He shuffled through some of his papers until he found what he was looking for.

"Can you hand me the codex pages?" he asked, looking up to Anna.

Anna made her way to the desk and fumbled in her bag for the obsidian case that held the codex pages then placed it on the desk in front of Fraser.

"Do you want the first translation too?" she asked.

"Go ahead and hold onto that until I translate these two first," he replied. "Then, we can determine the actual order of the pages, and see if I need to retranslate the first one."

"What should I do while you do that?" she asked. Fraser had already set his mind to translating using the cipher that she had discovered.

"You can look about the shelves if you'd like," he replied without looking up. "You might find something interesting."

Anna was a bit perturbed by his lack of attention to her but she couldn't really blame him for it. If she could translate the pages as fast as he could, she would likely ignore him too. She had her notes and such, perhaps she should devote a little bit of time to her dissertation as it was due in a few days.

As she sat in the old, leather reading chair, Anna was having trouble focusing. Now that events had finally settled down, her mind began to dwell on the man sitting at the desk. Fraser Adams had apparently fallen for her- whatever that meant. Was he in love with her? He had almost declared as much to her in the car. The real question that plagued Anna's mind though was- did she want his love?

She hadn't really had time to consider such notions until then. Everything had happened so fast. Winston Leigh's murder, the Jane Austen Code, the Codex- all of it. She had also jumped into bed with Fraser pretty damn fast and that wasn't like her at all. The thought made Anna angry, but with who exactly, she couldn't tell.

"You slept with me, knowing full well you were lying to me the whole time." Her declaration brought Fraser out of his translating focus and he looked up at her. He could sense how angry she was.

"That, uh...hadn't exactly been my plan from the start you know," he replied a bit sheepish. "I wanted to let you get your rest, if you remember." She did, and it didn't make her less angry.

"So it's *my* fault?" she asked in reply. "When I asked you to stay I didn't know you had been using me the whole time..." As she said it, she began to feel even more used. It made her feel a disgusting chill that didn't come from being cold and Anna hugged her knees to her chest. Her eyes focused on the floor.

Within moments, Fraser had left his place at the desk and was kneeling on the floor in front of Anna.

"Regardless of my lies, Anna. What we shared the other night was real. I regret that I was mixed up in all of this, that I couldn't stop Tom from murdering Winston Leigh, and ended up putting you in the middle of all of it." He reached up with the back of his hand to gently caress the side of her face. "But, if I hadn't thrown in with them I would never have met you; and I don't regret that."

"Nice try," Anna replied coolly and then looked Fraser in the eyes. "You did meet me, six months ago, and couldn't have cared any less."

A look of shock and embarrassment invaded Fraser's face of tender declarations.

"Helen's party," said Fraser once the memory dawned inside his brain.

Olivia had taken Anna to a party at the house of one of her friends from the Archaeology department. The friend, Helen, was a nice girl just a little older than Anna and she got along with her pretty well. Helen had apparently thought Anna and Fraser might hit it off and had introduced the two of them, then left them to banter, flirt, or whatever might happen. Fraser had immediately looked uncomfortable, made some quick small talk, then fumbled with some lame excuse before he quickly left her side. He must have slinked out because she didn't see him again the rest of the night. That had been the first time that Fraser had met Anna, and apparently she hadn't been very memorable.

"You were wearing a short, light tan dress with long sleeves over black tights," said Fraser, recalling the evening. "Your shoes matched as well and you've cut your hair about six inches shorter since then."

Anna was a bit caught off guard by such a detailed memory and had to stop and think to herself if she had worn that particular outfit that night- she had.

"We talked briefly about how dreadful the wine was before I had to leave. I was nervous that night, for various reasons. A few hours before, I was contacted by the Master and told that Tom was coming into town for my 'protection,' which meant he was growing suspicious of me." Fraser sighed. "I had to leave my conversation with you in order to meet Tom at a pub down the street from Helen's house."

Anna found herself relaxing slightly, though not enough to let it go. "If you remember, then why did you act like we'd never met?"

"Honestly, I was hoping you had forgotten about it. When I was first tailing you, I hadn't been able to really get a good look at your face but I did feel like I'd known you from somewhere. It wasn't until the night of the seminar, after your insightful comments, that I remembered you from Helen's party." Fraser looked embarrassed, like a young boy caught in mischief, at the memory of how condescending he had been to her. "When you didn't say anything about the party, I was hopeful that you hadn't remembered me and I'd get to make a better first impression. I blew that chance too, by being rude about your question..."

"It wasn't *that* rude," Anna replied. "I liked catching you off guard and making you squirm for it though."

Fraser smiled slightly at her teasing. "From then on, my interest in you was never fully professional. Pantagruel wanted you followed to see what you knew, but I also wanted to get to know you better. When you looked so bored during my tour of the baths, I thought maybe I wasn't exciting enough for a smart and witty, beautiful American girl."

Fraser looked genuinely sincere as he both complimented Anna, and recalled that morning in Bath; it made her feel ashamed for how she had acted. She had been dreadfully bored, but it had been quite rude of her to let it show so much. Fraser had acted much more enthusiastic and polite when she had talked him through Bath Abbey.

"Well, I'm sure we've proven to be more than exciting enough for each other," said Anna as she brought her knees down from their place at her chest and placed her feet on the floor.

"Isn't that the truth of it," Fraser replied with a smile. "I should get back to translating. The sooner we find the Casket, the sooner you will be safe."

Anna simply nodded a reply with a slight smile and Fraser went back to his desk. When he was back to being focused on the codes, Anna decided to walk over to the book cases and peruse the small library of tomes.

The collection of old books ranged a variety of subjects, from geology and biology, to more esoteric pursuits, such as alchemy and the occult. Fraser's great-grandfather had been a man of eccentric academic pursuits to say the least. Anna decided on an old book titled *Hermes Trimegistus as Moses,* took it off the shelf, and then sat back down in the leather chair.

Anna became lost in her reading and wasn't quite sure how much time had passed. When she finally heard Fraser make an inaudible sound of frustration, she put the tome down. He looked to be about to pull his hair out. "Are you ok?"

"It's not complete," he replied in anger, tossing the notebook he had been writing in back onto the desk.

"Are you sure there are only three pages?" asked Anna as she walked to where Fraser was sitting. She picked up the notebook and began looking it over.

"Of course I'm not one hundred percent sure of it," he replied with a tone of irritation. He calmed a bit once he realized that he had snapped at Anna, his look apologetic. "My great-grandfather, and the Pantagruel scholars, all seemed fairly certain that only three codex pages existed and were dispersed among the militant monastic orders."

"Winston Leigh's journal also seemed to point to that conclusion as well," Anna replied. "Are you sure you have the translations in the correct order? That could make a difference."

"I'm sure. The page that was found in Bath in Jane Austen's day actually seems to be the final page. The other two contain poetic references to the *Ordo Castum*, the Casket of Aion, The final bit there, at the end of the back of page two, makes mention of various chambers of trials. The strange liturgies that we found before apparently contain the ritual for the final chamber."

"And if we fail we die, obviously," Anna said matter-of-factly reading over the translations.

"Obviously," Fraser replied with sarcasm.

"We're missing is the first page- the one that describes the location of the Temple of Aion." Fraser nodded as Anna made the same conclusion that he had moments before. Before they could even attempt to complete the trials and obtain the treasure, they had to find the lost temple.

Anna's gaze shifted to the various papers, drawings, and photographs that covered Fraser's desk. The one that caught her eye was their RTI scan of the back of the Rosetta Stone. She dwelled on the Greek word *Axioma*.

"The Axiom of Maria," she declared aloud as the notion came to her mind. Fraser looked up at her with a confused look in his eyes. "'Out of the Third comes the One as the Fourth.'"

"I'm not quite following you Anna," said Fraser.

"Use the same sort of cipher technique we've been using, but instead, use the third page of the Codex as a cipher for the first page."

Fraser looked skeptical of Anna's theory but he quickly went about doing as she said. After a few minutes of word substitutions and translations, he put down his pen and looked up. "My god Anna, you were right." He took her by the wrist and pulled her down onto his lap, quickly kissing her to express his admiration.

She pulled herself away after a few moments, still not quite sure how to proceed with her feelings for Fraser. She was extremely conflicted. Anna had been used by him for his own ends from the moment that the detectives knocked on Amelia's office door. However, he had fallen for her, so he claimed. But was such a declaration enough to make her forget how he had put her in very real danger? Hadn't Anna put herself in that danger from the start, though, when she had decided to pursue the quest? She stood up from Fraser's lap and shook the thoughts from her mind. She would dwell on them later.

"Where do you think these clues lead?" asked Anna. "Is it someplace on the Continent?"

"I'm not entirely sure," Fraser replied as he turned the notebook to inspect his translations. "This reference to *Ultima Thule* has me thinking that the location isn't likely south of England."

"Thule- that's the place that the Nazi's claimed the Arian race originally came from." Anna had remembered reading such things in a book on Nazis and their alchemic pursuits to create an Atomic weapon.

"True, but the Nazis took the name from the writings of Classical authors, like Virgil, who used the name to refer to the northern ends of the Earth."

"So the hidden temple is somewhere in the north?" Anna couldn't begin to guess where to go next. She hoped that Fraser had at least some small idea of where to look.

"It would certainly seem so." Fraser brought his arm up and placed his elbows onto the desk. He folded his hands and leaned in to rest his face on them, deep in thought.

"We know that the Order of Castus had ties to the Roman army," said Anna. "Are there any places in the north that had a strong military presence?"

Fraser looked at Anna as if she had just asked if the sky was blue, though in England that would be a fair question. "Are you joking?" he asked in all seriousness. When Anna shook her head in the negative he looked astonished. "You've never heard of Hadrian's Wall?"

"I'm not a Classicist and I'm not from England, why are you so surprised?"

"I guess I've never really thought about it," Fraser replied. "British children learn quite a bit more of Roman history than Americans I suppose. Hadrian's Wall was a large wall with a series of fortresses that separated the Roman province of Britannia from the untamed Celtic north. It ran roughly along the line that separates England from Scotland."

"So the Romans built a giant wall to keep out you barbarian Scots," said Anna with a grin.

"They tried to beat us but they never could," replied Fraser with a proud smile.

"So, you're telling me that the empire that conquered the entirety of the Mediterranean world, and then some, simply failed the defeat the Scots?" Anna shook her head. "I don't buy it. They were just trying to keep you out. They knew you would taint their civilization with your bagpipes and haggis."

"Yes well, if the Scots were running the Empire it would still be around." Anna wasn't quite sure if he was joking or not. "Regardless, the Roman army was all over the north and the Casket of Aion could be anywhere between here and Orkney."

Anna began to ponder what she had learned. The *Ordo Castum* had designed some sort of elaborate temple or sanctuary to house the Casket of Aion. If the order thought to keep the location safe, somewhere in Scotland sounded likely. It was an area of the world in which Romans were likely not to venture into, situated behind a vast wall of fortifications.

"What do the clues say?" she asked.

"Have a look at them yourself," said Fraser as he gestured to his notebook and Anna began to read.

Brothers of Castus, Sons of Aion,
Seek Ultima Thule, the Dwelling place of the Lord of Eternity
Kiss Belisama at the Pasture of Millstones
Caress her Body, Stopping above her Thighs
There Aion dwells, Beyond the Veil of Mithras
Worthy Brothers, Pass through
Hear the Raven's Call

"That's certainly not cryptic at all," said Anna, her words dripping with sarcasm.

"Mystery cults knew how to make sure that only their members would be able to understand their messages," Fraser replied.

"Well, I guess we should start with Belisama. Do you recognize that name at all?"

"It sounds Romano-Celtic in origin," said Fraser as he stood up from his chair and walked over to one of the bookcases to search for a particular book. Quickly finding it, he turned a few pages and scanned for what he was looking for. "I was right. It's the name of a Celtic river goddess that the Roman's equated with Minerva."

"Just like the goddess of the spring in Bath," said Anna making the connection.

"You remembered," said Fraser with a smile. "And here I thought my lecturing bored you to death."

"Drooling coma at the most," replied Anna with her own smile.

"According to this, the river that was worshiped as Belisama in ancient times is now called the Ribble." Fraser became lost in thought. He had the look of someone who had once known something and was trying hard to recall the information.

Anna left Fraser to his musings and walked over to the shelves and picked up an old book on the geography of Great Britain. She perused the table of contents for viable sections until she found a section pertaining to the riverways of the northern counties. Eventually, she found what she was looking for-information on the River Ribble and a small map charting its course.

"The River Ribble runs seventy-five miles westward from a place called the Yorkshire Three Peaks," said Anna.

"Ribchester!" exclaimed Fraser once his mind had been invigorated by Anna's information. "Of course!" He now had the look of someone who had just gotten home from a hard day at work and could then relax. "There was a Roman auxiliary fortress there, situated along the river at an important crossing. I should have remembered the name of the river. Ribchester literally means 'fortress of Rib.'"

"Chester means fortress?" asked Anna.

"Sort of," Fraser replied. "It's an Anglicized form of the Latin *castrum*."

"So, every city in England with the word 'chester' in the name used to be a Roman fortress?"

"Exactly, though some ruins are easier to find than others. In large cities like Manchester, it's hard to do proper excavations."

"So, you think the hidden temple of Aion is somewhere in Ribchester?"

"It definitely sounds plausible. There was a strong military force in the Yorkshire area. York itself was home to a proper Roman fortress-city, where the Sixth Legion was housed. It's where both Constantine and his father were proclaimed emperor."

"Well, it looks like we're off to Ribchester then," said Anna with determination.

"We can work on the other parts of the Codex in the car," said Fraser as he gathered his things. "It's about a four hour drive from here."

"Is there any chance we can swing by the dorms on the way?" Anna pleaded. "I'd love a shower. I was locked in a cave-cell for quite a while."

Fraser shook his head. "Pantagruel probably has someone sitting in your room with a gun waiting for you." When Anna's face showed her irritation he added, "But there is a shower in the loo over there. It's small, but it's all I have to offer."

"After the day I've had, it's a waterfall in paradise."

Clean and refreshed, Anna was ready for the journey into the north. Fraser also decided to freshen himself and put on a change of clothes. He now wore a pair of dark brown khakis and light blue sweater over a white tea-shirt. It was cloudy and cool in the south, he was probably preparing for it to be even cooler in the north. Anna still marveled at English summers. Fraser's clean clothes filled Anna with envy. She still had cave dirt covering her pants.

"I can buy you some clean clothes before we go if you'd like," said Fraser as if reading Anna's mind.

"That'd be nice," Anna replied, a little too eager. She probably should have declined the offer first and then make him insist. "But don't think this makes us square. I'm still not happy with you getting me thrown in a dungeon."

Fraser took Anna into a quaint boutique on the corner, just down the street from the flat, and let her pick out an outfit. She decided on dark blue khakis and a long-sleeved shirt with blue and white stripes. She had wanted a cute blue dress with white anchors on it, but decided pants would be much more practical if she were going to be traipsing about ancient ruins looking for treasure.

When they settled into Fraser's car for the journey into the north, Anna found it to be a fine time to attempt to relax. Truthfully, Anna was quite thankful for the long drive. She had had barely enough time to process all that had happened to her over the course of the past few days. She would likely go mad if she did not at least *attempt* to address her feelings- to herself at least.

They were drawing ever closer to the end of their quest- one that Anna had only been a part of for a few weeks, but for Fraser, it was the culmination of his family's legacy. His ancestor, General Mackenzie-Fraser, had risked his own honor, and the lives of his men, in search for the lost Codex pages. Fraser's great-grandfather had squandered most of his fortune and academic prestige in the process. Fraser himself had practically sold his soul to the Pantagruel Society, in exchange for the money and resources he needed to solve the mystery of the Codex and locate the lost Temple of Aion.

After long centuries of toil, murder, and war, it had been the young Jane Austen, and her curious nature, that had stumbled upon the path that would ultimately lead Anna to the long-sought-after relic of untold power. Had Jane not crept about the forbidden places of Prior Park looking for adventure like a heroine in a Gothic novel, she would not have found the hidden page of the Codex and her family's own secret legacy. It warmed Anna's heart to know that she was fulfilling Jane Austen's dreams and finishing her quest. She considered herself the final member of Jane's secret sisterhood. Perhaps she should start calling herself by a clever pseudonym.

Anna opened the notebook in which Fraser had written his translation of the Codex and began to read over the bits pertaining to what they should do once they reached the Temple of Aion. It read more like some sort of epic poetry rather than instructions to pass through dangerous traps.

Hear O Seeker of Truth,

Behold the Raven, Herald of Mercury, and take ear,

*   Enter the Grave in Communion and he will guide you,*

Behold the Maiden, Herald of Venus, prepared for the Bridegroom

*   In Love you will know her and she will guide you*

Behold the Soldier, Herald of Mars, armed for battle

*   Prepare for War and may your aim be true.*

Behold the Lion, Herald of Jupiter, Regal and Just

*   Only in Balance may the Scales show Wisdom*

Behold the Shadowbringer, Herald of the Moon, the Evening Star

*   Drink from the Mother's Chalice and know life*

Behold the Lightbringer, Herald of the Sun, the Morning Star

*   Wear the Crown of the Unconquered One*

Behold the Father, Herald of Saturn

*   Reap that which was Sown at the Dawn of Time*

Behold Aion, Behold Thyself

Anna was no scholar of ancient cults but she recognized symbolic ritual language. She had read similar allegorical descriptions in the works of medieval philosophers contemplating the mysteries of creation. Even Wolfram's *Parzifal* contained similar language during certain stages of the Grail quest. As to the specifics, only time would tell for sure. Anna was certain that whatever they were to find in the Temple of Aion, there would likely be seven trials involved.

After a couple of hours of relaxing contemplation, Anna's ponderings and musings were interrupted by Fraser saying "bollocks" and suddenly changing lanes a few times.

"What's the matter?" asked Anna, more out of reflex than genuine enquiry, for she already knew the answer.

"We've picked up a tail. Probably sometime after we got onto the M6."

"Which one is it?" asked Anna, looking behind through the rear window.

"See for yourself," Fraser replied and then switched lanes. As he did so, a black Land Rover quickly changed as well. After a few quick moments, Fraser changed lanes again and the SUV did the same.

"It doesn't appear to be chasing us," said Anna. "They were probably just told to keep a safe distance and watch."

"I should've known better," said Fraser disappointed in himself. "Pantagruel has many patrolmen in their pockets keeping an eye on the motorways if they need to. All it took was for one to spot the black Peugeot with the shot-out headlight and the unique decoration of bullet holes..."

"They don't appear to be dangerous...yet. Is there any way we can lose them before we get close to Ribchester?"

"I think so. Just sit back and don't act like we've noticed them."

Anna did just that, occasionally looking in the rearview mirror to see if the Land Rover was still on their tail. After an hour or so Fraser had gotten off of the M6 and then gotten onto the M62, making his way to the greater Manchester area, driving casual and cool the entire time. When they were on what Anna assumed to be the Manchester outer-belt, Fraser changed course a few times until they were making their way north again- away from the city. Unfortunately, the Land Rover was still with them and appeared to be growing suspicious.

"I don't think it worked," said Anna, her voice beginning to sound alarmed. "They're speeding up."

"Bollocks to that," said Fraser accelerating. "No sense in driving with a cool head now."

Anna didn't reply, but instead, tightened her seatbelt and held on to the armrests. The Land Rover was closing in on them and she began to fear for her life. Either Pantagruel would capture her again and probably kill her, or Fraser was going to kill them himself in the car.

Fraser had chosen the middle lane of the motorway as his personal race track to challenge their pursuers. When he had to, Fraser would juke one way or the other to avoid slower moving vehicles, but when he could, he stayed in the middle. After what felt like hours of a chase but in reality had only been a few minutes, Fraser got into the left lane and suddenly hit the break. As Anna jerked forward and the car sped down considerably fast, the black SUV went speeding by before it completely realized what had happened. Once Anna's head was back up and in a place to see what had occurred, she saw that Fraser had actually quickly gotten off of the motorway and unto a smaller road towards a city called Bolton. The sign identified it as the A666.

"Is this seriously happening?" asked Anna in disbelief.

"What in the devil are you talking about?" asked Fraser "I just lost our tail. You should be happy."

"The devil is right. Did you mean to turn onto the A666, or was taking the Road to Hell an unexpected bonus?"

Fraser shook his head. "You Americans and your superstitious nonsense. There is no such thing as Satan, or hell for that matter. 666 isn't even the actual number of the Beast. In the oldest manuscripts of the Book of Revelation it is 616 and both numbers simply represent the Emperor Nero."

Anna shot Fraser an incredulous look. "I'm not being superstitious and I don't really believe in a Satan either. I just find it a super creepy coincidence that we were chased from the Hellfire Caves and are now driving towards a lost pagan temple complex, filled with god only knows what, by way of route 666."

"It's just a number," said Fraser with a shrug. "I do suppose that the coincidence does cast a shadow now that you brought it up."

The remainder of the drive to Ribchester was relatively peaceful and quiet, save for the lingering feeling of dread that Anna felt. In spite of it though, her excitement fueled her onwards. When they arrived Anna found herself in another typical small English village, though a bit larger than West Wycombe, which had essentially consisted of one main road. Ribchester had two main roads and a few side roads that led to various residential areas. Surrounding the small town was the vast, green, rolling hills of the northern English countryside and the River Ribble. Anna was surprised when Fraser turned right and began driving away from the town.

"Where are we going?" she asked. "I thought the temple was somewhere in Ribchester."

"The Roman fort was in the town on the banks of the river. The church is built overtop what was probably the *principia*."

"You lost me," Anna interrupted. "And what is a *principia*?"

"Oh right, sorry," said Fraser in apology. "It's sort of like a shrine to Rome and the emperor that was in the middle of each military complex. It was where the sacred eagles and banners were kept."

"Well, I'm glad that we cleared that up," said Anna with sarcasm. "Why are we not going that way?"

"The clues to the temple's location said 'Beyond the Veil of Mithras,' which means that the entrance is probably inside of a *mithraeum*. They were usually built outside and away from the forts. The ruins of the Ribchester *mithraeum* haven't been identified yet but they are mostly likely under a church just outside the town, in a little hamlet called Stydd."

As Fraser said the words they approached a lovely area of fields and trees. They turned onto a small road called Stydd Lane, which seemed to grow narrower as they drove down it, until it might as well have been a footpath. Each side was lined with bushes or wildflowers in front of a small, wire fence, beyond which was an open field with sheep standing about or lying on the grass. Eventually, the small road forked at a tree and Fraser turned to the left. They drove up a short lane that led to what appeared to be a small, stone and brick manor house next to a complex of three stone buildings joined together with a small car park in between them. The small manor house had a front entrance of three rounded arches, built in an Italian style, with a large staircase up the middle which led into the house.

As they approached, Anna saw a sign which designated the complex the Stydd Almshouses. The other building was St. Peter and St. Paul's Roman Catholic Church. While different in architectural style, by their look, both buildings appeared to have been built in the 18th century. As there were no cars and no one appeared to be around, Anna wondered if the almshouse and the church were closed for some reason. When they were out of the car, Anna quickly began to walk towards the church but was startled when Fraser began walking towards where they had driven in.

"Why aren't we going in?" asked Anna, confused. "Isn't this the place?"

Fraser stopped to look at her and shook his head. "I don't think so," he replied. "It's been a while, but I'm fairly certain the article I read mentioned the *mithraeum* possibly being underneath a medieval church just up the way. I thought it best to park here."

Anna shrugged and made her way to Fraser's side. They were soon back at the fork in the lane. As they turned left to proceed further up, Anna was struck by how beautiful the area was. Stydd was a sleepy little hamlet, essentially a small farming complex, half a mile or so outside of the small town of Ribchester. Looking around, one did not even need to close their eyes to imagine that they were a few hundred years in the past. Apart from the paved lane, barely anything terribly modern was in Anna's view. In spite of everything she had been through lately, and the unknowns that lay ahead of her, she felt a calming peace walking through Stydd.

Soon, Anna began to see a small, stone, church building in the distance that certainly looked medieval. Just beyond the church were a few other buildings of more recent construction including barns and grain silos.

As they grew closer, Anna was surprised by how small and plain the church building actually was. It had no bell tower and was built in a simple, rectangular plan of thick walls of random stones with dressed corners, supported by simple buttresses. The doorway was in one of the long sidewalls of the building rather than at the front end. The sign just outside said "St. Saviour's Church".

Anna walked around to the other side for a more complete look at the centuries-old stone building. The western wall contained a high window that was positioned just left of center, making it look unusual and off-putting. Another, smaller, window or possible doorway, had once been to the far right next to the buttress but had been blocked up. The north wall was much the same as its south counterpart, though Anna noted a couple of features that looked to be Norman- two narrow, round-headed windows and a doorway, now blocked up, decorated with a simple dog-tooth zig-zag pattern. As before, no one appeared to be in the area and Anna wondered if the church was closed. She was surprised when Fraser simply pushed the ancient, nail-studded oak door open and went inside.

When they entered, Anna felt transported back into the medieval period. The building was one of the smaller old churches that she had been in, consisting mainly of an open sanctuary with an altar behind a simple curtain of wooden banisters, with a small wooden pulpit to the right side. An aged stone baptismal font stood in the middle of the sanctuary left of center, just as the window was. Anna imagined the sun's early rays shining through the eastern window and hitting the waters of the font. There were no pews, rather a few wooden folding chairs were sitting along the sides. The floor was stone-flagged, and the walls plastered and whitewashed. It was a simple aesthetic. The pointed ceiling was made of trusses of dark wooden beams offset by the whitewashed plaster behind them. As with most churches, a table to the left of the entrance had small pamphlets with some information about the building, its history, and services. Anna grabbed one and looked it over.

"According to this, the church was originally built by the Knights Hospitallar in the thirteenth century," said Anna. She felt the dating seemed off as she remembered the Norman features outside, which were usually older than that.

"Sounds like we are in the right place then," Fraser replied. "Perhaps some Hospitallar brothers of the *Ordo Castum* had stumbled upon something early on about the Temple of Aion, but failed to follow through completely."

"At the very least, they knew something was significant about the site." Anna continued to look around the small sanctuary. There did not appear to be any electrical lights within the building, save perhaps one above the pulpit, but the large windows let in a good amount of light. The hour was getting late, but as it was the middle of the summer, the sun was only just beginning to set. "The real question is- how do we get down into the temple of Mithras? I don't see a door anywhere like in Bath Abbey."

Fraser appeared to have been pondering the same question. He did not readily have an answer for her, but instead, appeared to be looking about the room while making some sort of calculations in his head. As he walked down the middle of the sanctuary his eyes were mostly fixed on the floor. "Like most early churches, *mithraea* were usually situated from east to west, which is why a lot of the time they would simply be repurposed."

"Medieval churches were usually built that way too," Anna replied. "Something to do with a tradition about the sunrise on Judgment Day."

"Yeah maybe," said Fraser sounding doubtful as he kicked at some of the stones lining the floor. "In the century just before the Church took over completely, the cult of Mithras and other sun cults were very popular across the Empire. That tradition was most likely invented after the fact to explain why the Church would repurpose buildings rather than destroy them."

"It just sounds easier to me," replied Anna. "Why would they waste time and money destroying perfectly good buildings? I would have just reused them too." Anna tapped the side of her head with her index finger. "Common sense."

Fraser looked at Anna with his mouth slightly open, surprised by her argument. He apparently had been used to hearing people simply agree that the Church was wrong and invented traditions to rule over people. She wasn't ignorant and knew that was usually the reality of it, but it wasn't always sinister. Sometimes it was just good business.

Anna didn't wait for Fraser's reply but turned to investigate the western wall. Whatever retort he was about to say was abandoned in favor of continuing to figure out where the entrance to the *mithraeum* might be. She was also quite perplexed, as the simple small sanctuary was not large enough to contain any obvious secrets. *If only it were bigger.*

As if Anna's wish had been granted, her mind began to make connections. The church *had* been bigger at one time, or another, larger, building had once stood on the site and repurposed by the Knights Hospitallar. The few Norman features, blocked-up doorways, the off-centered window- it all made sense. It was also hard to tell what the building complex could have looked like prior to Henry VIII's dissolution and plundering of Catholic monasteries.

Anna walked towards the back western wall and looked up at the small, blocked-up doorway. She had seen similar doors in other medieval churches leading to balconies at the back of the sanctuary. Since there had been no evidence of a staircase outside, it was most likely that the sanctuary they were in had been a part of a much larger building. Even if she were right, there was no way to know if whoever built the original church building knew of the *mitrhaeum,* or had had access to it.

"What does the entrance of a *mithraeum* usually look like?" she asked Fraser.

"It depends really," he replied as he sat on the stone floor, looking frustrated. "Some were carved out of the sides of hills to look like caves, while others *were* actual caves. Inside towns they could look like little rectangular houses. We act like the cult of Mithras was some mysterious secret society but their temples were about as secret as Masonic Lodges are today."

"About how big were they?" she asked.

"Well, you were in the one under Bath Abbey. Usually about that size, though some could be bigger, like the one found in London. Some in Rome are quite large."

"I think this building was originally part of a much larger Norman building complex. Either the Hospitallars or someone else demolished it and just left this sanctuary standing."

Fraser thought over her theory and appeared to be pondering something. He quickly got to his feet and walked over to the arched Norman doorway that had been blocked up from the outside. Anna quickly followed him. Though the outside wall had been flush with the rest of the wall, the inside doorway still had a small area of a few feet that almost felt like a niche shrine.

"Hey America," Fraser said to Anna after a moment of investigating the stone floor in the niche. "Hand me that candlestick from over on the altar."

Anna made a squenched face at his America comment but quickly went to the altar and retrieved for Fraser the heavy metal object that he desired. Once in hand, he immediately began to pound the side of a particular stone with it. After a few moments, and a groan or two, a bit of the corner broke off and was gone. Anna leaned in for a closer look and then realized it had fallen down a hole.

"It's slate," said Fraser, catching his breath and looking to Anna. "It was made to look like the rest of the stone floor. "The Knights Hospitallar probably knew a temple was here and demolished your Norman buildings, setting up this sanctuary over top to protect it from more zealous members of the Church."

"Nice work," Anna replied. "Now get to bashing in the rest of it."

Fraser smiled and quickly continued to smash open the rest of the slate covering. After he had kicked in the remainder with his foot, Anna produced a flashlight from her pack and handed it to him.

"You're looking first," she said with a smile. "There could be spiders."

With a wry look that suggested that he thought she was silly, Fraser took the flashlight and turned it on. Lying on the ground, Fraser stuck his upper torso into the hole and shined the light. Anna heard a muffled "Amazing" and "You need to see this" then pulled himself up from the hole.

"No spiders?" she asked.

"Quit with your spiders woman!" he said with excitement. "There is a completely undisturbed *mithraeum* down there! Do you know how amazing that is? My doctorate is as good as finished!"

"Well Doctor Adams, you can document that later. We have more important things to do tonight."

Fraser appeared to be struggling at that moment with what he thought was more important- his research or his family's legacy. He must have made a decision then began to lower himself down into the long-sealed temple of Mithras.

Looking down into the dark hole that now had a bit of flashlight quickly flickering out from it, Anna had a moment of apprehension. She was about to literally jump into an underground world of ancient dangers. The moment passed quickly as her excitement got the better of her and she sat down beside the hole with her legs dangling. As she eased herself down and was about to drop, Anna was startled when Fraser's arms went around her legs. He gently lowered her down, taking her into his arms. Being in his embrace left Anna confused. She wanted to tell him to let her go and that she didn't need his help, but the words wouldn't come. He gently placed her on the ground and Anna didn't find herself pulling away.

Fraser appeared to sense her mixed emotions and wanted to address them but she cut him off before the words formed in his voice.

"Shine the light over there," said Anna, pointing to a large shadowy object a few feet to their left.

As Fraser moved the beam of light onto the object, a beautiful marble sculpture in the likeness of a bull came into view. By the terror in its eyes and the position of the creature, it appeared that it was wrestling with some invisible enemy that held the bull in its power.

"Amazing," said Anna as she approached the sculpture. She went to touch it but Fraser shined the light somewhere else and she lost sight of it.

"It looks like they built this temple by digging it out of ground," said Fraser. "I've never seen one like this in Britain before. They were usually just built in marshy areas that eventually silted up over the remains. This one was built completely underground and then covered by another building to hide it." He shined the light at the far wall to their right. "There is the original entrance. It looks like there was a staircase that led up to ground level in Antiquity."

As Fraser slowly shined the light about the room Anna took in the shape of the temple and its furnishings. From the entrance in the back a long aisle ran down the middle, stopping just before the sculpture of the bull. To the sides of the aisle were raised benches made of packed earth and stone, atop which were the tattered remnants of deteriorated woven objects- possibly pillowcases or blankets. Along the back part of the benches ran narrow trenches that ran continuously towards the bull sculpture. Anna then realized that it was atop an altar of sorts, that she was standing on. To either side of the altar were smaller marble statutes of young boys with curly hair, wearing tunics and caps; they looked identical save for that one held a raised torch and the other a lowered torch. Both were exquisitely carved and appeared to be staring at her.

"Cautes and Cautopates," said Fraser, keeping the light on the one to her right- the one holding the upward torch. "The torchbearers of Mithras. No one really knows for sure who they are or what they mean, but most tend to agree they represent the rising and setting suns."

"What do you think?" asked Anna, knowing full well that Fraser had his own theory and probably wanted to tell her all about it.

"I agree to an extent," he replied. "The names actually appear to derive from Persian epitaphs for Mithras that go back into the Medo-Persian period, possibly older. Since they usually look exactly the same as Mithras, they are probably just his aspects at dawn and dusk. Everything in here could be Mithras." He shrugged at his own theory. "But what do I know?"

"Shine the light over by the entrance again," Anna ordered when she noticed another strange shadow. When the light rested in its direction, Anna saw a strange sculpture of a curly-haired youth, naked save for the cap he wore, springing forth by the torso from a rock. In one hand he held a sword, in the other a torch. To each side of the sculpture was a similar looking rock. One held what looked to be a bronze torch while the other held a Roman gladius sword, blade down into a crevice, looking much like Excalibur in the legends of Arthur. "What are those for?" asked Anna in wonder.

"I have absolutely no idea," said Fraser shaking his head. "I've seen similar depictions of the birth of Mithras from the Stone, but never items like these. They must have been used for the mystery rituals."

Anna began to make her way towards the strange items with Fraser following close behind with the light. She took the bronze torch from its place in the stone and looked it over. It was about a foot and a half in length with a mouth about three inches in diameter. The rim was blackened by fire and Anna could see a dark gooey liquid inside. It smelled of a strange mix of pine and gasoline. "What do you think that is?" she asked Fraser, sticking the torch in his face.

Startled, he backed away a bit before leaning in to take a quick sniff. "Pine resin and petroleum?" Fraser said with a look of pondering. "I wonder if it's an early form of Greek Fire. That would explain how it survived this long. Greek Fire was a powerful weapon and couldn't easily be put out; water only made it burn hotter."

Fraser turned to inspect the sword and Anna put the torch back into its place. She then fumbled inside of her pack for a lighter that she kept in a pocket, just in case. She pulled it out and pushed the button to produce the small flame.

"What're you doing!?" asked Fraser with alarm in his voice once he heard the lighter but she had already brought it to the torch's mouth, immediately igniting whatever fuel that had somehow survived the centuries. "Be careful with that. You could destroy everything in here."

"Relax," Anna replied. "If it was that dangerous they wouldn't have used it on a regular basis."

The torchlight began to illuminate more of the cavernous temple with its dancing lights and shadows. To her right, Anna saw a metal basin of sorts that was embedded into a stone block next to where the benches began. She also noticed that, inside the basin, was the same slimy black liquid that fueled the torch. Anna moved closer and carefully placed the flame of the torch into to basin. When she did so, the fuel inside ignited with the sound reminiscent of jumbo sparklers. The flames began to grow and spread, creeping from the basin and into the small narrow trenches that ran along behind the benches. It appeared that the trenches also contained the fuel as the flames eventually made their way behind the benches, surrounded the bull altar, and then made their way back behind the opposite benches until stopping right in front of where Fraser was standing.

"I'd be mad at you if that hadn't been so bloody awesome," said Fraser looking about the *mithraeum,* which was now fully lit as it had been in ancient times.

"Look there!" said Anna, pointing to the far wall behind the bull. At the very far end of the chamber, carved from marble with terrible beauty and elegance, was the lion-headed, winged, image of Aion.

With excitement Anna quickly made her way towards the statue. As she drew nearer to it she realized that it stood in front of a sealed doorway of some kind- it had to be the entrance to the Temple of Aion. "Beyond the Veil of Mithras," she mumbled aloud and turned around.

Fraser hadn't followed Anna but was still standing a ways back, appearing to be deep in thought while staring at the doorway.

"I think it's an Alexandrian Thoth-door," he said finally. "I once saw one when I was touring Egypt with my gran when I was little."

"I know you are probably tired of hearing this," said Anna. "But can you explain?"

"Yeah, sorry," he replied and began fiddling about the room, touching things as he continued speaking. "In the Ptolemaic Period, early alchemists and others magus-types often hid their work in storehouses or desert tombs protected by doorways with ingeniously constructed opening mechanisms. No one really knows how they developed the technology, but the ancients usually claimed they learned it from Atlanteans."

"It always comes down to Atlantis," said Anna. "It's like the ancient version of 'the Devil taught them.' Though now I guess people would just say it was aliens."

"Of course!" said Fraser in excitement and Anna wondered if he thought aliens designed the place. "I knew something felt off about this *mithraeum*. It has everything but the Tauroctony."

"The whatctowhaty?" Anna was pretty sure that over the last hour or so she had sounded confused and ignorant whenever Fraser said anything. He looked more annoyed with himself than he was with her though, obviously failing to remember that Anna knew nothing about any of this.

"Every *mithraeum* had an elaborate scene of Mithras slaying the bull. It's usually called a Tauroctony. It could be a caved relief, a sculpture, or a wall painting. It was the focal point of the temple."

"And this one has a bull but no Mithras," said Anna after making the connection.

"Exactly, but *all* are Mithras," said Fraser with a strange smile as he grasped the sword from the stone, then pulled it out of its crevice. With sword in hand Fraser walked with determination towards the bull sculpture. When he reached it, he climbed on top placing one knee on the creature's back, with the foot of his other leg on the floor. He grabbed a horn with his left hand while his right still clutched the sword. Fraser looked as if he were actually wrestling with the great marble beast. There was something strangely powerful about the scene and Anna felt uneasy.

Seeing something he had been looking for, Fraser lifted the sword up and then plunged it deeply into the bull's back as if it were really made of flesh. Anna then realized that there had been a place in the sculpture's back meant for the sword. Once in place, she heard the clinking of metal followed by what sounded, and felt like, other mechanisms moving under the floor. It felt eerily similar to the hidden door at Prior Park. A few moments later, the stone doorway behind the statue of Aion slowly moved down into the floor, opening the path ahead.

Anna turned back around and something she hadn't noticed before caught her eye- the statue was holding an actual metal key in its hand. She carefully pulled it up through the hole in the marble hand and then inspected it in her own- it looked to be made of dark metal, possibly lead. She stuffed it into the back pocket of her pants, and with the torch still in her other hand, Anna slowly walked through the doorway. She found a stone spiral stairwell that led deeper underground.

"Shall we?" asked Fraser, who had suddenly made his way to Anna's side, his hand still clutching the sword. Anna did not want to dwell on the reasons why he felt the need to bring a weapon. She didn't make an audible reply but simply gestured for Fraser to take the lead down the stairs.

"Spiders," she said, readdressing the very real possibility of creepy crawlies. She'd seen enough movies to know that these types of places could be filled with all sorts of monstrous critters. Fraser just rolled his eyes and led on, deeper into the earth and into the long-sealed Temple of Aion.

CHAPTER 12

Anna expected nothing, but was ready for anything, as she entered the temple. Stories were often written of dangerous tombs and lost temples armed with deadly booby-traps and all sorts of other horrors meant for trespassers. Such tales had been Anna's favorites as a child but that's all she had believed them to be- tales. Since growing up she had never once read an article or a book, or a watched a program for that matter, in which such danger-ridden constructions had actually been discovered. Archaeologists always claimed that such things were the inventions of Hollywood and not the ancients. Anna hoped they were right.

The stairwell did not lead too incredibly far down into the earth, perhaps twenty feet or so. Once at the bottom, Anna and Fraser found themselves in a trapezoidal room about half of the size of the *mithraeum* above. The torchlight bounced over the stone walls, which were rough save one, giving the room a cave-like feeling. Fraser shined the flashlight's beam onto the only smooth wall, revealing the image of a bird, carved in relief, carrying a familiar looking staff in its talons. It looked to Anna to be a medical symbol. The image was framed by two lines running from the floor to the ceiling; written above and below it in Latin were the word *CORAX* and *DEFERO* respectively.

Immediately to Anna's left, about a foot and a half above her head, was another metal fire basin similar to the one in the *mithraeum* above. She lifted the torch above her head and touched the flame to the basin, which quickly caught fire. As before, the flames quickly spread about the trapezoidal room, which Anna could now see had been lined with reservoirs in the walls containing the fuel for the fires. As the flames made their way around the room, bringing more illumination to the darkness, Anna began to make out the details of the chamber. To her surprise, and disappointment, it was relatively bereft of ornamentation save for the carved relief and some Celtic scrollwork engraved above the entryway that they had walked through. In the middle of the room was a rectangular pit of some sort which was roughly the size of a man.

The flames did not go completely around the room but looked to make their way into a hole through the wall of dressed stone. She could now clearly see that the lines that flanked the image of the bird were actually spaces.

"It's another Thoth-door," said Fraser once he also saw the small spaces in the wall. "What was the first line of that poem about seven initiations?"

Anna took the notebook from her pack that contained the codex translations and quickly turned to the page with the mysterious riddles.

"Behold the Raven, Herald of Mercury," she read aloud. "Enter the Grave in Communion and he will guide you."

"*Corax* is raven and *Defero* is communion," said Fraser pondering the words. "The raven holds Mercury's caduceus."

"The medical thing?" asked Anna. "Is Mercury the god of medicine and healing?"

"That would be Asclepius," Fraser replied as he rubbed his eyes. He was beginning to look as tired as Anna felt. "About a hundred years ago the staff of Mercury was confused with the staff of Asclepius. With the power of modern branding and such, it sort of just stuck."

"Also, I thought Latin for communion was *communio*," said Anna remembering some of her mostly forgotten Medieval Latin.

"It is, but Latin tends to have a lot of words for the same thing in different aspects. *Defero* is the type of communication of sending a message to someone."

"Well, whatever," replied Anna with a shrug. *So much for knowing something for once.* "What do we do now? There isn't a whole lot in this room which can trigger the unlocking mechanism."

"Enter the Grave in Communion," Fraser repeated and gestured to the rectangular hole in the ground."

"That's all you, thanks," Anna replied. "I *know* there are spiders in there. I've watched *Temple of Doom* enough to know that much. As soon as you lay down in there, they will crawl all over you while try and find some sort of switch."

Fraser just laughed at her in reply and walked over to the pit and peered down into it.

"It looks to be a normal bug-free pit to me," he said. "I'm not entirely sure there even *is* a switch down there."

Anna made her way closer to the pit as Fraser hopped down into it to inspect it further. When she looked down, he was crouched and feeling the sides of the pit, which Anna now saw was lined with stone slabs. After a few moments, Fraser looked up at her in frustration.

"There isn't anything down here," he said.

"Lay down," Anna replied. "You've studied these mystery cults through academic eyes for so long that you forget that these cultists were real people, with real beliefs and rituals to go with them. You need to think like an initiate of the Brotherhood of Castus seeking an audience with Aion. We must be worthy."

Fraser grumbled something as he lay down in the pit and Anna thought she heard the word *phenomenology*. Anna watched him as he lay there in silence, eyes closed, wondering what was going through his mind. At first there was a look of annoyance on his face- that he couldn't believe he was actually lying inside an ancient cultic pit. As she continued to watch him the silence was deafening. Anna could hear the soft fizzle and crackling sound of the fire slowly burning the fuel within the bronze torch; in the distance she could hear the very faint sound of the wind blowing outside of the stone church that stood two floors above them. She also began to grow more aware of the musty smell of the stone room, which until then, had been overpowered by the smell of the torch fuel.

As she continued to watch, Fraser's face began to take on a blank, death-like quality to it- as if he were lying inside of his own grave. The image produced in Anna emotions that until then she did not know she had. The thought of Fraser Adams lying dead in a grave filled Anna with an intense feeling of possible loss, as if the entire world could be taken from her. The thoughts that her mind refused to dwell on further were interrupted before they began as muscles around Fraser's mouth twitched and a look of serene peace came upon his face. He brought is hand up and touched the stone lining the pit wall just behind where his head lay. It moved back and Fraser smiled before opening his eyes. Anna could feel ancient mechanisms moving as Fraser pulled himself out of the pit.

Just as he was on his feet, the door slab began to descend into the floor. Anna's eyes were drawn back to the pit as metallic liquid began to pour from several small holes towards the top of the pit.

"Liquid mercury," said Fraser with a chill as he looked down into the pit. "My foot moved another block when I climbed out and must have triggered something." After a moment he looked horrified. "That could have poisoned me had I stayed in there a moment longer."

The thought gave Anna her own horrified chill. There *were* dangerous traps after all. They definitely needed to be wary of them as they could be anywhere within the temple.

When they walked through the doorway and into the second chamber, they found it already lit by the torch rim. It apparently had crept about the entirety of the temple complex. The second chamber was an identical trapezoidal room with a carved relief doorway. The other walls were not bare but had elaborate reliefs carved into them, but not smooth like the one on the doorway. On the left wall was a large stone circle, with what looked to be some sort of bearded Sea-god with large, glaring eyes carved into it. There was a small hole, about the size of person's hand, where its mouth was. It somehow looked familiar to Anna. On the right wall was another stone, triangle shaped and pointed down, with a beautiful woman carved into it. Her arms were open wide, as if to embrace someone. Two holes, similar to the first, were situated just beneath her shoulders and next to her torso. Behind Anna and Fraser, to either side of the doorway, were two bronze statues of Cupid with traditional bow and arrow, standing atop pillars of hewn stone.

Instead of a pit, the room was dominated by what looked to be some sort of marble bed or reclining couch. The red woven material, either pillows or blankets, which had once adorned it had deteriorated over the long centuries. Behind the couch stood a marble statue of a beautiful goddess holding her arms out over the bed. In her hands she held a wreath-crown of copper leaves.

The carved relief on the door slab was of a young woman, barely wearing her flowing robe, caring an oil lamp in one hand and some sort of leafy crown in the other. Above and below were written the words *VIRGO* and *AMOR*.

"The virgin and love," said Anna, not needing to be told what the words meant. Fraser smiled at her even though a ten year old could have probably figured them out. Anna fumbled with the notebook and read the next line of the poem. "Behold the Maiden, Herald of Venus, prepared for her Bridegroom. In Love you will know her and she will guide you." Anna put the notebook back into her pack and began to look around. "So within the Maiden's Chamber is the Trial of Love."

"How terribly romantic," said Fraser with less sarcasm than Anna would have expected.

Anna walked over to the marble couch and inspected it, careful not to touch anything. It looked quite comfortable even though it was carved from stone, though she knew it was probably anything but. "What, are we supposed to go at it on this thing?" asked Anna and laughed at her own joke. She looked at Fraser, who wasn't smirking or laughing, but rather looked like such a thing might be a real possibility. "You can't be serious?"

"We can't rule anything out," he replied with a shrug.

Anna noted the slight look of mischief on his face. *Oh he would just love that*, she thought to herself. Briefly, her mind held the image of the two of them in a passionate, naked, embrace on the ancient stone couch, giving her a tingle in her lower regions. She felt her face go flush and tried to think about anything else.

"I wonder what trap could be sprung in here if we go about this the wrong way," she said breaking the awkward silence.

"Last time it was mercury- quicksilver," said Fraser pondering her question. "What metal is usually associated with Venus in alchemy?"

"Copper I think," replied Anna, though she wasn't 100% sure. She was only an amateur when it came to alchemy studies. She found herself wishing these trials had more to do with Arthurian lore than esoteric philosophies.

"Hmm," said Fraser making a connection. "That makes sense. In ancient times most copper was mined on Cyprus, which had close ties to the worship of Astarte, Aphrodite, or Venus-

'You don't need to do that,' Phoebe had said stiffly. 'You could take it out of my wages.'

'Take what out of your wages?' Johnno had winked then clapped his hands over his ears. 'Whatever you're going to drop from Mildred's Greatest Hits, probably neither a borrower nor a lender be, I can't hear you.'

Johnno and Mildred had met only the once when Phoebe had first gone to work at Johnno's Junk as a weekend job and Mildred had wanted to check that everything was above board. They had nothing, not one thing, in common but for some strange reason, even though Johnno had blue hair and was wearing cowboy boots and Mildred was in a tweed suit that she'd had for forty years, it hadn't been the disaster that Phoebe was expecting. There'd been some weird kind of mutual respect.

Mildred had died a few years before but it made Phoebe feel better about it, knowing that the two most important people in her life had come together, however briefly.

Freddy wasn't the third most important person in her life. He was just a smiley, easy-on-the-eye bloke who gave her butterflies and kept asking her out though she couldn't imagine why. But he was also a trained solicitor so she'd trotted off to his office with the dog.

'I can't go to prison,' Phoebe had said once she'd reached the end of her tale of woe. 'I mean, I could cope with going to prison but I was doing a good thing! He kept kicking her. What are the chances that he'll actually go to the police to report me for stealing his dog?'

'Slim to none, I reckon.' Freddy had put a hand out to stroke the dog who was sitting on Phoebe's lap and no doubt getting pus and flakes of infected skin on her dress, but the dog cowered away from his hand. 'I doubt she's got a microchip. You could just say that you found her tied up somewhere.'

'But what about the CCTV? The witnesses?'

Freddy had grinned and Phoebe, as she always did when Freddy grinned, felt something inside of her melt. 'I think the police have more urgent crimes to investigate than a woman rescuing a dog from a violent thug. It was very brave of you.'

'It wasn't brave. But it was the right thing to do. It's wrong to treat anyone, even an animal, like they don't matter,' Phoebe had said fiercely. 'Actually, it's worse to treat an animal like that because they can't stand up for themselves.'

Freddy had gone with Phoebe to the vet where they'd checked for a microchip, but the dog didn't have one. They'd cobbled together some story on the way there about the dog being a stray and although, by law, they were meant to inform the dog warden who'd take the dog for seven days, she was in such a poorly state that she was admitted to the vet's for emergency heartworm treatment.

It must have cost Johnno a fortune, but he never once mentioned it. Though the dog would be put up for adoption once she was better, Phoebe visited her every day. Phoebe was a cat person, of course she was, but there was something about Coco Chanel (the vet had needed a name for the dog and Phoebe hoped that the little French bulldog would have the same tenacity as her namesake) that touched her more deeply than she liked to admit.

Phoebe knew what it was like to be badly treated through no fault of her own. Knew what it was like to be an inconvenience. And she especially knew what it was like to not be wanted.

'Once she gets the all-clear from the vet, I think maybe I'm going to keep her,' she said casually to Freddy when he popped into the shop to see Johnno.

'Of course you are,' he said as if he wasn't at all surprised. 'Perhaps she can give me tips on how to win you over. Like, if she came with you when we go out for that drink.'

'What do you mean *when* we go out for that drink? Don't you mean if?' she'd asked, and Freddy had given her one of those smiles of his that made Phoebe forget exactly why she was still keeping him at arm's length.

'I'm an eternal optimist,' he said and, although she still didn't want him to get the wrong idea, Freddy had been very supportive and kept her out of prison and so it was only polite to . . .

'One drink,' Phoebe had said. 'One quick drink to say thank you for your help. And I'm buying.'

'Not only is she finally going on a date with me but she's getting her round in.' Freddy pretended to swoon and Phoebe had pretended that she was offended but her heart really wasn't in it.

'It's not a date, Freddy,' she said not-very-sternly. 'It's one quick drink.'

One quick drink was actually three drinks and then dinner at a Thai restaurant and the whole time they didn't stop talking. First they talked about what they thought they had in common – the shop, Johnno – and then they discovered that they had a lot more in common than that. They both loved living in London, Regent's Park on spring mornings, summer evenings in Soho, watching the firework displays across London from Primrose Hill in early November and in winter, hunkering down in a repertory cinema in Notting Hill, to watch a 1950s musical or a 1960s avant-garde film.

Maybe it was because Phoebe had been caught off her guard and maybe it was because Freddy really was an enigma, as Johnno often said. But she'd realised that there was more to him than she'd imagined.

Especially when he'd seen her home, all the way to her front door in Tottenham. 'I know that this was only a quick drink,' he'd said, eyes dancing in the streetlights. 'But I'm still going to kiss you goodnight.'

Also, Freddy was very daring to make a statement like that and then actually take Phoebe in his arms. But she hadn't protested, she'd even kissed him back because his first, tentative kiss had made her swoon like the time she'd found an Ossie Clark dress in a Cancer Research shop.

What would Phoebe's life have been like if she'd never encountered that awful drunk man that one December evening? Well, she'd be Cocoless for one thing. She might not love Coco Chanel, but yes, she spoilt Coco Chanel rotten because if anyone deserved to be spoiled rotten after her awful start in life it was Coco Chanel, who'd now overcome her tragic beginnings to transform into the beautiful, sassy and salty little princess she was always meant to be. And Phoebe and Freddy . . . ?

It had taken five years but he'd let her down as Phoebe always knew he would. Eventually.

As the day dragged on and time seemed to have slowed down without any customers to match with their perfect dresses, Freddy didn't call. That evening, he didn't even send his usual 'goodnight' text and Phoebe was damned if she was going to message him.

Like Mildred had always said, *'Sooner or later a person will reveal their true colours.'*

Chapter Eleven

It wasn't until the next day that Freddy finally deigned to put in an appearance.

It was late enough that they were open (Sophy had managed to arrive only five minutes late and had also managed to work out how to turn off the alarm) but still too early to have any customers.

Everyone was very subdued, even Coco Chanel who had left half of her breakfast, which was unheard of. The thought of spending another day toiling away in the basement filled Phoebe with despair. The basement had never been so tidy, the stock so well organised, everything so neatly labelled. There wasn't much else for her to do and then Freddy walked in, looking like he didn't have a single bloody care in the world.

'Glad you're all here,' he said, even though where else would they all be? He was also making sure that his gaze skirted over Phoebe, even though Coco scampered over to him and stood on her hind legs, front paws on his knees. Freddy didn't pick her up, but gave her a very perfunctory scratch under the chin. So, as well as not having Phoebe's back, now he was shunning her dog too.

Clearly, he was still angry with Phoebe, which was no match for how angry she was with him. He'd not listened to her side of things; he'd demoted her and threatened to sack her even though he knew that the shop, the dresses, were her whole world.

Phoebe felt her lips tighten. Her everything tighten, especially her heart.

'I won't be long. I need to talk to Phoebe about having some training,' he said airily, like none of this was causing him any anguish at all.

Whereas the word '*training*' caused an icy sensation to trickle down Phoebe's spine. 'Training?' she echoed in a croaky voice.

Freddy looked her straight in the eye, his face impassive. 'If you return to managerial duties then you need to have a better handle on the admin side of things. You can't just leave it all to Sophy and Bea.'

'Admin?' Phoebe echoed in an even croakier voice. 'If?'

'But we're happy to do the admin,' Bea said quickly. 'I like doing the admin. I have a system.'

It was true, Bea did have a system. While Phoebe might have a near photographic memory for every single dress that passed through the shop, or had passed, including its provenance, price, fabric and approximate age, Bea took all that knowledge and put it into some kind of stock inventory program on the computer then added it to the website. Plus she ordered things that they needed: till roll, their stationery and bags, coffee. She'd even recently dealt with some women who'd come round from the council to do a health and safety survey.

'I never mind doing the cashing up. Can't have all those years at BelleGirl going to waste,' Sophy said of the decade she'd spent at a horrible high-street fashion chain, which had gone bust forcing Johnno to give his biological daughter a job. 'Plus, I'm very busy with my rental dresses.'

'I hear you, but there's no point in having a manager if they don't manage,' Freddy said firmly because once his mind was made up about something, he would not be convinced otherwise. Whether it was wearing Phoebe down until she went on a date with him or deciding that a suitable punishment for her crimes would be to spend the day on the phone to Camden Council with a query about their business rates. 'So, Bea, I think a good plan for today is if you walk Phoebe through the website and the ecommerce side of things. Which will mean that she doesn't have to deal directly, or indirectly, with any of the customers.'

'You're being *so* unfair!' Phoebe hissed because she couldn't hold her tongue a moment longer. In fact, she was amazed that she'd managed to hold out for, oooh, at least ten minutes.

'What if Phoebe is walking through the shop and a customer asks her something?' Cress wanted to know, in a manner that suggested that she also thought Freddy was being completely unreasonable. 'And what about the brides and the customers who are looking for a really high-end dress? I'm not cut out to deal with those women. They're very demanding. Very high maintenance and Phoebe has a magic knack for . . .'

'I think you need to have a little faith in yourself, Cress,' Freddy said in a much softer tone than he'd used so far. 'I'm sure you can cope admirably.' He surveyed the staff with a keen glance that had something of the head teacher about it. 'No one here is irreplaceable. If a customer does approach Phoebe, then Phoebe will direct them to another member of staff and be on her way. Talking of which, I'm going to have to love you and leave you.'

He touched the side of his head in salute, gave Coco Chanel a little pat on her head as she stood in the doorway and tried to block his passage, and then he was gone.

The shop was still empty of customers so no one moved from their slumped positions in the back office. Although Phoebe liked to think that she always had her fight face ready to go, she was the most slumped of them all. She really would end up with a dowager's hump at this rate.

'I can't believe Freddy is being like this. To me,' she muttered. 'I thought we'd cleared everything up on Saturday night and he was fine . . .'

Then she remembered that the staff, except Cress, didn't know about her and Freddy. How right she'd been to keep things on the down-low.

'He really is overdoing it. I still say that you shouldn't have reacted the way you did, but Rosie Roberts did get fake tan on that dress,' Sophy pointed out, which was the last thing Phoebe expected her to say. She'd expected Sophy to be drunk on all her new power.

'And she ripped it,' Cress added indignantly.

'I took pictures for the insurance claim,' Bea said. 'There's actual photographic evidence.'

'Anyway, she's a terrible influencer,' Anita said with a roll of her eyes, even though if Phoebe had expected Sophy to be on a power trip, she'd have thought Anita would be dancing a victory jig by now. 'She couldn't influence me to do anything.'

'I should have done my homework a bit better, but I was wowed by her follower count,' Sophy said as she stood up and advanced towards the kettle. 'I've sourced a new influencer, who hasn't got so many followers but she does have the right vibe.' She took down a couple of mugs from the cupboard in front of her. 'And she doesn't wear fake tan, I already checked. Now who wants a brew?'

It was one of the most boring weeks of Phoebe's life. Toiling away in the basement like a Victorian orphan not allowed to see sunlight.

Though, to be fair, she wasn't *always* in the basement. Roughly half of her time was spent in the back office sitting next to Bea who was trying to show her how the website worked. She kept going on about things that didn't have proper names, just random groups of initials: CMS, SEO. The only initials Phoebe was interested in were CC for Coco Chanel, obviously, YSL for Yves Saint Laurent or even DvF for Diane von Furstenberg.

Their social media accounts were still going haywire although Bea and Sophy advised Phoebe it was best not to look.

'People can be very unkind when they're hiding behind a false username and their keyboards,' Bea said when Phoebe had a peek on Instagram and immediately found a comment that suggested they sold inferior vintage, which had given her heart palpitations.

She didn't care that people were calling her a bully and a bitch. *'Someone else's opinion of you is none of your business,'* Mildred always said, but to cast doubts on Phoebe's ability to source good vintage was another level of cruelty.

To make matters even worse, Sophy's new influencer was coming in the very next day.

'Not to do a shoot,' Sophy assured Phoebe even though Phoebe wasn't in charge of the shop and no longer had the authority to grant permission for another professional show-off to come in. She wasn't in charge of anything. Not even her own destiny. 'Let's see if she passes the vibe check. The vibes have got to be right.'

The vibes hadn't been right for days. On Thursday, Freddy came by just after the shop opened to issue yet another diktat about boring tasks he wanted Phoebe to accomplish. Today he wanted Sophy to take Phoebe through some role-play exercises for dealing with difficult customers.

'Because the customer is always right,' he said, his eyes fixed on Phoebe even though, time and time again, the customer was wrong and didn't even know their Biba from their

Bus Stop. It was hard to believe that this was the same Freddy who used to give her butterflies every time he smiled at her. Freddy's smiles were now in very short supply and Phoebe was getting used to the new leaden feeling when he walked through the door. 'We'll catch up again tomorrow.'

As soon as he left, Phoebe turned to Sophy with a pleading look. Forced to plead with Sophy! 'Even the idea of role play makes me want to break out in hives,' she said but it was more than that.

This whole week, having her many faults pointed out to her by Freddy, the person who claimed to have feelings for her, made Phoebe feel like the years had melted away. She was five again. Seven again. Ten. Twelve. Then a teenager who was never good enough to be given the things that other children took for granted. A space to call her own. People to call her own.

The two most basic things in life. A home. A family. But Phoebe never got them because she didn't deserve them. There was something about her that repelled rather than attracted.

Was it any wonder that every day she did her hair and put on her make-up and slipped into a perfect black dress and heels like they were a costume to hide her true self from the world? Because her true self was that girl with greasy hair scraped back and a grubby tracksuit who'd arrived on Mildred's doorstep all those years ago.

'I don't like role play either,' Sophy said, pulling Phoebe out of her memories. 'But it might be worth a try . . .'

'Please, Sophy, do you want me to quit? Is that was this is all about? Getting me to resign so you can take over the shop?' Phoebe demanded.

'What? No!' Sophy sounded shocked and offended enough that Phoebe maybe believed her. 'Yes, I want a bit more responsibility. Yes, I want to have my little rental dress thing so I feel properly invested in my job. Honestly, even after all this time, you're still determined to think the worst of me.'

'To be fair, Phoebe thinks the worst of everyone,' Anita shouted from the shop where she was meant to be working and not eavesdropping on other people's conversations.

'All I'm saying is that banishing me from the shop floor, from my dresses, is punishment enough,' Phoebe said plaintively. She wasn't very good at being plaintive but Sophy grudgingly nodded. 'Don't make me role-play. Do you want me to beg?'

There was a moment's awkward silence during which Sophy narrowed her eyes almost as if she was seriously considering making Phoebe beg but then she sighed. 'No role playing but when Birdy comes in, will you be nice to her?'

'Who's Birdy?' Phoebe asked.

'My lovely micro influencer,' Sophy said, as she added more hot water to her mug of tea, which had cooled in the time that they'd been chatting all this out.

Why did everyone assume that Phoebe's default position was outright hostility? It was more that she took a while to warm to people. 'I'll be polite and friendly, maybe even verging on charming,' she said.

Sophy looked extremely sceptical. 'Really?'

'Well, I'm going to try,' Phoebe admitted and Sophy had to be satisfied with that.

There was nothing left to do but to sit next to Bea while she explained about the SEO thingy again. It made Phoebe's head swim. Thankfully, she soon persuaded Bea that they should go on Instagram to look up this so-called influencer.

Birdy lived in London, she had just over twenty three thousand followers and according to her profile she was 'a vintage girly, a hopeless romantic, a teller of stories and the slave of Peggy Gug, a spoilt little pug'.

It was so twee and saccharine sweet that it made Phoebe's back molars ache like she'd eaten too much sugar.

A quick look at Birdy's grid showed that she'd done a brand campaign for Phoebe's favourite underwear company, who specialised in retro designs including the right kind of pointy bra to look good under vintage clothing. She'd also worked with a small independent parfumier, a bakery in Covent Garden and a very well-known chain of DIY shops who'd helped Birdy transform her bedroom into 'the boudoir of my dark floral romantic dreams'.

Birdy's photos, whether they were interior or exterior shots, all had the same aesthetic, a dreamy, nostalgic feel with pops of saturated colour.

'It's giving goth Cath Kidston,' Bea said because by now she'd abandoned any pretence at teaching Phoebe about the intricacies of SEOs.

There was no 'Felt cute, might delete later' or 'hashtag bliss'. Birdy preferred to write mini essays or little stories or quote from books and poems that Phoebe had never read or, in a lot of cases, ever heard of.

But even Phoebe had heard of William Shakespeare and *A Midsummer Night's Dream*. Accompanying a series of pictures of Birdy running through wildflower meadows in a floaty white dress were the words:

Over hill, over dale,
Thorough bush, thorough brier,
Over park, over pale,
Thorough flood, thorough fire
I do wander every where,
Swifter than the moon's sphere;
And I serve the fairy queen,
To dew her orbs upon the green:
The cowslips tall her pensioners be;

In their gold coats spots you see;
Those be rubies, fairy favours,
In those freckles live their savours:
I must go seek some dew-drops here
And hang a pearl in every cowslip's ear.
Farewell, thou lob of spirits: I'll be gone;
Our queen and all her elves come here anon.

What did it all mean? Who even knew?

Phoebe had more pressing concerns. That particular post was back in the summer when Birdy had long dark hair that fell in ringlets. However, in her most recent photos, she was sporting a very sharp, very precision-cut black bob. She was also featuring more and more little black dresses, which she accompanied with flicky liquid eyeliner and a bright red lip.

'Oh my God, she's stolen your look!' Bea exclaimed. 'Though, to be fair, you kind of stole your look from Coco Chanel.'

'My look is nothing like Coco Chanel's,' Phoebe corrected sharply. 'My look is *inspired* by the iconic style of the silent film actress Louise Brooks. Really, Bea, it couldn't be more obvious!'

'Coco Chanel and Louise Brooks are, literally, the same woman. I bet no one ever saw them in the same room at the same time,' Bea said and Phoebe didn't have the energy to point out the flaws in Bea's argument, especially when there were other far more concerning matters to be addressed.

'Talking of Coco Chanel, look!' Phoebe pointed at the screen where a black pug, no doubt Peggy Gug (which was a ridiculous name) bore a startling resemblance to Coco Chanel, the canine version. Right down to the pink tweed Chanel-inspired jacket it was sporting.

It went without saying that Coco Chanel wore it much better.

'To think I promised Sophy that I'd be nice to her,' Phoebe muttered. She didn't know how she was going to be civil, much less nice, to this pretentious, up herself, look-stealing little diva.

Chapter Twelve

Phoebe took a late and very long lunch to walk Coco Chanel who absolutely didn't appreciate that her human was going through something and needed some thinking time.

She waited until they were right at the top of Primrose Hill before she planted her backside firmly on the ground. Phoebe had to carry CC back to the shop and smile tightly at all the people, so many people, who felt the need to comment, 'Who's taking who for a walk?'

When she returned to The Vintage Dress Shop it was busy with afternoon shoppers. Their rail of black dresses was looking very sparse as everyone was shopping for Halloween looks.

Not that that was any of Phoebe's business anymore. Not her circus, not her monkeys, which wasn't one of Mildred's mottos but something Johnno liked to say whenever someone was trying to make him do something that he didn't want to do. Which had happened quite a lot.

How Phoebe missed him. And how she missed supervising the purchasing of dresses. 'You might want to restock the black rail,' she advised Bea who was now on the till while Anita was manning the changing rooms and the shop. 'Where's Sophy?'

'She's up in the atelier with Birdy,' Bea said, as she took a dress from a customer and folded it, before wrapping it in tissue paper.

'Why are they up in the atelier? There aren't any rental dresses up there? It's going to be like that Rosie Roberts nightmare all over again.'

Bea didn't seem unduly concerned. 'She seems really nice.'

'Oh! You're the woman from that TikTok video!' The customer looked at Phoebe in surprise. Then she held up her phone. 'Can I get a selfie?'

'No, you absolutely can't,' Phoebe said tersely, because she and Sophy could have role-played all day and it still wouldn't have prepared her for this. Then she summoned up a smile that was more of a baring of her teeth as the customer, who seemed like no stranger to fake tan herself, took a hasty step back. 'I hope you've enjoyed your visit to The Vintage Dress Shop. Do come again!'

As Anita and Bea clearly had enough to do, Phoebe went down to the basement and began to pull out more black party dresses, of which they had a huge number. Even without Halloween looming, there was something about a black dress that always made a statement.

Phoebe held up a black lace dress with cap sleeves and a boat neck, a nipped-in bodice and a full skirt that would need a full petticoat to achieve optimum swishiness. She was tempted to keep it for herself but then, even with a generous staff discount, she shouldn't be buying any more dresses. Not when she might be out of a job quite soon, and it wasn't as if she had that many parties to go to anyway.

There was the Vintage Christmas Ball at the beginning of December, which they always treated as their official Christmas party. Phoebe organised all the details, as she did for the Vintage Summer Ball in June too, including persuading Freddy to fork out for a glam squad, but that came under managerial duties and she wasn't a manager anymore.

She couldn't help the white-hot flame of anger that flared in her belly. It was Freddy who she wanted to singe. Not even Rosie Roberts anymore.

Why was he treating her like this? He hadn't even attempted to talk things out, just the two of them.

Phoebe didn't even know if there was a two of them anymore. What Freddy had done, what he was doing, it was going to be very hard to forgive. She'd given him everything that she was capable of giving and even that wasn't enough.

She thrust the dress away from her as if it were responsible for all her current woes.

'Phoebe? Are you down here?' called Sophy from the top of the steps.

'Where the hell else would I be?' Phoebe muttered under her breath. 'Yes! I'm just going through the black dresses so we can restock.'

Sophy's feet, clad in trainers like that was an acceptable item of footwear to accessorise with a vintage dress, appeared followed by a smaller, daintier pair of feet wearing fishnet stockings and an adorable pair of cotton-reel heel, two-strap, black patent Mary Janes.

'Phoebe, this is Birdy. She's been dying to meet you,' Sophy said as all of her came into view.

Phoebe doubted that very much. She tried to school her features into an expression of pleasant expectation but she suspected that she just looked constipated.

There were legs attached to the dainty feet, a green and blue pinafore dress worn over a black turtle neck and then the face that she'd been peering at on Instagram for most of the morning appeared.

Birdy was a tiny, elfin creature who jumped down the last step and approached Phoebe with her arms outstretched, a huge smile on her delicately pretty little face.

'Phoebe! I'm so pleased to meet you,' she said in a gaspy, breathless voice. 'Can we hug? Is this a hugging moment?'

Phoebe knew she looked more horrified than approachable. She tensed every bone, every muscle, every cell in her body and braced for impact but Sophy quickly said, 'Phoebe's not really much of a hugger.'

Birdy, thankfully, came to a halt mere centimetres away from Phoebe. Phoebe wasn't that tall without her heels but Birdy was a good half a head shorter. She looked like the fragile sort of woman that men liked to protect and who made other women feel like great galumphing hags.

'Sorry, I'm half Maltese, half Italian,' Birdy trilled, her big, liquid brown eyes fixed on Phoebe. 'I'm too much of a hugger.'

'It's very nice to meet you,' Phoebe said stiffly. Behind Birdy, Sophy looked very disappointed at Phoebe's pitiful attempt to roll out the welcome mat. 'I hope Sophy's been looking after you.'

'Oh, Sophy's been wonderful,' Birdy assured her, throwing Sophy a dazzling smile.

Phoebe couldn't work out what Birdy's angle was. Clearly, she had to have an angle. Nobody was this nice. This enthusiastic.

'And you've gone through the rental dresses?' Phoebe asked but then she couldn't help herself. This was probably (actually no probably about it) what Freddy, Johnno and a cast of thousands meant when they said she was her own worst enemy. 'What were you doing in the atelier? There aren't any rental dresses up there.'

'Pheebs . . .' Sophy began but Birdy held up one tiny, dainty hand.

'My fault. Sophy said that you had a Mary Quant dress up there and I *begged* to be allowed to look at it. I love Mary Quant,' she added, her huge Bambi-like eyes growing even wider. 'Did you go to the Mary Quant exhibition at the V&A? And the one at the Fashion Museum?'

'Of course,' Phoebe said, still unable to keep the suspicion out of her voice. 'So, you're all sorted, both of you?'

Sophy nodded. 'Birdy's going to come back on Monday morning when we're at our quietest to shoot some looks . . .'

'Yes, we're quiet but we're still going to have customers. I . . . we can't have a huge entourage like last time . . .'

'Oh, not a huge entourage. Just me and my boyfriend and a ring light,' Birdy assured her. 'The shop looks so gorgeous with the rainbow rails and the pink sofas. Perfect for the 'gram. Your doing, I guess.'

Phoebe nodded. Why was this woman still being so nice? What was wrong with her? Was she on drugs? She should definitely have a word with Sophy to make sure that Birdy wasn't . . .

'At the risk of sounding like a crazy stalker, just being here and talking to you is giving me such a fangirl moment,' Birdy said, her hand reaching out for Phoebe's hand but, catching sight of Phoebe's bemused expression, then retreating. 'I'm a big fan. Huge. I always look out for you at vintage fairs. At the Vintage Summer Ball last year, you gave me a safety pin in the ladies' when the strap of my dress broke . . .'

Birdy tailed off as Phoebe shook her head. She had a vague memory of dispensing safety pins.

'And I saw you at Glorious Goodwood having a go at that heinous woman who always tries to pass off 1970s revival 1930s dresses as genuine 1930s dresses,' Birdy continued.

'Ugh! I hate that woman.' Phoebe scowled. 'If I had my way, she'd be banned from every vintage fair and festival in the country.'

'I'd love to follow you on Instagram but your account is set to private,' Birdy said forlornly.

'Well, I'm not really active on the socials.' This past week Phoebe had locked down her accounts so she couldn't be messaged by randoms wanting to abuse her for caring about the welfare of fragile vintage dresses. 'Anyway, it sounds like you have everything under control.'

She tried to ignore the non-verbal cues that Sophy was furiously giving her from behind Birdy, until she mouthed very clearly, 'Oh, come on, Phoebe!'

'Well, I look forward to seeing you on Monday then,' Phoebe said though at this current point in time she didn't feel like she'd ever look forward to anything ever again. 'I hope it's quite a small ring light.'

'It's tiny,' Birdy said, as Sophy led her back up the stairs. 'You'll hardly know we're here. Oh! It's been *so* great to finally meet you properly.'

Birdy was a definite improvement on Rosie Roberts. She seemed to respect the dresses. She didn't appear to slather herself in fake tan. And most likely she'd be an *adequate* ambassador for the shop. Or the rental dresses anyway.

Chapter Thirteen

Friday was a much better day. And not just because it signalled almost the end of what had been a truly horrible week.

Phoebe had been woken by her phone ringing at some ungodly hour. Her first thought was that it was Freddy calling to apologise. Her second thought was that it was actually more likely to be someone in a call centre on another continent who wanted to scam her out of her life savings, though joke would be on them as her life savings were non-existent. Her third thought when she unearthed her phone from under her pillow and saw Johnno's name flashing on the screen was that he really needed to figure out the time difference between London and his parents' Australian sheep farm.

'It's not a sheep farm, it's a sheep station,' he said when Phoebe told him this. 'I get so confused with the clocks going back and forward and what have you at this time of year.'

'They're going back in a week or so,' Phoebe said, snuggling into Coco Chanel's sleep-warm and biscuit-smelling little body, the phone on speaker on her pillow. 'I love this time of year.'

'So, I hear you've been in the wars. Gone viral and all that,' Johnno said without preamble.

'You've spoken to Freddy then?' In the space of a few days, even saying Freddy's name made something in Phoebe's chest hurt.

'Might have exchanged a few words . . . Then I spoke to Soph last night. She's worried about you.'

Phoebe snorted like a furious little dragon. 'I doubt that.'

'Now, now, Pheebs,' Johnno said mildly. In all the time that Phoebe had known him, which was some sixteen odd (very odd) years, she'd never once seen him angry, or even heard him raise his voice. Not even when he was confronted by shoplifters, bailiffs or once the husband of a woman he'd been seeing who 'swore blind that they were separated'. 'How are you doing, kid?'

Johnno was also the only person who could call Phoebe 'kid' and not have their head bitten off. 'I've been better. Freddy says he's going to sack me.'

'Not exactly what he said, Pheebs,' Johnno corrected her in the same mild tone. 'But you can't get so aerated about a frock. It's just a frock at the end of the day. Not worth all this heartache and aggravation, is it?'

When Johnno put it like that, it wasn't. But then, Phoebe knew where she was with the frocks. It was the people who were an unknown quantity.

'He's been horrible to me,' she said because she had very few secrets from Johnno. Before she'd finally agreed to go on a date with Freddy, he'd always been bending her ear about how she should give him a chance.

'Kid, he's a good kid,' he'd say every time she turned Freddy down. 'You could do a lot worse.'

'The video doesn't look great though, does it, and between you and me, the shop could be doing better,' Johnno said and the unpleasant feeling in Phoebe's chest spread out to her neck and, when she looked down, she could see her skin was mottled and red.

'But we're always busy. We're especially busy right now.' Maybe she should have been keeping a better eye on the business side of things rather than just the frocky side of things. 'Are our takings down?'

'It's not that the takings are down. The problem is that our rent and our rates and the water bill and even the price of the fancy carrier bags have gone up,' Johnno said. The mottled rash now extended to Phoebe's arms and legs.

'You're going to have to close the shop!' Where would she be without the shop? What would happen to the dresses? What would happen to her and Coco?

'Nobody's closing the shop,' Johnno said firmly. 'But Freddy has been talking my ear off about overheads and growing our revenue streams and whatnot. So . . .'

'So . . . me reacting a little *fiercely* when some influencer ruined shop stock hasn't helped matters,' Phoebe supplied. 'Though I really don't understand how she was going to help Sophy shift a lot of rental dresses. Oh God, I'm going to have to just grin and bear it when people come in with coffee and burgers and get their greasy hands everywhere, just in case they decide to buy something. Bite my tongue! Even though we'll actually lose money if . . .'

'Hey, kid, do I sound like I'm in a panic?' Johnno asked gently.

'Well, no . . .' Phoebe admitted. 'But, quite frankly, Johnno, you could have one arm hanging by a thread and you still wouldn't sound like you were in a panic.'

Johnno chuckled. Such a rich, deep sound and, although Phoebe knew you couldn't rely on people and especially you couldn't rely on Johnno, who'd disappeared to the other side of the world with just a day's notice, she missed him so much. 'True that. But you only need to panic when I start panicking. Can you do that?'

Phoebe thought about it. 'Well, I can *try*.'

'Good enough, and be nice to Freddy.'

She didn't need to think about that at all. 'Well, Freddy hasn't been nice to me.' She flailed her legs just thinking about it. 'He's banned me from the shop floor. Threatened to

123

sack me if I don't turn into some simpering, smiling fool who lets customers walk all over me and walk all over the dresses. Literally! It's like he doesn't know me at all.'

'Oh, I think sometimes he knows you better than you know yourself,' Johnno said and, before Phoebe could protest that in the strongest possible terms, he said he had to go. 'Got to see a man about a dog,' he insisted though it was half ten at night where he was.

She and Coco were walking along the canal path when her phone pinged once more. Again, her first thought was that it was Freddy because that was what happened when you reluctantly let someone in your life against your better judgement.

But it wasn't Freddy. It was a message from her friend Marianne, who had her own tiny little vintage shop just down the road in Kentish Town.

Darling! You're all over TikTok. What's the story? Would rather hear it from you than believe some random and quite basic influencer. Charles and Sophy have invited us to their Halloween party tomorrow night, so I'll see you and Coco there. And Freddy of course!

It was a reminder that although The Vintage Dress Shop was a huge part of Phoebe's life, it wasn't all she had in her life. She had Coco and she did have friends. Friends who even knew about her and Freddy because what happened outside the shop, stayed outside the shop.

Me and Coco can't wait to see you, Phoebe messaged back and although she still felt heavy in her heart the feeling had definitely lightened a little bit by the time she arrived at the shop.

She was still trying to come to terms with the entirely new worry that the shop might not exist this time next year, another victim of the cost of living crisis and late-stage capitalism, but for the moment, it was there in all of its glory.

Freddy was nowhere to be seen that morning. Clearly, he'd got bored with issuing edicts and decrees and new punishments. Phoebe still headed down to the basement to slave away or rather to persuade Bea that instead of shooting all the dresses for the website as flat lays, they should shoot them on real people. It was an idea she'd had last night when she was still too cross about everything to sleep.

'You and Anita,' she clarified. 'Cress would never agree to it and Sophy' – she lowered her voice – 'she doesn't have the right look.'

'I'm not very photogenic,' Bea protested, which was a lie. Bea's vintage aesthetic was very much 1950s pin-up girl. In summer, she could even wear a sarong-style halter-neck dress (they'd been very popular in the 1950s) whereas when Phoebe had tried one on, it made her shoulders look like a pair of coat hangers. Very bony, very knobbly coat hangers.

'I have never once seen you take a bad selfie,' Phoebe insisted.

'That's because you haven't seen the hundreds of selfies I take and reject,' Bea said as Phoebe backed her into the little anteroom they used for a studio.

'Nonsense. And the camera loves Anita,' Phoebe said, as she approached the big ring light and wondered how to turn it on. She was learning new skills at a frightening rate this week.

'Anita also loves the camera.' Bea looked at Phoebe then she sagged in defeat. 'I can't argue with you anymore, Pheebs, it's exhausting. Take some photos of me; then when the website orders dry up because they're being modelled by a woman who resembles Shrek, you'll only have yourself to blame.'

Bea said it lightly, but Phoebe wondered if she really was that exhausting. Even before the events of this week, she'd imagined that Freddy seemed tired when they were together. Not even tired but defeated. How his eyes had lost their twinkle as if something, or rather someone, had made his glow flicker and fade.

'I just think we should try something new on the website. It can't hurt. Then we can also use the pictures on social media. Didn't you say that the algorithms prefer pictures of people rather than things?' Phoebe said in a soft, pleading tone, which felt very awkward. 'Now, could you give me a quick tutorial in how to use a ring light? I hope it's easier than understanding Camden Council's website portal.'

It was, but then manning the controls at NASA would be easier than Camden Council's online interface. They used a proper camera to take pictures and Bea, of course, looked stunning in the dresses that Phoebe put her in because, despite her many faults (and it seemed to Phoebe that currently certain people thought she was ninety-nine per cent faults and one per cent woman) she had a very good eye.

So, it was hardly a surprise when Sophy came down to the basement after lunch and didn't look very happy about it.

'Are you busy?' she asked Phoebe who wasn't at all busy but watching a YouTube video on how to increase web traffic. 'Can I borrow you?'

'Borrow me for what?' Phoebe asked. 'Have you found another soul-crushing menial task for me to do?'

'We've got a bride in for her first appointment and she's having an identity crisis,' Sophy said calmly but her face was red and then she gnawed her bottom lip anxiously. Phoebe hoped, for Sophy's sake, that she never tried to play poker.

'I'm not allowed to be customer-facing under pain of death,' Phoebe reminded her.

Sophy smiled weakly. 'I thought it could be our little secret. Freddy need never know.'

Not her circus. Very much not her monkeys. If Sophy had now stepped up as manager then she could get on with it.

But then again. A bride in need?

The success of her most special day hanging in the balance?

Phoebe was already sliding off the stool she was perched on and it took every last ounce of self-control that she possessed not to run up the two flights of stairs to the atelier.

Instead she walked slowly and sedately up the basement stairs, through the shop that was heaving, hopefully heaving enough that they might break even this month, and up the spiral staircase to find a despondent-looking woman standing on the dais in an oyster silk bias-cut 1930s wedding gown, which did absolutely nothing for her.

'I'm sorry but that's doing absolutely nothing for you,' Phoebe said. Sometimes you needed to be brutal and crush the dreams of a woman who'd been visualising herself in the wrong wedding dress for years.

Phoebe wasn't just being cruel for the sake of it, although Sophy and Cress both winced. Only then would the prospective bride be open to the possibility of having a new dream.

This woman was in her late thirties, with the pasty complexion of many a naturally pale woman during the winter months. Long brown hair pulled back in a low ponytail, which again did nothing for her but Phoebe would address that later. Blue eyes. Tiny waist, delicate wrists, but she'd chosen a dress that didn't make the most of any of those features but instead highlighted every lump and bump and washed out her complexion.

Phoebe thought for a moment and then approached the dress rail that went from champagne to pink and pulled out a blush pink 1950s dress . . .

'Oh no! I was thinking off-white, floor-length and definitely not a meringue.'

'It's not a meringue. It's a ballerina skirt,' Phoebe said, holding it up. 'It will be ankle-length. You have gorgeous wrists so I'm sure you also have gorgeous ankles. Why would you want to hide them?'

It was clear that the woman had never really considered her ankles because she lifted the hem of the bias-cut dress and stared down at her feet in wonder before rotating one elegant ankle.

'It's just not the dress I was picturing.' She raised her head. 'Do you want to see my Pinterest wedding dress inspo board?'

Judging by the woman's absolute inability to know what colours and styles suited her, Phoebe would rather stick pins in her eyes. She didn't say that though, because she wasn't a monster. Honestly, she really wasn't.

Instead she rustled the blush ballerina dress in what she hoped was a tempting manner. 'Humour me. Let's just try this on and see how you feel in a different silhouette.'

Cress accompanied the woman, Joanna, to the changing room and when she emerged ten minutes later, even the fact that she was still wearing ankle socks and completely the wrong size bra couldn't disguise the fact that the dress was perfect for her.

Joanna didn't seem convinced as she walked to the dais, plucking at the frothy tulle that made up the skirt. Then, as soon as she was on the raised platform and looking at herself in the mirrors, her fretful expression softened then disappeared altogether.

She was rapt. Transfixed. Turning this way and that.

'I never thought I could look like this,' she said at last. 'I never want to take this dress off. Can I take some photos? My mum, my family, are in Dublin. It's why I'm here on my own.'

Usually brides weren't allowed to take photos unless they'd committed to the dress and paid a hefty deposit. There had been occasions when women had taken lots of photos, then hadn't bought the dress but had had a replica dress made using inferior materials and craftmanship.

Joanna didn't seem like she had the audacity to pull that kind of trick and also, Phoebe could be flexible. Sometimes.

'You can take a couple of photos,' she said as Joanna handed her phone to Cress.

'It needs taking out at the waist,' Cress said once the photos were done. 'And maybe I'll raise the hem by just a couple of centimetres.'

'Is it a winter wedding?' Phoebe asked.

Joanna nodded. Her face fell. 'Yeah. Bit of a rush job which is why I'm here on my own. My gran's not very well so we've had to bring everything forward.'

Cress and Sophy made sympathetic noises but Phoebe felt she could be of more practical help. 'I love a winter wedding. A white faux-fur bolero or even a white velvet cape would be heavenly. I'll give you the details of a couple of vintage shops who are sure to have something suitable.'

'That would be great. Thank you.' Joanna held up her pony-tail. 'Then I was thinking my hair loose with maybe a tiara.'

Phoebe shook her head. 'Definitely not. You've got a great neck and collarbones, so I'd go for a relaxed chignon with some strands of hair framing your face. Jewellery, minimal. Maybe a delicate silver chain.'

It had only been a week since she'd last imparted her expert knowledge to a grateful bride-to-be but Phoebe had missed it more than she knew.

'Also, there's no polite way to say this, but you're wearing the wrong size bra,' she said enthusiastically as Sophy groaned in the background. 'Go to John Lewis and get properly measured before you come back for your next fitting.'

Joanna peered down at her bust. 'I've been a 32 C since I was twelve.'

'Then you've been wearing the wrong size bra since then,' Phoebe said, her eyes narrowed. 'I think you need to go down a band size and up a cup size.'

Before she could really warm to her theme, she was distracted by a hand on her arm.

'A woman downstairs said I should come up here and you'd help me.' It was a pretty young woman dressed from head to toe in designer gear. Phoebe pored over *Vogue* every month and even though she'd never wear it, she could recognise new-season Gucci when she saw it.

Even so, there was a system in place. You didn't just let anyone gain admittance to the atelier. Not without Phoebe's express permission.

Then again, if she could afford new-season Gucci then she had to be a big spender and they needed all the big spenders they could get.

'What are you looking for?' Phoebe asked because again, she could be flexible even when her system was being totally disrespected.

'I've got a Halloween party next weekend,' the woman said with a heavy sigh. 'Very fancy. Very black tie. I need something with Morticia Addams vibes but not something that looks like a costume. A gown . . . I mean, a black gown is a wardrobe staple, right?'

'Absolutely.' Phoebe gave her a quick once-over. 'I've got just the thing.'

Half an hour later, she was sent on her way with a sleek black dress with a fishtail hem that could have been made to her exact measurements and the details of a little shop in Mayfair, which did the best wigs.

Phoebe was on a roll. She was back doing what she'd been put on this earth to do.

She looked round the atelier for the next woman who needed her expertise but there was just Sophy wearing her fixed smile. 'OK, I think I can take it from here.'

'Are you sure?' Phoebe asked because she couldn't bear to be sent back down to the salt mines. Or the basement as it was known.

'It's nearly closing time on a Friday. Freddy could easily pop in on his way to The Hat and Fan and then it would become a whole thing.' Sophy sighed as if she had the weight of the world on her shoulders. 'He's been in such a crabby mood this week. Not like Freddy at all.'

Even though she was hurt and angry with Freddy, Phoebe wasn't going to comment. Especially now that she'd spoken to Johnno and could understand that maybe Freddy had worries about the future of the shop.

Then again, they were worries he could have shared with her. But he hadn't. In much the same way that he hadn't had Phoebe's back.

So, if anyone should be angry, it was Phoebe.

But when she walked into The Hat and Fan an hour later, behind the rest of the staff, and she realised that Freddy wasn't sitting with Charles and Miles because he was a no-show, she didn't feel angry.

She just felt sad.

They all agreed that as it was Charles and Sophy's Halloween party the next evening, that it would be a quiet Friday.

'I'm not even going into town afterwards,' Anita said virtuously as she clutched a large glass of Pinot Grigio. 'In fact, I might only have one of these.'

Without Freddy, Phoebe certainly wasn't motivated to stay for longer than the time it took her to drink her usual gin with slimline tonic, from a bottle and not the mixer tap, and lime, not lemon.

As she and Coco were walking back to *The Sheila*, Phoebe's heart beat a little faster in anticipation every time she heard a noise behind them. But it was never him. It was never Freddy.

Chapter Fourteen

Next day in the shop, without Freddy there to expressly forbid it, no one seemed to mind when Phoebe migrated up to the atelier. In fact, Cress messaged her to say that a bride was in for her final fitting and wanted Phoebe to sign off on the dress.

Things were still quite frosty between Phoebe and Cress. But when Cress showed her the dress she was planning to wear to the Halloween party that evening, Phoebe was effusive in her praise. The frock was a form-fitting deep red with fake ermine trim; a very bold choice for Cress.

'Inspired by Cruella de Vil in *101 Dalmatians* – and Miles is going to wear a black and white spotted T-shirt,' Cress explained.

'It's fancy dress?' Phoebe queried with genuine fear in her heart. She hated fancy dress as much as she hated fast fashion.

'Not really. Just Halloween-themed. Charles said that they were leaving it open to interpretation,' Cress said, her mouth full of pins.

Phoebe wished that Cress wouldn't put pins in her mouth when she was doing alterations. Inevitably the day would come when she'd swallow one, but she managed not to point that out. Just as she managed, with great difficulty, not to say huffily that she was surprised that Cress hadn't made a special dress for the party and was planning to name it after yet another person who wasn't Phoebe.

Just the thought of Cress's plans for a reproduction collection of dresses, which would mean her leaving the shop, and how she and Freddy had hatched this plan in secret, had Phoebe feeling cross and miserable all over again.

If she missed Freddy, then she also missed her friendship with Cress . . .

'Darling! Turn that frown upside down!' cried a tinkling voice and, with a genuine smile of delight, Phoebe hurried across the atelier to greet Chika, one of her favourite clients. 'Let's crack open the champagne. I'm parched. Then can you start pulling dresses for me. I'm going to need at least ten. I'm doing the party season in London, Paris and New York, then Christmas in the Maldives and New Year in St Moritz.'

Even though she was around forty (it was hard to pinpoint her exact age as she'd had a lot of very good cosmetic surgery and was a big fan of tweakments), Chika had already seen off three husbands, each richer than the last, and been awarded three separate alimony payments, each bigger than the last. She'd currently sworn off marriage but her latest boyfriend was a tech billionaire.

She had a wonderful, privileged life spent travelling to glamorous locations to attend parties and made no apologies for it. She was also terrific fun and always looked fantastic in any dress that Phoebe suggested. Talking of which . . .

'I hoped you might be in for your winter looks. I've already set aside some dresses for you,' Phoebe said, as Chika threw herself down on one of the chintzy sofas and shrugged off her fuchsia leather trench coat.

Chika was the only woman Phoebe knew who could get away with wearing a fuchsia leather trench coat and look absolutely fabulous in it.

Now, Chika threw a warm look at the bride-to-be who was having one final look at herself in an exquisite 1960s empire-line wedding dress. 'Darling, you look gorgeous! Even if you decide not to keep the man, you must keep that dress!'

Three hours and two bottles of Moët later, Chika left with eight dresses, including the most exquisite 1970s Jean Varon maxi dress in a champagne silk twill adorned with bright flowers with balloon sleeves, a pleated skirt and a matching cummerbund. She'd also tipped Phoebe a couple of hundred quid.

Chika's visits were both enlivening and completely exhausting. Phoebe felt rather shell-shocked when she came out of the back office after sticking her tip into the petty cash tin. They could put the money towards the staff Christmas dinner, which they always had the day after the Vintage Christmas Ball when they were all very tired and very hungover and very in need of a festive meal with all the trimmings.

Sophy was suddenly blocking her way with that fixed smile that Phoebe was starting to dread. 'Are you banishing me to the basement again?' she asked testily though she really needed a little time to decompress.

'I thought we'd all low-key agreed that you're wasted in the basement,' Sophy said, which was almost validating until she did her creepy smile again, which instantly made Phoebe suspicious. 'It's just . . . I was thinking, what with it being Halloween next weekend, that it might be fun to put up some decorations. What do you think?'

'I think that this is a quality establishment and not a fancy-dress shop,' Phoebe snapped. Because really, had Sophy learned nothing during her time at The Vintage Dress Shop? Then again, had Phoebe herself learned nothing from her basement banishment? She took a step back, hands raised in surrender. 'But, no. It's not my decision. You must do what you think is best.'

Sophy didn't seem that happy about getting her own way. 'They'd be tasteful decorations. No dismembered plastic fingers scattered in with the costume jewellery. I could nip down to the fancy dress shop in Camden and . . .'

Phoebe could bear it no longer. 'What about if I go to the craft shop in Camden and make some decorations instead? Some retro-style black bats and cats. That sort of thing.'

She couldn't have Sophy spraying fake cobwebs everywhere, especially on the dresses, and even though the shop was busy, it was nice to escape for a little while. Also the lovely man in the craft shop gave Coco Chanel a couple of organic dog treats and when Phoebe got back to the shop, she was happy to go down to the basement with the black card she'd bought and draw bats and slinky cats with their backs arched. She highlighted their features with some glitter pens then supervised their dispersal about the shop.

'These are really good, Pheebs,' Anita said with some surprise.

Phoebe shrugged. She'd always liked art when she was a kid but it was just another thing that had made her stand out at school, which was never wise. Outside of school, all too often she wasn't living anywhere where she had the space or supplies to draw pictures and by the time she landed with Mildred, she'd long given up such childish pursuits.

'Anyone can draw a cat,' she told Anita in an offhand way but Sophy, as usual, refused to read the room.

'These are fantastic and oh my God, learn how to take a compliment,' she said lightly so it was very hard to take offence, though Phoebe tried. 'Just you wait until you hear about my ideas for Christmas. How are you at drawing Santa Claus?'

'Is that a joke?' Phoebe asked. 'Please say that it's a joke.'

'You'll have to wait and see,' Sophy threatened as she stuck a bat on the front of the display unit that housed their costume jewellery.

'Is this a stealth way of getting me to quit?' Phoebe demanded, but it was without any of her usual fire and ice.

They both knew that there was no way Sophy could ever sneak a single decorative image of Father Christmas into the shop, not while Phoebe had breath in her body, and instead they were sharing a joke. As colleagues.

Which was very unlike them and quite unsettling.

Chapter Fifteen

There was enough time between the shop closing and the party starting that Phoebe was able to go back to *The Sheila* to get ready.

First of all she put Coco Chanel in the most adorable witch's outfit. Complete with a little pointy hat in between her ears and a little black tulle skirt. There were many things that Coco Chanel refused to tolerate – non-organic dog food, any dogs bigger or barkier than herself, people having the audacity to go past her on a skateboard – but she loved dressing up.

Phoebe, on the other hand, was not a big fan of dressing up. Or rather when you had such a distinctive everyday look, getting dressed up was just something you did every morning. Plus, she had a fear of looking costume-y. It was showing off by any other name.

Eventually she decided to wear a slightly spookier version of what she usually wore. A 1930s black silk crêpe dress with a starburst spider web and a spider crawling across one of the shoulders.

Then it was a short bus ride to Charles's beautiful flat with its art deco lines on the top floor of a mansion block in Bloomsbury. Although it was still comparatively early and the invite had said that things wouldn't properly get going until 'witching hour', the party was in full flow as Phoebe climbed up the many flights of stairs that led to what Charles called 'his garret'.

Packed into said garret were ghosts and gargoyles, witches and warlocks and, some people really hadn't understood the assignment, even a Barbie and Ken.

With Coco Chanel tucked firmly under her arm so she couldn't be trampled underfoot, Phoebe squeezed her way through the hall and into Charles's living room where she found him and Sophy in the tiny alcove that was the kitchen.

Charles was as impeccable as ever in black tie with tailcoat and spats. His Halloween concession was a pair of vampire fangs, while Sophy was in her favourite black velvet, Fortuny-inspired vintage dress, which Phoebe had seen on many occasions. To be fair to Sophy, she looked amazing in it, especially now that she was wearing the right size bra thanks to Phoebe, and she was also accessorising with fangs.

Their Halloween outfits met with her approval. However, the plastic cauldron on the worktop got a dubious look from Phoebe.

'Halloween punch?' Sophy asked, holding up a glass of dayglo green liquid.

'I'll pass,' Phoebe decided.

'Gin and tonic instead?' Charles was already busying himself by plopping ice cubes into a glass while Phoebe tried to remain upright with a death hold on Coco as the crowd swelled around her. 'No lime, only lemon, I'm afraid.'

'Lemon will be fine.'

Although they'd reached an uneasy understanding in the shop that day, Phoebe didn't really know what to say to Sophy now. If it had been just Charles, they could have talked quite happily for hours about vintage dresses and costume jewellery and the estate sales that Charles was planning to visit.

Out of work hours, Charles was now usually accompanied by Sophy. They were one of those couples who couldn't seem to function as two separate people anymore, because they'd thrown everything into their relationship.

'Happy Halloween,' said a familiar voice behind Phoebe and she didn't even have room to turn around but craned her neck to see Miles wearing a black T-shirt adorned with a life-size ribcage on it while Cress was behind him wearing a black vintage dress with a novelty print of Mexican Day of the Dead masks scattered all over it.

'You're not wearing the dress we talked about?' Phoebe said, unable to keep the disappointment out of her voice.

Cress shook her head. 'I wasn't feeling brave enough for a red dress with a faux ermine trim.'

Miles put his arm around Cress and kissed the top of her head. 'But you looked absolutely gorgeous in it, sweetheart.'

Cress and Miles were a relatively new couple. They'd barely been seeing each other for longer than a month or so but they also seemed to be joined at the hip.

'Don't let love make you weak,' Mildred had always warned her, usually when Phoebe was pining over Jason Mullins, a boy from school who would later do five years for armed robbery. *'Most times, it just turns out to be infatuation and you're left with a broken heart. Worse, you've completely forgotten the capable person you were before they toyed with you and turned you into a simpering fool.'*

So, once she had a gin and tonic clutched in her hand, Phoebe was happy to back away from the four of them.

She slowly made her way out of the flat to a little flight of steps, which led up to a service hatch. Phoebe had to climb over a pair of canoodling wizards but it was quieter and she could finally put Coco Chanel down and adjust her little witch's hat, which had been knocked askew.

She'd stay for one drink. She wasn't really a party person and she certainly wasn't in the party mood tonight.

'Ah, there she is! Phoebe!'

She looked up from contemplating the toes of her black suede stilettos to the far more welcome sight of her friend Marianne.

Marianne was a statuesque goddess of a woman. Six feet in her fishnet-stockinged feet with hair currently the same colour red as post-boxes and London buses. She was wearing a leopard-print catsuit, which wasn't unusual for Marianne, but in a nod to Halloween she'd added cat's ears on an Alice band and a tail. No wonder Coco Chanel barked out a warning.

'None of your nonsense, little miss,' Marianne said sharply as she scattered the two snogging wizards so she could reach Phoebe and air-kiss in her general direction. 'Claude has gone to get us a drink.'

Claude was Marianne's life partner. The real pussycat of the couple, despite the fact that he was covered in tattoos and piercings, Claude was an absolute sweetheart even if he did tend to clang when he walked.

'I persuaded Nina to come too,' Marianne said, sitting down one step lower to Phoebe to reveal that behind her was another of Phoebe's friends.

'I've come as goth Marilyn,' Nina said, giving a little shimmy to show off her look, which was a sparkly black version of the famous white halter-neck dress that Marilyn Monroe had worn in *The Seven Year Itch*. 'I'm a bit worried that this black spray-in hair dye isn't going to come out any time soon. I was platinum blonde this morning.'

'Worth it though,' Phoebe said, as Nina climbed over Marianne so she could scoop up Coco and sit down next to Phoebe. 'Sometimes one has to suffer for beauty.'

'Talking of suffering, what is the deal with you being the internet villain of the week?' Marianne asked. 'There was a lot of chat about you being a bully but what did you actually do? More importantly, what did that influencer do to make you behave like that?'

It was all about how you asked a question. Marianne was the first person who didn't automatically assume that Phoebe was entirely to blame.

'Even though she wasn't meant to, she tried on a 1930s wedding dress made of the most fragile silk. Got fake tan on it and then she yanked if off and *ripped* it,' Phoebe said and she could feel herself getting angry all over again. 'I know I'm not an angel but . . .'

'Oh my God, if someone had done that in my shop, I'd have ripped them,' Marianne said, though because she looked so imposing, people tended to behave around her. 'Not that I stock the really bougie pieces.'

'Your stock is beautifully curated,' Phoebe insisted because Marianne's little shop in Kentish Town was always full of the most covetable pieces of vintage fashion. 'I always know that I'm going to leave with the most gorgeous clothes and no money left for the rest of the month.'

'Not a single wedding dress to be found though. Not that I want to go traditional,' Nina said as she wafted her left hand about.

'You're about as subtle as a breeze block,' Marianne said fondly.

'Bridalwear is very specialised.' Phoebe perked up because this was one of her favourite subjects. 'But a good half of my bridal pieces didn't start life as wedding dresses. For one of my recent brides, she wanted a red wedding dress, so I asked some of my most reliable buyers to—'

'I probably wouldn't get married in red. Though you never know,' Nina mused, flinging her hand out again.

'You nearly had my eye out!' Phoebe complained. 'I know this can be a very emotive topic but—'

'For crying out loud, Phoebe, look at my hand!' Nina demanded, holding her hand up for inspection so that Phoebe could now see that on her third finger was . . .

'Is that . . . ?' She took hold of Nina's hand so she could inspect the beautiful art deco, pink tourmaline and diamond ring. 'Are you . . . engaged?'

'I am,' Nina confirmed with a beaming smile that was all teeth and gums. 'Noah popped the question a couple of weeks ago and I graciously agreed to be his old ball and chain.'

'Ball and chain, nothing! He's lucky to have you,' Phoebe said, because although Nina's boyfriend, or rather fiancé, Noah was perfectly pleasant, she'd never seen him wear anything other than navy blue. In fact, she was surprised that . . . 'He clearly has good taste. That ring is gorgeous.'

'I think that was more Charles's doing,' Nina said. 'Though Noah did remember that pink is my favourite colour. We're going to do a spring wedding. Can't see the point of putting it off, which means I'm in the market for a wedding dress.'

'What were you thinking?' Phoebe asked eagerly, trying to ignore the strange pang in her chest that Nina's news had caused. Even though hers and Freddy's undefined relationship was even more undefined than usual, even less of a relationship, she didn't think that they'd ever get married. If she wasn't the loving kind, then she definitely wasn't the marrying kind. Much easier to think about dresses rather than what it must feel like when someone picked you out of all the people in the world to be the one person that they wanted to spend the rest of their life with.

'Well, something that I can get my boobs and my booty into, which rules out ninety nine per cent of the frocks in The Vintage Dress Shop,' Nina said baldly because she never had any trouble saying the difficult things. Phoebe could respect that.

'I could make some calls . . .' Finding enough options for someone as demanding as Nina would be a challenging job but Phoebe was up for it.

'Don't get aggy but I was hoping you could ask your friend Chris if she'd make me something,' Nina said.

Phoebe's first reaction was to get aggy because did no one want to buy vintage anymore? Also, *Cress* would probably name the dress The Nina and add it to her line and . . . then Phoebe came to her senses.

This wasn't about her. This was about Nina's most special day. Though she still had every right to be cross with Cress. 'You mean Cress and she's here now. If she hasn't been crushed to death, I'll introduce you properly.'

'Oh, would you!' Nina squeezed Phoebe's arm affectionately. It was the first time in days that Phoebe felt as if she'd done the right thing. Then, as Noah arrived at the foot of the stairs, followed by Claude, Phoebe could say with genuine sincerity, 'Congratulations on bagging such a beautiful bride.'

Noah grinned. 'I know I'm punching . . .'

He and Nina were an odd match. She was a vintage queen, hair and make-up always on point, while Noah was a self-confessed nerd in his navy blue jumpers, but they clearly made each other happy. He was a definite improvement on Nina's past boyfriends, each one wronger than the last.

Phoebe couldn't help but sigh. Her sigh got even longer and louder as she saw that behind Noah and Claude was Freddy.

Their eyes met and Phoebe immediately looked away. Not so Coco Chanel who struggled to free herself from Nina's embrace.

Marianne picked Coco up to pass her to Claude who handed her to Freddy, who immediately cuddled her close to his chest so she could give his face a thorough tongue bath.

Then no one said anything, as if the frosty atmosphere between Phoebe and Freddy was covering everyone in its chilly embrace.

'I need a drink,' Nina said, although she still had an almost full glass of punch, a sentiment that was echoed by the others who quickly disappeared, leaving just Phoebe and Freddy alone to glare at each other.

Or rather Phoebe did the glaring. It was Freddy's turn to sigh. 'How long are you going to keep giving me the cold shoulder?' he asked roughly.

Phoebe couldn't quite believe what she was hearing. 'You've treated me abominably this week, Freddy. You knew what happened in the shop last Saturday. I thought we'd sorted things out on the weekend and then on Monday morning, once that stupid girl made that stupid video go viral, you were suddenly treating me like I was Public Enemy Number One.'

'I hadn't seen the stupid video until Monday morning and, honestly, Pheebs, it was quite a rude awakening,' Freddy said dully, like he didn't even have the energy for a proper argument.

Luckily Phoebe did. 'You should have stuck up for me, but you punished me instead. You're meant to be on my side.'

Freddy's shoulders dropped. Even his messy mop top of curls seemed to lack its usual energy. 'Sometimes it's very hard to be on your side.'

'Yet it's very easy to keep secrets from me.' Phoebe folded her arms. 'You didn't tell me that you and Cress are in cahoots . . .'

'It's hardly cahoots. We've had a conversation. One conversation . . .'

'About her designing a range of reproduction dresses.' Phoebe was outraged all over again. 'You know how I feel about reproduction vintage clothes.'

'Well, you know that I think that's ridiculous,' Freddy snapped back because he was clearly getting his second wind.

'The worst thing, the thing that's hardest to forgive, is that you didn't tell me that the shop, my shop, is struggling to break even and that we're all going to end up on the street. Is that why you agreed to let Sophy rent out her dresses?'

'It's one of the reasons but also because it makes good financial sense.' Freddy shifted Coco in his arms. 'I didn't tell you because I knew you'd kick off and start catastrophising about ending up on the street when that isn't even a remote possibility. But it will be if you insist on gatekeeping the dresses. It's a business, Pheebs. We are meant to actually sell dresses to anyone who wants to buy them.'

'I know it's a business. FYI, I sold over three thousand pounds of dresses to just one customer today . . .'

'I thought we agreed you wouldn't be interfacing with the public right now?' Freddy asked in a deceptively mild voice, though his posture was stiff, even with Coco Chanel loving on him. 'And what about all those prospective customers you've turned away because they don't fit into the narrow criteria that you have for allowing people into the shop, never mind actually trying something on?'

This was very unfair. 'Forgive me for weeding out time-wasters or people with sticky hands so we have to spend money having the stock cleaned,' she said huffily.

Phoebe didn't want to be huffy with Freddy. Even though this week had been awful, it had been, much to her annoyance, full of teachable moments.

'I'm making an effort,' Phoebe said tightly. 'I've come up with a new way of doing the photos for the website, which I think will be more effective, and I helped a prospective bride to find a dress when she was intent on walking down the aisle in a bias-cut gown that did her no favours and I've even reached a new understanding with Sophy, who by the way actually *begged* me to come up to the atelier.'

'We can't have a repeat of what happened with Rosie Roberts,' Freddy persisted.

Phoebe was fed up with talking about Rosie Roberts and Freddy not cutting her even the tiniest amount of slack. She stood up and stomped down the stairs, pausing only to take Coco from Freddy, who struggled as if she'd much prefer to stay with him rather than with the woman who'd rescued her from her former cruel owner then given her a life of unparalleled luxury.

'Sorry for being too much for you,' Phoebe said icily. She would have liked to majestically sweep back into the party but there were so many people that Phoebe couldn't majestically do anything. She had to squeeze her way through instead.

She formally introduced Nina to Cress and if the shop went to rack and ruin because its alterations expert was too busy designing her own dresses, then so be it.

Feeling miserable and out of sorts was always going to be amplified, when you were squeezed into a tiny flat full of people enjoying themselves.

It was time for what Mildred called 'the French goodbye', though in all the time that Phoebe had known Mildred, she'd never once attended a party. 'But in my younger days I did and I quickly learned that when one wants to leave an event, it's highly likely that one will miss the last bus home, if you stop to say goodbye to people. Far better to just do what the French do and leave without saying goodbye but send a letter of thanks to the hosts within the week.'

Phoebe drew the line at writing Charles a letter, a WhatsApp would do, and she'd see Sophy at work on Monday, so she quickly slipped out of the door and hurried down all those flights of stairs, until she was out on the street.

She took grateful gulps of the cold night air, although there was a fine mist of rain so Coco Chanel refused to put paws on the ground.

With an anticipatory sigh, Phoebe reached down to pick her up. She only had herself to blame for creating this monster.

'But you're such a beautiful monster, I can't refuse you anything,' Phoebe murmured as she made her way to the bus stop in her party heels, which unlike her work heels pinched her toes and made the balls of her feet feel like they were on fire.

It wasn't surprising then that her progress was so slow that it was easy for Freddy to catch up with her.

One moment she was trudging painfully to the bus stop, which didn't seem to be getting any closer, the next there was a gentle hand on her arm.

'You are, Pheebs, you are a lot,' he said and before Phoebe could ready herself for this next part of their row, which had lasted almost a week, he ran the back of his hand over her cheek. 'But you're not too much.'

'Are you sure about that?' Phoebe wasn't even being tart, she just wanting to know exactly where she stood.

'Quite sure.' Like Coco, when Freddy was looking at Phoebe like that, earnestly, maybe even a little bit adoringly, it was very hard to stay angry with him. 'I'm sorry.'

He didn't say exactly what he was sorry for; whether it was all of it or only some of it or none of it, but he took Coco's dead weight from Phoebe and with his other hand, he hailed a passing black cab.

'My treat,' he insisted when Phoebe opened her mouth to protest. 'I can tell that your shoes are killing you and if you come back to mine, I'll even throw in a foot rub.'

Chapter Sixteen

As Monday mornings went – even grey, cold October Monday mornings – Phoebe had a spring in her step as she walked to work. A metaphorical spring because her feet were still quite sore from Saturday night and she had a painful blister on her little toe. It almost made her envious of Sophy and Cress in their comfy white trainers, when usually she thought they looked like orthopaedic shoes.

She'd spent Saturday night and most of Sunday with Freddy, both of them keen to assure the other one that they were sorry. However, they didn't go into details of where the sorriness should be distributed. Phoebe, because she couldn't bear to go through the whole sorry saga again. And Freddy, probably because he knew how to quit when he was ahead.

Also, the thought of the shop being in financial difficulties gave Phoebe the same panicked feeling she got when she thought about what would happen if *The Sheila* had sprung a leak and which dresses she'd have time to save if such a disaster happened.

It was true that the shop was very quiet but again, it was a cold late October Monday morning and they were always quiet on Mondays. Even when it was glorious sunshine.

'So, it makes perfect sense for Birdy to shoot her pictures and whatnot,' Sophy said with an airy wave of her hands as she led the team through their Monday morning meeting.

Not that Phoebe had ever insisted on a Monday morning meeting when she was manager. Her team meetings had occurred on a random ad hoc basis as the need arose. The last one had been when she'd caught Anita snogging her then sometimes on/mostly off boyfriend in one of the changing rooms and had had no choice but to make an example of her.

Freddy hadn't mentioned if Phoebe's normal duties were to resume and Phoebe hadn't wanted to cause an argument by asking. (If nothing else, that showed how much she'd grown as a person over the last week.) So if Sophy wanted to waste everyone's time by banging on about her rental dresses and filling in the forms correctly, then Phoebe was happy for her.

She was less happy about having to see Birdy again. 'You mean your mini-me,' Bea said as they restocked the costume jewellery display unit with some dead-stock Scottie dog brooches. Charles had found them an almost inexhaustible supply of dead-stock Bakelite brooches in various animal shapes and Phoebe dreaded the day that they finally ran out.

'She wishes she was like me,' Phoebe said just as the bell tinkled and the mini-me herself walked in.

Phoebe waited for the inevitable entourage to follow her but it was just a slightly built man, buckling under the weight of a couple of vanity cases, a sizeable ring light on a tripod and a . . .

'What is that?' Phoebe asked, pointing a quivering finger at the podgy black pug in a bright yellow rain mac.

'Hi, Phoebe!' Birdy trilled brightly. She was obviously a Monday morning sort of person. 'Sophy said I could bring Peggy Gug. I'm going to use her in some of my pics and she doesn't like being left alone.'

'Yeah, she's been banned from doggy day care,' said the man, who on closer inspection was as pretty as Birdy, with a luxurious mane of Byronic dark hair, delicate features and the kind of thick eyelashes that Phoebe could never hope to replicate unless she wore two sets of false lashes.

'This is Faisal,' Birdy said, bringing a huge leopard-print wheeled suitcase to a halt. 'Is Sophy around?'

Sophy had popped to the big supermarket in Chalk Farm to buy teabags, coffee and biscuits. A managerial responsibility that Phoebe had been only too happy to relinquish.

'Why is your dog called Peggy Fug?' Anita asked from where she was lounging on one of the pink sofas. She wasn't meant to be lounging on the pink sofas at all but Phoebe's new reduced role didn't require her to reprimand Anita any longer. No matter how much she wanted to.

If Sophy were here, she'd have rushed to gush all over Birdy, but neither Phoebe nor Bea nor Anita had made any such move and Birdy's smile started to slip a little. 'It's Peggy Gug, not Peggy Fug,' she said in a voice that trembled slightly. 'After Peggy Guggenheim, the American heiress and art collector who lived in a Venetian palazzo and was never not fabulously dressed. Also, her father perished on the *Titanic* and . . .'

To be fair, Peggy Guggenheim sounded fascinating but whatever other facts about her Birdy was about to impart were drowned out by the most awful sound known to man.

The sound of a pug screaming.

Because Coco Chanel, having eaten her breakfast in the back office, had now entered the shop en route to the atelier where she'd spend most of the morning snoozing. She was a creature of routine.

But the mere sight of Coco had caused Peggy to rear up on her hind legs and start caterwauling. It was now quite obvious why she'd been banned from doggy day care.

'Sorry. Peggy doesn't play well with others,' Birdy said as she tried to shield Peggy from the sight of Coco who seemed to toss her head in disdain at the howling pug then trotted up the stairs.

Phoebe was so proud of her. At least Coco had good manners.

Alas, when Coco was safely halfway up the stairs, she turned to bark at Peggy whose decibel level rose accordingly.

'I'm so sorry,' Birdy said again.

'Anita, maybe you could show them out to the patio?' Phoebe suggested when the noise had gone on long enough. 'We've got a lovely view of the canal. It's very calming.'

Faisal shot her a grateful look as he gathered up the plump pug and followed Anita who'd risen from the pink sofa with a beleaguered air. She'd never have shown such attitude during Phoebe's reign.

'Hopefully there aren't any boats out there,' Faisal said as he hurried past. 'Peggy doesn't like boats.'

Peggy was clearly a very spoilt little madam who wasn't given proper boundaries, Phoebe decided. Talking of boundaries . . .

'So, you're just going to shoot the rental dresses?' Phoebe asked Birdy. 'Was Sophy quite clear about that?'

Birdy nodded. 'Very clear. But also, I'm going to try very hard not to buy any dresses while I'm here. Very, very hard.' She gazed longingly at a sea green chiffon kaftan, which was hanging up by the changing rooms because a customer was coming to collect it at lunchtime. 'Stay strong, Birdy. You know you haven't got the length of leg for a maxi.'

Where was Sophy? It showed very poor time management skills. Still, Phoebe didn't have anything pressing to do and there was a part of her that was curious to see what an influencer actually did. Also, it was probably best that she was there to make sure that no dresses were harmed during the shooting of this #sponcon.

'As we're quiet, you can use one of the changing rooms,' Phoebe offered graciously. 'Has Sophy already pulled some dresses for you?'

She hadn't. Of course she hadn't. 'Though she said it was probably best to wait until now as she only had limited stock and she didn't know what might be rented or returned over the weekend,' Birdy explained which all seemed very loosey-goosey to Phoebe.

Phoebe walked over to the rail of rental dresses, which were looking a bit sparse after a busy Friday and Saturday. 'Well, this would look good on you,' she decided, selecting a black 1960s A-line minidress shot through with silver lurex thread. 'Not sure how it will photograph though. And this 1940s cocktail dress.' It was adorned with champagne glasses and party hats on black rayon silk. 'Who doesn't love a novelty print?'

'Me! I love a novelty print,' Birdy said with genuine excitement. 'I'll try that one on first.'

While Birdy was getting changed into her first look, Peggy Gug was safely contained in the back office and Faisal set up the ring light. A couple of customers did come in while all this was going on, but Phoebe could tell that they were just idle browsers keen to spend a few minutes in the warmth. She had a nose for these things.

Birdy emerged from the dressing room in the cocktail dress, which she'd accessorised with black suede peep-toe heels she could hardly walk in.

'Your jewellery is all wrong. The dress is already making a statement. You don't need your necklace clamouring for attention too,' Phoebe said as Birdy fingered the big gold necklace she was wearing.

'Do you think?' she asked uncertainly.

'I know.' Phoebe was already unlocking the door of the glass display cabinet. 'I've got a couple of faux jet wrist cuffs in here and maybe these jet beads too. I'd double loop them.'

She had planned to be just a casual observer but Phoebe found it so hard to be casual when vintage looks were being put together. Once Birdy was dressed to their mutual satisfaction, Phoebe perched on a stool behind the till and watched as Birdy went through a series of poses from standing on one leg with the other leg kicked out behind her to gaily swinging her black beaded necklace about to elegantly sprawling on one of the sofas.

During all this, she and Faisal would take breaks to look at the pictures he'd just shot on an impressive-looking camera so they could reshoot if necessary. Then they shot some live action on camera and phone before Birdy disappeared into the changing room to try on another outfit.

She shot four separate looks then was back in the clothes she'd arrived in: a pair of black corduroy dungarees with a paisley 1960s long-sleeved top and the same pair of black Chuck Taylors that Phoebe had. Birdy shot some footage on her phone, her arm outstretched as she raved about 'the best vintage shop in London. Seriously, guys, I'm not even sure I want you to know about it because I want to gatekeep all these gorgeous vintage dresses for myself. So, like, when I found out they were offering a new rental service, I was first in line to check it out and it couldn't be any easier to use . . .'

By this time, Sophy was back from the supermarket. She'd been so long that Phoebe had begun to wonder if she'd had to milk the cow herself. Faisal shot some pics of Sophy standing in front of her little rental rail of dresses but only after Phoebe had fixed her make-up.

'You're not even wearing eyeliner,' she gently scolded as she gave Sophy's eyes more definition.

'Because eyeliner is more of an evening look,' Sophy protested though she wasn't protesting that hard.

It was approaching the lunchtime rush (or as much foot traffic as ever rushed on a Monday) when Birdy decided she had everything she needed.

'When will the first piece of content go live?' Sophy asked.
'Before the weekend would be great.'

'Well, we're going to go home and edit it now. That'll take the rest of the day, then I could send you something to approve tomorrow morning,' Faisal said as Birdy went to fetch Peggy from the back office.

This social media world moved very fast. Once, back in the days when the shop had first opened, Phoebe had done a little shoot for a fashion magazine and it had been months before the piece had appeared. They hadn't even credited her, whereas Bea was making sure that Faisal had the right social media tags 'there's no underscores', then they discussed the most effective hashtags to use.

'Phoebe!' Birdy suddenly hissed from the back of the shop and beckoned when Phoebe looked her way. 'You have to come and see this.'

Phoebe couldn't imagine that there was anything that interesting to see in the back office unless, God no, Peggy had peed on something. She had the look of a dog that wasn't properly house-trained.

So, she was unprepared for the sight that met her eyes. In one of Coco Chanel's many dog beds, this one a very expensive Harris tweed, was Peggy Gug curled up and snoring away and lying on top of her, also snoring, was Coco.

'So adorable.' Birdy had her phone held aloft. 'You don't know what this means to me. Peggy Gug finds it very hard to be accepting of other dogs. She's a classic only child.'

The same could be said of Coco Chanel, who wasn't so much unaccepting of other dogs as unpleasantly surprised whenever she encountered one. As far as she was concerned, she was the only dog in existence and she hated to be reminded otherwise.

Anyway, it was clear who was top dog in this meeting of canine minds. Phoebe felt a warm glow of pride and even nodded when Birdy enthused excitedly about 'setting up a doggy playdate'.

'Well, we'll see,' she said as the warm glow dissipated. Birdy wasn't so bad. To say that she was an improvement on Rosie Roberts was a huge understatement and Phoebe now had a new appreciation for how hard some influencers worked.

'Not an influencer, Phoebe, I'm a content creator,' Birdy said earnestly, her eyes especially wide. 'And if you could add me back on Instagram, well, I'd love that.'

'Oh, I hardly ever post on Instagram,' Phoebe said, which was true. Given the current climate, she doubted she'd ever post on there again.

'Well, you absolutely should,' Birdy said. Then she forgot that Phoebe wasn't a hugger and hugged her goodbye.

Finally she and Faisal and Peggy were gone and Sophy had that fixed smile back on her face. 'You were very helpful, Phoebe,' she said, barely able to keep the surprise out of her voice. 'Thank you for that.'

'I'm always helpful,' Phoebe pointed out, but they both knew that her words lacked conviction. 'And it's in all our best interests, if we can create more revenue streams, right?'

'Right?' Sophy echoed uncertainly as if she didn't really understand what Phoebe was getting at. How Phoebe wished that she too was still in blissful ignorance about the impending financial crisis that might befall The Vintage Dress Shop.

Still, it had been an interesting start to the week and because Phoebe wasn't officially back on the shop floor, she spent a lot of time in the atelier. Things were still stilted between herself and Cress – Phoebe knew that she wouldn't be able to bring up the thorny topic of Cress's plans for her own collection of dresses without getting angry about it. And she knew that Cress certainly wouldn't start the conversation for fear that it would make Phoebe angry, but they could still work together like the civilised, grown-up women that they both were.

In fact, Phoebe was more than capable of doing a little repair work herself, which freed up Cress to work on more major alterations. After all, she'd lived with a woman who'd been a seamstress all her working life. Mildred had taught her how to sew on buttons, to replace hooks and eyes, to take up and let down hems. Phoebe had always kept quiet about this skill, as she was worried that it would be another thing that would undermine her authority in the shop if she was being called upon to put right astray belt loops and loose stitching.

Now her authority had been well and truly undermined these past couple of weeks, what did it really matter?

Truthfully, if Phoebe could bear to admit it to herself, she didn't mind having less to do with the customers. They could be very wearying and the shop was managing adequately without her policing the changing rooms and telling people that they were a clear spring and not a bright summer. It still pained her that women might be going home with dresses that really didn't bring out the best in them, the dresses destined to languish, unworn, at the back of wardrobes but, right now, this wasn't a hill that Phoebe was willing to die on.

Though give it a couple of weeks and who knew? But for now, the shop was still in business and doing a roaring trade as the party season came into full effect. The rental business also seemed to be running as planned. Despite Phoebe's fears, all the dresses rented out had found their way back to the shop, and if there were a few late returns, they racked up penalty fees. Only one dress had suffered: an incident involving a glass of red wine and a pale blue satin sheath dress. Phoebe hadn't been able to resist a smug 'I told you so' (she was trying to be on her best behaviour but she was never going to be a saint) but she'd sent it off to the specialist cleaners they used and it had come back spotless.

As promised, the first of Birdy's videos had gone live on TikTok and Instagram the next day. She looked amazing, the shop looked amazing, they'd grown their own followers and Sophy was trying to frantically source more dresses to rent. As she lamented to Freddy when he popped in to make sure that Phoebe hadn't run the business into the ground.

Not that Phoebe ever would. Always, but especially now, she wanted the shop to thrive, not just survive. Even if it meant assisting Sophy with her rental dresses. 'I could ask a few of my contacts if we could buy some dresses from them wholesale?' she offered in a very offhand way and was rewarded by Sophy and Freddy both beaming at her.

It wasn't quite the type of bright smile that Freddy had used to gift her with, but they were friends again or whatever it was that she and Freddy were. The whole fuss with Rosie Roberts had died down now – although they still had lots of lairy young girls coming into the shop to corner Phoebe.

'Could you be mean to me? I'm absolutely desperate for clicks,' one of them had said and then deliberately dropped a dress on the floor, but Phoebe hadn't risen to the bait. But for hours later, she was still thinking hard about what she would have loved to have said to the little madam if her rule was still absolute.

Chapter Seventeen

Another week went by with Phoebe's role at the shop still unclear and her relationship with Freddy still a bit scratchy.

It was all quite unsettling but not as unsettling as the determined expression on Sophy's face at the Monday morning meeting (Sophy was being very inflexible when it came to these new Monday morning meetings) as she announced that it was time to put up Christmas decorations.

'Halloween is done. The clocks have gone back. It's now November and Christmas season has officially begun. Phoebe, why are you pulling a face?' she demanded because Phoebe might be a well-behaved shadow of her former self but it was very hard to school her features into bland acceptance of things she disapproved of.

'I told you before that we don't go in for Christmas decorations. Of course you were in Australia last Christmas so you don't know how we do things,' Phoebe reminded her, and reminded herself again that she wished Sophy had stayed there.

'That's a bit bah humbug,' Sophy said, folding her arms and tilting her chin in the stubborn way she did. To think that people thought Phoebe was a bully.

'We do Christmas accents, rather than Christmas decorations,' Bea said because she'd been at the shop the last four Christmases.

'Very tasteful Christmas accents,' Anita added. 'A few retro baubles here and there. Kind of boring, I always thought.'

Typical of Anita to be so disloyal. 'They're not boring. They're actually very lovely, very delicate Christmas tree decorations from the 1950s,' Phoebe pointed out. 'Imported from Poland.'

'Oh, so you do have a tree?' Sophy brightened. 'Because I was . . .'

'A Christmas tree? Pine needles all over the floor? Taking up valuable floor space? Are you mad?' Phoebe asked. 'The baubles are dotted about discreetly and, this is very important, in places where they won't get damaged.'

'I think we could have a small tree.' Sophy looked around the shop. 'Perhaps between the blue and green rails. Maybe some tinsel to go with the baubles. Also, hear me out . . .'

Maybe it was best to just let Sophy ramble on then put a spoke in her plans before they could come to fruition.

Phoebe wasn't Christmas's biggest fan. Growing up, Christmas was a time when everything she didn't have hurt more than usual. If she was a temporary guest in someone else's home, she always felt her transient status more keenly when presents were being opened, crackers were being pulled and extended family came to stay and talked about her in loud whispers. *That's your new one, is it? Sulky little thing. How much are the council paying you?*

It wasn't much worse being in a group home for Christmas. The staff were usually agency workers on overtime but at least they didn't pretend that they were there because they wanted to be. There were presents from charitable organisations, maybe a trip to the panto, but it was better than having to try and fit into someone else's happy family when you knew that you weren't going to be there for long.

Probably the best Christmas Phoebe ever had was her first Christmas with Mildred. Mildred also had Christmas decorations that she'd probably bought in the 1950s. A fake silver tree, but it had come from Harrods, and even though she

159

was long retired, she still got sent a hamper from Fortnum & Mason's from her former employers: Marvells of Mayfair.

Phoebe still had one of those empty hampers, which she used to store Coco Chanel's spare leads, collars and harnesses.

It was also the one time of year when Mildred allowed herself to indulge, instead of sticking to her usual calorie-limiting, unable-to-cook diet of cup-a-soups and finger sandwiches. For Christmas dinner, there was a Marks & Spencer's turkey dinner ready meal and on Christmas Eve, some of Mildred's decorative bowls were filled with Quality Street and mixed nuts which stayed out until January 2nd.

Of course, Mildred could make a small box of Quality Street last the whole of the festive period and still have chocolates left, but she made some allowances for Phoebe 'as you're a growing girl. Though you don't want to grow too much, Phoebe. Clothes looks better on slim people.'

That first Christmas with Mildred was when Phoebe received her first ever vintage dress. She hadn't been too impressed when she unwrapped the paper (*'carefully, Phoebe, I'll want to reuse it'*) to find a dress. An old dress – it had to be at least sixty years old.

It was the quintessential 1950s dress, sleeveless with a boat neck, a form-fitting bodice and a full skirt. Big pink roses ran riot on the white cotton. 'It hasn't yellowed at all because I know how to take care of my clothes. I'm afraid my days of wearing dresses like this are long gone but it should do quite nicely for you. Of course, back in the day I had a twenty-two-inch waist but you're developing a lovely figure so it should fit. And it will probably fit you for another forty years as long as you don't scoff all the Quality Street.' (To this day, Phoebe could still hear Mildred's dire and frequent warnings about 'little pickers have big knickers' whenever she was even thinking about eating chocolate.)

The girls that Phoebe knew at school, (and to her utter mortification, Mildred walked her there every morning to make sure that she actually attended) always had the newest of everything. Phones, make-up, clothes, and Phoebe just had a series of hand-me-downs and things bought with vouchers from the council.

Now it was Christmas once again and Mildred seemed to think she was doing Phoebe a massive favour by giving her a second-hand dress that she no longer wanted.

'It's not . . . I don't . . . Why would you . . .'

'When someone graciously gives you a present, you must always thank them, even if you don't like it,' Mildred said in her unperturbed way. She was always unperturbed in the face of all of Phoebe's rudeness and rule breaking. As if Phoebe didn't know any better because she'd never had anyone who cared enough to make any effort with her.

There were times that Phoebe wished that Mildred cared a little less.

That first Christmas there'd been another present too. Which Phoebe had unwrapped carefully this time, without being reminded, to discover a tiny bottle of Chanel No 19.

Even she'd heard of Chanel. The girls at school had fake Chanel bags adorned with the iconic double C logo but this bottle of perfume was the real thing.

'Oh my God, Mildred, this is amazing. I've never . . . This is like the best present ever,' Phoebe said, ripping off the cellophane not at all carefully.

'Well, you're nearly sixteen. About time you had your first proper scent. Much nicer than those awful body sprays you smother yourself in.' Mildred had allowed herself a tiny smile. 'I did think about getting you Chanel No 5 but it's not a young lady's perfume. Chanel No 19 is more youthful and springlike.'

Even though it was some sixteen years later, a Monday morning in the shop and Sophy was now banging on about playing Christmas music (dear God, no) in her head, Phoebe was back in Mildred's tiny, tidy but cluttered living room. Mildred was sitting in her favourite armchair with the spotless white antimacassars, wearing a periwinkle blue wool dress with a pussy cat bow, which made her blue eyes sparkle. Because it was Christmas, she was wearing her pearls and a lipstick that was a brighter pink than usual.

It was so rare that Phoebe had ever done anything to make someone else smile, so she remembered Mildred's smile on that long-ago Christmas Day as much as she remembered putting on the dress and spraying a little bit of perfume on her neck and wrists. ('Don't rub your wrists together. That's a common mistake women make but it actually breaks down the chemicals in the fragrance.')

When Phoebe had looked at herself in the mirror, even with her scraped-back ponytail and doubtful expression, wearing something that wasn't tracksuit bottoms and a hoodie, she saw the faintest hint of the woman she might become.

She was no longer youthful and she'd never been particularly springlike, but to this day, she still wore Chanel No 19 as her signature scent. Phoebe sniffed her wrist because smell was such a powerful time machine but also to remind herself that she wasn't that girl anymore.

Mind you, she still hated Christmas even though Sophy promised as Phoebe headed towards the atelier that, 'Yes! For the fiftieth time, I'm going to organise some tasteful Christmas decorations. I'm perfectly capable of being tasteful, Phoebe, thank you very much.'

'How do you fancy mending a dropped hem?' Cress asked, ever the peacemaker.

Phoebe would rather mend a hundred dropped hems than have to listen to Sophy for a second longer.

It was another quiet Monday without anyone booked in for an appointment in the atelier. It was just Phoebe and

Cress – things still awkward between them – so they were both pleased not to talk but to listen to a podcast about Peggy Guggenheim because Phoebe was keen to learn more about the fabulously dressed heiress. She turned out to be such an icon that, as Cress said, 'I'm surprised that Taylor Swift has never written a song about her.'

Phoebe didn't have any need to go back downstairs until later that afternoon. In an uncharacteristic display of kindness, Anita had offered to give Coco her lunchtime walk and fetch Phoebe a salad.

It wasn't until mid-afternoon that Phoebe had to answer the call of nature but found her way barred by Bea who stood on the bottom step of the spiral staircase.

'Did you need anything?' she asked, her voice quite shrill and her face quite red. 'Why don't you go back upstairs and I'll fetch it for you?'

'I need to powder my nose,' Phoebe said delicately but forcefully. One of Mildred's most stringent rules was that ladies (and gentlemen for that matter) didn't discuss their bodily functions in public.

'Oh! Your nose looks fine.' Bea peered at Phoebe's face. 'Do you want your make-up bag? I'll get it for you and take it up to the atelier.'

'Oh for goodness' sakes,' Phoebe exclaimed, continuing down the stairs so Bea had no choice but to give way or be mown down. 'I need a wee, not that it's any business of yours.'

'Well, let's get you to the bathroom,' Bea said holding out her arms to usher Phoebe's progress, though she was quite capable of visiting the tiny little bathroom tucked into an alcove by herself.

'What *are* you doing?' Phoebe asked suspiciously and although she was careful not to manhandle, she did push Bea out of the way so she could do a one-hundred-and-eighty-degree turn to see what was happening in the shop.

Then really wished she hadn't.

She went hot.

She went cold.

She could feel rage and her blood pressure rising in that way that always mottled her hands and throat. Phoebe began to count to ten in an effort to calm down before she blew her top.

She managed to get as far as seven.

'What the *hell* have you done?' she demanded of Sophy, who had tried to obscure a rail of dresses by standing in front of it with her arms outstretched, but judging from the cringing look on her face, she now realised that it was futile. 'What the hell have you done to my shop?'

Chapter Eighteen

It was too awful to contemplate.

Phoebe shut her eyes for a long moment and she prayed that when she opened them again, it had just been a minor hallucination brought on by the wasabi dressing she'd had on her salad.

Or maybe this was all a dream, or rather a horrible nightmare, and she'd wake up in bed and discover that the day was yet to begin.

But when Phoebe opened her eyes, she wasn't hallucinating or dreaming. Sophy – this had to have been Sophy's idea – had finally let the power go to her head and decided to rearrange the dress rails.

Instead of a painstakingly curated, beautifully graduated rainbow of colours – starting with black, then purple, blue, green, yellow, orange, red, pink and finally white – the dresses were now arranged willy-nilly, with no thought or reason.

An egg-yolk yellow 1970s maxi dress was nestled next to a deep red velvet cocktail dress, which was next to a purple and black chequerboard mini. All the colours clashing, so that Phoebe's eyes actually hurt.

She put a hand to her heart, which was racing, and her other hand on the till counter to steady herself.

'I just thought . . .' Sophy began but Phoebe couldn't bear to listen to her garbled explanation.

Also, she still needed to . . . powder her nose very urgently.

She spent long moments running her wrists under the cold tap, something Mildred had always sworn by when she felt herself getting upset, but it had no calming effect on Phoebe.

Quivering with emotions that were too strong to be contained, Phoebe left the bathroom and walked back onto the shop floor where Sophy, Anita and Bea were now taking the dresses off the rails and *dumping* them on the pink sofas.

'I didn't think that it would do any harm to maybe arrange the dresses by size,' Sophy said. 'You must admit that it's very confusing and quite hard to find things.'

'No, you really didn't think at all, did you?' Phoebe's voice sounded as if it had been coated in ice. 'I don't find it confusing or hard to find things, because all my brain cells are fully operational.'

Bea winced, Sophy's chin tilted up and Anita put her hands on her hips. 'There's no need to get personal,' Anita said chippily.

'I wasn't getting personal. I was talking about *my* brain cells.' Phoebe took a deep gathering breath, which was as much use as running cold water over her wrists had been. 'I couldn't possibly comment on *your* brain cells.'

'This way, at least, a customer can come in and won't need to ask if we have a dress in a size ten, because the size-ten dresses will have their own rail,' Sophy said in a stilted fashion like she was grinding her teeth.

'But this isn't the sort of shop where someone just wanders in for a random size-ten dress and then wanders out again. Coming to The Vintage Dress Shop is an experience. It's an adventure. It's about not knowing what you'll find but letting the dresses speak to you. Finding a dress that you're drawn to, that you didn't even know you'd need until you see it on the rail,' Phoebe said.

'Yes, but it's not much use being drawn to a dress in a size eight if you're a size twelve,' Bea pointed out, but she did it very quietly as if her heart wasn't really in it.

'So, then you put the dress back and look for another one or, and this is just a wild suggestion,' Phoebe said in the most condescending tone she could manage, which was actually very, very condescending, 'you could ask a member of staff to help you.'

'But it's very hard to remember the size or the provenance of every dress in the shop,' Anita protested.

'It's not at all hard. I manage it without any trouble at all,' Phoebe said. She turned around slowly to once again see the havoc that had been wrought while she'd been hemming upstairs and listening to podcasts about flighty heiresses, without a care in the world. 'This looks *terrible*.'

'It's not that bad,' Sophy said but her face said something else entirely.

'And if I had a pound for every time that a customer told me how beautiful our rails look on Instagram I'd be a wealthy woman and wouldn't have to work with . . . with . . . bloody imbeciles,' Phoebe snapped. Ok, that was quite a personal remark. 'Our rainbow rails are one of our USPs, like our pink sofas or the one black dress that we have in the window. In the space of a couple of hours, you've destroyed our brand.' She clapped her hands in a mocking manner. 'Well done! Good job, everybody!'

'We were going to put things back before you even saw it,' Bea said placatingly.

Phoebe could feel her eyebrows shooting up. 'Oh, and why was that then, Bea?'

Bea muttered something that Phoebe couldn't quite catch.

'What was that?' she demanded.

Sophy sighed. 'We quickly realised that it looked much better the way it was before.' Her eyes flashed. 'Even if it is really hard to find specific sizes and it's all very well asking for a member of staff to help, but if that member of staff is you then I pity that poor customer.'

'Rude!' Phoebe hissed.

'I don't know how you have the nerve to call me rude when you're the rudest person I've ever met,' Sophy said, stepping nearer to Phoebe and clenching her fists.

Even Anita, who lived for the drama, all kinds of drama, looked alarmed at how quickly the situation had escalated. 'Oh my God, everyone, calm down! We're going to put it back the way it was.'

Phoebe snatched up the nearest dress, a black and gold striped taffeta 1950s shirtwaister, and held it in front of her. 'You'll do no such thing. You've already made a complete mess of the shop. You can't be trusted to know your teals from your turquoises or your carmines from your crimsons.'

'You are a ridiculous woman,' Sophy said and as if she couldn't bear to be in Phoebe's presence a moment longer, she stalked out of the shop without even a coat on and slammed the door so hard that the bell nearly had a nervous breakdown.

Phoebe felt like joining it. Instead she gathered up more dresses. Her poor dresses, shoved about without any respect. 'Bea, you can help me. Anita, I don't even want to look at you right now.'

'It was Sophy's idea,' Anita said quickly because there was no loyalty among thieves or between completely incompetent shop assistants. 'Can I go home early then?'

'You can but I'm docking it out of your wages,' Phoebe said although she didn't have any idea how to do that.

All this time there had been customers in the shop. Goodness knows what they must think? Probably they pitied Phoebe for what she had to put up with.

She turned to the nearest one, a woman in an adorable navy blue princess coat, a silk scarf with a navy and pea green graphic pattern, tied just so around the collar. Clearly a woman of discerning taste. 'I'm so sorry that you had to witness that,' Phoebe allowed herself a careless laugh though the effort almost choked her. 'You just can't get the staff. Now is there anything in particular that I can help you with?'

The woman backed away slowly. 'I was just looking but I think I'll come back when things are a little less . . . chaotic,' she said, keeping eye contact with Phoebe as she sidled towards the door.

Although a very chastened Bea stuck around to help and Phoebe knew *exactly* where every single dress in the shop belonged, it still took a surprisingly long time to restore order.

By closing time, they were still only half done. Phoebe was just turning the shop sign to closed when Sophy returned. She was tight-lipped with two blazing patches of red on her cheeks and stuck around only long enough to grab her bag and coat, have a hissed conversation with Cress who'd just come downstairs, then flounce out again.

Good riddance, Phoebe thought as she slotted a lemon yellow chiffon fit-and-flare dress next to a sherbet yellow maxi with appliqué flowers trailing over the skirt and bodice.

'You might as well go home too,' she said to Bea sharply. 'This will be quicker if I do it myself.'

'Well, if you're sure . . .' Bea tailed off but she didn't need to be told twice and she left the shop very quickly after that.

Then it was Cress's turn to go, without words but with a reproachful, recriminatory look in Phoebe's direction.

'Honestly, CC, what I have to put up with,' Phoebe muttered. Coco Chanel, who was perched on one of the sofas, tilted her head in a sympathetic fashion.

Phoebe's hands were still a bit shaky but now that the shop was empty and she was alone with the dresses, matching all the colours, stroking her hands over jersey crêpe and soft lawn cotton, floaty chiffon and slippery satin, she could feel herself calming down. Her blood pressure lowering. It was cathartic. Mesmerising.

Phoebe loved to imagine all the women who had worn these dresses. What their lives were like. How they felt when they got dressed and looked at themselves in the mirror.

When she saw herself in a mirror, the person she'd created, she always felt not just a sense of satisfaction but also a sense of achievement.

She imagined that these other women, the dresses' former owners, felt the same. No matter how much life threw at you, the disappointments and the failures, when you put on the perfect dress, then you were back in control.

Phoebe felt in control too once she'd put the last dress back on the right rail. Then came a sharp, peremptory rap on the door and she looked up to see Freddy standing there. It was dark outside so she couldn't see the expression on his face but she didn't feel quite so in control anymore as she walked to the door to let him in.

Once he was in the shop, he said nothing, just looked around slowly, then his gaze settled on Phoebe and she could feel her blood pressure beginning to climb again.

He was looking at Phoebe as if he were seeing her for the first time. And not liking what he saw either.

'Sophy came to see me,' he said at last. His lips twisted, so far from his usual ready smile, when Phoebe shrugged at the mention of her arch-nemesis's name. 'Then I called Cress and she said that you'd be working late. Among other things.'

Phoebe could only imagine. 'Cress is hardly an impartial third party. She's always going to take Sophy's side on account of them being sisterfriends or whatever it is that they call it.'

'That's hardly fair,' Freddy said mildly, but his voice sounded tight. 'Cress isn't like that.'

'Well, I know why you'd stick up for Cress what with the two of you having a secret side project,' Phoebe reminded him bitterly.

Freddy shook his head and took a step back. 'No, I'm not getting drawn into an argument about that all over again.'

'Then why are you here?' Phoebe asked and she felt just as weary as Freddy. It was clear that he wasn't here to take her side or even try to understand where she was coming from. 'To tell me off, I suppose. Go on, then!'

She sat down on one of the sofas and picked up Coco so she could wrap her arms around her comforting, chunky little body.

'You called her an imbecile,' Freddy said, which admittedly hadn't been Phoebe's finest moment.

'Not specifically. And anyway, did she tell you why I called her that?' she demanded.

'She screwed up, she admitted that but your reaction was . . .' Freddy sighed and shoved his hands into his trouser pockets. 'Once again, it was a complete over-reaction and in a shop full of customers too.'

'There were maybe two or three customers and you didn't see what it looked like, Freddy. There were dresses everywhere, not just shoved onto hangers in a random fashion . . .'

'Sophy said that she arranged them by size . . .'

'Oh my God, will you just let me finish a sentence!' Phoebe exclaimed, flexing her fingers in frustration. 'Sophy had no business arranging everything. The shop has a system. I have a system, which has worked perfectly well since long before Sophy so-called Stevens turned up to show us all the error of our ways.'

'I don't understand why you're always so hard on Sophy,' Freddy said, running a hand through his hair so that it was in more disarray than usual.

'Of course you'd take her side even though she made a complete mess of the shop during our busiest period of the year and it's taken me *hours* to put it back.' The sheer injustice of it all, of Freddy, made Phoebe want to contort her body into odd shapes. She couldn't stay seated for a moment longer and slid Coco off her lap so she could jump to her feet.

'This isn't about taking sides,' Freddy insisted, his words sounding as if they were being forced out of him. 'The way you spoke to her was inexcusable . . .'

'Yes, I admit I shouldn't have called her an imbecile but she called me a ridiculous woman,' Phoebe recalled in an angry rush. 'I bet she didn't tell you that.'

'I know what she called you because the whole exchange, once again, has been posted online,' Freddy said, a muscle now pounding away in his cheek. He dug his phone out of the inner pocket of his Harrington jacket and swiped the screen a couple of times before handing it to Phoebe, who had to relive the whole unpleasant scene all over again. It had been shot from a very unflattering angle so she was all nostrils.

'Who took this?' She clicked on the username but their avatar was just a greyed-out silhouette and their name a random collection of letters and numbers. 'I hope it wasn't the woman with the nice coat and scarf. I'd expect better from someone so well dressed.'

'It doesn't matter who took it, what matters is you can't keep doing this, Pheebs,' Freddy said, his voice softening. 'It's not good for the shop; it's not good for staff morale. You can't enjoy being like this . . .'

'Being like what?' Phoebe asked, because she was who she was and she didn't know how to be anyone else. 'Do I care that people keep taking videos of me and putting them on the internet? Of course I wish they wouldn't but I'm always going to stand up for the dresses when they're being badly treated.'

She looked at Freddy in disbelief. If he knew anything about Phoebe at all, then he'd know that.

'But, at the end of the day, they're just dresses,' he said flatly. 'It's people who are important. It's people who will love you. A dress will never love you back.'

Phoebe thrust Freddy's phone back at him, flinching as their fingers brushed because she didn't like being touched when she felt this angry. 'What on earth are you talking about, Freddy? I do know that dresses aren't, like, sentient, but they are reliable in a way that people aren't. There is no better feeling in the world than when you're wearing your favourite dress.'

Phoebe's favourite dress in the world was a 1930s white silk jersey cocktail dress with the most exquisite drape and a scattershot pattern of crystals over it. It had originally belonged to a debutante, who'd been photographed wearing it in *Harper's Bazaar*. Whenever she slipped it on, which wasn't often because it really was a special occasion dress and was so precious that she saved it only for the absolute best, she felt beautiful. Invincible. Incredible.

There wasn't a person in the world, not Mildred, not Johnno and especially not Freddy right now, who could make Phoebe feel like that.

She realised that Freddy was talking, his mouth making shapes, his hands now out of his pockets, to make stabbing motions. 'We can't go on like this,' he was saying.

Finally, something Phoebe could agree on. 'You're right, we can't,' she said crisply. 'I'm not putting up with this absolute nonsense any longer. I don't care about silly people taking videos and trying to make fun of me just because I care about my job, about the vintage dresses that have been entrusted to me. It hasn't stopped our customers from visiting and quite frankly, if I was in the market for a vintage dress, I'd want to visit a shop where the staff were passionate about their work.'

Freddy folded his arms. 'Have you quite finished?'

'Not even close,' Phoebe assured him with a brittle smile. 'Also, I know that times are hard and we need to increase our profits and I'm going to do everything I can to make that happen, which is why I'm reverting back to my role as manageress and there's nothing you can do about it. You are *not* the boss of me and can't sack me. Johnno wouldn't hear of it.'

Phoebe was pretty sure about that. Johnno wouldn't take sides. He never did. He would just tell them to sort it out between them and he couldn't stick around to chat because he had to go and see a man about a dog.

'We can't go on like this,' Freddy said, his expression and his voice both flat.

'You've already said that.' Phoebe rolled her eyes.

'I'm not talking about the bloody shop. I'm talking about you and me,' he suddenly snapped in the most unFreddy-like way. 'It's been years now and in all that time I thought loving you would be enough to make you change. But it's not. I'm not.'

'You don't love me!' Phoebe spluttered because they'd never talked about love. In fact, she'd always been very keen to avoid the topic altogether. 'I never wanted or expected you to love me.'

Freddy turned his head away as if he couldn't bear to look at Phoebe. 'I do, I did, I wish I didn't, because there's no room in your heart for me.'

'You're just being silly, Freddy,' Phoebe told him sharply because this turn in the conversation, his words, sent panic shooting through her veins. 'Have you been drinking?'

'Is there even an outside chance that you love me? If not now, then one day?' he asked and now it was Phoebe who couldn't bear to look at him, at the desperate expression on his face, his eyes and his voice imploring. She hadn't signed up for this.

'You knew exactly what I was like before we got . . . involved,' she reminded him. 'I don't do . . . love. Never have and I never will. I'm just not wired that way.'

Time had proved, over and over again, that Phoebe wasn't lovable. And if she'd never known love then it stood to reason that she didn't know *how* to love. One could manage perfectly well without love. Mildred was proof of that.

They hadn't really gone in for heart-to-heart chats but Phoebe knew that there had been a man in Mildred's past. She'd been very vague on the details, but he'd promised Mildred the moon and hadn't delivered. Phoebe always suspected that he might even have run off with Mildred's sister because she was Mildred's only relative but they didn't speak. 'She did something unforgivable, Phoebe, and anyway, only fools forgive. It will only show people that they can take liberties again and again. Better to harden your heart so it can't be stamped on.'

Phoebe's heart was as hard as a diamond. Formed, shaped and polished by circumstance. Circumstances that she wasn't going to share with Freddy because then he'd feel sorry for her and she didn't need his pity.

'You knew that from the start, Freddy,' she reminded him and though her heart was hard, her voice was soft and shaky. 'I like you a lot, even now although you've hardly stood up for me at all, but I can't love you.'

'Yeah, yeah, because you only love clothes. Well, I'm not doing it anymore, Pheebs,' Freddy was already walking towards the door, but he stopped to turn and look at her. 'I refuse to come second to a load of old dresses anymore.'

For one long moment, they were frozen in time. It was odd. Phoebe had thought that she'd long since lost the ability to be hurt by other people, but Freddy's words were like a thousand tiny cuts slicing through her skin and leaving her exposed to the elements.

She hated feeling that way. Raw. Vulnerable.

All she knew how to do was to fight back. She scooped up Coco Chanel who'd been sitting on one of the sofas all this time, her head tilting first in Phoebe's direction and then towards Freddy, again and again. Phoebe held the little dog in front of her like a canine shield. Her hands were shaking again. Coco also trembled in her grasp.

Freddy had his hand on the door and Phoebe had to be quick, before he opened it and disappeared.

'Actually, Freddy, you don't even come second,' she said in her most callous voice, her words punctuated by the door closing behind him.

A full stop.

The end.

Chapter Nineteen

Phoebe wasn't sure if Sophy was going to show up for work the next day. In fact, she hoped that she wouldn't, but she was there on time, face looking like a bulldog chewing on a slow worm, as Mildred, most confusingly, used to say.

'I'm back on managerial duties,' Phoebe announced once everyone, even Anita eventually, was assembled. 'Normal service has been resumed, except Anita if you keep being late, I *will* dock it from your wages.'

She still wasn't any closer to figuring out how that could be done, but Anita didn't know that and Phoebe needed to establish her absolute authority once more.

Maybe that was why Bea raised her hand. 'Permission to speak.'

Phoebe gave a gracious nod of her head. 'Permission granted.'

'I'm not telling you what to do, I'm just a member of staff, but I do manage the shop's socials . . .'

'And you do a very good job,' Phoebe said because she wasn't just there for the nasty things in life like punishing Anita for her poor timekeeping or crushing Sophy's ridiculous notions. When someone was worthy of praise, she was happy to give it.

'That video that someone took of you yesterday, it's doing really big numbers, so like, maybe, this is just a suggestion – I wouldn't dream of telling you what to do – but perhaps you being on the shop floor isn't a great idea,' Bea said, with a cringing smile. She held out her phone to Phoebe, who took it gingerly.

She'd already seen it yesterday and she really didn't want to rewatch herself in all her full-nostrilled glory reading the riot act to Sophy, Anita and Bea. But, even with a night to sleep on it, though Phoebe hadn't done much sleeping but kept reliving the scene with Freddy that had followed, she still thought they deserved all her fury. But taken out of context by . . . Phoebe checked the numbers with a jittery little heart flip . . . over fifty thousand people on TikTok, she just came across as slightly demented.

Actually, a lot demented.

'I have quite a lot of things to do in the atelier, anyway,' Phoebe said, even though she didn't. She clapped her hands. 'Now, let's get to work. Please don't get any ideas about rearranging the dresses according to decades or fabrication.'

There was a stony silence. Sophy's features were set so tight that it looked painful. Cress wouldn't make eye contact with Phoebe. Anita was sullen and sulky, but that was just a normal Tuesday morning for Anita, and Bea still looked as if she wished the floor would swallow her up.

It set the tone for the rest of the day.

The atmosphere in the shop was horrible. Despite what *some* people thought, Phoebe wasn't without any feeling. She didn't like working under these conditions but everything she'd done was in the best interests of the dresses. It always was.

So, she was happy to spend the day in the atelier. It helped that she had a bride come in for a first fitting, but even she seemed to pick up on the fact that the relations between Phoebe and Cress were as frosty as the ground first thing on these November mornings.

Once the bride had gone, Cress stalked off back to her workroom (Phoebe hadn't even known that Cress knew how to stalk) and Phoebe was left to do an inventory of the designer dress room, not that it really needed inventorying.

Usually the dresses calmed her but when Phoebe wasn't thinking about how everyone she worked with hated her, and how strangers on the internet who didn't even know her hated her, she thought about how Freddy hated her.

But before he'd hated her, apparently, he'd loved her. Not that he'd told Phoebe that and even if he had, she wouldn't have known what to do with the information.

Certainly, she'd never done anything to make Freddy love her. On the contrary, she knew she was hard work for very little reward and she often wondered why Freddy had stuck around for as long as he had.

But even if it wasn't love, what she and Freddy were . . . had been . . . nice. Phoebe had never had time for relationships before Freddy. She couldn't really see the point of them but somehow Freddy had just fitted into her life. Probably because he had the patience of a saint. That was what Johnno always said about Freddy, because if Phoebe was high maintenance then Johnno was . . . beyond even high maintenance.

He lived his life in a state of chaos. Missed appointments, lost weekends, the time that he'd been on his way to the bank with a week's takings and had left them on a park bench. Freddy had been there to sort it all out.

Which was why Johnno had always said that Freddy had the 'patience of a cathedral full of saints. You've got a good one there.'

'I haven't got anything,' Phoebe had said. 'I don't have Freddy and he certainly doesn't have me. People don't belong to each other.'

'Whatever you say, kiddo.' Johnno had grinned and that had been the end of that.

And now it was the end of Freddy and Phoebe. It had been a whole day since she last saw him and she was going to have to get used to days, weeks, months, without him.

Maybe, in time, they'd be able to have some kind of working relationship but right now, when Phoebe thought of how Freddy had looked at her the day before, his hands shoved in his pockets, his eyes and voice cold, it made her shiver.

This unhappy train of thought was completely derailed by a terrible sound.

Not Sophy making good on her promise to start playing Christmas songs in the shop. Nor some horrible Instagram person loudly talking into her phone about fit checks.

It was the sound of a pug screaming. Again. Over that was the sound of Coco Chanel barking and who could blame her?

Phoebe stuck her head over the banister of the twisty stairs to see Coco on the third step from the bottom and Peggy Gug on the bottom step, both making their feelings known.

'Coco!' Phoebe said sharply. 'I've brought you up better than this.'

Coco turned to look at her, her eyes wide and imploring (in a way that always made Phoebe acquiesce to whatever Coco had set her heart on) then turned back so she could tell Peggy off for her impertinence.

'Hi, Phoebe!' Birdy came into view with a wave and a happy smile.

How many bloody rental dresses did she need anyway?

'Hi,' Phoebe said in a tone that she hoped wasn't at all encouraging but Birdy was already halfway up the stairs, Peggy on her heels as Coco took one look at the advancing guard and came scampering up to the atelier to hide behind her mistress.

'I was just passing,' Birdy said airily. 'Did you see the first couple of pieces of content I posted?'

'I saw one of them. Things have been quite busy,' Phoebe said vaguely.

Birdy turning up unannounced and so cheerful was quite annoying. Phoebe didn't know why it was but then everything was annoying her today. Including the adorable black and yellow tartan pinafore dress Birdy was wearing with a black polo neck and black stompy boots.

'Yeah, I saw that video that was posted. But you know what I always say?' Birdy asked cheerily as she ran a hand over an oyster silk 1920s flapper wedding dress. It was quite a respectful hand so Phoebe couldn't tell her not to touch.

'What do you always say?' Phoebe asked, because it was clear that Birdy was going to be here for a while.

'Never read the comments and if you do, remember that if those people aren't paying your bills, then pay them no mind, as the great RuPaul says,' Birdy imparted, which was quite close to Mildred's advice that someone else's opinion of you was none of your business.

'I don't care what anyone thinks of me,' Phoebe said, which wasn't strictly true. She cared, even now, what Freddy thought of her. She also cared that Sophy and Anita probably wished her dead and that Bea and Cress would probably help them hide the body, but she'd never admit that to anyone.

'Well, that's one of those ideas that's good in theory . . .' Birdy mused, which was more perceptive than Phoebe had given her credit for, but then she turned and sighed rapturously. 'Aw, look at them! I knew all that yapping was just them saying hello.'

Peggy Gug had managed to get her plump self up on one of the sofas and was stretched out, back legs splooted, while Coco Chanel was sitting on Peggy's bottom.

'Coco doesn't yap,' Phoebe said but Birdy had her phone out to document this canine meeting of the minds and didn't appear to have heard her.

'We should definitely arrange a doggy playdate!' she exclaimed. 'Let's swap numbers.'

'Oh, Coco doesn't play with other dogs,' Phoebe said loftily even as Coco gave her a quite bombastic side-eye then started licking Peggy's ear.

'They seem to like each other,' Birdy said, unthwarted. 'What's your number?'

Even Phoebe couldn't refuse to give Birdy her number. Though she did say suspiciously, 'I'm trusting you not to post it on the internet because the last thing I need is a whole load of rude people blowing up my phone.'

'I'm hurt that you'd even think that,' Birdy said with another keen look at Phoebe. 'I'll be in touch. Come on, Peggy, we've things to do, places to be.'

Her tone was now brisk and business-like and though Phoebe still didn't know why Birdy had popped in and why she was being so friendly, she knew that she'd behaved like quite the beast.

Phoebe gave Birdy a five-minute head start then went downstairs herself. The shop was briskly busy. It was lunchtime and half-term and Sophy, Bea and Anita were barely coping.

With some difficulty Phoebe fought her way through the space, her face slightly averted so no one would recognise her and thrust their phone in her direction. As she approached the till, Sophy, who was standing behind it, actually turned her back on Phoebe, which was very immature behaviour.

'Are you three all right to take a late lunch?' Phoebe asked. 'Bea, I can do the website orders if that would help.'

Phoebe wasn't going to apologise but she could be benevolent in her absolute authority.

'Are you sure?' Bea asked. 'I mean, are you sure you know how to?'

Anita sniggered but quickly turned it into a cough when Phoebe gave her a flinty-eyed look.

'Of course I know what to do,' she said. 'You were very good at explaining things. And as we're so busy, I think we'd better engage our emergency protocols.'

The emergency protocols were Bea on the door to only let people in, once she'd let people out. Anita policing the changing rooms and only allowing customers to try on three dresses or fewer and Sophy on till.

When Phoebe wasn't one of the most hated women on the internet and hadn't been cancelled for a second time, she'd supervise the operation, but that wasn't currently a viable option.

'I'll be in the back office if you need me,' she said, although she did have to venture onto the shop floor a couple of times to look for dresses that had been ordered online.

The second time, as Phoebe pulled a navy blue knit dress from the rail, the two young girls standing next to her nudged each other. 'It's her,' she heard one of them hiss with glee. 'That absolutely mental woman from TikTok.'

Keeping calm and carrying on was not in Phoebe's nature. How she longed to turn round, tell the pair of them off and then ban them from the shop for life. She didn't though, but once she'd finished doing the website orders, only four of them, which took no time at all, Phoebe was glad to have an excuse to pop out and go to the post office.

She still had no intention of apologising but she did offer to fetch lunch for them and Cress, who'd been called downstairs to help out.

They refused Phoebe's request with varying degrees of politeness and although The Vintage Dress Shop was meant to be her safe place, she couldn't wait for Bea to unlock the door and let her escape.

There wasn't even a long queue in the post office to delay her, nor in the little café where she liked to go to get her lunchtime salad. Coco Chanel wasn't in the mood for a long walk either and kept tugging on her lead in the direction of the shop.

All too soon, Phoebe had to return to a shop that wasn't quite so crowded but the atmosphere still had teeth and claws.

'I'll be in the office if you need me,' she said brightly and someone, either Anita or Sophy, Phoebe couldn't be sure which, muttered, 'Like I need a hole in the head,' in response.

Turning the other cheek was almost as hard as keeping calm and carrying on. As it was, Phoebe had no appetite for her chicken salad. For a moment, she wished she was the sort of person who ate carbs because her inner turmoil really needed something bready to squash it down. Possibly a doughnut.

Instead she found herself mindlessly scrolling through her phone. Or rather mindlessly scrolling through Birdy's Instagram feed and her colour-drenched, quirky pictures, which told a story just as well as the slightly breathless and gushy words that accompanied each post.

Phoebe was very careful with her fingers. She didn't want to accidentally like a picture from two years ago and have Birdy think that she was some crazed stalker. She'd rather that Birdy didn't think about her at all. Although Phoebe couldn't find fault with the two pieces of #sponcon for The Vintage Dress Shop that she'd posted already. One was a reel of Birdy running her hand over the rental rail and a commentary about how to rent dresses and the other was a series of pictures of Birdy frolicking on one of the pink sofas in the silver lamé minidress, which Phoebe had pulled for her.

They both had hundreds of likes and lots of comments, although a couple advised Birdy that they were unfollowing her because *I can't believe you'd do ads for a shop that employs BULLIES.*

Phoebe was saved from having to read any more uncomplimentary comments by the ping of her WhatsApp. Her heart lifted just a little to see a message from Johnno.

It was a photo of a fawn-coloured French bulldog frolicking on a beach, with the caption: *Coco is cuter.*

Phoebe was very much the sort of woman who kept her own counsel. But she never had to do that with Johnno.

Are you around for a bit. Fancy a FaceTime? she wrote back and her message had barely been in the ether and landed on the other side of the world before her phone rang.

She accepted the call, propped up her phone against the fancy tin that had once stored tea bags but now held a motley collection of pens, pencils and a manky pair of scissors, and smiled as Johnno's weatherbeaten face, sporting a huge grin, appeared on the screen.

'Love the hair,' Phoebe said, a smile on her face for the first time in days. 'Aren't you worried you'll scare the sheep?'

Johnno's close-cropped hair was currently neon green, which clashed with his ruddy cheeks. 'Had to leave the sheep for a week or so to come to Sydney to see a man about a dog,' he said with a grin. 'Talking of which, how is Madame Coco?'

At the sound of her name, Coco who'd been lying at Phoebe's feet in the hope of some chicken, raised her head. Phoebe scooped her up and sat her on her lap. 'There's your uncle Johnno,' she said and Coco's ears twitched as if she understood.

Then once Coco was back on the floor with a small piece of chicken for her trouble, Johnno launched into a long story involving a man he'd met in a pub, a darts match and how Johnno had 'won the fella's ute, fair and square, then he reported it stolen to the police. Thought they were going to bang me to rights but turns out the bloke has form for this kind of thing.'

Phoebe nodded and smiled and once Johnno had come to the end of his tale of woe, it was her turn to speak. Though every time she tried to think of a suitable opening statement, her words failed her.

'Everything's terrible,' she heard herself suddenly blurt out. 'There's a horrible atmosphere in the shop. Sophy and I argued, though she overstepped and took liberties with the dresses and people keep taking videos of me and posting them on the internet so that other people who don't even know me call me vile names and . . . and . . . and Freddy and me. There is no Freddy and me anymore.'

Johnno didn't say anything for a while. Phoebe always liked that about him. When it really mattered, Johnno listened and considered what he'd been listening to before he commented.

Now, much like Coco Chanel, he tilted his neon green head and processed everything that Phoebe had to say.

'It sounds like you're having a rough week,' he summed up.

'The absolute roughest,' Phoebe agreed.

'Did any dresses get damaged or destroyed?' Johnno asked.

'Well, no but . . .'

'If the dresses are all right, then everything else will come out in the wash,' Johnno said because he was the only person who understood how Phoebe felt about the dresses. He never made her feel bad about it either: that she could care for clothes, *stuff*, so much but when it came to people, she could take or leave them. Mostly leave them.

'Sophy's a good kid. You're a good kid. One day, you'll both find a way to co-exist and who cares what a bunch of people on the internet are saying?' He tilted his head again.

'I don't care,' Phoebe insisted because everyone from Mildred to Birdy knew that it was silly to worry about what people said about you, or to have any control over it. But if Phoebe hadn't said or done the things she'd said and done when people were surreptitiously recording her, then none of these recent unpleasant events would have happened.

'They don't know anything about you or your life. What makes you tick. What your story is, so sod 'em, pardon my French,' Johnno said. He knew more about Phoebe's life than anyone else. Because he'd known her since she was sixteen, almost half her lifetime, and even though she hadn't told him the details of how she'd ended up so surly, so displaced and living with Mildred at sixteen, Johnno wasn't stupid. He pretended that he was just a simple guy, but he was so good at reading between the lines. He'd always understood Phoebe without her saying a word. And, he'd never judged her for it. 'And as for Freddy . . .'

'Freddy will be fine,' Phoebe said sadly. Because it was true. She'd always acted as if she was doing Freddy a huge favour, right from the beginning of their awkward, protracted courtship, but in reality he could do a lot better than Phoebe. Or, at least, find someone who was much less hard work. He'd be much happier for it too. 'But you're not to let him sack me.'

'Nobody's sacking anyone,' Johnno said, which should have been a relief but wasn't. 'But it sounds like things can't carry on the way they are.'

'So, how do I make them better?'

'I think you already know the answer to that,' Johnno said, because the other thing about him, which was as infuriating as it was understandable, was that he never took sides. Even when it was quite obvious who was in the wrong. Even when that person wouldn't even admit it to themselves. 'It will all come good in the end, Pheebs. Always does.'

'Does it?' Phoebe rolled her eyes.

'I reckon.' Johnno looked past Phoebe just as she heard a noise behind her. 'Hey, kiddo, how are you? I know I owe you a phone call.'

With her heart sinking all the way to the soles of her feet, Phoebe turned her head to see Sophy standing there. A Sophy who mustered up a thin smile.

'You do,' she said shortly, then her face softened. 'What are you doing up so late anyway? The sheep causing you sleepless nights?'

'I'm in Sydney. Had to see a man about a dog,' Johnno repeated.

Sophy nodded. 'Of course you did. Are Bob and Jean good?'

'They're grand. I'm heading back to the station tomorrow. We're just heading into lambing season.'

Sophy and Johnno exchanged a few more incomprehensible words as they talked about lambing season on his parents' (Sophy's grandparents') sheep farm or station or whatever it was, as Phoebe tried to assume a neutral face.

It was hard when it was her phone propped up and Sophy was leaning down and across her to see Johnno on the screen. So close that Phoebe could smell her perfume.

'Anyway, you go and see that man about that completely fictitious dog and maybe we'll catch up when I call Bob and Jean on the weekend,' Sophy said, straightening up as Johnno touched the side of his head in a salute.

Then Sophy moved away to fill up the kettle and it was Phoebe's turn to say goodbye.

'You'll be fine,' Johnno assured her. 'This too will pass and all that.'

'Yeah, I suppose,' Phoebe said without much conviction. 'Let's speak soon. Oh and *Sheila*'s doing great, by the way.'

'I knew I could count on you to look after the old girl,' Johnno said. 'Right, I'll be off then. Be good!'

Johnno was never one to prolong a goodbye. The screen went black as he disconnected the call. Phoebe picked up her phone and risked looking over at Sophy, who wasn't watching the kettle but was staring at Phoebe with her hands on her hips.

'Since when do you speak to my dad?' she demanded.

Chapter Twenty

'Since always,' Phoebe said. 'I've known Johnno for years. He's my boss technically.'

She didn't explain things with her usual heat because she was mindful of Johnno's advice, such as it was, and also mindful that Sophy's relationship with Johnno was . . . complicated.

He was her father but in all the years that Phoebe had worked for Johnno, she'd never met Sophy. He talked about her sometimes but as far as Phoebe could work out, or even cared, Sophy was quite happy with her mum and her step-father.

Phoebe's life would have been so much better if Sophy had never come into it. Right from the start, Phoebe was sure that Sophy, who'd worked for BelleGirl, an awful fast-fashion high-street chain that had gone bust, had designs on her shop, her job, but the reality had been even worse than that.

First, she'd set her cap at lovely Charles then she'd broken his heart by emigrating to Australia and her grandparents' sheep farm. (No matter what anyone said, it was a farm. You didn't have sheep on a station.)

Phoebe had been delighted for Sophy to go and live on the other side of the world but she'd never dreamed that Johnno would decide to go with her. Then when Sophy had returned, it had been minus Johnno and with a few months' experience of working at Clive's bloody Closet, so she thought she was now a vintage clothing expert. Phoebe hadn't wanted her anywhere near the shop but back she came for an 'indefinite' period of time and with notions about renting out dresses and still she showed no inclination to leave.

So, she had good reasons for not liking Sophy but Phoebe could understand very well how difficult families could be. Especially families that weren't a one-size mum, dad, two kids fits all.

'He's my father,' Sophy said in a voice loaded with feelings. Lots of confusing, warring feelings. 'This is just *weird*. Are you doing this to get a rise out of me?'

'No! Johnno is . . . He's just the person I can always go to when I need advice,' Phoebe admitted, though it was the very last thing she wanted to tell Sophy. That there were times that she needed help and Johnno was the only person she trusted enough not to hold her weaknesses against her. 'He's your father but in some ways, a lot of ways, he's always been a father figure to me, you know.'

Sophy clicked the kettle so it would boil again as she'd now missed the peak hot water window. 'No, I don't know. Yes, Johnno's everyone's friend, and I'm glad that we have a relationship now, but just because he's a great guy, it doesn't mean that he's a great dad. He's so unreliable.'

'I don't know why that's such a problem.' Phoebe shrugged. 'He doesn't claim to be reliable. He's always been really upfront about his absolute flakiness. All that going to see a man about a dog when he's trying to wriggle out of something.'

'Thanks for explaining the ways of my own father to me,' Sophy snapped as the kettle clicked off and she picked it up.

Phoebe tried not to flinch. Sophy had a temper on her – all that red hair – but she hoped that she wouldn't start flinging scalding-hot water about. 'I'm sorry,' she said. 'I didn't mean to dadsplain.'

Sophy, thank goodness, put the kettle down. 'Oh my God, did you actually just apologise?'

'Only sorry for . . .'

'And then did you really crack a joke? Jesus. It's the end of days,' Sophy exclaimed, picking up the kettle again.

'I'm not *that* bad,' Phoebe said crossly, except she didn't even sound cross. She was tired mostly. She'd been cross now for what felt like weeks. Maybe months. Years. Her entire life. It was exhausting.

'But, Pheebs, you really are that bad.' Sophy sounded exhausted too.

'This thing with Johnno and his unreliability . . . I get that it's a very different situation for you but for me, well, I always expect people to let me down so he's never disappointed me in that way,' she explained as delicately and as diplomatically as she could, though neither of those adjectives were really in her wheelhouse. 'I've known him for years, Sophy. You think I'm bad but Johnno has seen the absolute worst of me and he's never judged me for it. He's come through for me, time and time again, in so many different ways. I owe him everything and I'm not saying that to upset you but . . .'

It was impossible to say what she wanted to say.

The tension between the two women, always there, shimmering like a force field that separated them, was almost visible.

It felt to Phoebe as if neither of them even dared to blink. 'But . . . ?' Sophy prompted very gently.

'If Johnno had been my father, not just a father figure, then . . . then I wouldn't have minded that and when you turned up, out of the blue, Johnno's actual daughter, oh God, I was so jealous of you I couldn't even stand it,' Phoebe said bitterly. 'And you don't appreciate him at all.'

'So, is that why you've always hated me?' Sophy asked flatly. Then she lifted up the kettle again. 'Do you want coffee?'

'Yes please and I don't *hate* you . . .'

'Dislike me intensely then. Potato potarto.' Sophy spooned coffee granules into Phoebe's mug, which Cress had got her for Christmas. A vintage Wedgwood mug from the late queen's coronation in 1953. Almost too nice to be used but Cress had insisted and Phoebe had been touched that Cress had given her such a thoughtful on-brand gift.

Cress was another one of the very small group of people that Phoebe had welcomed into her world. Yet now Cress was someone else who counted Phoebe as one of her least favourite people. But of those people, Sophy was the one who was currently in her eyeline and giving her grief.

Grief that was maybe just a little bit justified.

'Look, it's not my fault that we didn't become instant best friends,' Phoebe said, which probably counted as explaining but at least she wasn't complaining. 'I had no idea you were going to be working here. Even Freddy didn't know until Johnno sent him a message asking him to collect you from the station. Then you were very disrespectful about the dresses. For weeks you kept saying that people had probably died in them.'

Was that the ghost of a smile on Sophy's face as she held up the milk carton. 'Black or a splash of milk?' She'd remembered that Phoebe took her coffee in two different ways depending on her mood.

'Just a splash, please.'

'The odds are that at least one of the dresses that we've sold did have someone die in them,' Sophy muttered.

'Why would you say that? Are you deliberately trying to wind me up?' Phoebe demanded as Sophy handed her the mug.

'Yeah. Maybe.' Sophy sighed as she leaned back against the sink. 'It goes both ways. I was so jealous of your relationship with Johnno. It seemed too easy, so effortless. Like he didn't need to bother staying in touch with me because he had you.'

'But Johnno adores you!' Phoebe pointed out because even if there had been a distance between father and daughter, there was still no mistaking the way that Johnno's face always lit up when he talked about Sophy. More so, when they were actually in the same room together.

'I don't know if he does. I hope he does. I am really fond of him. One of the best things about working here has been this new relationship with Johnno . . .' Her lips twisted wryly.

'But I'm the worst thing,' Phoebe guessed.

Sophy shrugged. 'You said it, not me.' She sighed again. 'Look, I don't want your job. I don't want to be the manager and have all that responsibility. I just want to sell pretty dresses to interesting people and have a little piece of something that's my own, which is the rental dresses. I have no evil plans to take over your empire.'

Phoebe digested this information. 'Freddy would prefer it if you were manager.'

'No, he wouldn't. If he wanted anyone else to be manager, it would be Bea because she knows how to make Excel spreadsheets, how the inventory thingy on the computer works and how to order new bags and a hundred other things that I have no interest in because, again, I don't want to be manager,' Sophy said. 'But also, Phoebe, I like working here. I love working with Cress. But no job is worth this much stress and hassle, so if you really want me to go then . . .'

'No! No! Of course I don't want you to leave,' Phoebe said quickly, even though it had been her heart's true desire ever since Sophy turned up. But was Sophy really that bad? If she didn't have designs on the shop and stayed in her lane then . . . 'Do you promise never to get another hare-brained idea, like reorganising the dresses, then act on it without getting my approval?'

'I'm happy to sign something to that effect,' Sophy said with a grimace. 'Honestly, I knew I'd screwed things up.

When I heard you come down the stairs, I swear my whole life flashed before my eyes.'

'I'm sure we can find a way to work together,' Phoebe said, though she knew she was the one who needed to make the most effort. 'Also, happy Sophy means happy Charles and I really couldn't afford to lose him. All those dresses from estate sales that he'd pass on to another shop. That would be unbearable.'

'Was that another joke?' Sophy asked. 'It really is hard to tell.'

'It started off as a joke but then contemplating the loss of Charles quickly turned into my worst nightmare,' Phoebe confessed. She drained the rest of her coffee then stood up. She felt depleted. This conversation had been challenging and difficult but now it felt like the closing of one chapter, where nothing good had happened, and the start of something new. Hopefully, something much better.

'Well, this has been a good chat,' Sophy said with some surprise.

'It has,' Phoebe agreed.

'Should we shake hands or something?' Sophy grinned mischievously. 'Or hug it out?'

Phoebe's shudder wasn't entirely fake. 'That won't be necessary.' She paused on her way to the door. 'You know, if you want to decorate the shop for Christmas, then that's fine with me. Just, please, don't go mad. Tasteful. Even understated.'

'Yes to Christmas tunes too?' Sophy asked hopefully.

'If I were you, I'd quit while I was ahead.'

Phoebe and Sophy's new, friendlier relationship was clearly going to be a work in progress.

Chapter Twenty-One

A couple of days later Sophy put up Christmas decorations and in the time it took, the atmosphere in the shop changed completely.

From frosty with the threat of storms to a gentle breeze and the promise of sun.

Of course, if Phoebe had decorated, she'd have chosen either silver or gold. Not both. Never both. But this was clearly what people meant when they said you should pick your battles.

'Very nice,' Phoebe managed to say when she came down from the atelier after attending to a private client who'd tried on ten dresses and hadn't bought a single one. She knew her smile was quite brittle, but she nodded her head effusively. 'Very nice indeed.'

She couldn't resist adjusting a stream of tinsel – the bougie, very full tinsel, not the nasty straggly cheap kind, which was wound round the end of one of the dress rails. Still, Rome wasn't built in a day.

Then the bell above the door tinkled and Phoebe hurried to the safety of the back office. The shop was busier than she could ever remember from Christmases past. Though it was quite hard to tell who was there to shop or who was there to simply gawp at Phoebe and try to stealthily video her so she wouldn't notice.

Phoebe didn't really know what this business meant for their profits. If they were up year on year and far greater than their outgoings? It wasn't something she could ask Freddy. Not now. Not anymore. There was an accountant who handled their payroll, probably the best person to contact if she wanted to start docking Anita's wages for poor timekeeping too, but buddying up to accountants really wasn't playing to Phoebe's strengths.

It would be a far better use of her time if she could think up ways to get more people in the shop to buy more dresses.

Drumming up the good kind of publicity would be a start, instead of the bad kind. At least their social media numbers were through the roof (although the trolls and the mean comments continued apace) and so were their website orders. Bea said they'd hit 25,000 followers on Instagram and that they needed to finesse their TikToks and Instagram Reels and memes.

In between customers, she'd spent quite a lot of time filming Sophy and Anita as they decorated the shop. Then even more time trying to make a TikTok and swearing when it kept refusing to upload. Phoebe hadn't even known that Bea knew how to swear, unlike Anita who needed her mouth washing out with soap given how frequently she dropped the F-bomb.

Still, they felt like a team in a way that they hadn't in ages. Things were even cordial between Phoebe and Cress, though they could be friendlier, but last time Phoebe checked Cress had still gone behind her back to launch a business with Freddy. And – it was a really big *and* – hadn't even named a dress after her.

Talking of Freddy, though even thinking his name made Phoebe feel clammy, he'd stopped dropping in. Or rather it was now Friday and no one had seen him all week though Bea had mentioned that he'd emailed her a couple of times.

As Anita ushered the last customer out of the shop and turned the sign to closed and Sophy began to cash up, all

Phoebe could think about was Freddy. Though she'd been thinking about him, or trying not to think about him, all week.

If he was keeping a low profile then maybe he wouldn't even come to The Hat and Fan for the usual Friday night drinks. As soon as Phoebe thought it, Sophy's phone beeped.

Sophy frowned because she was in the middle of some heavy-duty counting, her fingers flying over the sturdy shop calculator as she tallied up the card receipts. Not that Sophy could ever ignore her beeping phone for long.

She wrote something down. Shuffled the card receipts into two piles, then picked up her phone.

'Charles, Miles and Freddy are already in The Hat and Fan and some selfish people are sitting at our table,' she reported.

'It's not actually our table,' Cress said as she rubbed Coco Chanel's belly while she sprawled next to her on one of the pink sofas. 'Though I do think that one of the bar staff should stick a reserved sign on it for us.'

'Oh my days! Not again!' Anita suddenly exclaimed. She was meant to be vacuuming but wasn't doing a very good job of it as she was staring at her phone screen too. Phoebe didn't have the emotional bandwidth to tell Anita off, which just showed how off her game she was. All her emotional band-width was currently being used to process the information that Freddy was in the pub and she'd soon have to face him. Neither Phoebe nor her frantically racing heart was ready for that.

'What? What's happened?' Bea asked from behind Sophy where she was breaking up some cardboard boxes to be left outside for recycling. 'Has that bloke from Hinge sent you another dick pic?'

'Why he even bothers I don't know,' Anita snorted. She looked up from her phone but held it aloft. 'It's actually worse than that. Rosie Roberts has reposted her clip of Phoebe going off on one.'

There was a collective sigh though no one sighed as loud and as long as Phoebe. 'She's already posted it once. I can't see what difference posting it a second time is going to make. I'm already cancelled and still the most hated woman on the internet.'

'You're not even close to being the most hated. I think Kim Kardashian would have something to say about that.' It was nice of Cress to stick up for her even in a half-hearted fashion, but Phoebe wasn't convinced.

Especially as Anita was still waving her phone around. 'Except this time she hasn't muted what you're saying.'

It all felt like it had happened years ago. 'I can't even remember what I did say. Something about women saving up for their wedding dresses, I think, but the rest of it is a blur,' Phoebe said, her stomach one gigantic, gnarly knot as she took the phone to watch herself call Rosie Roberts a monster. Phoebe's open mouth resembled a dark void. Her neck was very cordy and she looked utterly deranged. 'I absolutely don't need to see any more of this.'

She pushed the phone back to Anita. 'That's just part one of four,' Anita said with an undercurrent of delight, because whatever beef Rosie Roberts had with Phoebe, Anita's beef had been cooking for a good three years. 'You don't want to see any more?'

It was a very easy decision to make. 'I think I'll pass,' Phoebe said.

By now Sophy had completed the cashing up. Somehow Anita had finished vacuuming, though she'd done a very poor job of it, and Bea and Cress were waiting by the door so they could all go to The Hat and Fan because it was Friday night and drinks and devoted boyfriends were waiting for them.

Five minutes later, they were assembled outside the shop. In the distance they could hear the crackle and bang of fireworks, pink sparks lighting up the night sky. It was cold and there was a smell of autumn in the air; an earthiness from the damp leaves that had been swept up and placed in bags waiting for the council to collect them, chestnuts roasting from a street cart further down the road.

Phoebe wasn't the type of optimistic and carefree person who loved the regrowth and promise of spring or the long sultry days of summer. She was a clear autumn and a true winter, which could be why she currently felt like a small woodland animal. Instead of parading the frost-sparkled streets of north London in a variety of fabulous coats and accessories as she'd loved to do in previous Novembers, now Phoebe wanted to burrow deep into her den and not emerge until March.

Of course, if she did hibernate then she wouldn't be able to see Freddy when she wanted to see Freddy desperately. She missed his face. She missed his easy grin. She missed so many things about him. Then again, she didn't miss the way the light had gone out of his eyes, his strained voice, his disappointment, all qualities that would be much in evidence when he discovered that Phoebe had gone viral again.

'Actually, I'm not really in a pub kind of mood this evening.' Her words came out much croakier than she'd intended. Almost as if she were on the verge of tears, even though Phoebe was proud not to be a crier.

'Oh, come on, if anyone needs a drink then it's you,' Sophy said because they might never become friends but they were now friendly. 'There's a gin and tonic with your name on it.'

'It's Friday night,' Bea pointed out. 'It's bad luck not to come to the pub.'

'That isn't even a thing,' Phoebe said. 'I've got a headache and also last week I'm sure Coco ate a pork scratching off the floor because she had a very upset stomach. Very upset.'

'OK, more information than we needed,' Anita said, again positively delighted at the thought of Phoebe bowing out.

Probably so they could all moan about her. 'Well, we'll see you tomorrow then. Bye!'

'Do come if you change your mind,' Cress muttered but Phoebe could tell her heart wasn't in it. It was odd that of the two sisterfriends, it was Sophy who was currently on better terms with Phoebe.

Phoebe had never been surer of anything. She watched the four women walk down the street, then turn the corner. Once she was certain they were gone, she looked down at Coco who was straining at the lead, her face scrunched up in confusion as to why they too weren't going to the lovely place on the corner where there were always crisps on the floor and a lap for her to sit in. Usually Freddy's lap.

'I know, Coco. I know you miss him. As a special treat, I'll make you some chicken tonight,' Phoebe murmured.

Once they were on *The Sheila* and there were two chicken breasts gently baking, Phoebe slipped into something more comfortable. Something more comfortable usually meant an elegant pair of pyjamas or a caftan. But tonight she was going more for comfort than style – a very, very rare event indeed.

Buried right at the back of a drawer were a pair of fleece-lined leggings and some very thick woolly socks, which Phoebe paired with a loose freebie T-shirt she'd been sent when she ordered some skincare online. Over that, she pulled on a hoodie, which didn't even belong to her. It was Freddy's. He'd left it behind one morning and Phoebe had meant to return it but somehow it had slipped her mind, even though Freddy said that she had a memory like an elephant and never forgot anything.

She'd washed it several times over the year or so that she'd had it but she liked to think that it still smelt like Freddy. The lime tang of his aftershave, the clean, crisp scent of his laundry detergent but also something else, some undefinable pheromone or molecule that made Phoebe always want to bury her nose in Freddy's neck until she had to come up for air.

Instead, she had to make do with his hoodie that she'd borrowed indefinitely. And instead of a gin and tonic and pinching some of Freddy's chips, Phoebe had to make do with a glass of water and the chicken and rice that she'd made for herself and Coco. She'd managed to overcook them both so that the meat was like rubber and the rice was like sludge.

Not that Coco minded. She wolfed down her share then cast a longing look at Phoebe's bowl. She was just about to put it down for her when there was a tapping at the window, which made them both jump.

It wasn't the random knocking of someone, usually a quite drunk someone, passing, which was an annoying and thankfully only occasional drawback of living on a boat.

This was two taps and a pause. Then the same sequence again. The signal that she and Freddy had come up with so that Phoebe would know that it was him and not some drunken random.

She kneeled on the sofa to pull back her little curtain and there he was standing on the canal path. It was dark but she'd recognise him anywhere. He gestured with his hand to indicate that he wasn't going to come on board without her permission. Phoebe nodded and as she got up to unlock the door, she felt the boat shift in its moorings as Freddy stepped from the path to stern.

It was only as she opened the door and gestured for Freddy to come inside, bringing the chill of the night with him, that Phoebe wished she hadn't slipped into something quite so comfortable. If she was still wearing her work clothes, a black dress and heels, she'd feel more prepared to face him for the first time in days.

She'd even wiped off every last trace of make-up and had a conditioning treatment on her hair. That might have been why Freddy's eyes widened ever so slightly or it might have been because he recognised the hoodie that she pulled tighter around her body.

'I know you don't like people dropping by unannounced,' he said hoarsely when the silence between them had passed awkward and was heading towards excruciating. 'I tried messaging, calling . . .'

Phoebe's phone was still in her bag. She hadn't wanted to deal with the fallout from her latest appearance on Rosie Roberts's socials, even if it was messages of support from her friends.

'Have you come to tell me off?' Phoebe asked because she didn't know why else Freddy would be here. 'Though technically I haven't done anything wrong. Or rather I haven't done a new very bad thing because it was footage that had already been posted.' She tried to aim for a careless little laugh but it turned into a cough.

'Are you all right?' Freddy asked but Phoebe turned away from him, with her hand outstretched to ward him off, not like he was about to touch her anyway.

She managed to stop coughing and also dredge up a smile from somewhere. 'I'm fine,' she said. 'Why wouldn't I be?'

'Well, you didn't come to the pub,' Freddy said. He was wearing a navy wool jacket, a grey scarf tucked into the neck, but he made no move to take it off, hang it up on the hook by the door and make himself more comfortable. To sit down and ask Phoebe to stick the kettle on.

The only thing he did that was halfway normal was to crouch down to attend to Coco who couldn't hide how pleased she was to see him. Her entire back end was wiggling with joy, her paws skittering on the floor.

'How's my best girl?' he murmured throatily. Coco was now on her back, legs akimbo, so he could scratch her belly with his long fingers. 'Did you miss me?'

Phoebe wondered what might happen if she answered for Coco. *Yes, we both miss you. We both hate how things are.*

But she didn't even try. She knew the words would just get stuck in her throat. And besides, what would it even matter? Freddy wasn't on her side. He didn't accept Phoebe for who she was, good and also, yes, very bad. He wanted her to change. To become someone she wasn't in order to be someone that he wanted to be with.

'Is that the only reason you came round? To ask why I wasn't in the pub?' Phoebe folded her arms. 'Was there any other reason?'

If Freddy said that he missed her, Phoebe, not just her dog who now had one back leg pedalling in ecstasy because Freddy always knew how to find her sweet spot, then maybe Phoebe would say it back.

But he didn't. He kept stroking Coco but at last stood up. 'I looked at the accounts for the last couple of weeks and takings are up year on year,' he said because it was strictly business between them now.

At least that was some good news. It was even worth the influx of new customers these last few days even if they did want to shove their phones in Phoebe's face so they could get more likes for their social media accounts.

'I was wondering about that and trying to come up with some ideas for increasing our profits. Johnno will be pleased,' Phoebe said. She made a jerky movement with her hands then folded her arms tight again. 'So, was that everything?'

Freddy stood there, still and unknowable in that moment, even though Phoebe would have said, only a couple of weeks ago, that she knew everything about Freddy. How he took his tea. The sound he made when he slept, which wasn't snoring but wasn't that far off either. How his lips felt when they were on hers.

Then he took a step back and looked around Phoebe's eclectically styled living space. His eyes came to rest on her wood-burning oven, which was burning merrily, one of Coco's beds in front of it because she loved to toast herself like a loaf of bread. 'Did you ever get the flue on that thing checked?' Freddy asked.

Phoebe couldn't quite believe what she was hearing. 'Is that all you came round to say?'

Freddy's attention swung back to Phoebe. 'What do you want me to say?' He looked at Phoebe as if he could see past the uncharacteristic outfit and beyond even that. Like he was looking at the very bones of her and what he saw there was very disappointing. 'Seriously, what do you want me to say, Pheebs?'

There were so many things that she wanted Freddy to say. That he was on her side. That he'd always have her back. That he might not understand her or agree with her but he liked her enough that those things didn't matter.

Phoebe had things that she wanted to say to Freddy too. Not just to berate him either. That she knew she was difficult and prickly and she gave him a hard time pretty much always, and even though she *still* didn't trust him enough to tell him about how she came to be that way, she *wanted* to trust him. That had to count for something, didn't it?

It was always easier to pour her emotions into inanimate objects, her dresses, her *stuff*.

Instead, Phoebe just shrugged helplessly. Hopelessly. 'Well, if we have nothing to say to each other then you should probably go. It's getting quite late.'

Indeed it was far too late for the both of them.

Phoebe's phone chimed as Freddy left without another word, his face impassive even as Coco Chanel barked her displeasure at his departure.

She glanced at the screen impatiently, only to see that she had a message from Birdy.

Sorry that the internet/Rosie Roberts is still being vile. Would you and Coco like to come round on Sunday for a tea party/ doggy date?

Phoebe's first, second, third and quite a few instincts after that was to refuse. She hardly knew Birdy. They'd met three times now and that was hardly enough times to go round to her house to hang out. Like they were friends or something.

Then Phoebe thought of how after work tomorrow, the rest of the weekend stretched out before her with nothing to do and no one to see. Before Freddy, she was perfectly happy with her own company or seeing people from her very small and carefully selected friend group. Then it had happened that when she wasn't at The Vintage Dress Shop, she was with Freddy. His presence and his plans for the two of them filling up every minute. Also, she knew that Marianne and Claude had gone to see his parents in Scunthorpe for the weekend so she couldn't throw herself on their mercy either.

The thought of a Sunday spent on her own with nothing to do but housework and replaying all her past mistakes of the last few weeks was too awful to contemplate.

That would be great. Would you like me to bring anything?

The reply was almost instant.

Just yourselves. See you at three. Location pin attached.

Chapter Twenty-Two

Phoebe was never late. She was never too early either, which was another kind of rudeness altogether. If you had friends coming round and they turned up thirty minutes before the agreed time while you were still in the shower, well, that was just inconsiderate.

'Punctuality is the politeness of kings,' Mildred had been fond of saying, so at exactly five minutes to three, even though the bus from Camden had taken ages, Phoebe rang the bell to Birdy's basement flat in a quiet tree-lined road in Upper Clapton.

She didn't know why her stomach felt like it was on the floor and her hands were clammy inside her gloves. Like she was nervous or something.

There was the sound of yapping, which made Coco, who was waiting patiently at her feet, squirm and give a warning bark.

'Company manners, CC,' Phoebe said sharply, as she heard footsteps and the sound of a key turning then the door opened and Birdy was standing there with a delighted smile on her elfin face.

'You came,' she said as if she hadn't been sure that Phoebe would.

'I came,' Phoebe agreed.

They stood there for a moment, each sizing the other one up. Birdy was clearly one of those people who dressed strictly for comfort at home. She was bare-faced, her hair curling up at the ends and she was wearing a onesie. It was leopard print but it was still a onesie.

Phoebe was in one of her weekend outfits. Vintage-cut, indigo denim dungarees, a black and white polka dot rayon silk blouse with pussy cat bow, biker boots and her hair caught up in a black and white polka dot silk scarf, only her fringe visible. And of course full make-up. Phoebe never went anywhere without a red lip.

The sizing up was interrupted as Coco Chanel made an attempt to push past Phoebe probably because she could sense that Peggy Gug was near.

'Oh, you can just let her off the lead,' Birdy said. 'I think she and Peggy are going to be fast friends.'

Phoebe doubted that very much. There was every possibility that Coco might eat Peggy but she released the catch on Coco's pink leather lead so Coco could shoot through Birdy's legs.

'I got you this,' Phoebe said when she'd straightened up and handed over a stiff cardboard box, which had become a little squashed on the bus. 'For tea.'

There was a very fancy, very expensive bakery in Primrose Hill, which mostly specialised in cupcakes but cupcakes were so early 2000s and a triumph of frosting over actual cake. Instead Phoebe had brought a Victoria sponge. Classic, timeless, the little black dress of cakes.

'Oh, you shouldn't have,' Birdy said, sniffing with a little rapturous sigh. 'It smells delicious.'

'I could never turn up to someone's house empty-handed,' Phoebe insisted, another useful life lesson from Mildred and now that greetings had been exchanged, she stepped through the door and hoped this wasn't a big mistake.

Birdy's flat was on the lower ground floor of a Victorian house. From the outside, the house looked very done up. It's paintwork grey, its wooden trims and doors black as was fashionable, but the separate little basement flat wasn't as smart as its exterior.

It was very dimly lit, the weak November sunlight trickling in through tiny windows, and Birdy and Faisal had painted the walls black so the whole effect should have been quite sombre. Except all the doors, window frames and skirting boards, even the old-fashioned fire in the lounge, had been painted a cheerful deep yolky yellow.

As Phoebe followed Birdy along a narrow hall, the walls were crowded with pictures: paintings of flowers, portraits of sad-eyed Modigliani-esque girls, which had been popular in the 1960s, and postcards of everything from kittens to the Velvet Underground to vintage book covers, all of them in an eclectic variety of different frames.

They came to the kitchen, the walls black, the cupboard doors the same bright yellow, black and white chequerboard lino on the floor, where Coco Chanel got up on her hind legs to scrabble at the back door.

'I told Faisal to put Peggy in the garden so we could reintroduce them on neutral territory,' Birdy said. 'I looked it up on Google. Are you happy for Coco to go outside?'

Coco Chanel wasn't really an outside sort of dog. She preferred the sheets to the streets, as Freddy used to say.

Also, Coco didn't play well with others. She regarded them as beneath her.

'Well, it's worth a try,' Phoebe said doubtfully.

Birdy unlocked the back door, Coco wriggling through the gap before it was fully open.

Phoebe realised that she should have put Coco back on her lead and escorted her out but it was too late. Coco made a beeline for Peggy who was already screaming, bopped her on the snoot with a paw, then the two of them charged around the tiny garden, mouthing at each other. Occasionally one of them would drop and roll, then get back up to charge the other again.

'Um, should they be doing that?' Phoebe asked as she and Birdy stood on the back doorstep, and Faisal did a strange hopping dance on the lawn to avoid being mown down by two small but powerful dogs. 'It looks a bit like they're trying to kill each other.'

'Oh, they're just doing bitey face,' Birdy said airily. 'It looks aggressive but it's only playing.' She turned to Phoebe with a smile and misty eyes. 'It's so rare for Peggy to really connect with another dog.'

Phoebe didn't say anything at first. She was transfixed by Coco tearing around the garden like an actual real dog. It was the first time she'd ever seen Coco get the zoomies.

'Coco too. She never interacts with other dogs. It's not her fault,' she added defensively though Birdy hadn't said anything condemning. 'She's a rescue. I don't even know all the terrible things that had happened to her before I found her.'

Both coming from brachycephalic breeds, the zoomies and the bitey face didn't last long before Coco and Peggy splooted out on the grass, panting heavily.

Once they were inside, they drank from the same water bowl then curled up together in a plush dog bed under a radiator in the kitchen. Faisal greeted Phoebe then said he was meeting a friend to lay down some tracks.

'He's a composer,' Birdy explained once Faisal had left. 'Do you want tea? Coffee? I only have oat milk though. Or I have some kombucha if that's more your thing.'

It really wasn't. Phoebe requested black coffee and leaned against the worktop as Birdy got down mugs then started opening a lot of big Tupperware containers.

'I knew you were coming so I baked a cake,' she said with a grin. 'Cookies, brownies and some scones too.'

Phoebe was about to protest that she didn't eat any of those things but, then again, she did love a brownie. 'So, what does Faisal compose?' she asked. 'Anything I'd have heard of?'

'He's composed two symphonies and he's working on an opera about Peggy Guggenheim with a friend, but in the meantime we have to pay the bills so he also does music for adverts and video games,' Birdy said, as she arranged her home-baked treats on a vintage cake stand. 'Shall we go into the front room?'

Once they were settled on a comfy little sofa covered in a Welsh blanket and a variety of cushions, with coffee and cake, Phoebe dreaded the conversation grinding to a halt.

It never happened. They talked about *Peggy Guggenheim*, the opera; Peggy Guggenheim, the heiress; and Peggy Gug the Pug, which led to a series of confessions about how hard it was to be the owner of a dog who didn't like other dogs.

'Although it's more like other dogs don't like Peggy. What with the screaming and she's very bad at reading the room. It's like she doesn't understand Dog,' Birdy said and Phoebe could empathise.

'Oh, Coco hates most other dogs,' she said and went on to tell Birdy about the time she'd taken Coco to a Frenchie meet-up as a way of socialising her and Coco had peed on another dog's head. 'The organiser asked us to leave and never come back,' Phoebe recounted as Birdy shook with silent laughter. 'I mean, Coco is very judgemental. She judges everyone. Sometimes, I catch her giving even me side-eye and I'm the one who keeps her in the bougie lifestyle to which she's become accustomed.'

It wasn't very often that Phoebe met someone and felt any kind of kinship with them unless they instantly bonded over vintage dresses. That was how she had met and become friends with Marianne and Claude. Her social circle mainly comprised people she'd met at vintage fairs and vintage clothing swaps, which reminded her . . .

'Oh, I brought you something,' Phoebe said after an hour when there had been no uncomfortable silences and she'd eaten more cake than she had done in years.

'The Victoria sponge was enough. More than enough,' Birdy protested as Phoebe reached into her vintage straw bag, which some intrepid traveller had brought back from the Bahamas many decades ago. It had the country's name embroidered on it in red along with a bunch of bright pink hibiscus flowers.

'I was having a sort-through and I found this dress, which just isn't my style.' Phoebe produced a package, which she'd wrapped in white tissue paper and tied with a thin strip of pale green ribbon that she'd had knocking about. As Mildred used to say, it was better to reuse than to recycle. 'I don't know why I bought it originally. Probably because it looked so pretty and I couldn't bear to leave it in the shop, but I think it would look great on you.'

'Well, that's very kind. Absolutely unnecessary,' Birdy said as she carefully unwrapped the paper to reveal a 1960s crimplene sleeveless minidress with a swirling psychedelic pattern in white, green, blue and yellow. 'Oh, this is really cool!'

'I thought you could wear a black turtleneck under it like you wore the other day,' Phoebe explained. 'Although it might get a bit sweaty. I went clubbing in crimplene once and I really don't recommend it.'

'I've got some white vinyl boots that would look amazing with it.' Birdy held the dress up for closer inspection. 'Thank you, Phoebe. I really appreciate this . . . I mean . . . I never.' She shot Phoebe a sideways look. 'Shall we talk about the elephant in the room?'

'Which elephant in particular?' Phoebe asked, immediately on guard. She could feel a tingling sensation as every hair on her body stood to attention.

'Those awful videos that have gone viral. In that the people who have posted them are awful,' Birdy clarified. 'But also, I get that you're passionate about vintage clothes, like, really passionate so I didn't think you'd just give away a dress.'

Phoebe frowned. 'But I never wear it and it's silly to keep it tucked away. I'd much rather give it to someone who'd appreciate it and show it a good time.'

'I just didn't get the impression that that was your vibe,' Birdy said carefully. 'Like, maybe, you were more about keeping people away from the vintage dresses.'

'Only the wrong people,' Phoebe said with a little heat but she was a very long way from going fully nuclear, because Birdy didn't seem to be criticising her but genuinely curious as to Phoebe's policy when it came to the keeping, buying, selling and redistribution of vintage dresses. 'Like influencers who think vintage is cool but have no respect for the history of a dress and yank it about and get fake tan all over it.'

No, she still wasn't over *that*.

'By influencers, I guess you mean Rosie Roberts?' Birdy ventured and all Phoebe could do was snort in agreement. 'It was still quite hard to work out what the context of that video was even with the four separate parts she posted.'

'Let me fill you in on the details,' Phoebe said and proceeded to do just that, which took quite some time. 'Yes, at the end of the day, it's just a dress but think about your favourite dresses and how they make you feel, all the good memories that you've made while you were wearing them. Then if that dress is a vintage dress, it was someone else's favourite dress before you ever clapped eyes on it. That's why I gave you this crimplene number, why I'm happy to swap dresses with friends, because you can never really own a vintage dress. You're more of a guardian, keeping it for future generations. Does that make sense?'

Birdy nodded. 'Yeah, it does. And I get why you'd be cross when someone treats a dress that's survived all those years with as little respect as if they bought it from Shein for a fiver.'

'So, anyway, that's why I have to intervene when people aren't treating the dresses with the respect they deserve.

Though yes, sometimes my interventions get a bit too heated,' Phoebe said. She was relieved when Birdy smiled. She was smiling too.

'I don't want to be creepy but I really like you,' Birdy said matter-of-factly. 'I'm a great believer in just putting these things out there. I texted Faisal ten minutes after our first date to tell him that he was someone I wanted in my life.'

'That's very courageous.' Phoebe sighed. Life must be easier, if you were more like the Birdys of this world. 'I'm very good at telling people off for crimes against vintage fashion but I'm not brave like that.'

'It's the best way to make sure you only have good people around you,' Birdy said with a warm smile like Phoebe was one of those good people. 'Although me asking you to tea was my third attempt and then I was going to give up on you. If someone doesn't want to be in your life, there's no point in forcing them.'

Phoebe had only accepted Birdy's invitation because she couldn't bear the thought of being alone. She'd come here under false pretences but she was very glad that she had. 'I'm quite hard to get to know,' she admitted, not that she thought that was going to come as a shock. 'I'm not really a people person. We've already established that I'm more of a dresses person.'

'Maybe you just haven't met the right people,' Birdy said, getting to her feet and stretching her arms over her head. 'But now that you are here, it would be a pleasure and a privilege to let me show you my favourite dresses.'

Phoebe was grateful for the change of subject and she always welcomed the opportunity to rifle through someone else's wardrobe especially when that someone had fairly excellent taste. But as she followed Birdy to her bedroom, Phoebe wondered if maybe she had already met the right people but she hadn't given them a chance because she was simply too used to always expecting the worst.

It was impossible to brood though, when confronted with Birdy's main wardrobe in her bedroom and her overspill wardrobe, which was barely contained in a tiny box room. Birdy was a fashion magpie. Instead of settling on one look and one aesthetic like Phoebe, she refused to commit.

'I mean, one day I want to dress like a 1960s dollybird, the next I want to look like it's 1942 and I've been jiving all night with an American GI called Hank,' she explained. 'In fact, I was thinking of doing a time-lapse film showing ten different looks from ten different decades. Like, from the 1920s to the 2020s.'

'Someone would pay you to do that?' Phoebe asked in surprise.

Sadly, Birdy wasn't getting paid for it. But she explained that the brand partnerships and #sponcon she did subsidised her income enough that she could film content that was more indulgent.

Phoebe was happy to pull some outfits together from what Birdy already had. 'And I do actually have a 1920s flapper dress – it's gorgeous, covered in silver bugle beads – which you can borrow and I can give you some tips on make-up.' She remembered herself and tried to rein in her enthusiasm. 'You've probably got that all covered.'

'I'd love any input from you. You're the expert.' Birdy might have been shamelessly buttering Phoebe up but Phoebe didn't even care.

It was so nice to be appreciated for her quite limited skill set instead of being criticised for all her many failings.

'I'm happy to help out,' she said in an offhand way, like she wasn't that bothered but Birdy beamed.

'I would love that,' she breathed. 'Though I don't know why you're not more active on social media. You could have so many followers. Are you not tempted? Everyone I know wants to be a content creator.'

'I absolutely don't,' Phoebe said firmly. She and Birdy had come this far so they could probably go a little further with no hard feelings. 'Call me old-fashioned but it just feels a lot like showing off.'

Birdy didn't take offence but laughed and clapped her hands.

An hour later when Phoebe and Coco had finally been allowed to leave with a selection of uneaten treats in a Tupperware container and a beaded cashmere cardigan because Birdy didn't have the patience to repair the beading herself, Phoebe felt a warm glow that was nothing to do with a very fast walk to the stop so she wouldn't miss her bus.

It was the cosy little feeling that comes from meeting a kindred spirit and making a new friend. Something that didn't happen to Phoebe very often.

They'd barely been on the bus for five minutes when Phoebe's phone chimed. As ever, her heart did a weird backflippy thing in the hope/dread that it might be from Freddy. But it never was.

It wasn't this time either.

It was from Birdy.

Such a treat to spend some quality time together and eat lots of cake. So glad you came round and, I refuse to take no for an answer, we ARE going to be friends.

Phoebe pursed her lips but it was more to hide a smile than because she was bristling at Birdy's peremptory tone.

I had a lovely time. Thank you for inviting me. Are you going to the Christmas Vintage Ball at the Bloomsbury Ballroom? If not, you should. I'll text you the details.

Her phone chimed again.

Please do! I hear you on the whole showing off thing (BRUTAL, btw) but I feel like Coco and Peggy might have a future as fashion-forward dog influencers. Let's hatch a plan next time we see each other. Birdy xxx

The idea was ridiculous but not unappealing. It was a pity not to share Coco's grace, beauty and style with the wider world.

I'll get Coco's people to call Peggy's people, Phoebe messaged back. And she was still smiling even when someone with appalling body odour sat in the seat behind her.

Chapter Twenty-Three

Any lingering grudges that her colleagues might be holding on to were swept away when Phoebe opened her Tupperware container at the Monday morning meeting.

That was now a regular thing that they did. Or rather she said to Sophy as they were hanging up their coats, 'It's probably a good idea to have a quick catch-up on Monday mornings so we can see how the week is going to pan out. If you wanted to head that up.'

'We could do that,' Sophy agreed slowly. Then her eyes narrowed. 'Is this a cunning plan to offload a whole lot of paperwork on me? I thought we decided that I was quite happy being a humble sales associate but with a rental dress side hustle.'

Phoebe allowed herself one, and only one, eye-roll. 'Even when you stepped up for more responsibility, I don't remember you going near any paperwork. But you are a people person . . .'

'You always say that like it's a bad thing . . .' Sophy said with a grin.

It wasn't necessarily a good thing either. 'So I think your talents are better suited to running a Monday morning meeting because I'll just end up telling Anita off for having an attitude.'

Anita definitely had an attitude that morning. There was much huffing and puffing from her when Sophy asked everyone to gather round the pink sofas. A lot of sighing as Sophy said that as they were now in their busiest period of the year, customers could only take three dresses into the changing room at a time.

'Cress, could you make some signs? You do have lovely handwriting and a great selection of glitter pens.'

'I don't think glitter pens have enough gravitas for that kind of notice,' Cress said after giving it some thought. 'But I'm happy to use a more suitable sort of pen.'

'Oh God, how much longer is this going to take?' Anita groaned from her prone position on one of the sofas.

Phoebe suspected that she was hungover but refrained from threatening Anita with a breathalyser kit. (There had been an occasion when Anita came into work positively reeking of stale alcohol fumes and Phoebe had seriously considered Amazon Priming a breathalyser device.)

It wasn't one of Mildred's sayings, not at all, but supposedly you caught more flies with honey than with vinegar. Monday morning Anita was like a very annoying, very buzzy fly.

Sophy was winding things up now by suggesting that they put the kettle on, which was the perfect moment to hold up her Tupperware container. 'I have cake, brownies and some very nice shortbread if anyone needs a pick-me-up,' she said.

They all turned to look at her with varying degrees of suspicion.

'Have you poisoned them?' Anita asked.

'No, because that would be illegal and also completely traceable,' Phoebe said evenly.

'But you don't eat cake or biscuits,' Bea piped up. 'No carbs before something or other . . .'

'Which is why I'm sharing them out,' Phoebe explained with great patience. 'I ate two slices of cake yesterday and God knows how many brownies and I swear I had trouble getting my zip up this morning.'

'Nonsense,' Cress said, running a professional eye over Phoebe's figure. 'You look exactly the same as you usually do. It's more likely that your zip has got stiff with age. Vintage zips do that. I'll have a look at it later if you like,' she offered. 'But first yes, to cake. Always.'

It was the friendliest interaction Phoebe had had with Cress ever since their falling-out. Two brownies later, and even Anita had perked up, though Phoebe had to remind her twice to wash her hands before she touched any of the dresses.

Birdy's baked goods set a sweet tone for the week. Phoebe wasn't going to make cake a regular Monday morning feature but she'd much rather have a happy staff than a staff who were hoping for her early death.

On the surface, life was good. Business was brisk. Her colleagues were pleasant towards her. The weather was getting colder, which meant Phoebe could choose a different coat from her vast collection every morning.

The bulk of her collection was still at Freddy's flat, along with a good half of her dresses and also her very expensive GHD straighteners. At some point, they were going to have to have a painful and very unpleasant conversation about Phoebe moving her stuff out. Which wouldn't be half as painful and unpleasant as having to go round to Freddy's flat and remove all traces of herself. Like she'd never been there at all.

There were a lot of traces. Not just her clothes. Her *stuff*. But all the memories too. Much harder to get a man with a van to deal with them.

On a more practical note, Phoebe was sure that some of the dresses stored at Freddy's place were third-tier dresses (in her own personal dress ratings system, these were dresses that she hadn't worn in at least two years) that she might be prepared to part with and sell to the shop. They needed all the dresses that they could get their hands on.

It was almost halfway through November and they were deep, *deep*, into party season. They couldn't keep the dresses on the rails. So much so that Phoebe had made an executive decision to designate more dresses for rental. To her credit, Sophy hadn't even looked that smug about it.

Phoebe had also rung round every supplier she knew to source more dresses. After work the night before, she and Marianne (who was having the same problem at her little Kentish Town shop) had gone all the way to Loughton to visit the lock-up of Handsy Harry, a vintage dealer they knew. They'd had to take Claude with them for protection; there was a good reason why Harry had been given that nickname.

In the past, Freddy had always chaperoned Phoebe's visits but she hadn't felt comfortable asking him, even if it was official shop business. It was odd that a few weeks ago, even the thought of Freddy made her spirits lift and now the thought of him gave her a sinking feeling.

Even the dresses she'd selected from the lock-up couldn't raise her mood, though Harry had been holding on to a whole selection of dead-stock Chelsea Girl dresses from the 1960s and 1970s.

Phoebe was in the basement sorting through her selection, all of which would have to be sent out to be professionally cleaned before they could have them in the shop, when Coco Chanel who'd been asleep in her basket, in front of the heater, lifted her head, her ears twitching.

A second later, Phoebe heard the door open then a tread on the stairs. 'Are we still super busy?' she called out. 'I can come upstairs but I don't want anyone taking pictures of me.'

The footsteps paused and then a familiar voice said, 'All right, Kate Moss,' and Freddy's legs came into view, then the rest of him.

'I didn't mean it like that,' Phoebe said. 'It's quite hard to know who's here to buy a dress and who's here to shove their phone in my face and hope it will get a reaction out of me. Yes, I know it's my own fault,' she added before Freddy could get on her case about all that again.

She gave her full attention to a John Bates for Jean Varon turquoise chiffon 1970s vintage one-shouldered dress, which was giving Studio 54 vibes, so she wouldn't have to look at Freddy who'd made a beeline for Coco Chanel anyway. Out of the corner of her eye, she saw him scoop her up so he could bury his face in her neck.

They'd always agreed that Coco Chanel, especially when she'd been baking in the sun or in front of an artificial heat source, smelt delicious. Now, it seemed, it was still one of the few things that they could agree on.

'I didn't come here for an argument but we need to talk,' Freddy said grimly, which was at odds with the way he was cradling Coco in his arms like she was a little baby.

'Oh God.' Instantly Phoebe's mind was racing with possibilities each one more terrible than the last. 'Are takings down now instead of up? Actually I was going to get Bea to ask you if we could open late Wednesday through to Saturdays and maybe open on Sundays too? Just until Christmas.'

'That sounds like a good idea. I'm sure we could pay some overtime and offer days off in lieu,' Freddy said but he didn't sound very enthusiastic about Phoebe's plans to maximise their profits, which sent her deeper into panic mode.

'Are we going to have to close? Are you going to sack me? That's not fair! I've been making a real effort, not that you've been around to appreciate it, and you probably wouldn't even if you were because you're always so determined to think the worst of me.'

'Phoebe!' Freddy's voice and the way he looked at her were both sharp. 'It's nothing to do with work. And I don't always think the worst of you.'

It very much felt that way. 'You haven't been on my side for a very long time,' she said flatly.

'You make it very hard to do that sometimes, Pheebs, and after all these years I still don't know why, because you never let me get that close.' Freddy's voice was even flatter.

'I did let you get close,' Phoebe insisted at a quieter volume.

Freddy shook his head. 'Physically, yes. Emotionally, never.' He looked down at Coco in his arms. 'I didn't come around to talk about this.'

'Then why did you come round?' Once again, the possibilities were endless and none of them were good. 'Are you seeing someone else? Already?'

The thought of finding someone new hadn't even occurred to her. Before, even during, and now especially after Freddy, Phoebe considered herself to be one of those people who weren't really meant to be in a relationship.

'What? No! That's the very last thing on my mind.' Freddy looked at Phoebe like she'd dyed her hair pink or was wearing athleisure wear. 'Goes to show how well you know me.'

'I think, maybe, neither of us really truly knew the other one,' Phoebe said. If she sounded sad about it then that's because she was.

'Maybe,' Freddy conceded. 'But please stop guessing why I'm here because even though your imagination is quite frightening, you're not even close.'

'Go on then. Don't keep me in suspense.' Phoebe leaned back against the table and waited for Freddy to deliver the bad news. It was definitely bad. He wasn't giving good news energy.

'I had an email from Stefan, the guy who organises the vintage balls at the Bloomsbury Ballroom.' Freddy raised his eyebrows as Phoebe opened her mouth. 'No, it's not being cancelled. Yes, we booked tickets ages ago. It's not that.'

Phoebe was intrigued but still had a feeling of foreboding given Freddy's unexpected visit and his grave manner. 'What is it then?'

He looked down at Coco Chanel who was now happily asleep in his arms and snoring like a chainsaw. 'Promise you won't get mad,' he muttered, refusing to meet Phoebe's eyes, which had widened in alarm. 'Oh God, you're going to get mad.'

'I'm going to get mad if you don't just come out with it for goodness' sake,' Phoebe snapped because her last nerve had been well and truly worked.

'It's Coco. Stefan says that she's banned from attending the Christmas ball,' Freddy said quickly as Phoebe gasped in shock, outrage and a bitter sense of betrayal.

'He said what?' Her ears had to be deceiving her. 'Coco *always* attends the vintage balls. She's like the guest of honour.' She sat down heavily on the stool she'd only just vacated as she was reeling too much to stay upright. 'Stefan said that? But he *adores* Coco. Is this a change in venue policy? Who's the manager? I'm going to speak to the manager!'

Considering that Phoebe kicking off was the reason why she and Freddy were no longer she and Freddy, and even though this was prime kicking off, he wasn't getting that flinty look in his eyes and tightening his lips. Instead he came to sit on the stool next to hers.

'There was an incident at the last ball,' he revealed somewhat unwillingly. 'Consensus of opinion is that the culprit was this young lady.' He shut his eyes, probably so he wouldn't have to see Phoebe's face scrunched up in fury. 'After the summer ball, they found a . . .'

'What could they have possibly found and blamed my precious Coco for?' Phoebe demanded.

'They found a turd . . .'

'A what?'

'You heard me the first time,' Freddy muttered, his head hanging low. 'Under a table and Stefan said that it could only have been Coco.'

'Coco would *never!*' Phoebe all but exploded. Freddy put a hand on her arm as if that might calm her down, and it took all she had not to angrily shake him off. 'Were there actual witnesses?'

'Well, no . . .'

'So, I don't know how he can accuse Coco of such a thing. She's here all day, even in the atelier with its thick carpet and expensive dresses, and she's never disgraced herself like that. Not once in all these years.'

'I know but what other explanation could there be?' Freddy asked because it turned out he wasn't on Coco's side either.

'People have too much to drink and then they turn into animals,' Phoebe said immediately because that was a far more likely explanation instead of blaming it on an actual animal who was beautifully house-trained. 'Fine! If Coco isn't going, then I'm not going either.'

'Pheebs, you love the vintage balls,' Freddy reminded her. 'All the staff will be going so I think you need to go too. For shop morale.'

It was true that Phoebe enjoyed the biannual vintage balls, one just before summer and one just before Christmas. It was an excuse to get properly dressed up in the kind of looks you could only really bust out for a formal occasion. Unless you were Marianne's friend Gretel who would happily wear a ball gown to her office job in an insurance broker's. Still, Phoebe did have a lot of occasion dresses and not that many occasions to wear them to.

Plus, Freddy always agreed to pay for a glam squad for the staff, Phoebe's friends Vivienne and Roy, who specialised in retro make-up and hair looks.

It was always the best night out. They'd do predrinks and an after party then finally end up getting a kebab and chips at an all-night place on Southampton Row. But maybe the best part of the best night out was getting to dance with Freddy in a proper ballroom swagged out in red velvet and gold, the lights from the mirror balls shimmering in time to the fifty-piece orchestra. And wedged in between them, as always, was Coco.

'If Coco isn't welcome then I won't feel welcome either,' Phoebe said because although she wasn't officially licensed, in a lot of ways Coco was her emotional support animal. Just as Phoebe was her emotional support human. Which was another reason why Phoebe would have to bow out. 'You know she has separation anxiety, Freddy. I can hardly leave her on her own.'

'Can't you leave her with a friend?' Freddy asked. Even though they were no longer a secret us, Phoebe appreciated that Freddy was trying to find a solution to this problem so maybe he was still a little bit on Coco's side after all.

'But all my friends will be going to the ball.'

'What about your neighbours? The tie-dye hippies or the ones who grow carrots on the roof of *The Sheila*?' Freddy frowned. 'Are they the same neighbours? I get confused.'

'Two entirely different sets of neighbours but Coco hates Gunther because he always makes piggy noises when he sees her.' Which was why Phoebe also low-key hated Gunther. 'And on the other side, Sean is allergic.'

'Maybe their partners, the one who doesn't make piggy noises or the one who isn't allergic, could look in on Coco a couple of times,' Freddy suggested. 'You do leave her on her own occasionally. If you have to go to the big supermarket or the doctor's or something.'

'I don't know.' Phoebe was genuinely torn. Despite everything that had happened, maybe even because of it, she wanted to make some good memories with the people she worked with, and she still wanted to dance with Freddy and maybe see that soft, tender look he used to get when they danced together. 'Maybe. Maybe not, because if I turn up without Coco then it's like I believe Stefan's version of events even though in my heart of hearts I know that Coco would never do that.'

They sat there in a considered silence for a few moments punctured only by Coco's snoring, the dog blissfully unaware of the baseless accusations that had been flung her way. Then Freddy came to with a little start almost as if he'd drifted off.

'Anyway I should probably go now.' He handed Coco over gently to Phoebe as if she were a precious newborn. 'Thank you for not shooting the messenger.'

'It's not your fault,' Phoebe said, standing up so she could put Coco down in her basket. 'Although I will be having words, quite a lot of words, with Stefan the next time I see him.'

Freddy grinned. 'Yeah, he mentioned that in the email too. Something about hoping that the stab vest will fit underneath his best bib and tucker.'

'Stabbing's too good for him,' Phoebe muttered darkly, then caught Freddy's sudden panicked look. 'That was a joke! Kind of.'

'Glad to hear it.' Freddy was already halfway up the stairs but then he paused. 'The way you love Coco, it's always been one of my favourite things about you.'

Phoebe shrugged. 'I don't do love, Freddy. You know that. But when I adopted Coco, I made a commitment to always be there for her. To be all in. And yes, I do know that maybe I indulge her and spoil her a little bit too much but it's nothing less than she deserves. After everything she's been through in her life, she deserves to be absolutely spoilt rotten.'

'Impossible,' Freddy muttered, but before Phoebe could ask him what he meant, he was gone, disappearing up the steps so quickly that he stumbled over the top one and swore under his breath, which made Phoebe glad that she'd be giving the weekly trip to The Hat and Fan on Friday a miss.

It was painful not to see Freddy but it was more painful to see him and to obsess over every last thing he'd said, every micro-expression which had flitted across his face.

Maybe given time they could go back to being people who worked together in a friendly fashion but not right now. It was too hard.

Everyone, even Anita, begged Phoebe to come to the pub, but she was happy to head home, change out of her work clothes then cut through the back streets to Kentish Town where Marianne and Claude were having their annual late-night-opening party for friends and valued customers.

If they spent more than a hundred pounds then Claude, whose tattoo parlour was on the first floor, would give them a free tattoo. 'Nothing fancy. Not a replica of the Sistine Chapel on their backs, but their loved ones' initials in a heart or something,' he'd said when Phoebe, a little aghast, asked for more details.

Not that Phoebe would qualify for a free tattoo. 'I'm not buying anything,' she said to Marianne. 'Please don't let me buy anything, but I'm happy to help out if you need it.' She looked around at the cheerfully eclectic rails of clothes. Leather jackets mixed in with leopard-print coats. Paisley hippy shirts hanging next to mod-inspired dresses. 'Honestly, Maz, have you never thought about arranging the stock by genre and era? It would make your life and your customers' lives so much easier.'

'And not colour?' Marianne asked with an arch of one already exquisitely arched eyebrow.

'The thought of having to arrange all this by colour makes me want to cry,' Phoebe admitted, sweeping out her hand to encompass the cluttered, cramped little shop.

'Which is why, although you're a dear pal, if we worked together, we'd end up murdering each other,' Marianne said, putting an arm around Phoebe's shoulder to guide her over to the counter where a makeshift bar had been set up. 'Gin and tonic? I'm afraid it's just bog-standard tonic and there's not even lemons, let alone limes.'

'Is there bottled water for Coco?' Phoebe asked. If there wasn't, she'd nip to the newsagent a few doors down to get a bottle of Evian and hope it was chilled.

'Of course! Nothing but the best for Mademoiselle Chanel.' Marianne looked over Phoebe's shoulder to where a noisy crowd of people had just come in. 'Oh, there's Nina. Grab a drink, then come over and say hello.'

It was good to be surrounded by friends. Of course everyone wanted to know how Phoebe had managed to go viral three times over the last month but when she explained that there had been crimes against dresses, they seemed to understand. Or maybe because they were friends, they understood Phoebe.

Marianne's shop, Retro-a-go-go, was a much more rough-and-ready affair than The Vintage Dress Shop with that smell of vintage clothing, musty and a little *unfresh*, which Phoebe had sworn would never be smelt on her premises. Her clientele were a more rock 'n' roll crowd too; both men and women rocking quiffs and a lot of tattoos. Most of the stock focused on the fifties, sixties and seventies. She even sold some reproduction lines. It was something she and Phoebe had agreed to disagree on.

Inevitably, Phoebe did end up buying a few things. Marianne had recently made her annual pilgrimage to Palm Springs in California, the vintage capital of America, and had returned with some darling novelty items, including a set of brooches that celebrated the Las Vegas of yesteryear when the Rat Pack had ruled the Strip. A tiny cocktail glass with a swizzle stick. A miniature pair of dice. A roulette wheel. And, of course, the Welcome to Las Vegas sign. Perfect presents for the shop staff.

By then, although she didn't usually drink that much, Phoebe was on her third gin on an empty stomach so when she found the perfect shirt for Freddy, a 1960s Italian knit polo shirt that was almost the same shade of blue as his eyes, she had to have it. Which took her over the hundred-pound mark and somehow, the details were a little hazy by then, Phoebe found herself in Claude's chair about to get tattooed for the first time.

'Are you sure, Phoebe?' Claude asked, his tattoo gun poised. 'This is very unlike you.'

'Maybe I'm not like people think I am,' Phoebe said. 'Maybe I have hidden depths. Like the iceberg that hit the *Titanic*.'

'You're not an iceberg, Pheebs, you just want people to think that you are,' Marianne said, because Phoebe deciding to get a tattoo warranted her leaving the shop to witness this strange event. 'Also, how much have you had to drink?'

'Enough but not enough to have lost my senses,' Phoebe said, very carefully pressing a tip of one finger to the tip of her nose to prove that she still had perfect hand-to-eye coordination. 'Come on! Tattoo me.'

Chapter Twenty-Four

'And now it hurts like hell,' she admitted to Bea some twelve hours later as she sat in the back office of The Vintage Dress Shop. 'My head hurts too. All of me hurts. Just between you and me, I now have a greater understanding of why Anita prostrates herself on one of the pink sofas when she has a hangover. I feel utterly wretched.'

'Never mind you feeling wretched,' Bea said rather crushingly, 'can we rewind to the part where you got a tattoo. You got a tattoo! A tattoo of what? Let me see!'

Phoebe lifted up her arm, even that took a superhuman effort, and carefully unbuttoned her cuff and rolled back the sleeve of her dress to reveal her bandaged wrist. 'I can't take this off until tonight. The thing is I wasn't drunk when I got the tattoo, not really, but I may have had quite a lot to drink *after*.'

It was somewhat hazy but the gin and tonic had quickly run out and Phoebe had made the cardinal error of mixing grape and grain (or grape and sloe berries) and had switched to red wine. The devil's drink.

'But what did you get tattooed on you?'

'My favourite Chanel quote,' Phoebe said, pressing the tips of her fingers to her aching, pounding temples.

'Which is . . . ?' Bea prompted.

'Keep your heels, head and standards high,' Phoebe recited although she couldn't be one hundred per cent sure that those words were tattooed on her arm.

She could remember both Claude and Marianne, then Nina, questioning her decision but when Phoebe's mind was made up about something, then it was very hard to convince her otherwise. Really, it was the story of her life.

By lunchtime, the shop was frantic and there was no way that Phoebe could leave Sophy, Bea and Anita to manage the scrum.

At least she was feeling a lot better after Anita had insisted that Phoebe try her patented hangover cure. Bacon and fried egg on a toasted everything bagel, a can of full-fat Coke and a family-sized bag of Haribo Starmix. 'Every time you feel yourself flagging during the afternoon, just down another handful,' Anita had advised.

'You're enjoying this far too much,' Phoebe told her but she didn't have the energy to get annoyed about it.

'I'm absolutely loving it.' Anita didn't even try to hide her delight. 'It's like my best day ever.'

Now, dosed up on Starmix, Phoebe was on the till – even though her usually elegant fingers were like stabby sausages – where she'd have the least amount of contact with the majority of customers but a vantage point to supervise her team.

Not that she really had the emotional bandwidth to tell Bea that emerald green and Kelly green were not the same green. Or to signal to Anita that a customer had been in one of the changing cubicles beyond her allotted time. Or even to tell Sophy that she was going to get a written warning if she played her 'Christmas Choons' playlist one more time.

'Anita was right, this is the best day ever,' Sophy cheerfully remarked as Phoebe slumped against the till. 'You should drink more often.'

'I'm never drinking again. Not a drop will pass my lips,' Phoebe vowed, lifting her head as a customer approached the counter.

She was a young woman, not much older than twenty, with her hair in milkmaid braids and wearing an appropriately milkmaid-ish dress which wasn't vintage Laura Ashley but was a pretty good copy of a classic Laura Ashley design. 'Sorry to bother you,' she said to Phoebe. 'But . . .'

'If you're into that seventies boho, country girl chic then we've got a pretty Bus Stop maxi dress on the black rail.' Phoebe gestured in the vague direction of said rail.

'Absolute queen!' the girl said rather confusingly, then turned around so her back was to Phoebe and leaned in. 'Can I get a selfie?'

Phoebe didn't have time to refuse before the selfie was taken and the girl had been swallowed up by the crowd of shoppers.

Then three customers later as a woman paid for a 1940s Bakelite bangle and necklace set, which Phoebe wrapped up in their trademark Wedgwood blue tissue paper, she took the parcel with a grateful smile and said, 'Keep up the good work!'

There were more requests for selfies, which Phoebe graciously granted with a gritted smile and there were also a lot of approving smiles and comments, variations on 'Good for you,' and 'Don't let the haters win.'

'Am I still recovering from last night or are people acting weird?' she asked Sophy but Sophy was too busy on the shop floor to really notice.

Phoebe was pleased to escape to the relative calm of the atelier to attend to the one bridal party who were booked in. Then she had a walk-in, a beautiful and beautifully turned-out young woman, dressed in genuine vintage Chanel and her much older gentleman companion. 'Hard to tell if it's her daddy or her sugar daddy,' Phoebe hissed at Cress en route to the designer room to pull some dresses for her. 'Not that I like to judge.'

'You love to judge,' Cress pointed out as she got up from her sewing machine to have a discreet gawp at the couple who were now canoodling in a way that suggested that they weren't blood relatives.

It was another, very lucrative hour later before Phoebe took the spiral staircase, one hand gripping the banister very carefully, though usually she careered down it in her four-inch heels without a moment's thought, back down to the main shop.

There was still a crowd but it had thinned out and it was only an hour until they shut. Phoebe would have given anything to have a long, soaky bath that evening but she'd have to make do with a quick shower.

Things between her and Freddy were civil enough but her days of treating his flat like her second home were long gone.

'I can't wait for today to be over,' she muttered to Bea who was now on the till but mostly glued to her phone. 'You know, Bea, I am feeling recovered enough to remind you of how I feel about staff being on their phones during work hours.'

'Yup,' Bea murmured, eyes still fixed to the screen. 'It is work. Looking at our socials.' She raised her head to stare at Phoebe as if she should be behind glass at a museum. 'I can't quite believe it but you're going viral again. There's even a hashtag.'

Phoebe racked her brains for any heated interactions she'd had recently with customers who had conducted themselves in an unacceptable manner. 'I've been on my best behaviour for at least a week. Maybe two,' she huffed. 'Or is it some archival footage of me being justifiably annoyed when someone has come in to ask if we sell jeans?'

'Neither.' Bea put down her phone as a customer approached and, right on cue, came the Saturday final push. A sudden wave of shoppers in a panic because they had parties to go to and even if their own wardrobes were full to bursting, they still had nothing to wear. Or they longed for the transformative powers of a new dress. Even better if it was a new old dress with its very own particular brand of magic.

Phoebe didn't have time to ponder the reasons for her latest internet cancellation. Instead she was caught up in the last-minute drama of a woman rushing in on a mission to buy the perfect dress because she'd had reliable intel that her boyfriend planned to propose to her that night.

Ten minutes after they should have closed, Phoebe sent her on her way with a midnight blue satin 1950s halter dress, lace overlaying the full skirt, and a matching bolero jacket. 'Even if he hadn't been planning to propose, he will once he sees you in that dress,' Phoebe told her.

Then she shut the door firmly behind the grateful woman, locked it, turned the sign to closed and leaned back with a tiny exhausted sigh. 'Surely this has been the longest day since records began,' she enquired plaintively of the other women. Sophy was cashing up, Bea was returning discarded dresses to the rails, Anita was doing her usual very desultory job with Henry the Hoover. 'I long to slip my shoes off but I don't think I'll be able to get them back on again.'

Then Phoebe flopped down on one of the pink sofas with such force that Anita's mouth dropped open and she gasped. 'Those sofas are for customer use only, young lady,' she said in a prim voice, which if it was meant to be an impersonation of Phoebe wasn't a very good one.

'I'm sorry, Anita, I'm just too tired to rise to the bait,' Phoebe said sorrowfully then she swung her legs up so she was lying full length, eyes closed, and only stirred when Coco Chanel bustled down the stairs, followed by Cress, and hoisted herself up and then onto Phoebe's stomach. 'CC, you weigh a ton.'

'Now she's daring to criticise Coco Chanel!' And Anita was daring to poke the bear again.

Phoebe opened one eye. 'I might have to sleep here tonight. I'm unable to move.'

'Budge up, drama queen!' Sophy shoved Phoebe's legs to one side so she could sit down. 'Did you forget that you've gone viral again?'

'Don't remind me,' Phoebe groaned, putting her hands over her eyes.

'Oh, it's the good kind of viral,' Cress said, as she put her coat on.

'Surely there's no such thing unless it's a cute video of a dog on a surfboard?' Phoebe pondered aloud as Sophy took one of the hands that she had over her eyes and put her phone in it.

'Watch this!' Sophy ordered and to think that people said that she, Phoebe, was bossy.

This was clearly one of the many parts of the TikTok video Rosie Roberts had posted the other day because there was Phoebe, red in the face, as she said in a very shrill voice, 'These dresses aren't boring. These dresses represent so many different women's lives. They capture and preserve a magic moment in time. Their hopes and dreams on the day that they wore their wedding dress.'

Some appropriately rousing music started playing to accompany Phoebe's stirring speech. 'These women all had something in common, a shared sisterhood, as they slipped on a dress that they'd chosen so carefully. Sometimes a dress they'd scrimped and saved for. A dress that made them feel beautiful and special and like the best version of themselves because that's the alchemy of a good dress.'

Phoebe was all ready to thrust the phone away when the clip cut away to a head and shoulders shot of Birdy saying, 'I stand with Phoebe from The Vintage Dress Shop. You don't just own a vintage dress. You own a story, a piece of someone else's history and you have to respect that.'

There was a sudden unexpected prickle in Phoebe's eyes as if she might start crying. 'Well, that's very sweet of Birdy,' she mumbled.

'Not just Birdy,' Bea said, coming to stand over Phoebe so she could thrust her phone in Phoebe's face too. 'There's your mate, Marianne.'

It was the same clip of Phoebe with the speechifying and the anthemic music, then there was Marianne looking fierce as ever with her bright red hair freshly pin-curled and not even seeming the least bit hungover from last night. 'I abso-bloody-lutely stand with Phoebe and The Vintage Dress Shop. Respect the vintage, kids.'

'That's called a stitch,' Bea said knowledgably. 'When you combine someone's video with your own reaction video. Did we cover that in the tutorial I gave you the other week?'

They hadn't. Phoebe sat up. 'I'm glad that Birdy and Marianne have stuck up for me but two people isn't going viral. Even I know that.'

'But it's not just them,' Bea said, thrusting the phone at Phoebe again.

'You nearly had my eye out, Bea!'

'Sorry, but I'm very excited about this. There's two hashtags, #IStandWithPhoebe and #IStandWithTheVintageDressShop and our Instagram and TikTok follows are going through the roof. All the vintage sellers and vintage girlies are rallying around,' she said. 'Not just our vintage girlies, but people we don't even know from all over the place. America, France, Germany, Brazil . . .'

'Even Clive,' Sophy interrupted, her voice practically vibrating.

Phoebe frowned. 'Who?'

Sophy hissed in annoyance. 'My lovely Clive from Clive's Closet where I worked in Sydney.'

'Oh, that Clive,' Phoebe said in an offhand way because she was still feeling very fragile and if Sophy started wanging on about her glory days at Clive's Closet, then it would finish her off. 'Well, I appreciate the solidarity.'

She sat bookended by Sophy and Bea for a few more minutes to watch some more stitched videos, until Anita clapped her hands. 'Please!' she said with annoyance. 'It's half an hour since we closed. What the hell are we still doing here?'

'Yes, can we go now, please?' Cress asked from where she was standing by the door still with her coat on.

'You're free to go,' Phoebe said, as she took Coco off her lap and placed her on the floor. 'You didn't need to stay.'

'Oh, I'm having a sleepover at Sophy and Anita's,' Cress said, gesturing to the very laden tote bag slung over her shoulder.

'We still ordering a curry?' Anita asked as Phoebe stood up and winced as her feet protested. ''Cause I'm feeling more in the mood for some Korean fried chicken.'

'Are you not seeing Miles or Charles?' Phoebe asked. The thought of Korean fried chicken was quite appetising. She'd have to look on Deliveroo to see if there was somewhere close that delivered though the drivers never wanted to come down to the canal path so Phoebe always had to loiter on the street and wait for them.

'We are strong independent women who don't see our boyfriends every night,' Sophy said from the depths of the back of the shop where she was collecting her bag and coat.

'Also, Miles has gone up to Glasgow to do some location scouting and Charles is staying overnight in Dorset as he has an estate sale first thing tomorrow,' Cress explained. She smiled faintly. 'But yes, also we are strong independent women and Anita is between partners . . .'

'Is it my fault that the men of London can't recognise a good thing when they see it?' Anita asked as she did a little shimmy.

'While I am terminally single,' Bea complained. 'I can't even remember the last time I swiped right.'

'What about you, Pheebs? Are you seeing anyone?' Anita asked, her eyes alight not with mischief this time but with curiosity. 'Your life outside the shop is a bit of a mystery.'

Which was just how Phoebe liked it. For one agonising moment, her eyes met Cress, who was the only one who'd known about her and Freddy back when there was something to know. Usually Cress told Sophy everything and since their argument, Phoebe wasn't sure if Cress had kept the secret that she'd begged her to keep. Cress shook her head and rolled her eyes a little as if to say that she was offended that Phoebe would even think that she'd betrayed that confidence.

'There's nothing much to tell,' Phoebe said with a forced sort of lightness. 'No man. I just go home and catalogue my vintage dresses.'

'I've asked once, I'm going to ask again,' Anita said as Sophy emerged with not just her coat but Phoebe's too and even Coco's. Phoebe shot her a grateful smile. 'Your house is on fire. You can only rescue one thing. Is it Coco Chanel or your favourite vintage dress?'

Her favourite vintage dress was worth a good couple of thousand pounds but to Phoebe it was much more precious than just its monetary value. And maybe Coco Chanel might be able to rescue herself . . .

'Seriously, Phoebe, do you have to think about it? Of course it would be Coco,' Bea exclaimed. 'By the way, are you planning to set the alarm before we leave?'

'Oh God, yes! Thank you for reminding me.'

By the time Phoebe had set the alarm, she'd have expected the four women to have dispersed, but they were standing outside the shop in a huddle, talking in fierce whispers.

'Haven't you got homes to go to?' Phoebe said with the same forced jollity from before.

238

Sophy separated herself from the huddle and with a swift glance back at her three colleagues tilted her chin in Phoebe's direction. 'Bea's coming back to ours too.' She paused. 'If you haven't got plans then you and Coco are welcome to join us.'

Immediately, reflexively, Phoebe opened her mouth to decline the invitation but then she shut it.

There was no good reason not to accept. Unless they were just asking her to be polite?

Except Anita never did anything just to be polite and what was the alternative anyway?

She'd go home, still mildly hungover, and she wouldn't eat delicious fried chicken but brood and be miserable. It was no way to spend a Saturday evening.

So, Phoebe nodded. 'Yes, Coco and I would love to.'

Chapter Twenty-Five

Anita and Sophy lived in Hackney. During the walk up Chalk Farm Road to catch the bus from Camden, Phoebe almost cried off. Her shoes were pinching and simply putting one foot in front of the other was agony.

Then Bea tucked an arm into hers, which helped, and as soon as they finally reached the stop, the bus came and they were able to squeeze on.

It wasn't until they went past the stop where Phoebe had got off a week before to visit Birdy that she noticed that Anita and Sophy were getting a bit twitchy. They were sitting behind Phoebe and Bea and having a fierce whispered conversation until eventually Sophy tapped Phoebe on the shoulder.

Phoebe turned around, half dreading being given her marching orders, which actually would have been very rude. 'Pheebs, Anita and I have another flatmate,' Sophy announced with some trepidation. 'Please, don't be funny about this.'

'You're allowed to have other flatmates,' Phoebe said exasperatedly because really, she wasn't *that* bad. 'There's no law against it.'

'He works in a vintage shop in Shoreditch,' Anita revealed.

'Antik,' Phoebe said with a very slight lip curl because it was a ridiculous name and also . . .

'That's the one and he says that you've had several run-ins with his boss before,' Anita said. 'But that's not George's fault.'

'Of course it isn't,' Phoebe agreed.

They all settled back in their seats but Phoebe couldn't help herself.

'Unless George also sews fake Biba labels into nasty 1990s dresses that don't even look vintage,' she said and felt Sophy's huff of annoyance ghost the back of her neck. 'Sorry, I just had to get that off my chest.'

It turned out that George, an absolutely beautiful young man with the flawless complexion of a person with a very rigorous skin regime, was thrilled to meet Phoebe.

'The woman, the phenomenon, the legend,' he breathed, slinking down the stairs like a catwalk model, before Phoebe had even taken her coat off. 'Big fan of your work. But hear you're not a big fan of my boss Katy.'

'Do you want me to be polite because I'm a guest in your house or do you want me to be honest?' Phoebe asked.

'The latter. Always the latter,' George said with a wicked smile and though it had taken Phoebe three goes before she'd warmed to Birdy, when it came to George, she suspected that they were going to be instant friends.

'She's a monster,' Phoebe said baldly as George put a hand to his heart and gasped in delight. 'I don't know how you put up with her.'

'You can't say that about people!' Sophy tutted, pushing past Phoebe in the narrow hall. 'Shall we order some food? I'm starving.'

'But she really is a monster,' George insisted, putting his arm around Phoebe's shoulder to lead her into a small living room, its furniture IKEA standard issue and its walls painted renters' magnolia but livened up with vintage film posters and brightly coloured cushions. 'FYI, Sophy and Anita too, I'm very cross with you for keeping me and Phoebe apart all this time. I've been begging for an introduction.'

Anita made the sign of a cross. 'Oh God, what have we done?'

'It's like matter and anti-matter colliding,' Sophy added. 'I don't know how we've managed to keep them apart this long.'

Neither did Phoebe or why, because George was utterly charming and they didn't stop talking, only pausing the conversation briefly to eat the promised Korean fried chicken with a kimchi mac and cheese on the side.

As both of them had worked in vintage shops for pretty much their entire careers, they had loads of mutuals in common. They'd been to the same vintage all-dayers, must surely have shared the same air at Glorious Goodwood and had both briefly dated a rockabilly called Nelson who'd very quickly proved himself to be 'a total wrong 'un', Phoebe remembered darkly.

'The wrongest wrong 'un,' George echoed until Anita said that they were monopolising the conversation. So they threw it open to the floor where, apart from Cress who'd spent most of her career repairing ecclesiastical robes and hassocks at an obscure religious museum in Chelsea, they'd all worked in retail and had the war stories to prove it.

Phoebe couldn't remember the last time she'd laughed so hard, clutching her ribs, tears streaming down her face, as Sophy described disturbing a couple in a changing room who weren't just having sex but also livestreaming it to their OnlyFans.

After dinner, talk turned to the Vintage Christmas Ball, which was only a week away, on the first Saturday in December. In the past, Phoebe had tried to impose a first-look policy where she'd yay or nay her staff's outfit choices as they were ambassadors for The Vintage Dress Shop and the eyes of the vintage community, and everyone that Phoebe knew, would be on them. It had never gone down that well.

Now Anita treated Phoebe to a winsome smile. 'I have three different options. I need your opinion.'

'You've never wanted my opinion before,' Phoebe pointed out but Anita just shrugged.

'That was because you issued a decree. This would be more of a freeform discussion.' Anita was already on her feet and heading towards the door, but she stopped to shoot a sly smile at Phoebe. 'I mean, we both know that you're dying to have a good nose in my wardrobe.'

It was the absolute truth. Despite Anita's many other failings, she was always impeccably turned out and had at least three black shop dresses that Phoebe coveted.

Anita's room was a good size. 'I've lived here the longest so of course I've got the biggest bedroom.' But apart from the bed, every available inch of space, including built-in wardrobes, two chests of drawers and a free-standing clothes rail were given over to her huge collection of vintage dresses, separates, coats (the coats!) and accessories.

Phoebe sat down on the bed, Coco Chanel in her arms and took it all in. It was a lot. And very, very messy. 'Honestly, Anita, I'd have expected you to be better organised and *wire* hangers? Surely I've brought you up better than that, haven't I?'

Because they weren't at work and also because Phoebe was too full of carbs, the words lacked her usual bite.

'Every year I promise myself that I'm going to do a winter and summer edit, then store what I'm not wearing, and every year I can't be arsed,' Anita admitted, flopping down on the bed next to Phoebe, not even caring that she was crushing a 1950s red taffeta ball gown.

'Well, let's do it now. It won't take that long,' Phoebe said eagerly.

'But it's Saturday night!' Anita promised as Bea also squeezed into the room, but Phoebe wasn't going to put up with such feeble excuses and between the three of them it didn't take that long to sort Anita's clothes into seasons.

Then to sort them further into keepers, donators and 'fit for nothing but the knacker's yard,' said Cress who'd also come in to help. Phoebe was glad that, for once, it wasn't her saying the hard things.

'What do you do to your clothes, Anita? What have you done to this blouse?'

Cress held up the blouse in question. In a former life it had been a pretty pintucked, short-sleeved white cotton blouse with sweet pink piping on the cuffs and collars. In this life it was a wrinkled rag with torn armholes and missing half its buttons.

'It's my deodorant,' Anita insisted. 'I swear, it rots clothes.'

'Well, use a different one then,' Cress said sternly because in the eighteen months since she'd come to work at the shop, she'd transformed from mouse to a mouse with quite the attitude when she was riled up.

As Phoebe knew to her cost. It was all very well making new friends but she also had to maintain her existing friendships. She was still cross with Cress, or more hurt than cross, but now wasn't the time, not when Cress was sitting down next to her to scritch Coco behind her ears.

'We can send the really damaged stuff off to the charity we use,' Phoebe said because any dud stock from their suppliers or pieces that even Cress couldn't resuscitate got boxed up and shipped to an ethical textile recycling charity so it wouldn't end up as landfill. 'The clothes you're not going to wear, I'd sell. I'll have the three black dresses, which were always going to be too small for you, for the shop. Let Sophy have dibs on the other dresses for her rental thing and then, I don't know, don't you swap the dresses you're tired of with your friends?'

'Did someone say my name?' Sophy poked her head round the door. 'And what are you saying about my rental dresses?'

'It was nothing bad,' Anita said, from her cross-legged position on the floor, which was now no longer covered in a fine coating of clothes. 'Phoebe, of all people, is telling me that I should get rid of the dresses that I no longer wear.'

'Oh my God, the hangover has addled your brain,' Sophy said, squeezing her way into the room.

'My brain is far from addled,' Phoebe snapped but it was a very tame kind of snapping. 'Clothes swapping is the life-blood of the vintage community. There's no point in hoarding dresses you're never going to wear. It's not fair on the dresses. They deserve to be worn.'

'This from the woman who has point-blank refused to sell dresses to customers on occasion,' Cress said, but she said it affectionately and nudged Phoebe with an elbow.

'Only when I suspect that their intentions aren't honoura-ble,' Phoebe protested, as George was the last person on the premises to force his way into Anita's room. 'Maybe in January, when we're not so busy, we could have a little unofficial clothes swap at work.'

'A lot can happen between now and January,' Sophy said. 'In fact, come Monday morning, when you're firing on all cylinders again, you'll forget that we shared Korean fried chicken and retail horror stories.'

Was she really that much of an ogre? Phoebe wondered. Although she already knew the answer. Yes, yes she was. Prided herself on it. Because when you made yourself vul-nerable, you made yourself weak. Mildred had been quite vocal on the subject of how people would prey on your kind-ness and take advantage.

So, yes, Phoebe was nobody's fool but she liked to think that she was only an ogre during work hours. 'I'm sure come Monday morning, I won't have forgotten at all but I will be taking my managerial duties as seriously as ever,' she said.

'Too late. We've seen your softer side now,' Anita said. She levered herself upright with a groan. 'Now, let's go through my options for the ball. I was considering the red taffeta gown but is red too Christmassy? I don't want to look like I'm wearing fancy dress, though one of my other options . . . hang on . . .' she dived into her wardrobe, which was now much better organised but still, alas, had dresses hanging on wire hangers '. . . is this gold dress, which is more slinky but I'm not sure I can dance in it.'

'What's the other option?' Phoebe asked and once she'd advised Anita to wear a black strapless dress shot through with gold lurex thread, she then went through Sophy's options. Or rather it was one option: a stunning, 1930s halter-neck, bias-cut mossy green silk dress very reminiscent of the dress Keira Knightley had worn in *Atonement*.

'Charles bought it for me,' Sophy said, which wasn't a surprise because Charles had absolutely exquisite taste. 'But is it too much?'

'It's just enough,' Phoebe assured her, ignoring the pang of envy at not just the dress but that Sophy had Charles. A man who didn't just have an unerring eye for picking out vintage clothes but who seemed to adore Sophy without rhyme or reason. Although she and Sophy were on much better terms, Sophy could be annoying. Very, very annoying indeed.

Much more annoying than Phoebe and yet Phoebe had no man. Not that she wanted just any man. She wanted one particular man even though he was too intimidated to buy her vintage dresses, but he did have a knack for picking out delightful vintage pyjama sets.

Phoebe didn't even know why she was bothering to check her phone. Of course Freddy hadn't messaged her. He could manage without her very well. And she could manage without him. After all, here she was on a Saturday night, bonding

246

with her workmates. Or maybe they were her out-of-work-hours mates too.

It was hard to know. By the time they'd drunk the red wine and eaten the crisps that they'd ordered on Uber Eats and planned an ambitious charity clothes swap for the New Year, which would involve renting out a church hall, sorting out a bar and possibly a raffle, it was very late and the thought of having to put her shoes back on for the journey from Hackney to Primrose Hill made Phoebe want to cry.

Also, she'd had enough to drink that she couldn't be sure that she'd avoid detouring via Freddy's flat and begging him to take her in. To take her back, no matter how much she'd tried to harden her heart.

'It's too late to be waiting for buses and too expensive to get an Uber. You might as well stay the night,' Anita said when both Phoebe and Bea made very unenthusiastic noises about being on their way.

And so it came to pass that in a pair of Primark pyjamas borrowed from Sophy, Phoebe, Bea and Coco slept in Anita's bed while Anita slept with George ('but keep your hands to yourself, Neeta, I know what you're like') and Sophy and Cress doubled up as they'd planned to all along.

It wasn't how Phoebe had ever thought she'd spend a Saturday night but it hadn't been terrible. Not in the slightest. In fact, it had been the most fun Phoebe had had in ages.

Chapter Twenty-Six

It was only slightly awkward on Monday morning. Mostly because Phoebe had to return Sophy's trainers, which she'd borrowed the day before because drinking two nights on the trot had meant she was hungover again and couldn't do heels.

'It will be our little secret,' Sophy said. She cast her eyes to the ceiling of the back office. 'But only because I didn't have the foresight to take a picture of you yesterday morning in your tight little black dress with a pair of green Adidas Gazelles on your feet.'

'I hate you,' Phoebe told her but Sophy just laughed because Phoebe's power was no longer absolute. Her authority had been completely undermined with very little chance of ever returning.

'Actually, you don't. In fact, I think I'm growing on you,' Sophy said, which was sort of true but Phoebe just rolled her eyes.

'Stop talking nonsense and let's get the Monday morning meeting done and dusted,' she said and soon they were all gathered on the pink sofas to plan the week ahead.

The plan was much the same as ever: to sell dresses. A lot of dresses. It was now just touching December, their busiest month, and time for Phoebe to broach the subject of the shop opening late night Wednesday through Saturday and even opening on Sundays too.

There was a collective groan as Phoebe announced the extended hours. 'Yes, it's a lot of extra work but it makes sense to stay open longer. Not that the shop is in financial trouble, not at all, but there is a cost of living crisis and I'm sure all our outgoings will increase in the new year.'

'Oh my God, are our jobs in trouble?' Anita exclaimed with what seemed to be genuine panic. 'Who else would employ me?'

It was a very good question. Who else would employ Anita, or Phoebe for that matter?

'Everything's good,' Bea said firmly. 'But they'll be even better if we're making as much profit as possible. Especially when it comes to our annual bonuses.'

Johnno, bless his heart, always made sure there was a decent bonus in their last pay packet of the year, which was very welcome when January seemed to last forever and they'd all overspent on Christmas.

'Also, opening for slightly longer means that there will be overtime and the undying gratitude of a lot of disorganised women who've left their party outfits and Christmas presents to the last minute,' Phoebe said.

'I'd much rather have the overtime,' Anita muttered, her questionable work ethic back in the room with them.

'Well, I think that's everything,' Sophy said as the door opened and the first customer of the week walked in.

Except it wasn't a customer, but Freddy.

It used to be that Phoebe saw Freddy every day. Messaged back and forth constantly.

Now, it wasn't the case that absence made the heart grow fonder. Rather, just seeing him, standing by the door, hands in his trouser pockets, made her heart ache.

'Don't mind me,' he said, although all Phoebe could do was mind him. 'Just pretend that I'm not here.'

It was an order that Phoebe was happy to obey but Coco didn't have to hide her feelings. She went barrelling over to Freddy and did a drop and roll to get his hands on her belly.

Over the sounds of Coco's contented little grunts, Phoebe realised that Bea was saying something to her.

'Sorry, Bea, I didn't catch that.'

Bea held up her phone. 'I was just saying we've hit thirty thousand followers on Instagram, which is immense but also there's a lot of media requests coming in.'

'What kind of media requests?' Phoebe asked in alarm. 'Do they want to do a piece on the shop?'

Bea's smile drooped. 'Actually, they want to interview you.'

Phoebe didn't even have to think about it. She knew where her strengths lay and also what her many weaknesses were. 'I really don't think I should be doing interviews.'

Bea couldn't hide her relief. Her shoulders, which had been up around her ears, went back to their usual position.

'I couldn't agree more,' said Freddy, even though he was meant to be a silent presence.

His words were just a little more hurt to add to the pile of hurts Phoebe had already accumulated over a lifetime. Which was one of the reasons why she didn't want to go anywhere near a journalist. Not just because she was bound to say the wrong thing. Many wrong things. As soon as she got on to her favourite topic of vintage dresses, all bets were off.

But also she didn't want anyone prying into her life. Ferreting out all the secrets that she'd buried. It's not as if she was Kardashian famous but people seemed to end up in the papers and all over the internet for not very much.

'Maybe we could make a fun reel with Phoebe in it?' Sophy suggested. 'Give the people what they want without saying anything.'

'Like Kate Moss,' Cress added before Phoebe could analyse Sophy's statement for hidden meanings then take offence at them. 'She's had a whole career without giving interviews.'

'Phoebe's hardly Kate Moss,' Anita snorted as if the cama-
raderie of the weekend had already been forgotten. 'But you
are ridiculously photogenic and you wear a little black dress
like nobody else.'

'Are you after a pay rise or something?' Phoebe asked
because old habits died hard.

Anita shook her head. 'Dude, learn how to take a compliment.'

Phoebe could feel herself blushing both from the compliment and because she was so aware of Freddy's presence,
his gaze on her. It was as if the top layer of her skin had been
removed, leaving her exposed and sensitive.

'Maybe Birdy might have some ideas,' she mumbled and
she'd never been so glad to see the door open, hear the tinkle
of the bell as an actual customer came in to the shop. 'Right,
OK, I think we're done. Great work, team!'

'Are you *still* drunk?' Anita said teasingly as they dispersed,
and that was another thing that happened when you let your
guard down: people stopped taking you seriously.

Or maybe the lines between friends and colleagues had
become so blurred . . .

'Phoebe, can I have a word?' Freddy asked.

That was no longer the cue for the two of them to hide
in the basement and not actually do anything because of the
fear of being discovered but there'd still be some low-level
flirting.

'The back office?' Phoebe suggested because there was
going to be no low-level flirting so Freddy might as well say
whatever it was he had to say in plain sight.

Freddy followed Phoebe through the shop, then he closed
the door of the back office behind him, so it was just the two
of them.

'How are you?' he asked earnestly.

'I'm fine,' Phoebe said.

'Because you didn't come to the pub on Friday night. Is that a new thing then?' he wanted to know, which was none of his business anymore.

Not that Phoebe could tell him that. She wanted to but also she was tired of lashing out. She didn't want to be that person anymore. 'Marianne had her Christmas shopping evening,' Phoebe said. Then she blushed again because even though it was still a slightly throbbing ache on her wrist, she'd forgotten about the tattoo.

Just like she'd forgotten about it until she got home from Saturday night's sleepover. She'd been desperate for a shower so she hadn't even been paying any particular attention as she peeled off the bandage that was covering the tattoo then she'd glanced down at it and . . .

Well, it certainly wasn't her favourite Coco Chanel quote.

'I was walking past the boat last night and it was quite early, but you were out,' Freddy said casually.

Maybe if he wasn't so casual. If he was a little desperate. A little 'I can't live without you, Pheebs', then Phoebe could allow herself to soften.

'It was Saturday night. People do go out on Saturday nights. It's not unprecedented,' she said. 'Why were you even walking past the boat?'

'I just wanted to check that you'd had someone in to service the flue on the wood-burning stove,' Freddy said, suddenly finding the toes of his white Puma Roma trainers absolutely fascinating.

Why was it that Freddy cared more about her domestic heating arrangements than he cared about her? 'The flue on my wood-burning stove is no longer any concern of yours,' Phoebe told him gently. But then the hurt reasserted itself. 'Remember? You don't want to be with me anymore because I'm a horrible person.'

'That's not what I said. I would *never* say that,' Freddy protested indignantly. 'But you are bloody impossible, that's for sure.'

'I'm going to stay that way,' Phoebe said, drawing herself up so that with her heels on, they were almost the same height. 'I'm not going to let anyone change me. I like being impossible.'

'That must be why you're so good at it,' Freddy said. He turned away but not before Phoebe heard him mutter under his breath, 'I don't know why I bother.'

'I don't know why you bother either,' Phoebe said and she wasn't even being unkind. It was the absolute truth. She couldn't be the person that Freddy wanted her to be, so the sooner he got that message and looked for someone who'd actually make him happy, instead of someone who made him sigh and dim his light, the better.

Chapter Twenty-Seven

There was no rest for the wicked. Or no rest for the heart-broken.

Phoebe had thought that Bea's idea to have her star in a reel was just idle Monday morning chat. But no. If it came to doing a stocktake, Bea was the queen of procrastination but on Monday evening when Phoebe was back on the boat scrutinising the flue of the wood burner to see if it really did need a service, Bea messaged her.

Had a great chat with Birdy. I'm going to shoot three Reels with you tomorrow when the shop is quiet. Daytime to night-time. Let's try and do a jump transition. It should be fun. Don't forget your make-up bag.

Phoebe had no idea what a jump transition was. It didn't sound like fun but it had to be better than answering a journalist's probing questions.

She turned up for work the next morning with her full make-up case and a much better idea. 'I think we should all do a day-to-night look,' she stated in a tone that would tolerate no arguments, once everyone was assembled. Even Anita, lately, was managing to get to work on time. 'A Reel each. Because we all work here. Otherwise three Reels of just me? Well, that really is just showing off.'

'Oh, I don't think I want to do that,' Cress demurred.

'You have to,' Sophy insisted. 'No woman left behind. I've got some lovely rental dresses in your size that you'd look gorgeous in.'

It turned out that Anita was an old hand at a jump transition so she volunteered to go first, heading up to the atelier with Bea while the others welcomed the first customers of the day.

Anita came down an hour later with a full face of party make-up. Her already doe eyes had never looked so large and lustrous as she fluttered her false eyelashes. She had a gold lamé dress over her arm, which she'd been coveting for weeks. 'I knew this would look fantastic on me and so I'm now forced to buy it,' she said glumly. 'Even with my staff discount, it's a lot and I haven't bought any Christmas presents yet.'

'Nothing wrong with a bit of self-gifting at Christmastime,' Sophy said as she surveyed her rental empire.

'Think of it as an investment in yourself,' Phoebe added. In one hand, she had three different dresses for a customer who was already stripped down and waiting in one of the changing cubicles. In her other hand, she had her phone because she was in the middle of a WhatsApp chat with Birdy. She'd messaged to thank her for giving Bea advice and it had turned into counselling Birdy who was having a Clothes Panic about what to wear to the Vintage Christmas Ball. 'You do look good in gold, Neeta.'

'You're a cursed pair of enablers,' Anita muttered. 'I'm going to put it back on the rail and if it's still here by the end of the day, then God obviously wants me to have it.'

'He does work in mysterious ways,' Sophy said. 'Right I'm going upstairs to force Cress into one of these dresses. I may be some time.'

With Sophy, Bea and Cress otherwise engaged, it was just Phoebe and Anita left to deal with an increasingly busy shop.

There were still quite a few customers solely there to gawp at Phoebe and who seemed to be quite disappointed that she wasn't making impassioned speeches about vintage dresses and sustainable fashion. But most of the people were shoppers with a slightly desperate look in their eyes even though there were still a good twenty shopping days before Christmas.

'Ugh! Men shopping for wives and girlfriends are the worst,' Anita hissed to Phoebe after the man she was serving finally left empty-handed. That was only after making Anita try on five different dresses as he said that she was roughly the same size as his wife.

'Though she's got more in the boob department,' he'd said cheerfully not realising that Anita was clearly wishing that very bad things would happen to him in the very near future.

'I'm not convinced that he even has a wife,' Phoebe hissed back. 'Maybe that's just how he gets his kicks. Making poor sales assistants try on dresses for his own sick pleasure.'

'Don't even!' Anita pulled a gruesome face, which she quickly had to adjust to a more pleasing smile as she was approached by a customer.

There was a momentary lull just before the lunchtime rush and still no Sophy. 'I wish she'd hurry up,' Anita moaned. 'I'm gasping for a cuppa.'

'If you promise to stay behind the till until it's finished, then I don't mind you having a hot beverage so close to the dresses,' Phoebe decided, then shied away as Anita tried to put a hand on her forehead.

'Are you sickening for something?' Anita asked sweetly. 'Why are you being so nice?'

'Maybe you've finally worn me down,' Phoebe said. Or maybe these past few weeks had shown her that when it came to dealing with people, difficult people like Anita, then, as Mary Poppins had it, a spoonful of sugar could be very useful. Although that had never been one of Mildred's life philosophies. 'I no longer have the energy to fight with you. Though if you get coffee on anything, I will kill you and I will make it look like it was an accident.'

Anita grinned. 'I expect nothing less.'

It was after lunch that the shop got really busy. There was no time to make Reels or faff about with jump transitions. It was all hands to the pump. Cress was stuck in her little rooftop eyrie replacing the beading on a 1960s cocktail dress that a courier was coming to collect by five. Downstairs, Bea was on changing room duty, Anita on till, Sophy on the shop floor to mill about and be helpful while Phoebe assisted where needed and refused to take selfies with anyone. Politely but very, very, *very* firmly.

But at five minutes past six, when the shop had emptied out, Bea jerked her head in the direction of the stairs. 'Time for your close-up, Phoebe.'

'Maybe now that you've got everyone else, then I don't need to do a reel,' Phoebe said because even if she wasn't being probed by a journalist, she still didn't fancy an ill-informed army of keyboard warriors being rude about her in the comments.

'You're doing a reel,' Sophy said from behind the till where she was just about to cash up. 'You have to lead by example. Also, Cress said that there's a black backless satin 1930s dress in the designer room that you've been having an affair with for months.'

Phoebe managed to sigh both in annoyance and in longing. Even with a very generous staff discount, the dress in question was still far too rich for her budget. 'I'll do it, but only if Coco does it with me,' she said because even if she was being more *democratic* at work, she was still the boss and that had to count for something.

The infamous jump transition was actually more of a twirling transition. Still in her black day dress and her day make-up, Bea made Phoebe twirl until she was dizzy and worried that Coco, who was tucked under her arm, might throw up.

Then it was time for a quick change into the black satin, bias-cut gown of Phoebe's dreams. Sparkly clips in her hair and an even more flicky eye and redder lip than usual. And twirling. So much twirling until Phoebe was sure that she had motion sickness.

'So, you'll start the twirl in your day clothes then with some nifty editing, you'll finish the twirl in your evening finery then do a little pose,' Bea explained as she showed Phoebe footage of her twirling. 'For music, I was thinking of Glenn Miller's "In the Mood".'

'Perfect,' Phoebe agreed. 'You've really thrown yourself into this challenge, but tomorrow, no excuses, you're going to be twirling yourself.'

'I like to think of myself more as the person who makes the magic happen,' Bea said, even though it was clear to anyone with eyes that the magic also happened on her pretty face.

'No getting out of it,' Phoebe said sternly, though now her stern voice felt more of an effort than something she'd never had to think about before deploying. 'Also, you might want to bring travel sickness pills.'

'I hate my life,' Bea called out mournfully as she went down the stairs while Phoebe put her work dress back on in the changing room off the atelier.

She thought that she had the place to herself but when she emerged, the lights were still on in Cress's workroom and the woman herself was bent over her sewing machine.

Phoebe tapped lightly on the open door. 'Did you forget the time? It's gone seven thirty. You should have gone home an hour ago.'

Things were still a little stiff between the two of them. Almost as stiff as Cress's neck because she straightened up slowly then winced and put a hand to her nape.

'I'm working late on something that I can't do at home,' Cress said, her words as awkward as her posture. 'I need to use the overlocker. It's all right, I can lock up and yes, I'll remember to set the alarm.'

Even though Cress was the only person Phoebe trusted to lock up and set the alarm, she still felt a momentary panic at the idea. And then she was feeling other unwelcome things.

'Are you working on a dress for your reproduction line?' she asked. If her tone was accusatory then Phoebe just couldn't help it.

Cress sighed, then bent her head to finish the seam she was sewing on what looked like a peony pink organza dress. Then she looked up again at Phoebe standing in the doorway.

'It's actually a Christmas present for my cousin's little girl,' Cress said, lifting up the needle then holding up a pretty tiered dress, which had little foil stars embossed on the fabric. 'She's going through a pink and flouncy phase.'

Phoebe had never gone through a pink and flouncy phase but still she mustered up a smile. 'Nice.'

'Oh God, Phoebe, you know I hate confrontation! I hate it more than anything but we are going to chat this out,' Cress exclaimed.

'I'm fine with you making a dress for a little girl. I'm not made of stone.'

'Even if I decide to scale up the measurements and yes, think about including it in my small collection of reproduction dresses, which by the way only exists as sketches in my sketchpad and a really beyond basic business plan?' Cress snapped. She pointed at the inky blue velvet armchair where she liked to curl up and do her hand stitching. 'Sit!'

'I don't like your tone,' Phoebe said even as she followed orders and sat.

'Coming from the queen of tone, that's quite hypocritical,' Cress said because it was as if she'd been recently abducted by aliens and had been returned in a much sassier, much snarkier format. 'Now, I want you to explain something to me.'

'Explain what?' Phoebe folded her arms and crossed her legs though it was quite hard to look imposing in a very low-to-the-ground bucket chair.

'Explain how maybe, a couple of years from now, launching a small capsule collection of reproduction dresses will in any way impact on your life in a negative way?' Cress asked, her own arms folded, an exasperated look on her pretty face.

'Because it will stop people buying vintage dresses and new dresses aren't sustainable. It's just kind of unethical to design dresses that look like vintage dresses but aren't,' Phoebe said, which was just scratching the surface of why she was so hurt at Cress's plans. She already had two side hustles. Why did she need another?

'Rubbish! Absolute rubbish,' Cress huffed like a furious little dragon. 'This from the woman who literally hates selling vintage dresses to people unless those people meet a series of criteria known only to her . . .'

'That's hardly fair,' Phoebe protested but Cress wasn't done with her.

'And also, these hypothetical dresses that only exist as very basic prototypes, would be made sustainably in the UK and what copyright am I infringing by designing a little black dress when there are hundreds, even thousands, of similar black frocks that have been designed ever since Coco Chanel first came up with the concept?' Cress said. And still she wasn't finished. 'You certainly didn't mind when you asked me to make a replica of your little black dress that was destroyed during your Bastard Moth Infestation of 2019.'

'But you could have told me!' Phoebe spluttered. She'd been so angry when she'd discovered Cress's sketchpad but now she couldn't properly articulate *why* she was angry.

'I didn't tell you and Freddy didn't tell you, because for the umpteenth time, there isn't really anything to tell but also because oh my God, Pheebs, you get so weird and territorial about anything to do with vintage dresses,' Cress said as if it was hurting her a lot more to say this than it was for Phoebe to hear it.

Which wasn't at all true. 'Weird? Territorial? There's nothing wrong in being passionate about something.'

'You take being passionate to a whole new level.' It seemed as if Cress was finding a whole new appreciation for confrontation. 'I mean, there have been times when you've even argued with me about the correct way to wash vintage clothes as if putting them in a washing machine in a mesh bag on a delicate cycle is an act of cruelty.'

'I still say that handwashing is . . .'

'I HAVE AN ACTUAL DEGREE IN COSTUME CONSERVATION!' Cress shouted so loudly that from the atelier where she'd been sleeping on one of the couches, Coco Chanel gave a little whimper. 'I'm not going to do anything that is going to damage a vintage dress. This is ridiculous. You're being ridiculous . . .'

'I am not ridiculous and you're going to have your stupid reproduction line and you're going to leave the shop and I thought we were friends but you kept a secret from me, with Freddy of all people, and you haven't even named a dress after me,' Phoebe hissed, which was the ugly truth. Why she'd been angry but mostly hurt.

There was a tense silence. Phoebe angled her body towards the wall so she wouldn't have to look at Cress though really she should just get up and leave.

Out of the corner of her eye, she saw Cress rest her elbows on her desk, then put her head in her hands. 'You're an idiot, Phoebe. An absolute idiot.' Her voice was muffled but her tone was soft and gentle. 'I have no plans to go anywhere for the foreseeable future. I love working here even if my line manager can be a real pain in the arse sometimes.'

'It's not funny,' Phoebe mumbled. It was easy enough to rant and rave about cruelty to vintage dresses but when the cruelty felt personal, it was much harder to talk about it.

It never felt good to get things off her chest. Instead it felt as if Phoebe had crossed a line and soon she'd be asked to pack up all her belongings into bin liners and her caseworker would turn up to take her some place unknown but it would only be temporary because nothing with her was ever for keeps.

'I know it's not funny,' Cress said in the same gentle tone. 'There's something about this that feels kind of heartbreaking. Freddy and I are working together on this, yes, but in a fact-finding way and we didn't tell you because, again, there's nothing really to tell and you'd only get upset. Which turned out to be the case.' She got up from her stool and stretched. 'I don't want you to be upset especially over something that's really not worth getting upset about.'

'I am a prickly person,' Phoebe said, like that was going to come as a surprise.

'You are,' Cress agreed. Then she took the three steps to where Phoebe was sitting and perched herself on the arm of her chair. 'But you can also be very kind and fun and so, most of the time, I don't mind if I occasionally get scratched on the prickles.'

Cress rested her hand lightly on Phoebe's arm. The touch, Cress's words, formed a lump in Phoebe's throat, made her eyes sting. 'It's not an excuse,' she said hoarsely. 'More of a reason, but I didn't have a good childhood. In fact, I learned from a really early age that you can't rely on other people because they're always going to let you down. You can only rely on yourself. I was also moved around a lot, so there was never really an opportunity to make friends. Which is probably why I'm not very good at it.'

There was no immediate reaction and Phoebe cursed herself for oversharing and she was going to get up and go

262

and never look Cress in the eye again but then Cress's hand tightened on her arm. 'Thank you for telling me that,' she said simply, and somehow, that was exactly what Phoebe had wanted her to say.

Opening up to people meant opening up to the possibility of being hurt. Again. Of being abandoned. Again. Of realising that you just weren't good enough. Again.

But sometimes if you found the right person to be open with then the world didn't end.

'It sounds very lonely thinking that you can't trust anyone . . .' Cress said.

'I'm not lonely. Against all the odds, I do have some friends,' Phoebe pointed out because she did have friends. Or did she just have some people in her life who put up with her?

'I hope you count me as one of them.' The hand was taken away and then Cress's arm curved around Phoebe's tense shoulders. 'I've hated how things have been between us these last few weeks.'

'These last few weeks have been . . . not good,' Phoebe admitted heavily.

'Although there have been times that have been very good.' Cress nudged her. 'We all loved hungover Phoebe. And you know what, you were vulnerable and well, very hungover and you let us in and . . .'

'Since then, Anita has taken shameless advantage of it,' Phoebe said with the ghost of a smile. She moved away from Cress's arm. She felt more in control of herself. 'Well, I'm glad we had this little chat but it's getting late . . .'

'Never mind it's getting late, now what's going on with you and Freddy?' Cress asked baldly.

Chapter Twenty-Eight

There was only one answer. 'Nothing. Nothing is going on with me and Freddy. There is no me and Freddy.'

'Have you really broken up or is it just a fight?' Cress asked delicately.

Rather than clamming up, Phoebe realised that she actually welcomed the chance to talk about this with one of the few people who even knew that she and Freddy had been seeing each other.

'He rejected me,' Phoebe recalled bitterly. 'Said that he couldn't do it anymore but the thing is, Cress, he knew what I was like. He knew what he was getting into. I'm not a person who feels things very deeply . . .'

'Well, you certainly feel very deeply about vintage dresses, and what about Coco?' Cress asked.

At the mention of her name, the lady herself appeared in the doorway and then padded purposefully towards them. 'What about Coco? Yes, I'm fond of her. I have a responsibility towards her that I take very seriously but I just don't . . . I've never loved anyone. I don't know how to. I'm not saying that for sympathy. It's just how it is.'

'That makes me want to cry.' Cress did sound as if the tears were about to put in an appearance. 'I think you're . . . *fond* of Freddy too and I know he cares for you.'

'He might have done once but he undermines my position in the shop. He can't be my boss and my boyfriend,' Phoebe stumbled over the last word because she'd never even used that word in her head to describe Freddy's role in her life. 'Did you not hear me when I said he was the one to reject me? He can't take me as I am. Instead he wants to change me.'

'Everyone changes though . . .'

'Not me. I don't,' Phoebe stated categorically for the record.

'OK.' Cress pulled a face that suggested that she didn't believe Phoebe's non-changeable status.

'What's the face for?'

'Well, it's just we've had a very different Phoebe these last few weeks . . .'

'I went viral. I was cancelled. Is it any wonder that my behaviour's been a little off . . .'

'Sophy said that you'd had a heart-to-heart about Johnno and since then you haven't bitten her head off for at least a fortnight, and you hung out with us on Saturday night and generally you've been a little less spiky . . .' Cress tailed off in the face of Phoebe's frozen expression.

'I don't think I've changed that much. But yes there is a subtle difference between my work self and my not-work self,' Phoebe conceded. That was all she was prepared to give.

Cress still looked unconvinced. 'Everyone changes. Because life and whatever it throws at you, good and bad, has an effect on the person you are. Look at how much I've changed since I've been working here. What with finding myself creatively and ending a relationship that I'd been in for half my life and meeting Miles . . .'

'Yes but . . .'

'Look how much Sophy has changed too,' Cress continued.

Sophy was still as annoying as she'd been the first day she arrived at The Vintage Dress Shop. Or maybe not *quite* as annoying and at least she wore the right size bra now, which was all of Phoebe's doing . . .

'Those are minimal changes for the better while Freddy fundamentally wants to change who I am,' Phoebe said as she thought of the way he seemed to sigh so frequently over the last few months, the flat way he looked at her.

'You said that he's rejected you but that's a very strong word. A very negative word,' Cress said. 'I think really he just wanted you to be the best version of yourself. We're all happier when we're the people who we're really meant to be.'

Phoebe wasn't convinced. 'If Freddy can't handle me at my worst then he doesn't deserve me at my best.'

Cress had the audacity to roll her eyes. 'Pheebs, I'm so glad that we're friends again and I'm saying this as a friend and also from a place of love but no one, not even the most devoted of boyfriends, could possibly handle you at your worst.'

There was no point in wasting breath on arguing about it. 'Well, it's something to think about, I suppose,' Phoebe said grudgingly. Although Freddy had seen her at her worst, those evenings when it was just the two of them, he'd definitely seen, if not the best version of Phoebe, then a much softer side. It hadn't been enough for him though.

She sighed and hoisted herself out of the depths of the chair. 'It's so late. We should both be getting home.'

'I'll work on Holly's dress in my lunch hour tomorrow,' Cress agreed, stretching tiredly.

'If you haven't got much on workwise, I don't mind if you work on it during the day,' Phoebe said and Cress nodded.

But five minutes later, as they bustled out of the shop as the alarm beeped out its warning, Cress didn't immediately start walking to the station but lingered as Phoebe locked the door.

'I think you should talk to Freddy at the ball,' she said. 'It's neutral territory and you'll be looking gorgeous in a fancy gown and he'll be in his best suit, plus there'll be a fifty-piece orchestra and it will be romantic.'

At the mention of the ball, Phoebe felt sour all over again. 'I haven't even decided if I'm going yet,' she said.

'Oh Phoebe!' Cress's tone was of pure exasperation. 'Because of Freddy?'

So, then Phoebe had to tell her about Coco Chanel's ban. The very unfair, the very unjust ban. 'She wouldn't do that. She would never disgrace herself like that.'

Cress pressed her lips together tightly almost as if she were trying to suppress a laugh.

'Was there something you were wanting to say?' Phoebe asked, her eyebrows raised.

'She does fart a lot though,' Cress said with a hiccup, again as if the giggles weren't far off. And, besides, Coco's occasional flatulence had nothing to do with anything.

'She has *anxiety*, Cress,' Phoebe reminded her.

'I have never in my life met a creature so secure in herself as Coco,' Cress said fondly, looking down at the Frenchie.

'She's just putting a brave face on when actually I think you'll find that she has severe PTSD from her sad life before me so all the more reason not to leave her on her own while I dance the night away.'

'Yeah, OK.' Cress nodded but her face was saying something else.

Phoebe put her hands on her hips. 'What? Come on, out with it!'

'Oh, it's nothing. But goodness, if you treated Freddy half as well as a dog that you claim you're only fond of then it would be the love affair of the century,' Cress said.

'You're just being ridiculous now, Cress,' Phoebe said a little crossly. She was all for Cress being the best version of herself but the Cress of last year would never dare say these . . . these . . . silly, unfounded things to her.

'Sorry,' Cress said though she didn't sound that sorry. 'It's late. I need my dinner. Let's discuss your outfit options for the ball tomorrow.'

'I really think I'm not going,' Phoebe said but Cress was already walking away.

She lifted a hand to wave casually and her jaunty 'Whatever!' carried in the chill night breeze.

Chapter Twenty-Nine

There was no time to discuss outfit options to a ball that Phoebe probably wasn't going to.

The rest of the week was sheer, barely controlled chaos. Every year, Phoebe half forgot how manic the run-up to Christmas was in the shop and every year, she was surprised all over again.

Her new-found notoriety was definitely more of a help than a hindrance. Every day Bea presented her with a curated selection of Reels and TikToks from people who'd stitched the original video of her big speech, and the reaction to the shop's twirling Reels had boosted their social media follows yet again.

It also boosted the number of customers coming into the shop. Not just to demand selfies but also to demand that Phoebe match them with their perfect vintage dress, which she was always happy to do.

On Friday night, after the longest week, with the shop shutting at eight, instead of six, it wasn't just Phoebe who was crying off from their usual outing to The Hat and Fan.

'We're going large tomorrow night at the ball so I'm not even going to go very small this evening,' Anita said. 'I also haven't quite narrowed down my accessories either.'

'Post a pic of your choices in the group chat,' Sophy said. This was the group chat that Phoebe had only just been added to, though she suspected it had been in existence long before that. 'And yeah, definitely a quiet one tonight. Agreed?'

None of them even had the energy for a rousing chorus of assent. Instead they all trudged off to get their Tubes and buses and Phoebe and Coco headed home in the opposite direction.

Phoebe stopped off at the corner shop for the gourmet dog food that Katya got in for Coco on special order, a packet of gluten-free spinach and ricotta ravioli (though she actually quite fancied a lot of gluten) and Gunther, her neighbour, messaged and asked if she could pick up a copy of *The Guardian*, if they still had one, and a grab bag of Maltesers.

To think that he had the cheek to make piggy noises at Coco, Phoebe thought to herself. Which was just what Gunther did when Phoebe handed over his items. Coco was obviously in a good mood though because she arched against his legs like a cat and consented to having her back end rubbed.

'If I decided to go out tomorrow night, just for a couple of hours, could you look in on Coco?' Phoebe asked half-heartedly because she still wasn't sure what her plans were.

'What time? I think we're going to be out for most of the day,' Gunther said, squatting down to pet Coco's belly. It must be all the yoga that made him so nimble.

The decision had been made for her. 'Oh, it doesn't matter. I'm not even sure that I want . . .'

'Sadie!' Gunther bellowed. 'What time will we be back from seeing your sister?'

Sadie stuck her head round the stern of their boat, *The Lakshmi*. 'Pipe down, Gunther. You'll wake the dead!'

'Really, it's all right,' Phoebe said, shifting uncomfortably because it was cold and late and her feet had reached their high-heel pain threshold a couple of hours ago.

Gunther repeated the question at a more reasonable volume and Sadie said that they'd be happy to look in on Coco or even bring her around to theirs when they got back at around seven.

'We've still got Johnno's spare key,' Sadie chortled, which was news to Phoebe, but now she had the option of going out if she wanted to.

As she ate her sad ravioli, Phoebe couldn't help but think back to the summer ball. She'd worn a black lace gown and, even though it was quite a warm night, black satin opera gloves. Freddy had worn a slim-cut Italian 1960s black evening suit, and though he'd complained that it was too hot to wear a mohair and wool suit, he'd looked so stylish. Like the leading man straight out of a Federico Fellini film. And of course, Coco had been adorable in pearls.

The three of them had danced all night and afterwards they'd walked slowly home together all the way from Bloomsbury, and it had taken ages because they'd kept stopping for long kisses.

It felt like ages, even if it had only been a few days, since she'd last seen Freddy. He hadn't even been around to see that she'd unbent enough to be on better terms with her team. Even Anita. *Even Sophy.*

Could she unbend enough to be on better terms with Freddy too?

'The thing about relationships, Phoebe, is that men get more out of them than women do,' Mildred had said when Phoebe was sad and sullen after she'd finally kissed Jason Mullins at her Leavers' Disco, only to discover the next week that he was now going out with a horrible girl called Stacey who'd called Phoebe a 'pikey chav' on her first day at school. 'Men can't manage without women, but women can manage very well by themselves. Indeed, they thrive. Look at me!'

It was true that Mildred was perfectly content with her life. She'd had a career that she was proud of, a little home that she loved, full of carefully chosen possessions, from the collection of dresses that she'd stitched with her own hand and kept pristine over the decades to the fine bone china she used every day. More than anyone Phoebe had ever met, except perhaps Johnno, Mildred knew exactly who she was and made no apologies for it.

'I may not be the kindest person, I'm not a soft touch, but I know right from wrong,' Mildred had said when she told Phoebe that she could stay after her eighteenth birthday, which was when society and the local council deemed her to be an adult and old enough to look after herself.

It had been something that Phoebe had been worrying about for weeks. Turning eighteen wasn't a cause for celebration. There'd be no big family party and extravagant presents. The horrible Stacey Baxter had gone to New York for her eighteenth.

Phoebe was working at Johnno's Junk full-time after scraping together a handful of GCSEs at not great grades. She wasn't earning that much and the prospect of having to pay rent and live who knows where, with who knows who, felt a lot like her life before Mildred. As if she were going backwards rather than striding forward into a glorious future.

Mildred, with her inflexible rules but that little twinkle in her eye, had been the making of Phoebe. She'd changed the way that Phoebe talked – she didn't dare drop an aitch in Mildred's presence. She'd changed the way that Phoebe dressed. The tracksuits had gone and instead of wanting to blend in, Phoebe didn't mind standing out in the big foofy 1950s dresses that she had first dibs on when they came into Johnno's Junk.

Most importantly of all, Mildred had changed the way that Phoebe saw herself. She wasn't a burden. She was a person. Her own person. It didn't matter who had let her down in the past 'as long as you don't let yourself down, Phoebe'.

That morning of her eighteenth birthday, there'd been a card propped against Phoebe's mug on the little kitchen table, which Mildred always laid for breakfast. There'd also been a present, the little string of pearls that Mildred had been given by her parents on her eighteenth birthday, which had touched Phoebe so much that she and Mildred had shared a very stiff, very rare hug.

'I've been thinking,' Mildred had said as she cracked the top of the boiled egg ('four and a half minutes, Phoebe, for the perfect soft-boiled egg.') 'I don't have the energy to take on another waif and stray and I do worry about you having to fend for yourself.'

Phoebe had hardly dared let herself hope because hopes dashed were the worst kind of pain. 'I'd be all right,' she said, because somehow she would be, eventually.

'You probably would, thanks to my expert guidance.' Mildred allowed herself a small smile. 'But we rub together fairly well so if you wanted to stay, then I'd be happy to have you.'

'Thanks, I'd like that too,' Phoebe said casually because Mildred had told her, countless times, that nobody liked a gusher.

And that had been that. Once the foster allowances had stopped, she paid Mildred a small sum for rent and housekeeping, and they'd continued to rub together fairly well for the next couple of years. Then Mildred had slipped over one winter and broken her hip and it been a quite a fast decline after that.

Phoebe pushed away her plate now. The ravioli had been so unappetising that she didn't even offer the last pieces to Coco. Once she'd done the washing up and put a conditioning mask on her hair and a nourishing skin mask on her face, she opened her wardrobe door and rummaged on the top shelf until she found her jewellery box. Not that there was much jewellery in it, most of it was costume pieces. Not even the high-end, semi-precious stones that Charles dealt in but glass beads and plated metals.

But in a flat velvet box was the strand of pearls that Mildred had given her. Phoebe didn't wear them that often even though Mildred had said that pearls should be worn. That leaving them to their own devices would make the pearls dehydrate and lose their lustre.

Phoebe didn't want the pearls to lose their lustre. She didn't want to lose her glow either and she decided then that, like Cinderella before her, she would go to the ball. She'd dance with Freddy then she'd lead him upstairs to one of the little boxes that overlooked the ballroom so they could be alone together.

Freddy would talk and Phoebe would try not to bristle. Then she'd try even harder to talk to Freddy, to explain who she really was and where she'd come from. Why she was such a difficult person. In short, to be vulnerable with him in a way that she'd never allowed herself to be before.

But she wasn't looking forward to it. Not one little bit.

Chapter Thirty

It was one thing to have good intentions late in the evening, when you were tired and full of nostalgia.

Quite another thing in the cold, cold light of a December day when you were managing a busy shop and a staff who were far too giddy and excited about the impending ball to provide good customer service.

'And for goodness' sakes, Anita, I've told you a hundred times not to leave dresses that have been tried on hanging up outside the changing rooms. Put them back on the rails!'

The glam squad, Phoebe's friends Vivienne and Roy, arrived at three. Even though they'd, yet again, had to lock the shop door and let customers enter on an in-and-out basis, because they were so busy, Phoebe had no choice but to let each member of staff disappear into the back office for at least half an hour to get their party glam on.

Up to that point, Phoebe was still not one hundred per cent certain about her plans for the night but then a delivery from the chichi florist on the corner arrived. Beautiful white camellia corsages for Sophy and Cress, courtesy of Charles and Miles, respectively. Anita and Bea hadn't been forgotten either. They too had white camellia corsages sent . . . 'with love from Freddy' And Phoebe? Phoebe had as Johnno would say, 'Sweet F A!'

That was that then. Freddy had made his feelings perfectly clear and there was no point in Phoebe going to the ball. Turning up all hopeful. It was the hope that did her every time.

'Are you all right?' Cress whispered to Phoebe as she put her corsage, a token not just of appreciation but affection from Miles, in the fridge in the back office to keep it fresh. 'I bet Freddy has something special planned for you. Or maybe he's going to deliver it in person. Or maybe . . .'

'Or maybe he hasn't got me a corsage because he's glad that we're not together anymore and he decided that if he did get me flowers, it would only give me the wrong idea,' Phoebe whispered back, as she took her . . . her disappointment out on the poor defenceless office desk and viciously rammed shut the drawer she'd just opened.

Cress frowned. 'I'm sure that's not true. Freddy would . . .'

'Enough!' Phoebe snapped, holding one tense hand in front of her to ward off Cress's effusive sympathy. She was glad that she and Cress were friends again but as Mildred always used to say, no one likes a gusher. 'I don't want to talk about it and I certainly don't want to talk about *him*.'

Inevitably, Phoebe was in an absolutely foul mood for the rest of the afternoon. It had already been agreed that she wouldn't need the services of Vivienne and Roy. 'It would just be gilding the lily,' Roy had gallantly said but Phoebe couldn't stop bitching about her staff being otherwise engaged when the shop was an absolute madhouse.

'How long does it take to do a few victory rolls and a bold red lip?' she kept hissing to herself, except her hissing was loud enough that all her colleagues could hear.

Even though they'd agreed that this wouldn't be a night that they'd open until late, she still kept the team back long after six thirty because Anita hadn't vacuumed to her liking and when Sophy cashed up, there was a fifty pence discrepancy.

There was lots of muttering and angry glances thrown Phoebe's way, which she ignored because even though she hated her hectoring tone of voice as much as they did,

Phoebe couldn't find it in herself to stop. She'd reverted back to all her bad, old habits. Cress, in particular, kept looking at Phoebe as if she wasn't just angry with her but very disappointed too.

But when Phoebe finally, grudgingly, released them from their duties and they could sashay off in their finest evening looks, it was Cress who paused in the shop doorway. She looked absolutely stunning in a fit-and-flare red satin dress, her curly hair braided and pinned, her lips as crimson as her frock. 'We're having predrinks in The Hat and Fan until eight, if you change your mind.'

'I'm not going to change my mind,' Phoebe insisted tightly and she couldn't really blame Anita for loudly whispering, 'Well, thank God for that.'

Phoebe's mind *was* made up. She marched Coco back to *The Sheila* and she was going to do what she always did when she was heartsore and unhappy. She was going to reorganise her closets and absolutely not think about Freddy.

But how dare he? How dare he send corsages to Anita and Bea yet he couldn't even care enough to get one for her? It was painfully and abundantly clear that even if Phoebe did go to the ball and got him on his own, there was nothing that she could say, nothing that Freddy would listen to. Freddy had always been such a great listener. It was one of the qualities that Phoebe most liked about him.

Well, she didn't like him now. She tore off her work clothes and pulled on the one tracksuit that had survived every wardrobe cull she'd ever had and started pulling out clothes and boxes.

Part of Phoebe knew that you should never reorganise while angry. Then you made irrational decisions and got rid of clothes and accessories that a few weeks later, you realised you couldn't live without. But another much larger part of her was too angry to care.

She stood on tiptoe to pull down a box that was right at the back of her wardrobe. It was caught on something until she tugged hard and the lid flew off and a shower of paper rained down on her.

'For fuck's sake!' she swore though Phoebe never swore because of all the times Mildred had threatened to wash out her mouth with Fairy Liquid.

Thinking of Mildred, and Phoebe had been thinking a lot about Mildred these past few weeks, the first piece of paper that she picked up from the floor was a list written in Mildred's careful and precise handwriting.

Three nighties.
My good quilted dressing gown.
My blue slippers.
My washbag (it's in the cupboard under the bathroom sink).
Pack it with soap, toothbrush (in its proper case) toothpaste, deo-
dorant, my nail kit and hand cream. Shampoo, conditioner and
hairspray. Brush and comb.

And so it went on.

A list from when Mildred had broken her hip and after a very uncomfortable night in A&E on a trolley, had been admitted for surgery.

She'd been in hospital for not even two weeks and she'd never come home to the little flat. She'd had her broken hip replaced but the surgical site had become infected and although Mildred was the strongest person Phoebe had ever known, so utterly sure of herself, in reality she was a frail, old lady. The infection hadn't responded to treatment and had ravaged Mildred so that every day when Phoebe went to see her, Mildred was a little less. Then a lot less. Then as her organs shut down, one by one, she was a husk of a human being, until at just after eleven o'clock one drab Tuesday morning, Mildred died.

Her indefatigable spirit evaporated into nothing. Which was unthinkable and yet it was suddenly a reality.

It had been a terrible time. The council had given Phoebe two weeks to vacate the little flat and she'd had to clear out all of Mildred's possessions. All those precious little things that she'd cared so much about and taken so much care over.

The funeral had been utterly heartbreaking. Already organised and paid for by Mildred and attended only by Phoebe and Johnno, because just as she was the only person to be there for Mildred at her passing, Johnno was the only person there for Phoebe as she drifted through those dark days. She'd needed him in a way that Sophy with her mother and stepfather and family and friends had never needed him.

Phoebe was on this trip down memory lane for the long haul now. And so again she reached up on tiptoes to retrieve the big, flat box she'd found on the top of Mildred's own wardrobe. It was much like the boxes they used at the shop to carefully pack wedding dresses between layers and layers of acid-free tissue paper.

Inside this box was also a wedding dress. A beautiful ivory crêpe de chine dress with delicate beading. There was also a handwritten receipt, including her staff discount, plus a list in Mildred's careful script of the alterations she still needed to make.

But she'd never made them because, as Phoebe had realised when she packed up Mildred's life, the dress was never worn and the wedding never was. The man, who'd made Mildred so reliant on herself and so determined never to rely on others, had called things off. Maybe to marry Mildred's sister, maybe some other woman, or maybe he'd decided he was better off unwed. Phoebe would never know.

She put the lid back on the box but instead of saying a fierce but silent thank you to the woman who'd rescued her, for the first time, Phoebe wondered if it was a good thing: to have been raised in Mildred's own image.

A whole life lived. Over eighty years and Mildred had nothing to show for it but a wardrobe of old-fashioned dresses that she never wore. A collection of fine bone china that was really too delicate to be used for every day; its pattern almost indistinct after being handled and washed too many times. And one lost girl who'd been there for the last five years of Mildred's life because there had been no friends, no family, no one else to care, as Mildred lay dying, then dead.

Phoebe wasn't ungrateful. Mildred had saved her life in so many ways. What would have become of that snarling, terrified girl if Mildred hadn't taken her in and given her a crash course in being able to stand on her own two feet?

Now, as she sat on the floor, surrounded by Mildred's sad legacy, Phoebe realised that she didn't want to follow all of Mildred's life lessons to their inevitable conclusion. Phoebe didn't want to end up on her own with no family, very few friends, just her own pride and a self-reliance that had been forged from all the bad things that had happened to her. You needed to build a wall to protect yourself but the wall needed a door that you could open to let the light in. To let other people in.

Phoebe needed, desperately, to open the door.

Just like that, once again, this Cinderella was going to the ball.

It took half an hour, a personal best, to get Phoebe ball-ready. To shed her tracksuit like a snake shedding its skin. Then to style her hair until it was gleaming, paint her face with lip powders, paints and pencils.

Then she carefully removed her favourite dress from its garment bag and padded hanger. That white, beaded sheath dress, which had once been worn by a debutante and photographed for *Harper's Bazaar*. White in winter was so chic and white felt like a new beginning. A fresh page to write the next chapter on.

Phoebe packed essentials into a tiny silver clutch bag. Slipped on a pair of matching, three-bar heels and added a white faux-fur cape to complete her ensemble. She was going to be freezing but sometimes you had to suffer to look this good.

Although she was done with suffering, which was why she was going to find Freddy and fling open that door, which had been shut for far too long. She turned on the wood-burner stove and tried to settle a very put-out Coco Chanel who couldn't believe that she wasn't coming too.

'You'll be toasty warm here and it's only for about ten minutes until Sadie and Gunther arrive to take you back to their boat.' Phoebe stroked behind Coco's ears as the little dog turned her face away like she didn't even want to look at her human caregiver. 'If Gunther makes piggy noises at you, then you have my permission to bite him.'

Phoebe felt a pang of hurt pierce the fizzy mix of nerves and excitement in her belly. 'I'm going to be two hours tops. I just need to talk to Freddy and maybe, he might just, he might just . . .'

She couldn't finish the sentence. It was hard enough to even think the words, never mind say them out loud.

Instead she gave a stiff Coco one last cuddle and then stood up, straightened her shoulders ('you're slouching, Phoebe, you don't want a dowager's hump, do you?') and prepared to go out to fight for her life.

Chapter Thirty-One

Phoebe's plans didn't get off to a great start. It was very hard to navigate from boat to slippery-with-frost canal path in a long, heavy silk dress and very high heels, especially when she could hear Coco whimpering.

She sent a quick message to Sadie, who was far more reliable than Gunther, asking her to let Phoebe know as soon as they'd released Coco from her very cosy, very warm, very-one-hundred-of-your-favourite-toys-in-close-proximity prison.

It was the kind of chilly, damp night you felt in your bones. The kind of chilly damp that could ruin a good hairdo even with a heck of a lot of Elnett hairspray holding it in place. The Hat and Fan was only a five-minute walk but Phoebe slowed her steps down. Not just because her shoes were hard to walk in but because she didn't know what to say when she pulled back the heavy door of the pub to see everyone, her friends, her colleagues, her . . . Freddy sitting there.

Probably she'd have to start with an apology. Possibly even grovelling. Phoebe placed a hand on her stomach, which was quivering with nerves, even as she shivered with cold, and eked out at least another two minutes by standing under a streetlight so she could scrutinise her make-up in her compact mirror.

She looked the same as she always did. But the perfect make-up – the armour of arched eyebrows, perfect cat's eye flicks, flawless alabaster skin and the boldest of red lips – couldn't hide the hesitation that Phoebe felt.

She could manage perfectly well on her own.

Then again, perfectly well wasn't the same as being happy.

Full of resolve once more, Phoebe tucked her mirror back into her bag and started walking again. She took a deep breath as she turned the corner and The Hat and Fan came into view. The warm glow from its steamed-up windows was a welcome sight on a dark night.

'Don't slouch, Phoebe,' she whispered under her breath as she crossed the road and even the ringing of her phone wasn't going to distract her from her mission. It would only be Sadie to say that she had Coco.

Another deep breath as Phoebe opened the door so the still night was drowned out by the hum of lively chatter and laughter, the smell of beer and bar snacks, and in their favourite corner, the staff of The Vintage Dress Shop plus their significant others and the most significant other of them all, Freddy, were gathered.

They were all dressed up in their best, even Miles who Phoebe had never seen in a suit, and so engrossed in their conversation that they didn't even notice Phoebe approach. Then Sophy lifted her head just as Phoebe's phone began to ring again. Not just ring but beep and chime too.

She lifted her hand to wave at Sophy who, not surprisingly, didn't look too thrilled to see her. Phoebe reached for her phone, which had stopped ringing but, as soon as her fingers closed around it, started again.

Phoebe stopped in her tracks when she saw she had three missed calls from Sadie, plus messages from Sadie, Gunther, Emma and Sean on the other boat and . . .

'Hi, Sadie,' she said as she answered this latest call. 'Have you got Coco?'

'Phoebe!' Sadie's voice was shrill with panic. '*The Sheila* is on fire! We've called the fire brigade but . . .'

'But Coco . . .'

'Gunther's using our fire extinguisher but he can't get the flames out and I can hear Coco . . . You have to come . . .'

Phoebe didn't need to hear any more. Panic ripped through her like an earthquake and she gasped out loud. Her bag fell to the floor as she pressed a hand to her heart, which was thumping hard and fast enough to break free.

'Phoebe, there you are!' said a voice behind her. As if she was in a dream, she turned around to see Charles, impeccable in black tie and tails, coming from the bar with a tray full of drinks. 'A sight for sore eyes!'

'I have to go,' she said, her voice a hoarse, croaky thing. 'Oh God, Coco! There's a fire and she's all alone and she must be so scared and she needs me . . .'

She pushed past Charles so the tray went flying, drinks going everywhere, people shouting and swearing, the sound of glasses breaking. Phoebe didn't even feel the liquid soaking her hair, her cape, her dress. She stumbled through the crowd, not caring who she knocked into. Behind her, she could hear someone call her name but there was no time to stop. No time to do anything but shoulder open the door and run back out into the night.

Phoebe picked up the heavy skirt of her dress as she raced through the streets. Then she stopped only to wrench off her stupid, slippery shoes. She could still hear the echo of her name but she ignored it as she began to run again.

The pavements were hard and unforgiving under her feet. The cold, cold night snatched the breath from her lungs, but Phoebe barely noticed. She ran as if the devil himself was at her heels.

Then came the acrid scent of smoke and Phoebe was sure she could hear the crackle of flames as she came to the narrow path that led down to the canal. Finally she was on the towpath and in the near distance she could see the people gathered around *The Sheila*, which was lit by a fierce orange glow as Gunther and

Sean aimed fire extinguishers at the bow of the boat where the fire was concentrated. Sadie and Emma were scooping up canal water in buckets and flinging it at the boat but . . .

'Coco! Where's my baby?' Phoebe screamed as she reached the terrible scene.

Sadie said something to her, but it was lost in the commotion. Phoebe didn't ask her to repeat it but instead ran to the other end of *The Sheila*, which wasn't on fire but the boat was made of wood and it was only a matter of time. She might already be too late.

'Coco? Coco?' she shouted again. She was sure over the commotion at the other end of the boat, over the ominous hiss and roar of the fire, she could hear the sound of barking. The short, offended barks that Coco always gave like she couldn't believe that she needed to raise her voice.

Phoebe tore off her cape and hitched up her skirt so she could leap on to the back of the boat where her bedroom was and beyond that the fuel tank. If the fire reached the fuel tank, then there was no hope.

You had to have hope. Without it, life would be absolutely unbearable.

And for now, there was hope. Phoebe gathered herself, tried to summon all her strength but suddenly there was an arm round her waist, hauling her back from the boat.

'Phoebe!' It was Freddy. 'It's not safe.'

For one fleeting second, she let herself rest against him, her hand covering his.

'I'm so glad you're here,' she said. 'I'm sorry. I'm so sorry for ruining everything.'

'It doesn't even matter,' he mumbled into her hair. 'It's not important.'

But some things were important. Some things were a matter of life and death. Even though Phoebe could hear the sound of sirens getting nearer, there wasn't time.

'Coco needs me,' she said and she pulled free of Freddy, using her elbows to knock him down because she knew he'd try and stop her again. Then she jumped onto the side of the boat, clinging on to the rail as she inched along until she reached the stern, where the fuel tank was.

'Phoebe! Come back!' Freddy shouted, but he was just one more voice in the crowd that had assembled and who collectively gasped as Phoebe hoisted herself up the side of the boat so she could climb onto the roof where the little vegetable patch was. She lay belly down in the soil so she could lean over the other side of the boat and see into the little window by her bed, which she gazed out of every morning.

Over the sound of people shouting to her, she was sure she could hear Coco. Yes, she could definitely hear Coco barking and she sounded royally pissed off.

Phoebe knocked on the glass. 'Coco! Get on the bed! On the bed! Please, get on the bed.'

Usually Coco needed help getting up and down from the raised bed; she only had little legs. Phoebe realised that she'd have to break the window to get to Coco. She hoisted herself up so she was standing again and looked around wildly for something heavy that she could aim at the glass.

'Phoebe! Please come down!' Freddy shouted. 'The fire brigade are here now. They'll get Coco out.'

It was just her. The only person she could rely on was herself. The only person Coco had to rely on too.

Phoebe gathered up the skirt of her dress once more and ripped it in two. Then she wrapped the heavy silk around her hand several times and lay down again, her torso hanging over the side of the boat.

'Coco! Are you on the bed? I'm here!'

Phoebe took the deepest breath she'd ever taken, clenched her fist then smashed her hand against the window. It took three goes before the glass shattered and she could push her upper body through the small window.

Immediately smoke, thick and noxious, swirled around her. Phoebe's first instinct was to rear back; she could hardly breathe, but she tamped down her fear and blocked out the noise from outside and listened for Coco's imperious barking.

There was nothing. She was too late. It had all been in vain.

'Oh, Coco . . .' Phoebe moaned, smoke curling into her open mouth. But then she felt it. The faintest damp touch against the hand that wasn't covered in silk, then something warm and furry press against her wrist.

Phoebe grabbed Coco by the scruff of her neck and pulled her through the window, trying to avoid scraping her precious little body against the shards of glass that were still embedded in the window frame.

They lay there for a second, both panting and shaking, Phoebe pressing kisses all over Coco's face.

'Phoebe! Please! I am begging you, get off this bloody boat!' she suddenly heard Freddy shout.

It was hard to move. Phoebe's limbs felt like lead and she could hardly catch her breath but she managed to crawl over the roof of the boat, cradling Coco to her with one hand. Then she lowered her legs and suddenly there was an arm around her waist again, pulling her and Coco to safety.

Coco wriggled frantically in Phoebe's arms, panic seizing hold of her, and just as they were pulled to freedom, she felt Coco slip from her grasp. She landed on firm, solid ground at the same time as Phoebe but clearly disorientated the little dog ran haphazardly along the path, until she missed her footing and fell into the murky water.

Phoebe tried to scream but she had no voice left. Before she could gather what little strength she had left, the arms holding her up were gone and Freddy pushed past her, toeing off his shoes so he could dive into the greasy, dark, freezing depths of the canal.

'Oh my God, oh my God,' Phoebe wheezed, limping over to where Freddy's head was bobbing above the water.

'Phoebe! Are you OK? Of course you're not OK,' a voice panted in her ear and then Cress was hugging her tightly, Sophy launched herself at Phoebe from the other side while two men in fancy suits, Charles and Miles, lay down on the bank with their hands outstretched to pull Freddy from the water.

Freddy and Coco. Freddy lay on the path on his back, Coco splayed out on his chest and, over Sophy's shoulder, Phoebe stared in horror.

The two halves of her heart were still.

Chapter Thirty-Two

There was one awful moment that lasted several lifetimes. Then Freddy suddenly rolled over, one arm around Coco, and coughed as the little dog licked his face.

He glanced over to where Phoebe was still sandwiched between Cress and Sophy and managed to stagger to his feet as Phoebe wriggled free so she could limp towards Freddy and Coco.

She started crying before she even reached him. 'I couldn't bear it if anything happened to you,' she sobbed. 'To either of you.'

'Right back at you,' Freddy said, then screwed up his face in disgust. Water was dripping off him and his face was ashen in the light of the fire, which was still raging. 'Christ, I must have swallowed half of the canal.'

'I don't care,' Phoebe said, scooping Coco up in her arms, then launching herself at Freddy so hard that he staggered with the force of her embrace. Phoebe grabbed hold of the sodden lapels of his jacket with one hand so she could pull him to safety then pepper his face with kisses.

She didn't even care that he probably had swallowed a good litre of canal water, which even on its best day still looked dank and green and had an oily slick floating on top of it, she kissed his mouth, tangling one hand in his wet hair.

Freddy kissed her back. Then they just held each other, delayed shock and the biting chill of the cold December night making both of them shake. Between them, Coco was a damp, wiggly weight, licking whichever one of their faces she could reach. Phoebe didn't think she'd ever let either of them go until she could no longer ignore the insistent tapping on her shoulder.

She reluctantly turned around to be confronted by a very angry firewoman who proceeded to read Phoebe the riot act for her rescue mission.

'You need to leave it to the professionals,' she finished very sternly as Phoebe looked beyond her to where the woman's crew were rolling up their hose and *The Sheila* was no longer on fire but literally a husk of what she used to be. 'Look, I get it, I have a cat that I'd run into a burning building for, but you're bloody lucky to be alive. Now, needless to say but I think you're the sort of person who needs me to say it, you are *not* to get back on that boat. It's unsafe and we need to establish the cause of the fire.'

Behind Phoebe, she felt Freddy stiffen. 'I was meaning to get the wood burner serviced,' she said weakly, as the fierce firewoman looked very unimpressed.

'Well, meaning isn't the same as doing,' she said and even on her most impossible day, Phoebe didn't think she'd ever made any customer feel as small as she felt right then. 'Lecture over. The paramedics have just arrived to check the two of you over. They're parked on the street. Can you walk or do you need a stretcher?'

Phoebe was about to say, quite indignantly, that she could walk but as soon as she thought it, her legs started wobbling and Cress and Sophy were there again to hold her up.

The adrenalin that had given Phoebe huge amounts of bravery and a superhuman strength so she could tear heavy silk and smash windows was suddenly gone. Now, she was a shuddering, trembling woman whose feet felt as if they'd been walking on razor blades and her right hand was stinging and throbbing. She looked down to see that she was bleeding in several places.

'This is the most beautiful, expensive dress I've ever owned,' she rasped, as Freddy, still dripping fetid canal water and shaking himself, took her hand, his other arm clutching Coco to his chest, and Sophy pulled her and Cress pushed her very gently along the path. 'It's worth over two thousand pounds and it was once owned by a debutante who was photographed in it for *Harper's Bazaar.*'

'Oh, Pheebs, I'm so sorry,' Cress said because even she couldn't work her magic on a dress that had had half the skirt ripped clean off it, huge tears in the bodice and sleeves and covered in rusty red streaks of blood, not to mention greasy, green waterlogged stains from where Phoebe had been pressed against Freddy. 'Maybe I could make a replica of it for you.'

Freddy squeezed Phoebe's fingers and she waited to feel inconsolable about the loss of the most beautiful dress that she'd ever owned. 'I think I will be very sad about the dress. All my dresses. And my capes. You know I've been deep into my cape era. I can't imagine many of them have survived . . .'

'Anita and Bea did talk about us forming a human chain to rescue your dresses but then we got shouted at by the fire lady,' Sophy said, as they carefully manoeuvred Phoebe up the narrow path that led to the street.

Anita and Bea, Bea convulsed with sobs, were waiting for them. 'I'm so sorry about your dresses,' Bea hiccupped.

'They are just dresses,' Phoebe said slowly. She was still waiting to feel grief-stricken about her dresses but mostly she was concerned about Freddy – he could have E.coli from the canal water – and Coco. In fact, as soon as Phoebe was helped into the back of the ambulance she insisted Coco was checked over first. 'She must have inhaled a lot of smoke, not to mention swallowing that rank canal water, and she's a brachycephalic breed. Have you got a little oxygen mask you could put on her?'

Bea and Anita handed over all the items that Phoebe had dropped during her panicked run. Her phone. Her clutch bag. Even her shoes that had been abandoned in the middle of the street, like a true Cinderella. And they'd also brought the little box containing her corsage: a red rose the exact same shade of Phoebe's favourite lipstick, which Freddy had planned to give her in person.

Then they gathered around the open back doors of the ambulance, even though one of the paramedics said that they didn't need an audience, and Phoebe asked in a croaking voice, which hurt her throat, 'But aren't you going to the ball? There's still time.'

'Not really feeling the vibes for a ball now,' Anita said. She shrugged. 'Seeing your friend's home go up in smoke is a bit of a mood killer, you know. Even I'm sad about all your dresses.'

Phoebe was still more worried about Freddy who was sitting next to her on the gurney and looked an awful grey colour. 'Are you all right? You look terrible.'

Freddy's grin was a shadow of its former self. 'I would say that you don't look that good yourself but to me, you always look beautiful.' His eyes were fixed on Phoebe like he wanted to memorise every last millimetre of her face. 'Especially when you were standing on the roof of *The Sheila*, like some kind of warrior queen. But I've never been so terrified, Pheebs. It could have all ended so differently, so badly.'

He shuddered at the prospect but it had ended the way that it had. *The Sheila* was a write-off. Her dresses were probably just ash by now. But the three of them were still here. Bloody, bruised, maybe a little broken but gloriously and happily alive.

Even though it hurt when she leaned towards Freddy – it was very possible that she'd cracked a couple of ribs – Phoebe had to kiss him again. Just to make sure that this wasn't a dream. It was real. He was real. 'I meant what I said before,' she told him gently. 'I couldn't bear it if anything happened to you. I know that I don't show it and I never ever say it, but honestly, Freddy, you mean the world to me.'

There was a shocked gasp from the peanut gallery. 'I'm having trouble taking this all in,' Sophy said in a shocked whisper. 'Not just that Phoebe lives on a boat but Phoebe and Freddy? Since when?'

'I couldn't tell you – it was a secret,' Cress said at the exact same time as Anita and Bea chorused, 'Since forever.'

So much for keeping things on the down-low so Phoebe's authority wouldn't be undermined.

'My personal life is nothing to do with you,' Phoebe said grandly, which was ruined when she started coughing hard enough to hack up a lung.

'Right, your little dog is OK. Best to get her checked over by a vet tomorrow, but really if anyone needs checking over, it's you,' the paramedic said, lunging at Phoebe with a blood pressure cuff.

'You know what?' Anita suddenly grinned. 'This does answer the question once and for all, that if Phoebe's house was on fire, what would she save?'

In the end, Phoebe hadn't even had to think about it. It turned out that she could love after all. She gently scooped up Coco, who was huddled next to her on the stretcher, and pressed a kiss to the top of her head, though Coco really didn't smell that good.

On the other side of her, Freddy was being hooked up to an EKG machine, his face still grey, his hands trembling.

'You're going to have to say goodbye to the dog now,' said the paramedic who had tightened the blood pressure cuff to

293

the point of maximum pain, although compared to all her other aches, cuts and bruises, it hardly registered.

'Coco isn't going anywhere,' Phoebe spluttered, hugging her even tighter. Coco was limp in her embrace, completely devoid of her usual sass.

'Your blood pressure is very high.' Which really wasn't any wonder given the circumstances. 'And even if it wasn't, you both need to go to hospital. No dogs allowed.'

Coco whimpered faintly and Phoebe would have whimpered too except it felt as if someone had taken sandpaper to her throat. 'I promise I'll go to hospital tomorrow,' she managed to say though talking really hurt.

'No, Pheebs, you go to hospital and I'll stay with Coco,' Freddy insisted, but then he went even greyer and lurched forward as his paramedic shoved a kidney bowl at him just in time.

'Oh Freddy, your poor thing, you're not going anywhere,' Phoebe croaked. 'You're the one who should go to hospital.'

'Both of you are going to hospital,' Cress said very sternly. 'I'll take Coco.'

'But . . .'

'But nothing, Phoebe!' Sophy added just as fiercely. 'Coco spends half the day hanging out with Cress so it's not like she'll be with strangers.'

Phoebe's paramedic was already lifting Coco up to place her in Cress's outstretched arms. It felt like Phoebe's heart was being removed from her chest. Maybe that was a slight exaggeration but Coco needed her and she really, really needed Coco.

Coco cuddled into Cress's chest. 'She'll be fine, Pheebs, I promise,' Cress said, trying not to wrinkle her nose as her nasal passages met the stench of wet dog and fetid canal water. 'But can I give her a bath?'

'You have to test the water with your elbow and she likes to be dried by a hair dryer on the lowest setting and there's an emergency vet open all night in Belsize Park and . . .'

'We'll call you to let you know how she is,' Sophy said very firmly, as Phoebe's paramedic climbed out of the ambulance. 'But she will be fine.'

'She'd prob . . .'

The doors shut so Phoebe couldn't explain that when Coco was feeling poorly, she was very partial to some chicken noodle soup.

'Let's get you both strapped in,' said Freddy's paramedic. 'We'll have you at A&E in no time at all.'

It was a quick ride to the Royal Free, Phoebe and Freddy clammy hand in clammy hand. Though every time they went over a speed bump, Phoebe moaned as it jolted her ribs and Freddy groaned like he was going to throw up again.

As soon as they reached the hospital, Freddy was led out of the ambulance then Phoebe was wheeled out on the stretcher and whisked straight into triage, then resus and a curtained-off cubicle. There she was poked and prodded, ultra-sounded and got told off every time she tried to explain what had happened or asked where Freddy was because 'you need to rest your throat'.

Phoebe was diagnosed with three broken ribs, which would take time and rest to heal. The cuts on her stomach and her feet were cleaned and dressed. The cuts on her hand and wrist were stitched up. Then to counteract the effects of the smoke inhalation, she was put on oxygen administered via a nasal tube.

It was there that Freddy found her. Phoebe had been instructed to sit propped up but she tried to get off the bed when he poked his head around the curtain.

'No! Stay where you are,' he said in a hoarse voice. 'I'm fine. I'll grab a chair.'

He returned with a plastic chair and sat close enough to Phoebe that she could take his hand and entwine her fingers through his.

'You're not fine,' she said, though by now her voice was nothing but a hoarse whisper. 'You don't look fine.'

It was true. Freddy was still grey, but a very pale grey. 'I feel much better than I did. But my new suit's a write-off,' he said tugging at his trousers, which were still shiny from his dip in the canal.

'You were so brave,' Phoebe croaked. 'You didn't even take your jacket off. You just dived straight in to save Coco.'

Freddy raised Phoebe's ice-cold hand to his mouth so he could press a kiss to her knuckles. 'Got to look after my girls,' he murmured against her skin.

'Am I still one of your girls?' Phoebe asked, her words a pained little whisper because she was meant to be resting her voice on a night when she had so many important things to say.

'Of course you are,' Freddy replied just as hoarsely. 'Not just one of them. My best girl. My favourite girl. Except, I know you're not a girl. You're a woman.'

It was something, yet another thing, that she used to chide Freddy for whenever he called her a girl. 'Not a girl, Freddy,' she'd say. 'A woman. A fully grown up, adult woman, thank you very much.'

But now Phoebe just squeezed his hand. 'Your woman, I hope.'

'I hope so too,' Freddy said gravely. His eyes in his pale grey face were soft and tender. 'But should you even be talking at all?'

Phoebe shrugged, then winced as her ribs protested. 'Probably not, but I have a lot on my mind.'

'I'm sorry about your dresses. Sorry about the dress you were wearing tonight.'

Phoebe was currently sporting a fetching hospital robe. 'They had to cut it off me,' she whispered.

Freddy pressed another kiss on the back of her hand. 'Sorry, Pheebs. I know it was your favourite.'

Phoebe was still waiting for her heart to shatter over that dress, all of her dresses, her *stuff*. But her heart had already shattered once tonight when she'd seen Freddy and Coco lying motionless on the ground after being pulled out of the depths of the Regent's Canal. And now that Freddy was safe and she'd been sent a picture of Coco wrapped up in Cress's mum's favourite pashmina and sleeping in Cress's bed, her heart was healed and, all things considered, beating out quite a steady rhythm.

'I know that you think I care too much about the dresses. I probably do but I always think that the dresses need me to stand up for them. It's so easy to throw something away just because it's a little old-fashioned or a button's come loose and the hem has dropped but it still has worth, it still has value,' Phoebe said, her voice scratchy, her hand movements not as extravagant as they usually would be. 'Like you wouldn't throw away a person because they were a bit broken, would you?'

'I see what you mean,' Freddy mused as Phoebe's pulse began to thunder and she could actually see her blood pressure increase on the monitor she was hooked up to. It was easy to say these things to a load of faceless people on the internet. There was less at stake. It was much harder to say them to someone you'd grown to really care about but who might throw you away once they realised how damaged you were. 'But I think the best people are a little bit broken, a little rough around the edges. Life might have been a bit hard on them but they've come through it and it's made them stronger.'

'I'm not strong, Freddy,' Phoebe said so faintly, that he had to lean closer to catch every word that she managed to force out. Not just because it hurt physically but because emotionally, each letter, each syllable was wrenched out of her soul. 'I've always been broken and I'm terrified that people are going to find out.'

'Why do you think you're broken?' Freddy asked.

Phoebe shut her eyes, took a deep breath, which made her poor swollen throat throb, and then she started to tell her story. To tell Freddy the story that she'd never told anyone, though there were people, Mildred, Johnno, who had filled in some of the blanks themselves.

She told Freddy about the three-day-old baby who'd been taken into foster care. She told Freddy about Annabel, the mother who didn't want her, and all the other families that she'd lived with who hadn't wanted her either. The group homes and the caseworkers and a care system that didn't seem to care very much about her at all, until she'd landed on Mildred's doorstep.

And she told Freddy about how Mildred had rescued her as much as she'd rescued Coco. That she'd raised Phoebe to rely only on herself. That she'd spent all these years following Mildred's edict that she shouldn't let people into her heart because they'd only take advantage and stamp all over it.

'What kind of person am I when I can't even admit that I love Coco?' she asked. By now, her voice was barely there and Freddy was on the bed with her, pressed up close so he could hear her confession. A nurse had come in at one point, but had obviously decided that trying to separate them was far beyond her pay grade and had left them to it.

'Phoebe, everyone knows that you love Coco. Everyone except you,' Freddy said gently. Phoebe's head was tucked neatly under his chin so she couldn't see his face, but she could hear his smile.

'But does everyone know that I love you?' Phoebe lifted her head so she could watch the emotions, surprise, hope, then joy, play over Freddy's face because he never hid what he felt.

'You love me?' he clarified.

It was too hard to say it again. To make it a statement of fact instead of a question so Phoebe just nodded.

'Well, good, because I love you,' Freddy said as if it was as simple as that.

'Even though I'm a very prickly person?'

'Even prickly Phoebe.' The twinkle was back in Freddy's eyes. 'You can't have a rose without a few thorns, can you?'

'You can't,' Phoebe agreed and then she really couldn't talk anymore.

Except, he had one last question. 'So, is it Freddy before the frocks then? If, God forbid, my flat was on fire, would you save me first?'

'You can save yourself. I'd have to pick Coco first,' Phoebe said apologetically. 'But then you and then, and I can't quite believe I'm saying this, way, way down the list, would be the frocks.'

'Only second?' Freddy smiled as Phoebe stretched out her hand so he could see the underside of her wrist where her ill-advised tattoo, an F and a C entwined within the outline of a heart, was now clearly visible. 'I can live with being second. In fact, being second sounds pretty good to me.'

Epilogue

A couple of months later . . .

Something old, something new.
Something borrowed, something blue.

Everyone said it would be romantic to get married on Valentine's Day; however, there was only one place that Phoebe wanted to get married.

Her happy place. Which was the atelier.

And there was *no* way that Phoebe was going to close the shop on Valentine's Day, which fell on a Saturday that year. A working day but also it would mean that 'we'd be letting our customers down. Have you any idea of how many women suddenly wake up on February fourteenth and decide that they need the perfect dress for their dates later that night? Or how many men come to the shop to buy a red dress for their special person, even though it turns out that they have absolutely no idea what size their special person actually wears?'

'I just thought it would be romantic,' Freddy said mildly. 'If you feel that strongly about it, then let's do it on the Sunday instead. You can have the wedding any way that you want it but the honeymoon is non-negotiable.'

It was their new improved couple strategy. They were each allowed one, only one, red line on any given topic. A red line that couldn't be crossed.

So if Phoebe had the wedding of her dreams on a Sunday afternoon (they'd done the legal thing at Camden Town Hall a couple of days before) in the atelier with Charles officiating then Freddy was in charge of the honeymoon. A week in Paris, a whole week away from the shop and away from Coco Chanel, who was going to stay with Birdy, Faisal and Peggy Gug, even though Phoebe was sure they'd return to find that Coco had become a fully fledged doggy influencer.

'You're not financially savvy, Coco,' she said to her chief bridesmaid, who looked beautiful in her own little white veil and pearl collar. 'You'd sign your life away for a pig's ear.'

Phoebe fingered the pearls that were around her own neck. Mildred's pearls, her something borrowed, which were one of the few things to survive the fire. It was lovely to have something of Mildred's on this special day.

Her 1930s bias-cut dress was her something old. Once it had been repaired and the fake tan had been painstakingly removed after Rosie Roberts's harsh treatment of it.

Phoebe's something new was the going-away outfit that Cress had designed exclusively for her. The Phoebe was a French navy wool crêpe dress with satin accents, but it didn't count as her something blue. That was the diamond and aquamarine (her birth stone) engagement ring sourced by Charles and placed on her finger by Freddy at the end of that strange week after *The Sheila* had caught fire.

Even though it was the busiest shopping week of the year, Phoebe had been confined to bed in Freddy's flat. She had to rest her broken ribs, she had stitches where she'd cut her arm and hand, and her feet were still sore and throbbing from being torn to ribbons. Also, she'd kept bursting into tears every time she looked at either Coco or Freddy.

Freddy hadn't been much better. He hardly let Phoebe or Coco out of his sight. There had been a lot of sleeping off the worst of their symptoms. A lot of *cuddling*. A lot of gazing at each other because Phoebe couldn't get enough of the expression on Freddy's face when he looked at her; it was tender and soft in a way that she couldn't quite describe.

'It's so good to have my two best girls back with me,' Freddy had said at one point. 'We're our own little family.'

'I love our own perfectly imperfect little family,' Phoebe whispered because it was still easier to say that than to remind Freddy that she really did love him. Loved him more than all the vintage dresses in all the vintage shops in the world.

But he didn't need reminding because later that week when he was still a lighter shade of grey but well enough to go into town for a meeting, he came home with a cheeky Nando's for them and the ring.

He even went down on one knee.

Phoebe didn't even have to think about it. 'Very much yes. Definitely yes,' she rasped. 'But are you sure about this? I'm still prickly.'

'I wouldn't have you any other way,' Freddy said, with a grin. 'I can cope with the odd scratch.'

It was quite hard to remember to be prickly when Phoebe was now something of a heroine. She'd gone viral yet again (she'd stopped counting how many times that had happened) after someone uploaded footage to TikTok of her leaping onto the blazing *Sheila* to rescue Coco. She was officially uncancelled now and there was even talk of a Pride of Britain award.

It would also have been churlish to not thank her friends who'd all visited, bringing flowers and vintage dresses from their own wardrobes, to replace all those dresses that were now lost for evermore.

The Vintage Dress Shop had *somehow* managed without Phoebe while she was indisposed. Although someone would pop over every lunchtime to give Phoebe the low-down on that day's business. Still, after all that she'd been through, it was quite hard to get even a little bit stressed about their ever-dwindling stock of black party dresses or that Cress's overlocker was making an awful clunking sound and might be out of operation until the end of the year.

'I miss the old Phoebe,' Anita said mournfully, when it was her turn to come round. 'Can't you think of something to tell me off about?'

'I'm sure that in another couple of days, I'll be back to my true self,' Phoebe said but her heart wasn't really in it. She wasn't sure who her true self was anymore.

Probably not the chilly woman she'd forged out of the ashes of that lost girl she'd used to be. There had been so many different Phoebes and over the last few weeks, she realised that she was transforming into yet another version of herself.

A version that was learning to compromise. To appreciate the people in her life instead of insisting that she didn't need anybody. To prioritise what was really important. Coco. Freddy. Her friends. Her shop and yes, the dresses were always going to matter to her and that was OK too.

'Pheebs, we're ready for you,' she heard Sophy call down the stairs and Phoebe, who'd been sitting in the back office, hidden from sight of all the guests who'd assembled in the atelier, stood up.

She checked her reflection one last time in the changing room mirror, then she lifted up Coco Chanel, who as well as being chief bridesmaid was doubling up as her bouquet, and walked through the empty shop.

Past the three rails of rental dresses. Valentine's Day notwithstanding, it was a quiet time of the year. People not quite so keen to splurge on a new dress so it made sense that maybe they'd prefer to rent one instead.

Past all the other dresses on their padded hangers. Past the red hearts that Sophy and Anita had stuck all over the shop when Phoebe had agreed that maybe this year they could decorate for Valentine's Day.

She reached the foot of the stairs, hefted Coco to her other side because her ribs were still a little sore and looked up to see a familiar face gazing down at her.

'Oh my God, what are you doing here?' she gasped.

'Had to see a man about a dog,' Johnno said, with a shrug. 'And while I was in the neighbourhood, I thought I'd swing by.'

'I can't believe it,' Phoebe said, widening her eyes because she wasn't going to cry. It would absolutely wreck her make-up.

'Did you really think I was going to miss your wedding?' he asked as Phoebe slowly walked up the stairs towards him. 'There isn't an aisle and you're your own woman who's here of your own free will so I'm not giving you away, but if you want to take my arm, then that would be cool.'

'I'd like that,' Phoebe said.

It was a very narrow, very twisty staircase so it was quite hard to walk arm in arm with Johnno, especially when you were also holding a wriggly French bulldog, but Phoebe managed it.

Then she was in her happy place. Surrounded by all those dresses that had their own stories, their own memories, there to bear witness to one more story, one more memory, as Phoebe walked towards the spot where so many other prospective brides had stood.

Freddy was the first bridegroom to stand on the dais, nervously shifting from foot to foot. But as he caught sight of Phoebe and Coco, he stilled and a slow smile crept on to his face, banishing the clouds of uncertainty.

He was there to hold out a hand to Phoebe as she let go of Johnno and stepped onto the platform. 'You look beautiful,' he said. 'Coco too.'

'We do,' Phoebe agreed, because there was no point in being modest about it. She brushed away a speck of lint from the lapel of his exquisitely cut charcoal Italian wool suit. 'You don't look so bad yourself.'

And as Phoebe looked at the many Phoebes reflected back in the mirrors that lined the room, she didn't think any of them had ever looked as happy as she did now.

Acknowledgements

As we close the door on The Vintage Dress Shop, some heart-felt gratitude is due!

Thank you to my wonderful agent, Rebecca Ritchie, and the also wonderful Alexandra McNicoll, Lucy Joyce and the rights team, plus everyone at A.M.Heath Ltd.

It's also been a joy to work with Audrey Linton, my amazing editor, Cara Chimirri and all at Hodder & Stoughton. Thank you to Daisy Woods for the beautiful cover. A very honourable mention to Helena Newton, the copy editor of dreams.

And last but by no means least, thank you to all the readers who have visited The Vintage Dress Shop. I've loved writing this series and I hope you enjoyed reading it. What a thrill it's been to write three books all about beautiful dresses!

Go back to where it all started
with the first book in the series

Thirty-year-old Sophy Stevens is freshly fired, recently dumped and sleeping on her mum's sofa. So when her dad offers her a job at his vintage clothes shop, it's one she can't refuse.

With each new treasure Sophy uncovers, she begins to wonder if, like these vintage clothes, the store is the key to her second chance . . . and then there's Charles, who might just end up mending her broken heart . . .

Don't miss the previous book in The Vintage Dress Shop series

Cressida Collins is the queen of makeovers. But when her boyfriend of fifteen years drops a bombshell, it explodes all the carefully laid plans Cress had for her future.

It's going to take more than needle and thread to put Cress's own life back together. Will she ever be brave enough to say goodbye to her old dreams and start over?